Crumbs from Heaven

Crumbs from
Heaven

a novel

Rick Smith

Charleston, SC
www.PalmettoPublishing.com

Crumbs from Heaven

First Edition

Hardcover ISBN: 979-8-88590-456-8

Paperback ISBN: 979-8-88590-457-5

eBook ISBN: 979-8-88590-458-2

For my three girls: Juli, Meredith and Parker

The Experiment Begins

It's truly fascinating what the mind can remember given the proper stimuli. Forgotten ghosts, hidden in the darkest corners of our memory, pushed closer and closer to extinction by life's daily clutter, suddenly appear fresh and new, brought to life again by the simplest spark. For me, the greatest time machine ever invented is music. Mundane concerns quickly vanish when the opening notes of an old song blare from my car radio, drenching me in youthful euphoria. Adjusting the volume to a thunderous roar, I screech along in a spirited off-key karaoke. Suddenly a teenager again, I recall the sweet recollection of that first kiss or the gut-wrenching pain of a broken heart.

With the exception of my wife Lynne, these impromptu concerts of mine are strictly solo performances, sparing any would-be passengers the anguish of auditory misery. For those fleeting seconds nothing else matters as I surrender to the moment while playful spirits toy with my emotions. After strumming a few sentimental notes on my heartstrings, they crawl back inside their magic bottle, waiting in silence until summoned once again.

An admitted closet romantic, it doesn't take much to send me skipping gleefully down memory lane. Rummaging through a drawer, I might run across a faded old picture and suddenly I'm back at my senior prom or sitting with my family opening gifts on a special Christmas long ago. For the most part, I welcome these gentle spirits with open arms, allowing a momentary return to a cherished triumph or to relive pleasant recollections from a simpler place and time. I can assure those with wrinkle-free foreheads and others who still enjoy their original hair color, that this fondness for the past greatly enhances with age. With more miles behind me than in front, I don't mind the occasional diversion.

Unfortunately, these sentimental homecomings aren't always pretty. Good-natured apparitions are often swept aside, replaced by scar-faced phantoms. Wielding accusing swords of regret, they gleefully carve open painful scars inflicted years ago by a myriad of bad choices and stupid mistakes.

On a warm April morning, these collective apparitions gathered for yet another raucous appearance. Brandishing thick volumes from my childhood, these restless ghosts ambushed my unsuspecting family, forever altering our future.

The eve of this unexpected turn of events offered no hint of an approaching transformation. At least I thought so at the time. With wine glasses in hand, Lynne and I had just settled back on the screened porch watching soft twilight shadows begin their sluggish crawl across the yard. Suddenly a lone hummingbird appeared at the feeder hanging from the porch awning. A small bib of red clearly visible on his throat as he shoved his needle-like beak in and out of the plastic shaped flowers. I knew they were back as the feeder was only half full, but I hadn't seen one till now. Lynne saw it too and we both acknowledged his presence with a smile and quiet glance. As I watched him dart around the feeder, I thought of his arduous journey, flying thousands of miles from South America. And somehow this beautiful creature winds up in my backyard. After a quick drink, he disappeared into the shadows.

The call came in just after seven. Although the phone's mechanical pulse offered no clue as to the caller, I knew full well who waited on the other end of the line. Lynne's eyes met mine, sending us into our standard rapid response mode.

There was a time when I lived for that enticing computerized ring. Its tantalizing tone confirming acceptance of my client's real estate offer or perhaps another lucrative listing appointment awaited me. It could have been Ronnie calling to rub it in after another victorious afternoon on the links or perhaps the caller was someone on the other side of the world deeply concerned about my car warranty.

Retirement changed all that. Now the staccato ringtone possesses the ear-piercing quality of a fire alarm. Although rarely used, Lynne and I were simply too old fashioned to give up the landline. Besides, my aging parents always called the house phone, never my cell phone. Seeing Dad's number on the display sent the familiar twinge pounding through my chest as the shameful nudge of dread rose again from its selfish lair. From my earliest recollection, life has been a series of distractions, something I'd come to accept. Things were finally coming together in our golden years. Or so I thought. As heartless as it sounds, the latest irritation consuming my precious time centers around my aging parents. With our child and adult roles painfully reversed, simple phone conversations explode into dire emergencies. Perhaps a slight wobble has begun on the ceiling fan or the magnets have fallen off the refrigerator again, making their lives totally unbearable.

Of course, these calls occur at the worst possible time, screwing up my self-absorbed plans for the day. When that happens, I usually grab a beer, some peanuts, settle back on the couch, and listen while my desperate parents describe in panicked detail, the latest anthill that has morphed into an erupting volcano. After an exasperating thirty minutes of reliving the same conversation we had the day before, I'm more upset with myself than anything else. Instead of glorious days spent cruising the intercoastal waterway sipping margaritas, I now chug down a weary cocktail of guilt and frustration.

To make matters worse, I'm actually quite comfortable justifying these contemptible feelings under the arrogant notion that the direct deposit of my Social Security check somehow entitles me a carefree retirement. Where the only major decision is whether to use a seven- or eight-iron while Lynne and I chase golf balls around the lush fairways of the country club with other pensioned couples.

Sometimes I actually find time in my stingy schedule to make the two-hour ride from Wilmington to my parents' home. Of course, these few and far between trips, layered with good intentions, leave me totally frustrated. Certain my greedy irritations guaranteed me the hottest corner of hell, I confessed my loathsome self to Lynne who admitted similar feelings before her mom passed away, chalking it up to the stress of it all.

Taking a quick sip from my wineglass, I reached for the phone before the second ring. The unexpected excitement in my father's voice was refreshing for a change. Not the slightest hint of complaint or mention of the standard list of grievances. He understood the invitation was last minute, but I had to come home for the weekend or just Saturday if I could. Dismissing my questions, he guaranteed I wouldn't be disappointed.

To describe my father as simply spontaneous insults his spirited and impulsive nature. Wild-haired, spur of the moment pursuits, his once upon a time signature trademark had all but vanished. One of the things I missed about him. I agreed to come home; besides Suzie would be there.

Having my younger sister home charged Dad's battery, restoring his soul and sense of humor. She was a calming medication he desperately needed. As usual, she'd taken the hour and a half flight, leaving her husband David to tend to their Orlando insurance business. Something she did once a month since Dad's cancer diagnosis seven years ago.

Like a bloody and beaten boxer struggling to stand, endless rounds of chemo and radiation left him exhausted and disillusioned. Declared "cancer free" and convinced he was cured, the disease's sudden return sent him into a tailspin. This wasn't supposed to happen to Will Harrison. He'd played by the rules. No smoking or drinking. Busy with a wedding shower, Lynne couldn't join me on the trip. I arrived late Friday night.

I found out later that Suzie unknowingly initiated the whimsical scheme following an offhand 'Oh, by the way' remark during a phone conversation with a friend. Passing the tidbit along to Dad, she figured nothing would come of it. If anything, the news might bring a much-needed smile to his face. A soothing reminder of an earlier time. The idea quickly mushroomed into one of Dad's patented adventures. "A little experiment" he'd say later. He knew if he didn't give it a shot now, he'd never have the opportunity again. Suzie, a willing accomplice, made the arrangements.

More animated than usual, Dad joked of his "little secret" the next morning over breakfast, goading my curiosity. Growing up, humor drifted through our house like a warm summer breeze, breathing life into all it touched. Healing the bumps and bruises of childhood, assuring us everything would be all right.

My parents' usual quick wit and scalding banter had all but vanished, washed away by an angry tide of pain and indignities brought on by failing health, leaving only weary smiles in its wake. What laughter they now shared became short-lived, forced, and fatigued. Resisting the implied finality of updated wills and power of attorneys, Dad predictably buried his head in the sand, assuring us that everything was fine.

Being home evoked the standard menu of childhood memories. Treasured recollections that would stay with me forever, along with countless missteps I wished to forget. Stumbles and mistakes brought out Dad's devious wit and unfailing recall. Relishing awkward moments from my youth, he filed these tantalizing incidents away, waiting for an opportunity to throw them back in my face as an adult.

Dad's legendary primetime performances were a staple at family get-togethers. Waiting for just the right moment he'd gleefully ask, "Remember the time when you...?" His smoky nightclub delivery holding the audience captive as he embellished the story into a shattering crescendo sending everyone into hysterics, leaving me gawking at my shoes while inventing shades of red. But again, I provided him with a continuous supply of scandalous material.

There was a time in my teenage years when his playful humiliations got to me. Struggling to fit in, I didn't need the constant reminders of awkward childhood stupidity.

That is, until I had kids of my own. Whether I was nine or ninety-nine, I was still his child. Over the years, I came to appreciate these momentary indignities, especially after Dad got sick, realizing that all those years he'd been telling me that he loved me in a twisted sort of way.

Suzie insisted on cooking despite Mom's protests. Seeing my parents for the first time in months, I was stunned at their frailty. I studied the weary lines on Dad's face and the slight tremor in his left hand. Seated at the head of the table, 'the king' barked orders from his throne, convincing himself and the rest of us that he still had it. That no matter what, he remained the stalwart captain of the ship.

A remorseful spur stuck me in the gut as I watched Suzie rummage through the refrigerator. A scalding ember that typically made its humbling appearance during holidays and birthdays. Although she lived six hundred miles away, Suzie visited our parents more than I did. It was one of the many regrets that I'd taken immense pleasure beating myself up over as I sipped my coffee.

Eager to get the show on the road, Dad hustled us to the car. Tapping her fingers on the steering wheel, Suzie stared out over the hood as if she were leading some top secret mission. The family chauffeur his entire life, Dad appeared out of place as a passenger in the backseat. Although he occasionally drove, he didn't argue when Suzie took the keys.

Gripping a half-filled plastic bottle of water causing an occasional crackle, Dad peered out the backseat window into the bright morning through dark oversized sunglasses. Once mighty shoulders sagged under the weight of a long-sleeved flannel shirt. A light blue driving cap masked a desolate landscape of peach fuzz and darkening age spots. Blue jeans that fit him a few months back hung loosely over his shrinking frame. The thin belt twisting through the angled belt loops had found yet another notch, closing around him like a noose.

Another wet cough hit him, deep and guttural. Suzie and I made eye contact as he took a long swig. Not today. We would try again later. There would be another opportunity. We always thought so anyway. Together with Eddie, our nomadic brother, we'd danced around the grim subject countless times. Tiptoeing down the cumbersome path with good intentions, continually stopping before any decisions were made. Worried that considering a parent's death somehow hastened its arrival. Affectionate proposals were met with fierce resistance. Dad was going to beat the disease and be his old self again. You just watch.

Mumbling her disdain at another one of Dad's "harebrained schemes," Mom fidgeted beside him in the backseat. The fact she came dressed in her jeans and buttoned up long-sleeved top, complete with wide-brimmed hat, said in no uncertain terms that this nonsense better be quick. Her plants were waiting. In her late eighties and two years Dad's senior, Mom still managed to putter with her beloved containers and flower beds. A day was wasted if Dottie Harrison couldn't get her hands dirty.

I didn't have to peek underneath her hat to know there wasn't one strand of white hair. For decades her hairdresser, Miss Vickie, had poured enough chemicals on Mom's head to evoke a cease-and-desist order from the EPA. Before our adventure, she'd spent the good side of an hour in front of her makeup mirror.

Her descent into darkness, subtle at first, rode the slow-moving glacier of simple forgetfulness, routinely dismissed in the momentary humor of lost glasses and misplaced car keys. Repetitive questions and embarrassing lapses replaced her quick wit and pointed conversation. The dominos of dementia were falling.

Crumbling tobacco barns passed by my window, blending into an unkempt nondescript landscape, like forgotten pictures on a wall. Rusting tin roofs offered little protection for lacerated gray boards dying in the sun. I imagined the late summer bustle of activity that once surrounded these now decaying sheds. Wooden wagon trains laden with golden leaves, pulled along by smoke-belching tractors. The delicious smell of curing tobacco. Faded signposts of a different time and place.

Highway 119 segued into Second Street at a green "Maybin City Limit" sign. Dad kept me informed, but the quiet scene bathed in the brilliant morning sun bore little resemblance to the town of my youth. Main Street's stately nineteenth century brick structures, once home to barber shops, clothing, and hardware stores, catered to a new generation of eclectic boutiques, bars, and antique shops as the town struggled to find itself amid the exodus of business and industry to the interstate.

The portrait of Maybin I remembered, painted in heavy earth tones by weary brushstrokes of sweat, noise, and smoke, basked in the promise and confidence of postwar 1960s America. Weathered brick exteriors of monolithic furniture factories and cotton mills rose mightily from red North Carolina clay.

I recalled the stench of diesel fumes streaming over long silver trailers of grinding transfer trucks. Sweeping tailfins of brawny steel behemoths floating down the street atop wide whitewall tires. The stern melody of clicking cotton looms, blaring trains, and factory whistles playing its busy soundtrack. A typical southern town where everyone had their place and was expected to stay there. A place of haves and have-nots.

I imagined stern-faced men walking the streets dressed in dark business suits, thin neckties, and fedoras. Ladies in summer dresses and high heels, beehive hairdos, and bright lipstick relaxing on inviting front porches. The sweet smell of freshly cut grass drifting through the air while screaming children played in quiet streets.

And then there were those in the shadows. Humble women, their hair sprinkled with cotton dust, garbed in mismatched clothing, glumly punching time clocks. Forgotten oily-haired men with rolled up shirtsleeves and stained work pants. Cigarettes dancing on their lips as they spoke. Maybin's true heart and soul whose resolute work ethic stamped their signature on furniture, mattresses and cotton, forever charting the town's destiny.

A place wrapped in a comfortable cocoon of conformity and rules. A town everyone ran away from after high school.

"Dottie, 'member when Rose's 5 & 10 used to be there?" Dad asked, pointing to a row of glass windows. "You spent a lot of time and money in there."

"Yeah… reckon I did," came an embarrassing chuckle. Something she did when she wasn't sure.

"Ok, turn on Fifth," Dad ordered, knowing full well Suzie knew the way. The tires recoiled as we passed over the railroad tracks. Squinting through the sunlight, I watched the lazy trickle of a two-tiered water fountain flanked by two metal benches. I envisioned the green one-story frame depot, razed years ago to make way for the small park. A thin lightning rod pointing to the sky from its copper-topped cupola. "Maybin" printed on a leaning wooden sign, marking a long ago stop on the railroad.

"Heard from Eddie?" I asked.

"Called yes'day," Dad replied.

"Anything happenin' with him?"

"Said he's comin' home next week for a few days." Retired military with no ties following his second divorce, my younger brother sold used cars somewhere outside Atlanta.

"Bet I haven't seen him in a year."

"Talked like he might move back home. But I've heard that before," Dad sighed.

The warm April sun forced its way through spring's thick haze, kindling neatly kept lawns of vivid dogwoods and brilliant azaleas. Licking my lips, I tasted the chalky pollen. A white-haired lady on her knees, wielding a trowel, pawed relentlessly at stringy weeds that dared to invade her promising impatiens. Mowers, leaf blowers, and trimmers droned their noisy Saturday morning chorus. A blinking caution light above the familiar intersection caught me by surprise.

"When did they put that up?"

"Been up a while… take a left." The turn signal began its clocklike pulse while Suzie waited for an opening in the procession of oncoming traffic.

"Oh! So, *this* is your little surprise?" I laughed, trying to remember the last time I'd been anywhere near Circle Drive. Thirty? Forty years maybe?

"Hold on!" Seeing her chance, Suzie gunned the accelerator.

"Slow down Suzie Q! I ain't quite ready to go just yet." Suzie shook her head, playfully frowning at Dad in the rearview mirror.

As if witnessing a tennis match, my head turned back and forth at the vintage 1950s ranch style homes nestled in colorful yards of spring blooms and trimmed hedges. Long ago saplings from my youth towered like sentries, guarding an unassuming neighborhood where I once knew every tree, rock, and hiding place.

Tar-patches trapped the aging street in black webs as if it were the only force holding the road together. Soft grassy ditches ran on each side. Protective incisions where once upon a time little boys dressed in army regalia shielded themselves from imagined artillery barrages, spilling out into yards in screaming bayonet charges.

The brown planks and stucco of an aging Tudor emerged from the trees. An older man in gray overalls and sunglasses, oblivious to the Buick creeping past his yard, orbited a green John Deere lawnmower around the sprawling base of a massive magnolia. My chest welled, seeing the shadowy backyard remained a dark thicket; "Ashley Woods" to a ragtag army of crewcut-topped boys who chased each other beneath a canopy of oaks and pines in daily fights to the death.

"What was the lady's name who used to live there?" Suzie wondered.

"Mrs. Ashley," I sighed.

"Who lives there now?"

"Jimmy Hooks used too," Dad said, clearing his throat. "He was a big wheel down at Knight's Furniture 'fore they closed."

Whispered voices from the past grew louder as the familiar one-story came into view. Covered now in cream-colored vinyl, the sprawling ranch once belonged to my friend Bucky Watkins.

Bucky Watkins. Now there's a classic southern name for you. His real name was Harold, but he didn't look much like a Harold, given his flaming red hair. Why Bucky, I don't know either. Southern names bestowed on young baby boomers never made much sense anyway. In those days, parents possessing a lack of originality christened their children with an array of names with most of them ending with the letter "y" or an occasional "ie." There were more Jimmys, Dickies, Rickys, Timmys, Ronnies and Tommys in my school than there were No. 2

pencils. There were plenty of Cindys, Vickies, Wendys, and Suzies on class roll books as well. If a teacher called out the name Billy, half the boys in class would turn around.

Then there were parents who took a more southern aristocratic approach to names, often bestowing double titles on newborns as if the lifelong label would give them some sort of advantage. Following this noble line of thinking, my parents christened me John David Harrison where I entered the upper crust fraternity of Billy Joes, Carl Waynes, and Darrell Lees in town. Of course, girls couldn't escape the admired double moniker as there were plenty of Bobby Sues, Jane Carols and Barbara Anns pushing toy baby carriages around Circle Drive. Realizing early on that my dubious conduct didn't quite fall in line with the legacy of principled southern blue bloods, my parents took to calling me J.D. where I joined the limitless A.J.s and C.F.s of the world. And don't get me started on nicknames.

A metal pole extending from the front porch of Bucky's old house proudly displayed a Philadelphia Eagle flag. Two SUVs, one with thirty day tags, sat side by side in the driveway. Catching a quick glimpse of the swimming pool in the backyard, I noticed the screen porch that once fronted the cinderblock bathhouse had been replaced with a graceless metal awning.

"Oh, if that pool could talk," I mumbled.

"I heard way too much about that damn pool," Dad chuckled.

"Hush up Will," Mom gasped, swiping his arm. Hearing profanity spew through Dad's trembling lips seemed alien. Words I never heard growing up now tumbled out, increasing in severity during post chemo hell.

Across the street stood a white brick ranch-style house where Billy Ray Satterfield used to live. I smiled, remembering us boys chasing each other around the front yard in spirited games of tag. Below a large picture window, a long planter once filled with burgeoning annuals now sported faded plastic figurines resembling a troop of bleached rodents.

Surely Mrs. Satterfield had turned over in her grave.

"Remember old Benny Clark?" Dad laughed, nodding as we approached a brick story and a half. At first, I didn't recognize the name. Then a familiar flicker sent me into hysterics.

"Who's Benny Clark?" Suzie snickered.

"Old Benny," Dad said between breathy chortles, "liked his booze pretty good. Saerdy nights he'd get purdy snocker'd. 'Round midnight he'd stagger out to his backyard and fire up the motor on his fishin' boat. Woke up the whole damn neighborhood!"

"Will," Mom nudged in a futile rebuke.

Skeeter Crabtree's brick ranch appeared atop a hill above a sloping curve. The one car garage had been enclosed. The front porch light was still burning while a forgotten water hose twisted a dark green track through the patchy grass. I thought of the giant snowman we built once upon a time in his front yard. The one Billy Ray bestowed proud manhood with a strategically placed carrot, sending Skeeter's mother into a panic.

Slowly we drove through the neighborhood recalling families of yesteryear. Intimate places I knew in another life, where I played in sprawling yards and climbed the spidery limbs of a hundred trees. Homes where I spent the night and ate supper with my friends. An innocent world all its own snuggled in the shadows of comforting pines.

Circling the old neighborhood both thrilled and disappointed me offering an odd sense of both belonging and intrusion. Something wasn't right. An essential and necessary component was missing. It hit me when an empty swing set appeared in a backyard. Except for a few weekend gardeners, the neatly manicured lawns sat alone and still. No children in sight.

I could almost hear the playful cadence of soprano voices echoing down these same streets. Kids whose scraped knees peeked through the shredded holes of their grass-stained jeans. Thunderous bicycles with baseball cards pinned to the wheel spokes, patrolling the neighborhood. Girls in colorful dresses jumping rope and hopscotching between crudely drawn chalk outlines. Suzie pulled over to the curb.

There it was: 209 Circle Drive. A plain, ordinary one-story ranch just like every other house on the block. Unruly shoots from overgrown foundation bushes blocked a bedroom window. A red, white, and blue "For Sale" sign tilted slightly in the front yard that desperately needed mowing.

"You're kiddin'."

"Bank took it back. Foreclosure," Dad announced.

"Robin said there's two showings this afternoon," Suzie said, putting the car in park.

"Robin… Robin Crawford?"

"Robin Reinhardt. She's on husband number three now. Still doing real estate. She gave me the lockbox combination."

"Look at that Dottie," Dad pointed.

"You remember the house, don't 'cha Momma?" Suzie asked.

"I think so."

"Look how big that Fraser fir is? Remember you and Daddy planted it after Christmas one year?" Suzie's mention of the yard did the trick. Slowly the confused frown melted away from Mom's wrinkled forehead.

"Circle Drive. Is that our house? Well, I'll be!"

"Sure is." Dad smiled, patting her forearm.

Easing into the driveway, Suzie stopped the car in the same spot where Mom used to park her green Pontiac station wagon on what was then a gravel driveway. Wasting no time, Dad quickly opened the car door. Leaving his cane in the backseat, he waved off Suzie's outstretched hand, determined to show he could still do it.

Lost in memories, we stood in the driveway, surveying the house's bland profile. Two large picture windows flanked both sides of a small front porch. Eves and soffits, clothed in ugly lime-colored vinyl, drooped beneath a worn roof. The beginnings of a tropical rainforest flourished in the sagging gutters. Like an old friend, covered by the wrinkles of time, we knew without saying a word that the sweet enduring spirit still remained inside. No matter who lived here, this would always be our house. Our home.

"I reckon I won't be needin' this." Tossing her hat on the seat, Mom surveyed the lonesome yard. "Where are my flowers?" Contents of an overturned trash can lay strewn on what used to be a raised bed of mixed perennials. Gone were manicured island chains of azaleas and fruit trees she'd tenderly planted and nurtured.

"You remember it, Ma?"

"A little bit… it was a long time ago."

"Well come on then. Let's go visit!" I said, taking her hand.

"Lockbox's on the front door," Suzie announced.

Staring at the ground like a determined runner, Dad charged towards the front yard, slowing to a crawl when his feet hit the thick grass. Like a parent coaching a child on a set of training wheels, Suzie stepped beside him, keeping her hands a respectful distance. Blinding sunlight ricocheted off two thin parallel windows on the side of the garage.

"Remember when I busted that bottom window out with a base-ball?"

"Wish I had a dime for everything you busted," he chuckled. "I could have retired ten years earlier!"

Reaching for the porch's wrought iron railings, Dad paused to catch his breath. I recalled a red front door with half-moon glass fanning across the top. An abused dent-laden steel replacement stood in its place. Suzie worked the lock's combination, retrieving the key. Dad gushed like a kid at an amusement park.

"Here we go!"

The front door whined like a rusty gate. Our footsteps were amplified in the empty room as the musty stench of a million cigarettes slapped us in the face. Angled sunlight blasted through the massive windows, bathing the room with a dust-filled beacon, giving it life. Tiny tumbleweeds of lint lay scattered on the floor.

"Holy crap! It's a frickin' dump," Suzie whispered.

"Not exactly the Taj Mahal," I mumbled.

"Need your coat?" Suzie asked Dad, extending his blue jacket.

"Naw. Feels pretty good… a little dusty." Slick hardwood floors that once served as a skating rink for our sock-covered feet now resembled a pool of dingy brown water. A grimy popcorn ceiling covered with dark water stains reminded me of frozen gutter sludge three days after a snow.

I envisioned our toys scattered on the floor. The only furniture in the room back then had been a dark mahogany desk and Mom's piano. Standing there, I remembered an impromptu dodge ball game that resulted in a broken lamp. We moved to the country soon after my twelfth birthday, leaving my earliest memories as a child boarded up inside these walls. Where life's first recollections emerged from a foggy shroud entering the glow of light for the first time.

"It's so small," Suzie sighed. "Didn't a desk sit there?" she asked, pointing to a dingy interior wall.

"Sure did. Had a record player on it. Surprised you'd 'member that." Dad smiled.

A two-foot-tall brick planter bullied its way from the front wall to the center of the room. A once upon a time plastic jungle filled with artificial ferns. A make-believe South Pacific island where I dispatched a force of tiny green Marines whose mission was to flush out hidden snipers. Where I lost a pet lizard whose body was never recovered.

"Think I'll sit and rest a spell. Sit with me Dottie," Dad said, collapsing on the empty planter. Inspecting the filthy walls, Mom searched for a spark. "Recognize anything, honey?"

"It's dirty." Our laughter rebounded in the empty room. Mom grinned at our response.

"Pop? Why in the world did y'all build a honkin' brick planter—"

"Oh… let me tell you," he interrupted. "Your Momma just had to have it. Saw one in some magazine. Tell you what though, a brick flower planter in a new house was big stuff back then. Uptown! Makes a good seat though."

Faded outlines of old picture frames lined the yellowish-brown walls like a ghostly art gallery. Specks of black soot crawled up the fireplace's brick profile that sat catty-cornered at the far end of the room.

"Whoever lived here was a lot harder on this place than y'all ever were," Dad laughed. Taking a red bandana from his back pocket, he wiped his face.

"Wonder who lived here?" I asked, stepping to the middle of the room.

"Don't know. I'm sure it's been sold several times. Lost touch with this place when we moved to the country," he said, clearing his throat.

"You left your water bottle in the car. I'll go get it," Suzie said, darting out the door.

My parents' eyes swept the walls as they sat crammed beside each other on the narrow planter. A wistful smile stretched across Dad's face, while Mom appeared baffled as if trying to recall the name of an old song. They had built the house in the late 1950s. Both had been in their twenties then, strong with endless energy. An exciting and unknown path was ahead of them.

A cracked electrical outlet beneath the large center window kindled memories of our Christmas tree that stood there every year, supplanting for a moment the dirt and stench with a fresh bouquet of Fraser fir. I could see my exasperated father centering the tree under Mom's fickle direction. Bright multicolored lights wrapped from the tree's cotton-skirted bottom to an angel-topped crown. Glittering strands of fake icicles shined alongside an array of red and green glass ornaments. A supernatural beacon summoning Santa through the dark night to our house. I smiled remembering Suzie, Eddie, and me laying on the floor under the soft glow of the tree's reflected ellipse on the ceiling, whispering of Christmas Day and shiny new toys.

A dirty band of baseboard and cracked quarter round, sealed with endless coats of paint, wrapped the base of the walls. Taking a knee, I ran my fingers across the wood's imperfections, searching the dings and gouges for physical evidence that I'd been here. Lived here. Played here. A forever signature, like lovers' initials carved in a tree.

Dad's eyes followed me as I stepped to the fireplace. Running my hand across the coarse brick, I felt the holes of a missing wooden mantel. I imagined the twisted greenery draped across a hewed board. A bulging white candle centering Mom's carefully assembled creation. Below the mantle hung neatly spaced handmade Christmas stockings slumped from angled nails.

"You're thinkin' of Christmas, ain't 'cha?" Dad asked, reading my mind.

"Of course! This room *was* Christmas."

Christmases followed a distinctive and cherished pattern every year in our house, punctuated by standard holiday rituals that were observed to the letter. The spacious living room served as a glorious stage for our traditional Christmas play, where every actor knew their part. The only props that changed from year to year were the mountains of magnificent presents.

It was the way Dad sat on the planter, his legs crossed at the ankles, that sparked the memory. Christmas. *That* Christmas.

"There's one Christmas I'll never forget," I chuckled, shaking my head.

"Which one?" Dad wondered. I laughed out loud as the memory came alive.

"It was that traumatic Christmas every kid faces at some point, blowing their innocent world to bits." I grinned as I sat down on the hearth. "That was the painful year when I learned the horrible truth… about Santa!" Staring straight ahead, I recalled the memory.

THE SWEET AROMA OF freshly baked cookies drifted from the kitchen. A cold steady rain pelted the giant double windows of the living room. With our outside battles officially canceled, the squad took cover in our living room for a quiet afternoon of warmongering with the contents of five green army men sets. Spread out before us on the floor of our living room laid a stunning replica of Omaha Beach, enhanced by the waxed hardwood floors, giving the added appearance of beach sand. Bucky, a true artist, crouched beside the brick planter arranging German fortifications he'd made from painted shoe boxes while the rest of us attended to landing craft packed with tiny green invaders.

It was the Friday after Thanksgiving, although we didn't refer to that day as Black Friday back then. The date was more of a red-letter day, permanently marked in crayon by every fun-loving kid. The day when the official countdown to Christmas began.

A stack of Christmas records softly crooned from the record player atop the mahogany desk as we laid sprawled on the floor. Nat King Cole, Bing Crosby, and Perry Como topped the playlist. But for me, the true meaning of Christmas could be found in the touching and powerful lyrics of "The Chipmunk Song." A Christmas classic.

With festive music setting a holiday tone, our conversation naturally turned to the Big Day less than a month away. By now our squad knew the toy section of the Sears and Roebuck Catalog by heart. Skeeter hoped for a Lionel train set and transistor radio while Junior wanted a new bike and lever action rifle like Lucas McCain coolly wielded on the TV show, *The Rifleman.* It had been a perfect afternoon of glorious childhood dreaming. Everything was going along just fine when squad buffoon, Billy Ray, blew my wonderful little world to pieces.

With his ankles crossed, he leaned back against the brick planter fumbling with a toy army tank.

"Hey y'all, guess what? A couple of older kids at church told me and crossed their hearts and hoped to die, that Santa Claus ain't real."

No big deal. We'd heard it all before. Blasphemous accusations like Billy Ray's occurred every year, sending stalwart Santa believers into hysterics. When the seamy element of Christmas crawled out from the swamp on its slimy belly, hell-bent on destroying the joy for the rest of us. Would-be Scrooges shouting from the town square, denouncing Santa and all he stood for.

At first, no one flinched, refusing to acknowledge Billy Ray's scandalous statement. If we'd only ignored his stupid comment nothing would have happened. But the gauntlet had been cast down and we weren't about to let the little snot get away with it. Exchanging glances, Skeeter and I wondered if it was worth the trouble.

"Billy Ray, if you had a brain, you'd take it out and play with it," Skeeter laughed.

"That's what Aiken Campbell said." A nervous hush fell over the room. The only sound was the steady rain pecking at the windows. A sixth grader and Big Man on Campus at Maybin Junior High gave Aiken instant credibility. Three years older than the rest of us, he was almost a teenager. This wasn't some stupid fourth grader making wild assertions on the playground.

"OK, Smarty Pants. If there ain't no Santa, then where do all the presents come from?" I snorted.

"Your mom and dad." Breathing a sigh of relief, I continued loading soldiers into the miniature landing craft. Nothing new here. Just the same old tired 'mom and dad' argument we heard every holiday. Undaunted, Billy Ray continued.

"They just use this Santa Claus mess to make ya behave. You know. Santa's watchin' and listenin' and all that crap. If you ain't been good, then you ain't gettin' nothin'."

"Well, I heard Santa's goin' to be down at the dime store tomorrow," Junior smirked.

"Santa ain't nothin' but store clerks dressed up in red suits," Billy Ray snapped. Reading our hesitance, the Grinch moved in for the kill. Like Perry Mason ripping apart a shaky witness, Billy Ray carefully laid out the evidence.

"Think about it, ya'll. Ain't no way a big fat guy in a red suit can get down a little bitty chimney with a bag full of toys. Besides, he'd have to stop somewhere and pee or take a dump."

Take a dump! I'd never considered such a thing. Suddenly, a horrible mental picture exploded in my feeble brain: Santa himself sitting on the throne in our hall bathroom. His red pants pulled down around his ankles. An avalanche of fat dangling off both sides of the toilet like oversized pancakes on a saucer. With his pipe in one hand and toilet paper in the other, Santa flashes a satisfied smile of relief. The idea of the Big Guy taking a whiz or anything else at my house was more than I could handle. This would definitely be the year we stopped leaving him milk and cookies.

"Listen y'all," Billy Ray continued, climbing to his knees. "Tell me how Santa can carry all them toys to everybody in the whole world in just one night? One big fat man. One sleigh. All those presents. Think about it."

Panicked eyes darted around the room. *Think about it! Are you kidding?* What I wanted to do was stick my fingers in both ears and hum the "Star-Spangled Banner!" Why would anyone question Santa's existence? Hands down, Santa's the best thing about being a kid. All we have to do is follow a few rules and we get presents. And Santa brought them. It's that simple. Now take your gifts and shut up!

"Billy Ray's right y'all," Bucky said, breaking his silence. "I've known it for a long time, but I didn't say nothin'. Didn't want to mess it up for little kids."

It was the ultimate insult. The insinuation became a sharp kick in the gut. If we believed in Santa, we were just "little kids." Time to pull out the big guns or bow to ruthless peer pressure. Skeeter stepped to the plate.

"Look stupid! We know he can't do it all in one trip. He goes back to the North Pole and gets another load of toys... and probably pees then."

With the argument raging, I glanced towards the brick fireplace at the far corner of the room. Easing from the fray, I crawled to the base of the hearth. Drawing open the metal chain curtain, I stuck my head inside, peering into the black funnel. *No. No! This can't be true!* There in the sooty darkness, I saw it with my own eyes. The narrow flue was so tiny, Donnie Bright, the skinniest kid at South Maybin Elementary, couldn't squeeze his tiny butt through, much less a fat guy with a bag of toys!

"*See* J.D.! What'd I tell ya?" Billy Ray smirked. Knocking over scenery and kicking soldiers across the room, everyone scrambled to the fireplace. Sinking to the floor, I leaned back on the hearth, pleading to the ceiling. What was happening to my comfortable little world? I knew dang well there weren't no Tooth Fairy but played along hoping for a quarter under my pillow. And the Easter Bunny? Give me a break. But Santa?

With our childhood innocence tossed out the window like a cigarette butt, no one felt like playing. After the guys went home, I sat on the living room floor, staring at the army men scattered about the room. I thought about my Mickey Mantle baseball glove and the scooter I got two years ago. My train set. The Jim Bowie knife with carved wooden handle. Toys of Christmases past. Had it all been a lie?

This could not be happening! Santa never let me down. No matter how bad I'd been all year, he always came through. Well one thing's for sure, there was no way in the world I would dare question my parents about this newly discovered "Santa Conspiracy." In the unpredictable world of kiddom, parents are parents and kids are kids. There are certain subjects kids just can't approach their parents about and this might be the biggest question in the history of the world. I decided to wait and observe until I got some answers on my own.

After supper that night, the season's first commercial appeared during an episode of *The Flintstones*. A camera panned out from an angel atop a beautifully decorated tree revealing a typical Christmas morning somewhere in America. A sleepy-eyed mother shook her head at the clutter piling up in the living room as the happy family eagerly unwrapped their gifts.

"Hey Mom. Why so glum?" came a voice. "Not to worry! Remember your loving husband gave you that brand new Hoover vacuum cleaner as a present. Relax. And have a Merry Christmas!" The mom smiles. No mention of Santa.

The first Christmas commercial of the year was akin to waving the green flag at the Daytona 500. The race to the Big Day was officially underway and for the first time in my life I felt absolutely nothing. Not the first twinge of holiday excitement. Christmas was less than a month away and I didn't care. The revelation of the day had taken its toll.

The next morning the squad assembled in Ashley Woods for a day of wargames. Muddy from the previous day's rain, the battleground was in no condition for warfare. We stuck it out, playing until lunch when we finally threw in the towel.

Barricading myself in my room, I searched for something to do. Anything to take my mind off Santa's sudden demise. Grabbing an unfinished plastic model of a P-51 Mustang and a tube of glue, I'd just sat down at my desk when I heard the phone ring in the kitchen.

"J.D.! Telephone… Billy Ray!" Mom yelled down the hall.

Wonderful. The little shrimp called to rub my nose in it. If Mom hadn't been standing there, I would have cussed him out.

"Hello."

"J.D.! Ya gotta come over!"

"Why?"

"I gotta show ya something! Hurry up! You gotta come over right now!"

Trudging through the garage, I jumped on my bike. A sharp wind bit through my flannel shirt as I pulled out of the driveway. Dang it Billy Ray, this better be good. Rounding the block, I pulled into the yard. Standing on the front porch stood Billy Ray holding a flashlight.

"What's goin' on?"

"You'll see," he smirked. Leading me inside, we ran down the hall, pausing outside a closed door.

"Mom's sewin' room. She was in such a hurry to go shoppin', she forgot to lock it," he beamed, opening the door.

Bundles of folded fabric lay piled on a chair in front of a black Singer sewing machine. A headless mannequin stood in a corner, partially clothed in an unfinished dress. Rolls of festive wrapping paper, tape, and ribbon lay strewn on the bed. Dropping to his knees, Billy Ray stretched out on his stomach.

"I found 'em under here," his voice strained as he pushed aside shoe boxes full of spools. Clicking on the flashlight, he shined the light under the bed. "Look at that!"

Through balls of dust, I saw them. A brand-new Louisville Slugger baseball bat laid alongside a brown leather Spaulding glove. A gasoline-powered Spitfire airplane sat inside a large box with clear plastic top. Under the exposed bed slats laid a Chatty Cathy doll and an Etch-A-Sketch for Billy Ray's little sister Laura. My heart sank like a torpedoed warship.

"Mom's just gotten started. I asked for the bat and glove, but dang. I didn't know about the Spitfire." Rolling over, I closed my eyes, refusing to acknowledge the overwhelming evidence. "What do ya think about Santa Claus now?"

Taking a deep breath, I surrendered. There'd been no reindeer, no bearded fat man in a red suit. It had all been a lie. Riding home, what little hope I had about Santa vanished along with my breath in the cold wind. Just when I didn't think things could get any worse, they did.

Returning to school after a hellish Thanksgiving weekend, I didn't know what to expect, fearing Santa's true identity would be on everyone's lips. As soon as I hit the front door of the school, I could tell the fever had returned. Walking to my classroom felt as if I were strolling the crazed corridors of an insane asylum. Maniacal laughter echoed from open doors and I knew in an instant that Christmas Fever had consumed every boy and girl at South Maybin Elementary with a vengeance. Sparks of excitement, buried in kids' hearts all year, ignited into a four-alarm blaze. From now until Christmas break, no one would sit still for five minutes. Classrooms would soon disintegrate into chaos while exasperated teachers struggled to keep order.

When the final bell rang to go home for the day, I caught up with the guys at the front door for the walk home. Exhaust climbed into the frigid air from idling cars. A bitter gust of wind switched my face. Time for another glorious afternoon of playing war with the guys.

Somewhere in the excitement, a familiar voice called my name. Searching the masses, I spotted Mom standing in front of her car waving at me. Oh joy. Having your mommy pick you up after school was the ultimate embarrassment, particularly for a sophisticated fourth grader. Usually, this shameful occurrence meant something painful awaited, like a trip to the dentist. Suzie stuck her tongue out at me as I slid into the back seat.

"Have a good day?"

"Yes ma'am. Ma, we ain't goin' to the dentist, are we?"

"No. No dentist today. We're goin' Christmas shoppin'."

"*No*," I yelled. Giving my best bratty pout, I slumped down in the seat. No Santa Claus and now this? Boys didn't go shopping with their mommies. I should be outside, playing with my friends.

"We're goin' to Kenan's, so knock it off Buster!" She glared. Suddenly, I perked up. Hold on a second. Spending an afternoon at Kenan's meant Mom had some serious shopping to do. Seeing "The Pro" in action might shed some light on the newly discovered Santa Conspiracy. Besides, Kenan's had the largest toy department this side of the North Pole. Well, at least in North Carolina anyway.

Dressed in festive holiday splendor, Durham was a picture postcard of green and red. Swaths of tinseled lights stretched across busy streets, tethering power poles together in vivid color. Wreaths, bells, and shiny trees glistened from store windows. A city bus spit fumes at us as we made the congested turn at Five Points. Mom lucked out and found a parking place across the street from the huge two-story department store.

In one of our determined races to be first, Suzie and I charged up the sidewalk, when suddenly I stopped dead in my tracks. Just outside Kenan's tall revolving front door stood Santa himself. Shifting on one leg then the other, the bored imposter shivered beside a dangling red kettle, ringing a tiny bell with all the enthusiasm of a bored sloth.

While Mom dug through her pocketbook, I gave "Santa" the once over. This guy was as phony as a three-dollar bill. Black eyebrows and a cheap stringy cotton beard were dead giveaways. His pathetic *Ho-Ho-Ho* was about as sincere as a bull chewing his cud. The charade continues.

Shaking her head, Mom grinned when I took an extra spin inside the store's large revolving door. Packed with holiday shoppers, Kenan's buzzed with the excitement of the season. Stern-faced ladies on a mission hurried down aisles crammed full of countless holiday displays. Their determined high heels snapped across the hardwood floors, keeping time with Christmas carols that drifted through the store. In the distance, a huge Christmas tree draped in a million lights reached for the high square-tinned ceiling.

"Let's go see the tree!" Suzie squealed at Mom's suggestion. Navigating the crowd admiring the giant fir, we joined a line of squirmy kids that formed to one side. There was no mistaking the Big Man, sitting on a golden throne flanked by two giant candy canes. Santa Claus himself! Or Santa's helper or Rodney from hardware.

Shepherding my suddenly deranged sister into the giddy queue of excited kids, Mom and I fell in behind her. When Suzie's turn came, she bolted for Santa's lap. My heart sank, remembering a time when I felt that same incredible rush, busting at the seams to tell Santa what I wanted for Christmas. And I had loved every minute of it. After reciting her exhaustive list, Suzie gripped Santa in a lethal bearhug.

Mom turned toward me and waited. For a second, we stood there staring at each other. Her expectant look and nodding head said it all. I was next. All those years I'd lived for this one special moment. Knowing the Big Guy always came through despite my extensive list of sins during the year. To discover it was all a lie was more than I could take.

Suddenly the prospect of sitting on Santa's lap seemed silly and stupid. A major embarrassment. Something naïve little kids did.

Shaking my head violently, I backed away. Mom's playful expression quickly changed at my hesitation. With a loving smile, she gazed at me as if I were a two-week-old puppy. She knew I knew.

"Please Ma. Don't make me!"

"Do it for Suzie," she sighed.

Humiliated and shamed, I ambled over to Santa's throne, determined to get this embarrassing ordeal over with as quickly as possible.

"My goodness! You've grown so much since last year," he said with surprise, like he remembered me personally. "What would you like for Christmas this year?" he gushed, inches from my face with cigarette breath that could derail a southbound freight.

"A camouflage Marine fighting suit... and a rifle," I rattled off.

"I bet you'd like a baseball and glove too!"

"Gee that'd be swell," I said, playing along. *Playing along. Oh my gosh! What on earth was I doing?* I was being used! Exploited! Duped! Controlled! Manipulated! Another meaningless pawn in the Santa Conspiracy!

"HERE DAD," SUZIE SAID, pulling the front door closed behind her. Dad's probing eyes never left mine as he took the water bottle.

"Say Billy Ray ruined it for ya?"

"He ruined everything he touched. He was good at that."

"I seem to recall him being a little snot," he said, taking a long pull from the bottle. "Hey, I 'member that Christmas too." He grinned. "I believe that was the year we took our first Christmas ride!"

The Christmas Ride

The sentimental recollection of our first Christmas ride unlocked a childhood door to a one-of-a-kind Christmas. A beautiful chapter in our lives, lovingly written on a cold Christmas Eve long ago, suddenly came to life once again in the smiling face of my father. Another one of his spur-of-the-moment adventures.

THAT AMAZING DAY BEGAN like every Christmas Eve as we fell into our standard routine. The blur of chaotic excitement sent stress levels soaring off the charts in an all-day gift wrapping and cooking marathon, interrupted by last minute dashes to purchase one more gift for someone we'd forgot or to the grocery store for that missing ingredient. Unaware Mom was pregnant with our brother, Eddie, something our parents would share with us on Christmas morning, we settled in for the final push. By early afternoon, the sprint to the finish line was clearly in sight.

The unholy revelation of Santa that had haunted me the entire Christmas season magnified as the hours ticked away. Just when the thrill of the season knocked at my heart, the horrible thought of no Santa Claus cut me off at the knees. As usual, Suzie remained an annoying ball of energy, bouncing off the walls. Something I used to do before I learned the truth.

Surrounded by festive wrapping paper and miles of colorful ribbon, Mom crouched over the dining room table. Howling orders like a drill sergeant, she delicately wrapped an array of presents.

Dad, serving as subservient gofer, handed Mom another gift. Blowing unruly bangs from her forehead, Mom's mussed Jackie Kennedy hairdo resembled a tangled squirrel's nest.

"J.D., you drew Cindy's name at Grandpa's. Come sign the tag and put it under the tree." Scribbling my name quickly on the card, I ran to the living room, placing the gift on the growing expanse of colorful boxes. With one eye on the door, I picked through the pile, careful not to ruffle Mom's flawlessly woven bows. To my horror, I found just two dinky presents bearing my name. With Santa out of the picture, I didn't know what to expect.

Experiencing few hiccups, the Harrison team buzzed through the day, completing our Christmas rush in record time. Stuck in adrenaline overdrive, Mom wandered around the house as if she were forgetting something. When she finally dismissed the troops and started supper, the work was over.

Past Christmas Eves found Suzie and me floundering in giddy anticipation until our parents became fed up with our holiday rowdiness and sent us to bed. Instead, the hideous Santa Conspiracy transformed what was supposed to be a wonderful, exciting night into an agonizing hell. Given the endless list of capital crimes I'd committed over the past year coupled with the horrific realization that my fate rested solely in the hands of my unforgiving parents made me a nervous wreck.

After supper, we gathered in the living room surrounded by the soft light of the tree, observing another one of our time-honored Christmas traditions. Dressed in our pajamas, Suzie and I lay on the floor while our parents took their usual seats beside each other on the hearth.

Opening her Bible to the book of Luke, Mom read aloud the Christmas story. Up next, Dad retrieved the familiar tattered red book from the den bookshelves and recited 'Twas the Night Before Christmas. Although I knew the stories backwards and forwards, listening to their overly dramatic portrayal still gave me goosebumps.

When the stories ended, we settled back in silence. Lost in Christmas magic, a comforting quiet flooded the room, drawing us together. I don't know what prompted her. Perhaps it was the stillness of the moment, the soothing glow of the tree or the unexpected downtime. Mom's soft voice broke the silence.

"There's one Christmas I'll never forget," she started, bordering on a whisper. "I was about your age, J.D. I 'member that Christmas real well 'cause it was the year the war started; 1941. We'd just left Grandma and Grandpa Newlin's. They lived on a farm at the end of a dirt road south of Graham. I can still see the black woodstove in the dinin' room that heated the whole house. Grandma cooked every meal on that stove." She chuckled softly. "Momma's family always went there for Christmas Eve supper. Grace, Shelby, and me were so tired, we begged Momma to leave. It was real cold that night and the three of us bunched together in the backseat, tryin' to stay warm. Only sound was Daddy's car bouncin' along the dirt road. Santa didn't bring much back then. Some clothes and a few toys the three of us shared. I 'member thinkin' Santa might not come with the war and all."

Frozen in time, Mom stared into the shadows, speaking to the vision.

"I 'member layin' my head on the window of the car door, feelin' the cold glass against my hair, lookin' up in the sky. No clouds or nothin'. Clear as a bell. Stars shinin' everywhere. Moon was so bright I could see frost on the fields. I 'member thinkin' right then that Christmas Eve was the most peaceful night of the whole year. I believed with all my heart that the whole world stopped what it was doin'. Nobody fightin' no wars or nothin'. That everybody 'membered Jesus was born that night. Even the animals and birds all got quiet and still," she said, as she tucked her prayerful hands between her knees. "I 'member thinkin' that here I was, lookin' at the very same moon and stars that the shepherds, Mary, and Joseph saw that first Christmas. For some reason, I always thought about them poor shepherds sittin' out there in a wide-open field. Sheep layin' down, covered in the light of the Star. That being out there in an open field had to be the most peaceful place on earth... I'll never forget that night as long as I live."

Dad watched her in silence, allowing the story to breathe.

"Well... I know the perfect place," he said, offering his hand.

"Huh?"

"I know the perfect place. Come on. Git'cha coat on!" Staring back at Dad in stunned silence, Mom's mouth flew open.

"Oh boy," I screamed. Throwing a jacket over my pajamas, I sprinted to the car. An unknown adventure awaited us somewhere out there in the dark. The thrill of Christmas was back!

Turning left at the church, we drove past houses draped in strands of colored lights, gaudy plastic Santa Clauses, and manger scenes. Windows sparkled with electric candles and flickering Christmas trees. The dim outline of South Maybin Elementary, lit by a solitary streetlight, stood lonesome and dark as we drove past.

Festive houses transitioned to thick woods and open pastures. The car dipped when the pavement ended and the town of Maybin slipped away in the night. The jet engine sound of crushing gravel filled the car as we bounced over the road.

"Where we goin'?" Mom asked playfully.

"You'll see."

Eerie shadows from the car's headlights danced over ditches and rickety fences. Turning onto a rutty path, Dad pulled the car into the edge of a large field. In the distance, I recognized the tall silos of Gibson's Dairy silhouetted against the night sky. I thought of sweaty fall Saturdays that Dad and I spent dove hunting in the massive field that was now a dead landscape of twisted stems and wheel ruts.

"Here we are!"

"You're crazy," Mom snickered.

"I know."

Suzie and I stepped into the cold night holding tight to each other's hand. Following our parents to the front of the car, we huddled on the bumper trying to stay warm. Except for a few ghostly clouds, the night was crisp and clear. Stars flickered like tiny embers of a dying fire while a quarter moon smiled overhead.

The distant lights of Burlington haloed on the horizon. A far-off train moaned. The night was exactly the way Mom described in her childhood story. Peaceful and quiet. No breeze. Just an open sky that seemed to go on forever. Standing behind Mom, Dad wrapped his arms around her like a muscular blanket. Flashes of breath appeared as he spoke.

"Look y'all, there's the Big Dipper! And the Little Dipper!"

Seeing my parents cuddled together that night gave me a safe comfortable feeling. No matter what, they would always be there. Strong, protecting. Having all the answers.

"Momma? We gonna miss Santa?" Suzie whimpered.

"No, honey. He won't come till ya go to bed."

I'm not sure how long we stayed out in Mr. Gibson's field that night, but I didn't want it to end. Wiping tears on the sleeve of her coat, Mom slid over on the front seat, riding close to Dad on the way home. Leaning my head against the cold window, I stared up at the stars.

And so, it began. A new and thrilling Christmas ritual was born. One we observed without fail for years to come. Rain or shine, bundled up in our pajamas, we rode out to the same open field at Gibson's Dairy every Christmas Eve.

And then life got in the way. Distracted by foolish teenage pursuits, I succumbed to momentary laughter with friends. Riding gleefully along on a swerving ship of stupidity, I willingly grabbed the enticing coattail of fleeting pleasure, leaving behind something lasting and enduring that my family enjoyed without me. The last time I remember tagging along on our Christmas ride was sometime in high school.

"I'll never forget that night as long as I live." A standard declaration I heard my mother make all her life whenever the remarkable happened. Astonishing episodes of life's journey that were sure to stay with her forever.

STARING AGAIN AT THE empty hearth, I knew that the heartfelt narrative of a childhood Christmas ride she'd taken long ago, along with endless chronicled volumes that had once been Dottie Harrison, were gone. Stolen by dementia, erased by time. I wanted to ask to see if by chance she would remember. That by mentioning that magical moment, some faint spark somewhere would ignite a fire of recollection and it would all come rushing back.

"Those were some great times." Dad smiled wistfully.

"When was the last time y'all went out to Gibson's?" Suzie wondered.

"Went every year for the longest time. Missed goin' a few times back in the eighties when we had big snows. We quit for good when I got sick the first time. Now Gibson's a housin' development, so I reckon we won't be goin' back," Dad said, putting his arm around Mom.

"Momma? You 'member us riding out on Christmas Eve... to Gibson's Dairy?" Dad started.

Regrettably, Mom's life had morphed into a series of unexpected cross examinations. Good intentions became embarrassing grillings, putting her on the spot, forcing her to answer while we waited in an awkward silence. Pondering the question as if on a game show, she looked up, searching the ceiling.

"You 'member Christmas Eve? We'd ride out to Gibson's Dairy? Look at the stars?" Dad repeated, his voice a notch louder as if increased volume would help.

"I think so," she said in a nervous laugh. Backing off, Dad turned toward me. A reserved smile washed his face.

"J.D.? You 'member?" he started. "That was the same Christmas ya got that first letter," he said, catching me off guard. Another remarkable childhood moment from that Christmas of Christmases suddenly appeared. How in the world did Dad remember that? A lump rose in my throat. "You 'member the letter, don't 'cha?"

"Of course, I do. How could I forget? I thought that Christmas Eve was going to kill me!" I laughed.

The Cycle

ecalling that harrowing Christmas Eve, I took a seat beside Suzie on the fireplace hearth. Dad's eyes glowed at the memory while Mom, laden by the details of our stories, offered a disinterested glance.

THE UNEXPECTED ADVENTURE AT Gibson's Dairy had Suzie and me in a whirling frenzy. Wide-awake and wired for sound, we burst through the back door, racing each other to the living room, just in case Santa had visited while we were out. Carefully navigating mountains of packages, I reached for the twisted brown cord buried beneath the presents and plugged in the Christmas tree. The sudden explosion of festive light in the dark room amplified our enthusiasm. Tight on our heels, Dad paused at the mahogany desk.

"Listen, y'all need to calm down and get ready for bed." Ignoring his directive, Suzie and I wrestled on the floor in giggling excitement.

Turning on the record player, Dad started a stack of Christmas music, adjusting the volume up an extra notch. Slipping into the den, he gently pulled the door closed behind him. Nat King Cole's version of "The Christmas Song" drifted through the house. A musical cover, masking my parents' clandestine movements in the next room. The show was about to begin.

"OK. You two, off to bed," Mom ordered, peeking through the door. "Talked to Margie on the phone. Said she saw Santa flyin' over on Fifth Street!" Scampering down the hall, Suzie yelled at me as I blew past her bedroom.

"Wake me up in the mornin'!"

"I will!"

Fulfilling another Christmas ritual, Mom retrieved the plastic alarm clock from her nightstand and plugged it into the socket beside my bed. The orange dial would serve as my faithful companion on this exciting night of nights. Following prayers, Mom issued her standard Christmas Eve warning: Under no circumstances was I to open my bedroom door before five o'clock. Last year I made the mistake of going to the bathroom in the middle of the night, forgetting that Dottie Harrison possessed the super ability of detecting the slightest of noises, even in her sleep. Hearing my footsteps in the hall, she burst out of her bedroom and blessed me out.

Exploding with enough energy to run a marathon, I stared at the shadowy ceiling tiles covered in the auburn glow of the nightlight. A headlight ghost from a passing car scampered along the back wall, making a right turn in the corner before fading away.

For me, the possibility of sleeping on Christmas Eve was akin to dozing off while skydiving. Tossing and turning, my mind raced along, fueled by a million sounds that never bothered me other nights of the year, now exploded in my ears at 130 decibels. Passing trains blasted through the restless night as if they were plowing through my bedroom door. Somewhere around ten o'clock, every dog on Circle Drive gathered for a noisy canine version of "Jingle Bells." Wrestling with my pillow, I stared back at the orange clock dial as its lazy second hand wound sluggishly measured orbits.

Desperate for sleep, I counted the 128 ceiling tiles twice along with several herds of sheep. Nothing worked. The exhaustive list of questionable decisions gleefully orchestrated this past year by yours truly would surely come back to bite me come daylight.

Like every other brazen nine-year-old boy, I knowingly pushed my parents to the limit every day of the year in a brutal and vicious cycle of mischief and wrongdoing. Floundering in a churning sea of disobedience the entire year, I never took my actions seriously until Thanksgiving. Faking pitiful sincerity and repentance, cramming a year's worth of manners in those last few weeks, I kissed my parents' butts at every turn, playing to their frazzled emotions as the big day approached. Of course, I'd wake up to a room full of toys every Christmas, proving once again that I'd been worried for nothing.

But that was before I discovered the gut-wrenching truth. Discovering Billy Ray's hidden toys sealed the deal. My hesitation with Santa at Kenan's department store the icing on the cake. The jig was up and my parents knew it. As long as I danced gleefully in the innocence of Santa's existence I was safe. Parents, no matter how vengeful they happen to be, couldn't be so cruel as to reveal Santa's true identity and ruin a naïve little boy's Christmas. With Santa out of the picture by my own admission, Christmas spoils rested solely in their vindictive little hands. Fully justified, my coldhearted parents could gleefully stiff me and get away with it!

To be honest they had every right to crush my spirits come Christmas morning. The past twelve months had been an exceptionally brutal year. Without a doubt, my worst childhood performance ever. Despite regular beatings and lost privileges, the frequency and sophistication of my felonies reached unimaginable lows. Nothing in my tainted past came close in comparison.

In a few short hours, excited children around the globe would scamper from their bedrooms and be gloriously showered with gifts from doting parents. Now, for the first time in my life, I wondered if I would join in the wondrous celebration. Drowning in an uncontrollable case of the fidgets, sleep was simply out of the question. It was just me, the orange clock dial, ceiling tiles, and plenty of time for reflection.

Slowly the rusty wheels began to turn. Sturdy walls of denial that shielded me from the painful memories of the past year crumbled under the weight of my countless transgressions. Crimes exploded like fireworks in the night sky, cascading down in specks of lethal fire.

Summer came to mind. Three magical months of joyous freedom where my offenses reached epic proportions. Naturally, I thought of Larry.

Larry Sizemore was, without question, the smartest kid on Circle Drive. Tall with oily brown hair, his eyes stared back at me like giant golf balls through thick glasses that hung on his nose like a hood ornament. An assortment of pencils filled his shirt pocket in case the urge to perform a few algebra equations hit him. He probably slept soundly every night with a slide rule tucked under his pillow.

With his nose stuck in a book, Larry never took time to play army with the rest of the guys. Too intelligent for the likes of South Maybin Elementary, Larry attended a ritzy private school in Hillsboro for smart rich kids. I never saw him much until summertime, when he drifted mysteriously in and out of my life, conjuring up new and fascinating ideas. One afternoon raised its ugly head as I scrunched the pillow under my head.

The last of spring's cool breezes rustled through the trees before the hot breath of summer rushed in to take its place. Larry and I were playing in our garage engaged in various pyrotechnic pursuits. Warnings never to play with matches became just another irresistible challenge. Out of the blue, Larry declared that gasoline would burn when mixed with water. Somehow, I found the assumption hard to believe, but I wouldn't question Larry's scientific prowess if he told me I was radioactive.

In the middle of his intense oration, Larry spotted a bucket of water sitting beneath a downspout next door.

"Come-on! I'll show ya!"

Grabbing the gas can from our garage, we sprinted up the Sykes' driveway. Peeking around for potential witnesses, Larry confidently poured gasoline into the water, filling the tub to the rim. Reaching inside his pocket, he retrieved a pack of matches.

WHOOSH!

Flames shot up the side of the house like a blazing geyser, licking the porch awning! Hearing our panicked screams, Mr. Sykes ran outside. Reaching inside the inferno he managed to pull the flaming bucket away from the house. Someone called the fire department. After some soul searching inspired by Dad's friend, Mr. Belt, I felt the painful incentive to focus on more positive pursuits. Out of school less than a week and I was gaining notoriety as an arsonist.

Rolling over I cringed at the recollection. No damage really except for raised welts on my backside. The sudden thought of smoke sparked another memory so to speak. The Fourth of July. A truly patriotic disaster.

The summer day dawned in typical North Carolina heat. Afternoon clouds ballooned into fluffy pillows of gray, hinting of a storm. Mom outdid herself meticulously decorating the backyard for our annual neighborhood cookout. Festive bunting draped the patio in patriotic colors. Red, white, and blue tablecloths flapped gently on several folding tables topped with miniature American flags. The laughter of grownups sang harmony with the piercing screams of kids playing in the yard. Twisting streams of smoke rose from two grills filling the air with the tempting aroma of burning charcoal.

The screen door slammed behind us as Skeeter and I rushed to the kitchen for a quick water break. Mom and several other women scurried around, assembling the feast.

"J.D., you and Skeeter grab those trays right there and bring 'em outside."

A stunning patriotic hostess, Mom led the way through the back door wearing a dazzling red and white ensemble, complete with a dark blue apron. Balancing a tray of condiments, she glided through the crowd like a movie star on her way to a premiere. Dad's face lit up in a sneaky smirk the moment Mom stepped outside. Unfortunately, there were times when my father's brain short-circuited, sending ill-advised messages to his tongue. These occurrences seemed to happen at the worst possible time. As Mom sashayed across the patio in her celebratory outfit, Dad raised his spatula high in the air.

"Well! Would y'all lookee here. Here comes Old Glory herself!" Dad quickly realized from the raging expression on Mom's face that he would pay dearly for the obvious tongue malfunction. Off to an awkward start, things quickly deteriorated.

A chorus of "hey y'alls" briefly diverted the crowd from Dad's famous last words. As usual, Ray and Patty Allen arrived fashionably late. With his arm wrapped around his wife's waist, Mr. Allen flashed his signature cocky smile through a cigarette clutched tightly between his yellow teeth. Chestnut-colored sunglasses atop his forehead shoved his greasy dark hair back in an unkept wave. Raising his right hand, Mr. Allen took a long swig from a patriotic can of Pabst Blue Ribbon. *My gosh! Alcohol! On our patio!* Surely our home would be swept away by the wrath of God! Steam rolled out of Mom's ears and for a moment I thought she might solidify into a pillar of salt.

Perpetually the center of attention, Patty Allen purposely ditched the idea of holiday attire, settling instead on a multicolored top and matching pair of sprayed on green pedal pushers. Making their way onto the patio, the Allens shook hands like candidates at a rally. Retrieving a cigarette from her purse, Mrs. Allen grabbed Dad in a tight embrace, sending his spatula tumbling to the patio. On the verge of spontaneous combustion, Mom forced a smile.

Everyone in town knew the juicy details of the Allens' sordid lives. Gossiping was one of Mom's most fervent passions, right up there with collecting F&H Green Stamps, and Patty Allen was, without a doubt, her favorite subject. By simply listening to Mom whisper on the telephone I knew that Mrs. Allen's platinum blonde hair came straight out of a bottle. That there wasn't a doubt in Mom's mind that Mrs. Allen wore "falsies," whatever they were. I learned the Allens had both been married before and were the first couple on Circle Drive to get a divorce. And every Friday night, they drove all the way to Roxboro just to go dancing. But of course, Mom said a lot of things on the phone, never considering for a moment that Suzie and I were eavesdropping.

Seeing the Allens join the party, Suzie scampered across the patio. Reaching up, she tugged at Mrs. Allen's arm.

"Well, hey there little Suzie!" Looking up with her bright green eyes, Suzie twisted excitedly.

"Mrs. Allen? Can I ask ya somethin'?"

"Sure, you can Sweety. What is it?" she answered, bending down, stretching her pedal pushers to the limit.

"Are you really a fwoosy?" Suzie asked as one finger fidgeted on her bottom lip.

At that moment, the humid atmosphere in central North Carolina completely disappeared, violently sucked from the planet and deposited somewhere deep in space, leaving behind a cold silent vacuum. The spirited people on our patio suddenly transformed into stunned statues. "Floosy" along with "hussy" were terms I'd heard Mom use a thousand times on the telephone, usually when Mrs. Allen was the topic of conversation. Unfortunately, Suzie had heard these terms as well. No correction of my sister's mispronunciation was needed. But of course, I insisted.

"No Suzie, it's not 'fwoosy.' It's 'fl-o-o-sy,'" I said, languishing the syllables into a painful southern drawl.

The astonished faces of our catatonic guests quickly changed into sneaky grins. Everyone at the party knew exactly where my little sister had heard that word. Cutting eyes found Mom whose mouth resembled a railroad tunnel. Smiling sweetly into Mrs. Allen's horrified eyes with the purity of an adorable five-year-old, Suzie had no idea. Had it been me who uttered the innocent question, I would have been hogtied and thrown headfirst on the blazing grill with an apple crammed in my mouth.

Desperate to distract her shocked dinner guests, Mom hastily announced a lemonade break for the kids while escaping to the safety of the kitchen. Leaving the scene of the crime I joined the others when Billy Ray came running up.

"Hey. Git the guys together," he puffed, "Got somethin' to show 'em." As a mob of thirsty kids descended on the patio for refreshments, the squad huddled at my tire swing.

"What's goin' on?"

"Follow me," Billy Ray said with a wink. Strolling innocently to the back of Dad's storage shed, Billy Ray peeked around the corner, making sure we weren't followed.

"Look what I got!" Reaching into his jean pocket, he produced a crumpled pack of Lucky Strikes. "You know what they say: Lucky Strike means fine tobacco!"

"Whoa," Skeeter howled.

"Where'd ya git those?" Junior wondered, fingering curiously at the pack.

"Dad left 'em on the front seat of his car. He's got two cartons in the kitchen. He'll never miss 'em."

Smoking was something I'd witnessed all my life, especially at Grandpa Harrison's, where family get togethers became a serious threat to the environment. The cloudy fog of cigarette smoke was so thick in their house that voice recognition was essential to determine another's general location. Although I'd observed the adult pastime with mild curiosity, it never dawned on me to take a puff. Opening the pack, Billy Ray doled out the cigarettes.

Lacking basic smoking etiquette, I examined the thin cylinder as if it were a rare coin. Placing the roll between two fingers, I did my best James Dean impersonation to the delight of my friends. The hesitant looks on my friends' faces revealed they were tobacco virgins as well. Fumbling with the cigarettes in goofy poses, we giggled at each other while Billy Ray stole another peek around the corner. Always prepared, he pulled a silver cigarette lighter out of his pocket featuring a risqué picture of a woman in a grass skirt. Flicking the lighter with his thumb, he held the flame while we circled around him. Remembering how Grandpa did it, I placed the lit cigarette between my lips and sucked as hard as I could. *I thought I was going to die!*

Convinced that I had inhaled the smoldering flame from the tip of the cigarette into my lungs, I sputtered and hacked, trying to eject the fiery ember! *How in the world did Grandpa do this?* How did *anybody* do this? Like a choir of sputtering lawn mowers, we hocked and wheezed as our coolness vanished with the swirling smoke. Unfazed by our smoke-induced choke fest, Billy Ray resembled a cool and calm Edward R. Murrow in the middle of an interview. Watching him blow a perfect smoke ring, I wondered if he was up to three packs a day.

"Hey! Take it easy y'all. Not so fast," he laughed.

Coughing uncontrollably, I almost threw up. Skeeter fell back against the building. His face as white as a sheet. A string of snot blew out of Junior's nose as he heaved violently.

"What in the Sam Hill are y'all doin'?" Lost in the agony of group choking, no one noticed my dad, Mr. Satterfield, and Mr. Crabtree standing at the corner of the building.

Surprised by the interruption, we nonchalantly dropped our cigarettes on the ground, stepping on them as if that would help.

"Oh, don't do that," Dad laughed. "Everyone wants to see just how grown up y'all are!"

Jerking the pack from his son's hand, Mr. Satterfield pulled out four more flamethrowers.

"OK boys. Light 'em up!" Continuing to hack, I tried as hard as I could to choke myself to death.

"Follow me," Dad ordered. Leading the procession across the yard, he joyfully announced our grand entrance to the stunned party.

"Ladies and gentleman! May I have your attention please!" With cigarettes dangling from our mouths, the four of us trudged along as if on our way to the gallows.

"May I introduce to you our Fourth of July firecrackers! J.D., Skeeter, Billy Ray and Junior!" Shaking their heads, women's eyes narrowed in disgust. Beatings would surely follow. Men chuckled under their breath. On the other hand, I'd never been so happy in all my life to see a backyard full of company. Mom wouldn't dare kill me in front of this many witnesses.

When the Fourth of July farce finally ended, Mom sat me down for a screaming lecture, grounding me from TV, playing army, eating, drinking, sleeping, and anything else she could think of. Despite her continuous pleas to beat me, Dad surprisingly spared me a whipping, figuring that mortified embarrassment was enough punishment for one day.

With a heavy sigh, I rolled over to check the time, sure that my pitiful impersonation of the Marlboro Man would no doubt command a heavy price, paid in full in just a few hours.

The smoky recollection of that hot July afternoon ignited a firestorm. Suddenly the floodgates opened. Wrongdoings and misdeeds crashed over me like a giant tidal wave. None of which were more dramatic than the endless monkey business concocted while swimming at Bucky's.

His dad was one of only two physicians in the entire town, so they were rich. Nestled beneath a grove of tall pine trees in their backyard stood the only inground swimming pool south of the tracks. A cool refreshing oasis that drew neighborhood children to the Watkins' house on hot summer days. For our squad, the welcoming sanctuary from the summer heat became a cesspool of sins, where our wildest schemes and conspiracies were conceived.

Swimming and mischief weren't the only temptations luring us to this relaxing retreat. The outside chance of feasting our eyes on Bucky's stunning thirteen-year-old sister Gloria in a skimpy bathing suit kept our squad on high alert the whole summer. Blessed with long auburn hair and gorgeous green eyes, it was obvious that God had spent a little extra time creating this beautiful goddess.

Closing in on adolescence, it didn't take much to push our rowdy fraternity's stupidity and curiosity pedals to the floor. When the word spread of a "Gloria sighting," our squad descended on Bucky's pool like hungry vultures. Suddenly a hot afternoon in midsummer came gushing forth and I shamefully buried my face into my pillow.

Well into the nineties, the steamy sun baked itself in a cloudless sky turning the heavens white with heat. The humid shade of Ashley Woods offered little respite as we gathered at the rock trench for a game of Ambush. Sweat streamed down my face while a group of annoying gnats found me irresistible.

"Bucky comin' or not?" Junior whined. "I'm burnin' up!"

We were just about to start the battle when our tardy friend came traipsing through the woods wielding a silly grin.

"Where ya been?" Skeeter asked. Ignoring the question, Bucky jumped straight to the point.

"Guess what? I heard Gloria on the phone. A few girls are comin' over to go swimmin'."

Tossing our weapons aside, we charged through the woods. Catching our breath at the edge of the yard, we stared at each other in eager anticipation. The moment we'd fantasized about all summer had finally arrived. A tantalizing mission awaited, requiring stealth and cunning. One false move and the whole operation would be compromised.

Taking charge of our breathless herd of sheep, Bucky led us single file to a mass of shrubbery at the corner of his house. Checking that the coast was clear, we sprinted across the yard, taking cover behind a storage shed. The pool was deserted.

"Where are they?" Junior puffed.

"Won't be long," Bucky said, wiping his sweaty face on his sleeve. Lost in dreamy images, the five of us crouched down, fanning ourselves with our plastic army helmets. A car slowed and turned into the driveway.

"Car y'all," Skeeter said. "It's Mrs. McPherson's red Chevy."

"Oh my gosh! Are you kiddin'? Wanda McPherson? Lord help me," Junior broadcasted a little too loud.

"Shh!" we sprayed in unison. Pulling a pair of binoculars from his backpack, Skeeter focused on the three girls as they skipped to the front door.

"Barbara Sue, Wanda, and Elaine," he whispered.

Junior began to drool. We'd hit the jackpot! In a few moments, three cheerleader knockouts from Maybin Junior High would join Gloria for an afternoon at the pool. I elbowed Junior who was now visibly shaking.

"Junior. You OK?"

"Yeah, yeah, I'm fine."

"Ya look kinda weird. Maybe ya oughta sit this one out."

"And miss a bunch of half-naked girls? No way!"

A slamming screen door sent us jumping. Peeking around the corner, we gawked in little boy amazement as the four beauties danced down the path toward the pool. Colorful bags swung back and forth in their hands, no doubt packed with itsy bitsy teenie weenie yellow polka dot bikinis!

Carrying a small radio the goddess herself led the troupe. Once inside the gate the girls disappeared into the dressing room while Gloria stepped out on the pool deck. Adjusting the volume, she placed the radio between folded lawn chairs, then darted back to the pool house.

"Let's go," Junior yelled. Grabbing his arm, Skeeter jerked him to the ground.

"Dammit Junior, shut up! You're gonna screw it all up!"

"Listen y'all. Stay close," Bucky whispered. "And keep your mouths shut," he said, glaring at Junior. "OK, move out."

Lumbering through the yard, we collapsed behind a wall of thick azaleas that ran alongside the pool's chain-link fence. We couldn't have planned it any better. The blaring radio along with our green fatigues blending perfectly with the foliage offered the perfect cover. All we had to do was sit back and enjoy the show!

The unforgiving sun frowned overhead, boiling us in our own sweat. Fighting the urge to move, I tugged on the soaked shirt plastered to my skin. Music echoed across the pool as we wrestled each other for the best vantage point.

Suddenly the dressing room door flew open to a chorus of giggles. Floating onto the pool deck wearing two-piece bathing suits were four of the most beautiful girls on the face of the earth. Gloria was simply stunning. Her long hair fell over her tan shoulders as she swayed along. As the girls made their grand entrance, the song "The Stripper" blasted over the radio. "Oh, my Lord," someone mumbled. Everything moved in slow-motion. Curves, arms, and legs swirled seductively in time with the music while the squad melted into a sun-drenched stupor. Crouched on his knees, Junior's head bobbed up and down like a lost ship in a hurricane.

"Junior," I whispered. "Junior! Be still!" The combination of blazing sun and supercharged spectacle was just too much. Like a giant oak tree sawed off at the base, Junior fell face first into the bushes in front of him. Reaching over, I shook his arm.

"I think he's dead," I mouthed.

Absorbed in preteen heaven, we took in the amazing sight before us. The slightest gesture of a bare arm or the slight twist of hair became a life-altering moment forever burned into the imaginations of five little boys.

The sudden ring of the pool house phone broke the alluring spell. Leaving her chair, Gloria ran inside to answer the call. A few minutes later she returned, whispering something to the others. Nodding their heads in excitement, they retreated to the dressing room. Reaching over, I grabbed Junior's arm.

"Junior! Wake up!" Unconscious, he laid there like a log.

"Follow me," Bucky motioned. Leaving Junior to decompose in the sweltering sun, we sprinted through the pool gate. Tiptoeing past the closed door, we could hear their muffled conversation and faint laughter. Holding a finger to his lips, Bucky led us to the boys' changing room. Once inside, he raised his hand high to get our attention, then pointed to an opening under the bathroom sink and grinned.

Light filtered through a small gap in the plumbing lines. It hit us all at the same time. Holy smokes! We could peek at the girls from under the sink! Stampeding over each other, we raced to be the first, knocking over a pile of deck chairs in the process. At that moment, Junior burst through the door with the grace and style of a drunken Otis Campbell.

"Bucky! I'm gonna kill you!" Gloria shouted.

Flying out the door, we shot past the dressing room.

"I'm tellin' Dad!" Running as fast as we could, we didn't stop till we reached Ashley Woods.

Once my parents found out, a hasty conference was arranged with Mr. Belt, leaving red furrowed rows on my legs that resembled our summer garden. Life as we knew it came to an end as all pool activities at the Watkins' were banned indefinitely.

Branded an arsonist, an aspiring Marlboro Man, and now a Peeping Tom, my mind shifted into overdrive. With my guilty conscience on a roll, Bucky's tenth birthday reared its ugly head.

With our infamous pool fiasco hanging over our heads, salvaging our precious swimming rights took some doing. After a celebratory birthday supper, a trip to the movies followed by shameless begging, Bucky's parents consented to a squad sleepover in the pool house. Skeeter and Billy Ray brought sleeping bags while the rest of us threw a few sheets over lawn chairs. Somewhere around midnight, we went for another swim. With soft moonlight reflecting off the cool water, we splashed to a pleasant chorus of tree frogs and katydids.

"Skinny dippin' time," Bucky announced. This daring undertaking became standard fare when the pool was ours. As long as the tall pole lights at the four corners of the fence remained dark, we were safe. Who'd be awake this time of night anyway? Inhibitions quickly vanished along with any semblance of intelligence. Before long we were chasing each other around the pool deck in a naked and dangerous game of tag.

Out of nowhere, the pole lights exploded in a blinding flash! The pool lit up like a meteor! Wearing nothing but my Yankee baseball cap, I lost my balance, falling into the water. Unfortunately, Billy Ray happened to be relieving himself through the chain-link fence while singing "Popeye the Sailor Man." The sudden interruption sent him falling backwards, holding himself in agony. A screen door slammed somewhere in the dark and Dr. Watkins appeared at the gate a few seconds later. Dad got wind of our midnight shenanigans and blessed me out. By the grace of God, he didn't tell Mom, figuring the image of me running around naked at the Watkins' swimming pool would be too much for her to handle.

Somewhere along the way, you'd think I'd learn. Scrapes and bruises soon heal, but brazen stupidity never dies. A few weeks later, the squad was enjoying a leisurely afternoon swim when Bucky suggested we go skinny dipping in broad daylight.

"Are ya crazy?" Junior objected.

"We'll stay in the pool the whole time. No runnin' around. Ain't nobody gonna see us," Bucky assured. Considering there would be no brazen demonstrations of boyhood, we figured nothing could happen.

"What we gonna do with our bathin' suits?" Skeeter wondered. "We can't just throw 'em on the side of the pool. Somebody might see 'em."

"I know! Let's put 'em on the bottom. At the deep end," Billy Ray laughed. The teasing thought of our bathing suits lying ten feet underwater was just too exciting to pass up. Slipping our trunks off, we dove down, depositing them on the pool floor.

Skinny dipping in the middle of the afternoon didn't offer the wild rush of a night swim, but it was certainly daring and adventurous. I'd just broken the surface after a handstand to the sound of panicked screams. Strolling leisurely down the path towards the pool was the goddess herself. This time, the vision of Gloria Watkins in a two-piece bathing suit was positively terrifying.

Churning through the water like angry piranha, we dove to the pool's deep end. My ears screamed their displeasure as our whirling hands groped through the submerged pile of bathing suits. Squinting, I reached into the mass of blurred color. With my lungs on fire, I grabbed a suit and shot to the surface just in time to see Gloria ambling through the gate. Coughing and sputtering for air, we frantically bobbed in the water. Putting on a bathing suit in the water felt like floundering in a sea of wet cement. Working feverishly, I managed to get my feet into the suit but couldn't pull the twisted mass past my knees. In a moment of absolute horror, I realized the trunks weren't mine.

"Lookin' for this?" Standing at the shallow end, Billy Ray grinned from ear to ear, playfully twirling my red bathing suit on his finger. Returning a middle finger of my own, I plowed through the water, pinning myself against the side of the pool.

"Hey guys. Mind if I join ya?" Stepping onto the diving board, Gloria gazed down at her trembling prey.

"How's the water, J.D.?"

"Go on Gloria," Bucky pleaded.

"Guess I oughta call Barbara Sue, Wanda, and Elaine. Great day for a swim!"

"Go on!"

Satisfied she had extracted her revenge, Gloria meandered back through the gate, laughing hysterically. Turning one last time she grinned at us as we cowered in the water.

"Wait till I tell Cindy Lou."

Oh no! Not Cindy Lou Hunter! Circle Drive's resident big mouth! Our afternoon escapade would be all over town, church, and school. None of us would be able to show our faces, or anything else for that matter, in public ever again! For exposing myself, I was forced to apologize to Gloria and her entire family. Mom was positively mortified. Again, the squad was grounded from the pool and as usual, I felt the hot wrath of Mr. Belt.

Shaking my head, I stared up again at the ceiling tiles. Yep. Baring it all to Gloria Watkins sealed the deal. Might as well forget about Christmas and pray for a playful basket of candy at Easter. Mom had probably taken my stocking off the mantel by now.

Resigned to my fate, I listened as the grind of another train approached in the distance. The blaring horn cried louder with every blast. From the echo, I knew the train was passing in front of Knight's Furniture about to cross Fifth Street at the depot.

The depot! The unexpected recollection of that horrible night summoned a deep inhale. I'd tried my best to bury the rotting corpse of that awful memory, purging that hot summer night from my soul. The Blunder of all Blunders politely waited its horrific turn aboard my Christmas Eve Shamefest, bringing the curtain down on the final act of a sickening play.

It happened during the waning days of summer. School was starting back in less than a week. The night would be our last summer hurrah. A final bash before the grind of school stole our souls. Threatening to kill us if we stepped out of line, Dr. Watkins reluctantly agreed to one more sleepover at the pool house and laid down the law: No nudity. Be quiet and behave. Promising a mischief-free evening, we blissfully gathered for what would be the last time we would ever spend the night at Bucky's pool.

Lounging around the pool house, we recalled the glorious freedom of our fading summer, reminiscing about lazy days of Ambush, riding bikes, and playing baseball. In less than fifteen minutes we were bored out of our minds. Like inmates in a prison dayroom, we occupied the time playing War with a deck of cards. The only excitement was the occasional flash of the outdoor lights illuminating the pool like a search-light, reminding us that Warden Watkins was standing guard. As the night wore on the frequency of flickers diminished and after eleven o'clock the lights went off for the last time.

Antsy and restless, we weren't ready to call it a night. Besides, demons never sleep. Billy Ray had never sat this still for this long his entire life and was on the verge of exploding.

"Hey y'all! I got an idea! Let's ride bikes!" Excited suggestions from Billy Ray usually ended very badly, accompanied by extreme pain.

"Naw, Billy Ray. Let's just stay here," Skeeter said, laying back on his sleeping bag. "Let's not push it."

"What could happen? We'll ride for a little bit. Come back. Nobody'll know we're gone… Come on y'all," he begged. "I'm goin' crazy sittin' here!"

What we should have done was tie a cinderblock around Billy Ray's legs and thrown his skinny ass in the pool. A bad feeling came over me that something awful awaited us if we ventured outside the pool fence.

"What if Dr. Watkins turns the light on again or comes down to check on us?" Junior wondered.

"I know!" Bucky laughed. Running into the dressing room, he returned with an assortment of floats and inner tubes.

"Here. Stuff these in your sleepin' bags! Dad won't know the difference. He ain't gonna come down here no way. Probably snorin' to beat the band!" For the first time all night, we smiled at each other. Grabbing my Yankee baseball cap, I joined the others.

Strange how the mind plays tricks when you're in the middle of committing a crime. Pushing our bikes through the backyard, I peered into the shadows at Bucky's dark house wondering if someone were watching. Riding single file through a break in the bushes, we moved by the glow of a full moon. Exiting the trees onto Fifth Street, we jumped curbs and circled manholes with our bicycles, drifting towards downtown.

No one spoke as if the slightest noise would summon our parents from the dark. Heat rose from the street like a giant floor furnace. Flashes of heat lightning lit the sky in silent fireworks while droning window fans and air conditioners sang a monotone refrain. Crickets and other hidden night sounds announced our arrival at the depot.

That night was the first time I remember seeing downtown completely still. Bathed in the glimmer of streetlights, the three-story brown buildings resembled a lonely picture hanging on a wall. The only movement came when the three stoplights changed in unison. Behind the depot the black outline of the mattress company stood against the night sky like a giant mountain, quiet and deserted. In the distance, the constant whine of third shift looms from Tarheel Textiles echoed through the canyon of brick buildings. Across the tracks, yellow lights burned through the elongated windows at Knight's Furniture, giving the massive factory the appearance of a gigantic ocean liner passing in the night. The distinctive smell of burning wood from its invisible smokestack made the night seem warmer.

"Race ya to the dock!" Billy Ray's tattletale voice shattered the quiet. The first words spoken since we'd left Bucky's were loud and frightening. Laying our bikes down in the gravel parking lot we took the depot's rickety wooden steps two at a time.

"Beat 'cha!" Billy Ray laughed. A welcome westerly breeze floated through the open cargo dock sheltered from the elements by a green plank roof.

"You're it!" I said, punching Skeeter's shoulder. We scattered through the maze of stacked wooden shipping crates, screaming as we ran. Lost in the thrill of being chased, staying one step ahead of an outstretched hand just inches from fluttering shirttails. My chest pumped like the pistons of a train, inhaling the night air. Freedom on a hot summer night. Sneaking around made it all that much sweeter. At that moment, Maybin belonged to a bunch of little boys without a care in the world. Nobody there to tell us what to do. An exhilaration I can't explain. Perhaps deep down inside, I knew it would never happen again.

Running as fast as I could, I leaped off the dock crashing to the dusty parking lot three feet below, marking my landing with two distinct impressions.

"Beat dat!"

Junior followed, yelling as he left the platform. No one came close to my sandy divot. Bucky was the last to take a shot. Assuming a three-point stance, he charged to the edge of the dock. With his arms flailing in rapid windmills he crushed my footprint.

"Beat 'cha!"

"Nuh uh! You landed on mine! We tied."

"I beat 'cha fair and square!"

"Did not!"

"Did so!"

Leaving us to our eloquent debate, the others dashed into the middle of the empty intersection. Skeeter turned a cartwheel in the illuminated pyramid of a streetlight. Cocking his head, Billy Ray sized up the overhead light whose triangular metal casing resembled a conical straw hat.

"Watch this," he said, grabbing chunks of gravel. "Jimmy show'd me this the other night over on Sixth Street. If I hit it just right, it sounds like the bell at church."

Raring back, he threw the rock, missing everything. Improving his aim with each try, he tossed a perfect strike. The rock ricocheted off the light's covering with the thud of a muffled bell.

"See! What I tell ya!"

Our shadows danced on the asphalt as the streetlight recoiled overhead. Selecting another projectile, Billy Ray tried his luck once more. This time the rock struck the softball-sized bulb. A blue spark shot through the night, synchronized with a sharp pop. Specks of glass showered down in the now dark intersection.

"Boy! You done done it now!" I shouted above the wild hysterics.

Our raucous laughter abruptly died when a sudden flash of headlights lit up the canopy of trees overhead. Dad always told me that the only people out late at night were police and thugs. I didn't wait around to find out which one crept slowly towards us.

Racing to our bikes, I shuddered as white beams rose slowly over the hill like a ghostly sunrise. Falling in behind Bucky, I pedaled as hard as I could. High beam headlights exploded, capturing us in a wavy arm of light! I didn't dare look back. Screeching tires and a racing engine pursued us down the street. Starting low and rising in pitch, the cutting sound of a siren ripped through the night, drowning our collective screams. The spinning light atop the cruiser painted the surrounding buildings a bloody red.

In numbing fear, I willed my burning legs to pump faster. Following his every turn, I closed in on Bucky. At the last second, he cut sharply into a narrow alley. Barely missing a fire hydrant, I followed him through the dim passageway. The police car roared past, racing us to the corner. Darting through yards and driveways, I trailed Bucky's moonlit outline.

"Look out!" At the last second, Bucky spotted the clothesline. Ducking my head, the black wire clipped the baseball cap off my head as my bike rushed underneath. Jumping a curb, we rushed into the car strewn parking lot of the textile mill. Exhausted, I jumped off my bike and collapsed beside a pickup truck. The others sailed in behind me.

"Where's Junior?" I asked, my lungs gasping for air. No one answered. A beacon of headlights swept overhead. The siren stopped as the police car slowly drifted past the parking lot leaving us shivering in a chilling silence. Searching for us the cruiser eased to a stop at an intersection. Its flashing light went dark as the car turned left.

"He's callin' for backup y'all!" Skeeter screamed. "This place will be crawlin' with cops—"

"Shut up Skeeter," I panted.

The blunt smell of rubber and oil filled every breath as I leaned back against a truck's muddy tire. Suddenly the tremors of an approaching train cut through the night. Its blaring horn and steady drumbeat of railcars slammed through downtown in a deafening roar. Clapping my hands over my ears, I began to cry. Thankfully no one saw me whimpering in the dark. *How did this happen? Why did this happen?* Like a passing summer storm, the westbound freight disappeared, leaving only the hum of whirling looms from the mill.

"OK ya'll, let's go home," I said, wiping my face.

Pausing at the parking lot entrance, we squinted at the line of street-lights stretching down the street. Taking a different route, we quietly pedaled home. Reaching the Fifth Street intersection, I saw something move in the shadows.

My hasty shout created a chain reaction, sending everyone into a screaming frenzy.

"It's me! It's me!"

Bleeding from his knees and elbows, Junior sobbed as he limped towards us, clutching his right arm. Any other time, he would have been dubbed a "crybaby." But not tonight.

"Can't move my arm. Hurts bad."

"Where's your bike?" I asked.

"Fell makin' the turn at the alley. Bike's all busted up."

"We gotta git 'cha home. Stay out of the light goin' back," I said, surprising myself. Cutting through yards and side streets, we ducked onto the familiar path leading to Bucky's house. Circle Drive had never looked so beautiful.

One of the many consequences in choosing a life of crime is conjuring up the endless list of lies required to cover up the myriad of loose ends. Bucky's convincing story to his sleepy parents described in remorseful detail a midnight chase around the pool when Junior tripped over the diving board. Presenting our sobbing friend did the trick. After a phone call to Junior's parents, Dr. Watkins took him down to his clinic. Bucky rode along while the rest of us waited nervously in the pool house. No one said anything as we tossed about on our makeshift beds, pondering a million "what ifs."

"The bike," Billy Ray blurted out, scaring us all half to death. "They got Junior's bike! Prob'bly on its way to the FBI lab right now!"

"Oh no," Skeeter whined, on the verge of tears.

"We'll go by in the mornin'. See if it's there," I sighed, shuddering at the prospect of returning to the scene of the crime. Restless hours slogged by before car lights appeared in the driveway.

"They found us! I knew it! We're goin' to jail," Skeeter cried.

"It's Dr. Watkins," I said, spotting his dark outline in the shadows. A few minutes later Bucky hurried through the pool gate.

"Junior's arm's broken. Dad put it in a cast… his parents met us and took him home," he panted, wiping sweat from his face on his shirtsleeve. "I think we pulled it off." He nodded. Breathing a sigh of relief, I fell back on my lawn chair. Bucky's assuring words were like a cold drink of water in a dry desert. Overwhelmed by exhaustion we settled down and drifted off to sleep.

We woke to a yellow sun filtering through the sleepy pines. Hungry and running on fumes we debated our next move. With so much unfinished business, no one mentioned the prospect of going home. Somehow we had to recover the one piece of evidence that could send us up the river.

"Listen y'all. Billy Ray and I'll go to the alley. Look for Junior's bike," I said, tying my tennis shoes. "Y'all wait here and don't say nothin' to nobody." I was sure that if we survived all this, there was a high-level job waiting for me in a New York crime family.

Unable to shake the temptation, Billy Ray and I detoured by the depot. The more we shuffled down the street, the madder I became. None of this mess would have ever happened if it hadn't of been for Billy Ray! Glancing out of the corner of my eye, I watched him stare solemnly at the sidewalk. It was all his fault! *He* suggested going bike riding. *He* broke the streetlight. A cold shiver ripped through me. Oh my gosh! The rock! We forgot about the rock! Any moment the police would pull Billy Ray's grubby little fingerprints off the lethal stone that broke the streetlight. It would all be over!

Suddenly both of us stopped dead in our tracks. A block away, a police car sat sideways in the intersection beside the depot, blocking traffic, while a man in the arm of a yellow bucket truck replaced the streetlight. Panicked, we sprinted in the opposite direction, circling back to the alley. Surprisingly, we found what was left of Junior's bike leaning against the alley wall. Limping the twisted heap of metal back to Circle Drive, we hid the wreck in Ashley Woods.

My parents never suspected a thing. "It was a shame about Junior's arm," they said. "You know better than to be runnin' at the pool." Satisfied we'd beaten the rap, we decided to let that horrible night die. Never to be spoken about again. A terrible secret we'd take to our graves.

That hot summer night scared the living daylights out of me. I'd done some pretty stupid things in my short life, but this had been the worst. Deciding to go straight, I vowed to the moon and stars there would be no more nighttime excursions, no more nudity and never again would I entertain another one of Billy Ray's stupid schemes. It was time I made something of myself before it was too late.

A few days later I was enjoying a relaxing afternoon in my room, putting together a plastic model airplane, when Dad came in. Closing the door behind him, he tossed my New York Yankee hat on my bed. My heart stopped beating.

"Sergeant Edwards found it in Mr. Landry's backyard. Said you were the only kid he knew in town with a Yankee cap." Leaning against the wall, Dad crossed his arms, which was never a good sign. "He told me that last Saturday night, he chased a bunch of kids that broke out a streetlight at the depot. Ain't that the night you stayed at Bucky's?"

Before Dad finished his question, tears began rolling down my face.

"I ain't tellin' your ma. She'd blow a fuse. This 'tween us. Now put your shoes on. You and me gonna take a ride."

At that moment I knew I was going to get it big-time and I deserved every painful lash. I was nine, unsure if I'd make it to ten. Peeking up, I expected to see fire consuming Dad's face. Instead, a sad, hurtful expression filled his blue eyes. Over the years, I'd made Dad angry more times than I could count. But this was different.

A slick combination of snot and tears streamed down my cheeks as I slid in the DeSoto's front seat. Driving downtown, we pulled to the curb in front of the police station. A few minutes later we were escorted into Chief Clark's office. Staring at the floor, I closed my eyes while Dad explained how ashamed he was of me, assuring Chief Clark that I would be paying the town back for the streetlight. Humiliated, I just stood there and cried.

On the way home, Dad informed me how much the light would cost and that I would be paying for the damage in weekly installments out of my allowance. After some quick figuring, I realized that I'd be paying restitution to the town of Maybin till I was eighty-two.

My reputation as Maybin's youngest hoodlum had reached epic proportions. Naturally, I received a brutal whipping. Mom didn't ask why. She'd gotten use to the beatings over the years. Surely it was warranted, whatever I'd done.

Staring up at the ceiling tiles, I relived the nightmare one more time. Destroying city property was the last straw. No more guessing or hoping. There would be no last-minute reprieve from the Governor. It would be tough, but Christmas would pass like any other day of the year. The eventual acceptance of my fate gave me a strange sense of peace and it wasn't long before I fell asleep.

A terrifying nightmare featuring my mother firing at me from the turret of a Sherman tank shook me awake. Rolling over, I squinted at the clock, 4:48; T-minus twelve minutes and counting! The longest night of my life was almost over. The familiar Christmas morning tingle of excitement and hunger rose in my stomach. In a matter of minutes, this year's edition of The Cycle would officially come to its exciting conclusion. For me, playing The Cycle had always been the ultimate challenge. One I pushed to the limits every year with all the mischief and cunning I could muster, gleefully walking a tightrope across a bottomless ravine without a safety net. But this year I'd gone too far, devilishly stepping over the line and never looking back. I'd played the Cycle one too many times and this time, I lost.

Squinting again at the black hands of the clock dial, I read the time: 4:54. Close enough. I had to know! Bursting into Suzie's room, I plopped down on her bed.

"Suzie! Suzie! Santa Claus came!" Throwing back the covers, she grabbed me in a squealing embrace. Creeping through the pale outline of a streetlight angled on the den floor, we felt our way through the dark. In years past, I'd come close to ripping the living room door off its hinges with excitement. This time, I hesitated.

"Come on J.D.!"

The hinges softly whined as I pushed open the door. My heart pounded as I stared into the darkness. This was it. Taking a deep breath, I ran my hand across the wall, feeling for the light switch. Squinting, my eyes fought back at the blinding explosion. The tantalizing scent of hard plastic and metal permeated the room, blending with the aroma of Fraser fir. Santa never wrapped anything at our house, leaving high priority gifts in the open for full visual effect. Unleashing a primal scream, Suzie bolted for her toys stacked neatly beside the brick planter.

Disoriented, my burning eyes adjusted. Standing in the open door-way, I saw them. Toys! Lots of toys! Too many for just Suzie! Frozen in sensory overload, I spotted a Marx Battleground set. That would make number six. It was official. I now had more soldiers stationed at my house than Fort Bragg. An Erector Set leaned against the hearth next to an Untouchables play set. Camouflage Marine fatigues were laid out and neatly folded, held in place by a green plastic helmet and canteen.

A spark of intelligence ripped through my brain. *Santa had come! Or Mom and Dad! I didn't care. There were toys! Wonderful, magnificent, thrilling, too good to be true toys.* The inborn lust of selfish materialism drove my feet forward. Sluggish steps became a frantic sprint. Sliding to my knees, I glided across the hardwood floor in my pajamas. Sliding to a stop at the Marx Battleground set, I embraced the cardboard box like a newborn.

A frantic bee in a meadow of spring flowers, Suzie darted from one toy to another, lovingly caressing each one. Any other Christmas morn-ing I would have torn into my presents with reckless abandon. Feeling both relief and wonder, I sat there in stunned amazement. Christmas had come and I had not been forgotten!

Bursting into our parents' bedroom, Suzie and I screamed as we mercilessly trampolined above the covers. A few minutes later, Mom and Dad emerged like a couple of bleary-eyed grizzlies roused from hibernation. Forcing weary smiles, they collapsed near the hearth. Lis-tening to us ramble on about our gifts, Mom waited for the right mo-ment.

"Have ya looked in your stockin' yet, J.D.?"

"No ma'am," I said halfheartedly. I never quite understood the overdone Christmas stocking obsession. Here I was up to my shoulders in shiny new toys and Mom was concerned about a sock full of brown bananas. With the excitement of a snail, I offered the red and green stocking a cursory glance.

"Might want too. Ya just never know. Might be a surprise in there."

I almost declined but then again Mom and Dad had come through for me big time. I owed them that. Standing on the hearth, I lifted the fruit-filled sock off the nail. A white envelope protruded from the top. Curious, I looked over at my parents who smiled at my every move.

Examining the cover, I noticed my initials written on the front. Inside I found a letter written on lined notebook paper.

Dear J.D.,

I hope you like everything you got for Christmas this year. You'll be ten in a couple of months and won't be a little boy much longer, so enjoy every moment. I heard from some of the Elves that you don't believe in me anymore. That's OK. There are a lot of people out there that don't. Still, I want you to remember one thing. Never forget that I still love you. It's OK if you don't believe in me. But never forget that I will always believe in you!

Love,

Santa

THERE WAS NO MISTAKING the familiar swirls and arcs of Mom's flawless cursive. Looking into my parents' eyes, I saw something different. Without saying a word, their expressions became crystal clear. The three of us now shared a special secret that Suzie didn't need to know right now. As Big Brother, I was expected to be the keeper of that secret, safeguarding Suzie as long as I could. Grinning back, I realized we were now playing on the same team. Their welcoming devilish grins officially accepted me as a card-carrying member of the Santa Conspiracy.

My first performance as a new cast member was certainly Oscar worthy. Feigning wild surprise, I showed Suzie the letter, signed by Santa himself. In crazed excitement, Suzie discovered a letter from Santa in her stocking as well and just like that, another Christmas ritual was born in the Harrison house. From that day forward one of the highlights of Christmas morning was experiencing the thrill of discovering personalized letters from Santa.

The jam-packed day of celebration, including two family get-togethers and eight tons of food, didn't end until after nine o'clock. Exhausted, Suzie fell asleep before we backed out of Grandpa Harrison's driveway. The quiet ride home became a welcome respite from the day's bombardment of noise.

Before going to bed, I stood in the doorway of the living room one last time as the soft lights of the tree glistened on the mound of toys like a full moon shining on a calm sea. I thought about The Letter and the secret I now shared with my parents. I'd experienced some pretty amazing Christmases in my nine years, but without a doubt, this was the best.

I also realized that I'd been granted one more chance. Never again would I tread on thin ice while carrying an anvil. Never. This was it. No more shenanigans. My hoodlum days were officially over once and for all. Twenty-four hours ago, all was lost. OK. So Santa wasn't real. Well, maybe not in the way I had always believed, but Christmas came anyway.

With the big day behind us, our exhausted family relished in a welcome few days of relative peace as parent-child hostilities observed the official Christmas ceasefire. Glorious days were spent with my friends, basking in the glory of Christmas spoils. Worn to a frazzle, my parents slowly recuperated, surviving yet another holiday, counting the days till I was back in school.

The holiday that took forever to arrive ended in a flash. Tired and depressed, I moped through the doors of South Maybin Elementary where in two short weeks, I'd forgotten everything I'd learned since the beginning of the school year.

A deceiving January sun greeted us that afternoon when the day's torture came to an end. The freezing air danced with tiny breath flickers as we jabbered away. For some reason, Billy Ray was in a hurry.

"Slow down stupid," Skeeter yelled. Giving a wink, Billy Ray charged ahead. Knowing another dubious adventure awaited, we sprinted to catch up. Fishing inside his jean pocket, Billy Ray thrust open his hands.

"Get a load of this!"

There was no mistaking the cork-shaped objects resembling sticks of dynamite huddled in Billy Ray's open palms. M-80s! The ultimate firecracker! Rumor had it the famed explosive was manufactured in the same factory as the A-bomb.

"Where'd ya git those?" Junior marveled.

"Got 'em last summer at South of the Border. Shot off a bunch on New Year's Eve. Stole a few when Dad wasn't lookin'." He winked.

Billy Ray's passion for explosives created exciting yet dangerous situations. He carried such an assortment of fireworks in his pocket that we kept him away from open flame. But M-80s! This was heavy artillery, even for Billy Ray.

"Wow! Three of 'em," admired Skeeter.

Billy Ray's face lit up.

"Find a mailbox!"

Although we took the same route home from school every day, we'd never paid any attention to mailboxes. To our surprise, none were positioned on the street, instead perilously attached close to front doors. Pointing at old man Collingsworth's house, Billy Ray's pace quickened. Taking cover behind some bushes, we watched in awe as he twisted the firecracker fuses together, creating a semi-nuclear device.

As if storming an enemy pillbox, Billy Ray sprinted up the steps to the front porch. With his back against the house, he pulled out a cigarette lighter and lit the fuse. Opening the top of the black mailbox, he dropped the smoking bomb inside.

Jumping from the porch, Billy Ray's feet hit the ground the exact instant of detonation. The explosion echoed through the neighborhood, vibrating in my chest. Apparently old man Collingsworth hadn't checked his mail. Smoldering bits of confetti shot through the air, raining down on the porch. Hesitating for a moment, the wounded mailbox tumbled off the wall, slamming against the porch floor in a metallic thud.

Consumed with laughter, we staggered down the street in a cackling dash. Alive for the first time in months, I laughed so hard I couldn't breathe. At that thrilling moment, vows and promises made under extreme duress faded in the crisp January air. A whole year of fun and childish schemes waited for me to take the first step. And once again, The Cycle begins.

"I'd heard the story about the skinny dippin', but you busted out a streetlight?" Suzie marveled.

"No… you weren't listenin'… Billy Ray broke the streetlight. Not me. I was always the perfect angel. Just ended up in the wrong place at the wrong time with the wrong people."

"First I've heard about the mailbox," Dad chuckled. "Not surprised though."

"So, you remember the letter, Pop?" I smiled.

"Lord yes," he laughed, taking another swig of water. "Your momma cried like a baby when she wrote it," he said, patting Mom on the knee. "Said her little boy was growin' up… ain't that right Dottie?" Mom's face shined at the banter. Knowing her response, I asked anyway, hoping.

"Mom? Do you remember writing those Christmas letters?"

Her face shrunk in embarrassment at my question. "That was a long time ago."

Smiling at her, I felt like an idiot for putting her on the spot. Gazing at the empty fireplace at the far end of the room, I imagined a young boy standing there in a pair of Roy Rogers pajamas on a glorious Christmas morning opening that first letter. As I stood there looking at the apparition, I wanted so much to feel the treasured piece of paper in my hands again. To recite her heartfelt words, admiring the pristine loops and swirls before tremors stole them. A sappy love letter was just like Dottie Harrison. Someone who could bite my head off one minute and wrap her arms around me and hug me the next.

"Mom, what do you remember about this room?" I asked, shifting gears.

Searching with her eyes, she grinned.

"Oh, I remember… some things," she said, trying to convince herself. "My piano sat right there, didn't it?" she asked, pointing to the back wall.

Heart and Soul

The tight lines on Mom's face relaxed into a broad grin as she proudly pointed to the empty back wall of the living room.

"It sat right there. Got it for my birthday." Occasionally, the old Dottie surprised us all, breaking through the haze, leaving us thirsty for more.

"I couldn't drag you away from that thing," Dad chuckled. "I thought you, Shelby, and Grace were gonna wear the keys off the first day!"

"You loved it too, didn't ya J.D.?" Suzie laughed.

"Sure, I did. Loved it with every fiber of my being," I smirked. "Sometimes I wished I'd stuck with it."

"You? Playing the piano? Ain't no way. You were all boy!"

A defining understatement. In those days, I couldn't imagine why any red-blooded American boy would spend a beautiful sunny afternoon inside, banging away on piano keys unless forced to do so at gunpoint.

Stepping across the room, Suzie and I stared at the empty space, imagining the auburn-colored piano positioned against the wall. Kneeling down, I ran my hand across the dusty floor. Somewhere in the myriad of wounds and scratches, I felt the divots where something heavy had left its mark. Like dates on an old tombstone, four small caster incisions appeared in the worn hardwood floors.

"This has to be it."

Suzie knelt beside me. "I think you're right."

"I remember the day you got it." I chuckled.

"Me too!" Mom grinned.

THE TIMING COULDN'T HAVE been worse. A hopeless endeavor driven by good intentions, doomed to failure. Most mothers would have recognized the futility of it all, but Dottie Harrison was just as determined and bullheaded as her nine-year-old son. Looking back, I certainly understood her motives. Frankly, she'd tried just about everything else under the sun to get me to straighten up and make something of myself before it was too late.

Her grandmother had lovingly sowed the musical seeds early on, teaching Mom to play on a church piano. Never having one to call her own, she played every chance she could at Aunt Shelby's, Grandma Harrison's, and every weekend at Sunday School assembly. She even filled in during worship service one summer after our organist, widow Hanford, died.

Basking in my little boy world, I had no idea that Mom's musical passion could possibly present a threat to my comfortable existence. For me, life centered around splendid afternoons darting through Ashley Woods with my friends in spirited games of Ambush. Nights found me snuggled on the den floor, my eyes glued to the TV, marveling at the dangerous and fascinating lives of nighttime heroes who captured the heart of an impressionable little boy.

Still, the heartbreaking indignities of childhood hid around every corner, waiting for a chance to pounce. The greatest fear kids have at that tender age is the agonizing fear of embarrassment. The slightest misstep and suddenly you're the laughingstock of the entire school. Such is the unpredictable and fragile existence of a timid fourth grader. One minute, life rolls along like a well-oiled machine and then out of the blue something horrible happens, forever destroying your wonderful little world. For me, that life changing experience ran aground shortly after a joyous and wonderful Christmas.

My mother was one of the luckiest people on the planet having been born in early January. Just days following a deluge of Christmas gifts, Mom got the chance to load up again with mountains of birthday presents. But January 5th, 1963 was unlike any birthday in the life of Dottie Harrison. One that turned both our lives upside down.

That fateful day dawned cloudy and cold. A dreary fog hung over the backyard, giving the appearance of a steady rain. Lost in the bliss of Saturday morning cartoons, I didn't notice Dad pacing around the kitchen, nervously checking his watch. The lively opening refrain of *The Jetsons* blared from the TV when the phone rang.

"I'll get it!" Dad shouted. Cupping his hand, he whispered into the receiver.

"Dottie? It's Shelby! Wants ya to pick Grace up on the way."

Storming from her bedroom, Mom glared at Dad as she put her arms into her coat.

"Where ya goin' Mommy?" Suzie asked, still in her favorite pair of footed pajamas.

"Shelby wants me to come over to her house sweetie," she said, forcing a smile. "I'll be back in a bit."

"I ain't got time for this mess," she whispered through gritted teeth as Dad backed away. It was her birthday and Mom knew the drill. That afternoon she'd spend hours in the kitchen, fixing herself a nice birthday supper. After opening a few gifts, she'd clean up the kitchen, wash the dishes and go to bed. Short and snippy, she slammed the back door behind her with authority.

Glancing out the window, Dad waited till the Pontiac cleared the driveway before reaching again for the phone.

"Hey y'all, go get dressed," he said with a devilish smile. "I got your momma a surprise for her birthday!"

"What is it? What is it?" Suzie asked, tugging at his trousers.

"I'll show ya," he said and winked, dialing a number. "Now scoot you two! Git 'cha clothes on." After changing, we joined Dad in the living room. Suzie continued her interrogation while the three of us peeked through the curtains of the large picture window into the cold gray morning. Soon a large delivery truck made a slow turn onto Circle Drive. Written boldly on the truck's door were the words "Sutton Music" bookended by two music staff symbols.

"Here they come," Dad said, sprinting gleefully to the garage. Having a delivery truck show up at your house on a sleepy Saturday morning was about as subtle as sending a marching band booming down the street. One nosy neighbor could ruin the whole surprise. After a quick meeting with Dad, three men connected a long metal ramp to the back of the truck. Opening a retracting door, they climbed inside and rolled out a huge object bound in thick blankets. I easily recognized the outline.

"Momma's gonna love this," I said as Dad held open the door.

"I hope so!"

"What is it?" Suzie begged.

"You'll see!"

After some tricky maneuvering, the men lugged the giant bundle into the house. Leading them into the living room, Dad showed them the empty spot against the back wall. The quilts were removed, revealing a chestnut-colored Story and Clark piano. Once a matching bench was put into place and the instrument tuned, the men shook hands with Dad and left. Grinning from ear to ear, Dad retrieved a wrapped present from the mahogany desk and handed it to me.

"This is from you and Suzie. Hide it beside the piano for now."

Rubbing his hands together like an excited magician, Dad hurried to the kitchen and dialed Aunt Shelby's number. It wasn't long before Mom pulled into the driveway. Of course, Shelby had shared the secret with Aunt Grace and the two of them accompanied her back home. Suzie met them at the back door.

"Momma! Come see!"

"Uh… let your momma come in," Dad chuckled, pulling my sister against his knees. "Glad ya brought Grace and Shelby with ya. Come with me!" Taking her hand before she could speak, Dad pushed open the living room door.

"Happy birthday, honey!"

"*Oh…* Oh Will! It's *beautiful!* Glory be," she squealed, hugging Dad's neck.

"Yippee," Suzie yelled, banging on the keys.

"No, no! Stop that, honey. Wait for Momma," she said, grabbing Suzie's feisty hands.

Marveling at the sight before her, Mom ran her fingers lightly across the piano's glossy finish as if the slightest touch would break the instrument. Taking a seat on the bench, she shook her head, laughing and crying at the same time.

"Don't cry Mommy, it'll be all right," Suzie assured her, patting her leg. Sniffling, Mom hugged her confused daughter. Dad nodded and I reached beside the piano.

"This is from me and Suzie." Wiping tears from her eyes, she opened the package of assorted songbooks.

"Oh Will, this is so wonderful," she mumbled, as if reveling in a dream.

On his latest trip to the Home Plate of Super Surprises, Dad smacked this one right out of the park. Jumping up from the bench, Mom grabbed him and kissed him right on the mouth. I'd seen people kissing a million times on TV but watching my parents lock lips was totally disgusting.

"Well, let's break it in!" Shelby suggested, interrupting the sickening display of affection. The Andrews Sisters, as Dad called them after the famous girl trio from the 1940s, proudly sang at every family gathering, whether we wanted them to or not. Selecting a songbook, Mom shifted on the bench, touching the keys for the first time. The sound of piano notes drifting through the house seemed odd and out of place.

The three of them quickly burst into a lively rendition of "I Could Have Danced All Night." At any moment I expected Lawrence Welk to appear, joining the melody with a thrilling orchestral accompaniment. For two solid hours, the Andrews Sisters sang and played, never once coming up for air.

I must admit, Dad's surprise was pretty exciting at first. But after fixing a peanut butter sandwich for me and my starving sister, I'd had about enough for one day. Enduring the song fest as long as he could, Dad escaped through the patio door into the cold wind, wearing nothing but jeans and a thin flannel shirt. The fact that my father willingly risked freezing to death rather than stomach another chorus of "Some Enchanted Evening" said it all.

That night, Dad frantically ushered us out to the car. I wasn't sure if dinner plans were part of the original birthday agenda or if he made it up on the fly, hoping to drag Mom away from the piano for an hour. Before we left, Mom paused at the living room door one last time, staring helplessly at the piano as if she were abandoning a litter of newborn puppies.

Life at the Harrisons was never the same. I felt as if we were living on the set of *The Liberace Show*. The only thing missing was a pair of white candelabras. Every night after supper, Mom insisted on serenading the family, cutting in on my precious TV time. Watching her blissfully playing and singing, I had no idea that underneath this happiness lurked an ominous and sinister cloud. That cloud burst into a violent thunderstorm a few weeks later.

Surprising Suzie and me one Saturday morning with French toast, Mom seemed more animated than usual. Busting at the seams, she flitted around the kitchen brandishing a silly grin. Drowning my plate with half a bottle of maple syrup, I indulged myself in a sugar-induced frenzy.

"How do ya like my new piano?"

"It's purdy Momma," Suzie giggled.

"Dad surprised ya, didn't he?" I asked, inhaling another bite.

"Oh, your daddy is such a rascal. Now I have a little surprise for you," she announced, sitting down at the table. "Guess what? I signed both of ya'll up for piano lessons with Mrs. Byrd! I called her yesterday and she has two openin's. Both ya'll start next week. Isn't that exciting?"

"Momma!"

Bouncing out of her chair, Suzie jumped up and down in place, hugging Mom at the same time. *Oh, this was quite a surprise all right! Kinda like the surprise attack on Pearl Harbor! This could not be happening! Not piano lessons.* What would my squad think? Drum lessons and guitar lessons, maybe. But piano lessons? Choking on a mouthful of toast, I managed a garbled response.

"Ma, I ain't takin' no lessons. That's for sissies!"

"It certainly is not young man," Mom snapped, shocked by my insubordination. "Look at your cousin Stanley. He can play almost as good as Shelby!"

Oh, now I get it! Mom must have dreamed up this little nightmare one day while belting out the blues with her sisters. Stanley, Aunt Shelby's twelve-year-old slug, had never played outside the house a day in his life. The boy couldn't climb a tree with a ladder.

"Ma, please. I… I… I have to study to keep my grades up. And well… uh… baseball starts up soon and—"

"Baseball don't start till summer. Your daddy and I think piano lessons will help you in school." Are you kidding me? *Dad agreed?* Deserted by my own father?

"Please, Ma. Let Suzie take 'em but please don't make me."

When the veins protruded on Mom's neck, I knew it was over. Sensing a brain malfunction, my body took over. Stumbling to my room, I climbed in bed and assumed a fetal position.

Staring at the ceiling tiles, I wondered what would become of my wonderful little world. How could I, J.D. Harrison, squad leader and Ambush legend, face my friends with the specter of piano lessons hanging over my head? What fighting man worth his salt would follow an accomplished pianist into battle? I could just imagine Sergeant Saunders from my favorite show *Combat,* sitting on a piano bench with his Thompson submachine gun slung over his shoulder, a Chesterfield hanging from his lips, pounding out "Chopsticks" on a baby grand! The idea was beyond reasoning and understanding. If this horrible blemish were discovered by the authorities, West Point was completely out of the question!

Of all the battles I had faced in my young life, piano lessons would by far be the toughest. If the squad ever found out my military career would be over. Finished! Dishonorably discharged. The biggest scandal to hit Circle Drive since Rhonda March and Jimmy Whitfield got caught naked in her daddy's storage shed. Somehow, I had to keep this horrible humiliation from the rest of the world.

As the last days of freedom slipped away, I became a hopeless basket case. Concentrating in class was simply impossible, more so than usual. Then came that ill-fated Friday. When the last bell sounded, ending life as I knew it, the traditional Friday stampede began. Smiling children ready for a weekend of fun and laughter brushed by me as I moped down the hall.

"Hey, ya comin'?" Skeeter asked, looking back at me.

"No... uh... got a... dentist appointment," I lied. "Mom's pickin' me up."

Moving like a turtle with the flu, I was the last child to step out the front door. Staring at the ground, I shuffled down the front steps. Leaning on the side of the Pontiac with her arms crossed, Mom frowned at me and pointed to the car door. Sliding into the front seat, I pleaded my case one last time.

"Momma, listen. I'll clean the house. Mop the floors. Clean the bathrooms. I'll cook for you and Daddy. Please!"

Ignoring my pitiful appeals, Mom stared straight ahead. Resigned to my fate, I slumped down in the seat. Turning onto Oakland Street, Mom pulled the car to a stop in the gravel drive of a white Victorian. It was my last chance. Desperate, I busted out in a fake cry like a babbling two-year-old. What in the world was happening to me? What had I become? A once brave and courageous soldier and here I was reduced to a whining crybaby!

"Stop that mess right now," Mom yelled, turning off the ignition. "You're gonna take piano lessons and that's all there is to it. Now git out of the car before I beat 'cha to death!"

Feigning a whimper, I trudged sadly behind Mom. Standing on the wraparound porch, Mom's eyes glowed a fiery red as she rang the doorbell. A pleasant older lady with white hair and plenty of wrinkles answered the door. Wearing a plain green dress, she smiled and shook hands with Mom. The wife of a retired Presbyterian minister, Mrs. Byrd politely welcomed us inside.

"Mrs. Byrd, thank you so much for workin' us in. We're so excited!"

"Oh, I'm delighted to have Suzie and J.D. join our little family. As I mentioned, J.D. is set for Fridays and little Suzie on Tuesdays. Does that still sound fine?"

"Oh yes. It's perfect!"

Helpless against those who held firmly to the reins, I stood there like a mule in a harness.

"You must be J.D.," she said, extending her hand.

"Yes ma'am," I sighed, offering a dead fish handshake. Strolling through the foyer, we entered the ghostly inner sanctum of the dismal house. Specks of light struggled through tiny creases of velvet tasseled curtains. Crammed with stuffy antiques and ancient furniture, the musty brown paneled den reminded me of an old black and white Vincent Price horror movie.

Row after row of thick leather-bound books filled an entire wall of laddered shelves reaching to a ten-foot ceiling. Suddenly a terrifying discovery hit me. Panicked, I looked everywhere. I examined the bookshelves and gloomy furniture nervously for signs. Honest to God, I didn't see a TV anywhere! What was wrong with these people?

A buttery colored cat the size of a small pig lay curled up on the fireplace hearth. Its coal black eyes followed me across the room. No doubt the fat feline had seen students come and go over the years. Surely, he knew a phony when he saw one. Lodged inside a paneled alcove sat a glossy black Baldwin piano. Two spotlights illuminated the sacred instrument like a holy shrine.

After discussing a few particulars, Mom left. It was just me, Mrs. Byrd, her Baldwin piano, and the yellow mountain lion.

"Here J.D. Have a seat on the bench."

Sitting down, I stared at the keys as if they were crawling with snakes. Taking a seat beside me, Mrs. Byrd smiled at her newest lump of clay. Blessed with the attention span of a starving housefly, I knew in less than ten seconds that playing the piano was the most boring thing I'd ever experienced. Struggling from the start with the simplest of concepts, I just couldn't get the hang of it. When the lesson mercifully came to an end, I groveled again to Mom on the way home to no avail.

Once upon a time, I'd looked forward to Fridays. Counting down the last boring moments of school, ready for a delightful weekend of playing with my friends. Piano lessons changed all that. Fridays became a miserable day of suffering. My life quickly turned into an endless act of lying and deception. Coming up with excuses for my continued absence from Friday afternoons' war games made me a nervous wreck. Finally, I settled on the consistent story that Friday was "Chore Day" at the Harrison house, full of running errands and working all afternoon. Lying quickly became as natural as breathing. I hardly believed anything I said anymore.

After weeks of pitiful begging, I managed to score a small victory, convincing Mom to grant me the simple dignity of riding my bike to my torture sessions with Mrs. Byrd. Again, I hadn't fully thought things through.

Leaving the garage, I paused at the end of the driveway when another paranoia attack kicked in. Wait a minute! What if the squad saw me riding my bike? I told them I was doing chores. Surely, they'd suspect something was up. Gliding past Ashley Woods, I peered into the darkness. Thankfully I didn't see anyone.

"Hmm. Wonder where they…" The words hung in my throat.

Oh no! What if the squad were following me? They didn't seem very convinced about my pitiful "Chore Day" excuse.

Panic-stricken, I detoured through downtown. Glancing over my shoulder to see if anyone was following me, I nearly plowed into a parked car. The trip to Mrs. Byrd's that should have taken five minutes turned into a twenty-minute Tour de Maybin. Circling past Knight's Furniture, I pulled my bike onto the railroad tracks. Bouncing along the crossties, I exited down a grassy bank near Oakwood Street.

The final approach to Mrs. Byrd's would be the toughest part of the mission. Those last precious seconds could make or break my reputation. Never slowing down, I blew past the white Victorian, turning into a patch of woods at the end of the street. Covering my bike with dead leaves and tree branches, I scouted the surroundings. Dashing from tree to tree, I took cover behind a large oak. Confident no one was around I sprinted the last few yards to Mrs. Byrd's front porch. Ringing the doorbell, I ducked behind a gray cement statue until Mrs. Byrd answered the door. *Piano lessons were going to kill me!*

Time stood still for those agonizing forty-five-minute lessons. One of the first things I learned during these grueling sessions was that the notes "EGBDF" stood for "Every Good Boy Does Fine," which explained everything. Not only was I not a good boy, I wasn't close to doing fine. In fact, I was downright pathetic! Although the obese feline, whose name was Marcus, left the room when I arrived for lessons, my collection of missed notes and disinterested facial expressions never fazed my dedicated teacher. Sitting attentively beside me on the bench, Mrs. Byrd smiled, patiently enduring my countless mistakes.

Proud of her budding prodigy, Mom bragged for hours on the phone about her cultured and refined little boy. Knowing sooner or later my friends would find out, my double life started to get to me and it wasn't long before my performance on the battlefield took a nosedive. Known for my fearless concentration and intensity, nothing ever escaped me during Ambush. Unable to focus, my life of deception soon clouded my fighting skills, usually ending with my demise. Whispers spread through the ranks that I'd lost my edge.

My cover was nearly blown one day when the squad took a break from hostilities. We were sitting around the rock trench when Skeeter spoke up.

"Hey, J.D. Y'all get a piano?"

My body went numb. All eyes turned towards me with looks of disbelief.

"Uh—"

"Mom said ya did. She watched 'em haul it in y'all's house."

No surprise there. Mrs. Crabtree's inquisitive nose was so large, she probably used a shovel to pick it. With a crimson face, I fumbled for a response.

"Uh… yeah. Mom plays it all the time." Nervous and panicked, I contracted a sudden case of diarrhea of the mouth. I just couldn't shut up.

"Yeah, uh, her and Suzie… they play a lot. Suzie's takin' piano lessons. Yeah, piano lessons! Wow! But I ain't takin' no piano lessons… No… not me. That would really be sissified, wouldn't it?"

"Ha," Billy Ray interrupted, unwrapping a Zero bar. "Guess what I heard? Johnny Nelson's takin' piano lessons! Can you believe it?"

"You're kiddin'," hollered Bucky.

"Man, that's awful," chuckled Skeeter. "I feel sorry for 'im."

"Me too," I sighed, swallowing a lump. That's when I noticed my right foot wouldn't stop shaking.

Suffering through lessons once a week was bad enough, but the worse part of this stupid fiasco was the horrible punishment of daily practice. Every night after supper, I plopped down at the dreaded piano for twenty minutes of dumb exercises. Before beginning these evening torture sessions, I went through the standard ritual of closing all the curtains and locking doors. Standing over my shoulder like a prison guard, Mom ensured I took my practice time seriously.

After weeks of pitiful suffering, Mrs. Byrd presented me with my first two masterpieces: "Swanee River" and "Ode to Joy." When Mom discovered I was training for Beethoven's classic she bragged about it to all her friends. Of course, I didn't know the difference between Beethoven and Jerry Lee Lewis. Convinced I'd finally exited the highway to hell that I'd been traveling on all these years and was now headed down the road to stardom, Mom increased my practice time to a dreadful thirty minutes.

Taking the backroads to Mrs. Byrd's house like a wanted criminal slowly drove me insane. After a while I just couldn't take it anymore. Feigning sickness and every other excuse short of self-mutilation to avoid my weekly suffering, I finally snapped. Leaving the house for another mind-numbing lesson, I circled around, stopping at Ashley Woods. Finding no one there, I rode over to Bucky's house, hiding my bike in the backyard.

"Hey. Thought 'cha were doin' chores?" Bucky asked, answering the door.

"Got done early so thought I'd come over."

In a flash we were on his bedroom floor playing with model cars. Thoughts of Mrs. Byrd, Mom, and piano lessons melted away in the bliss of playful laughter. It was the happiest I'd been in months. The sudden ringing of the doorbell sent me into a panic. Running through Bucky's house, I peeked through the curtains. Assuming the standard "I'm going to kill you!" stance of crossed arms and gritted teeth, Mom fumed on the front porch. Fearing Bucky would discover my terrible secret, I eased out on the porch, closing the door behind me.

"John David Harrison! I figured I find you here!" Addressing me by my full given name meant severe pain was imminent. "Git yourself in the car right now Buster!"

"I will Ma. Let me say bye to Bucky!"

"Make it quick. Mrs. Byrd called. You're late!"

Moping back to his bedroom, I explained that I had to get back to my chores. Without a word, Bucky and I exchanged devilish grins. In a flash, we shot out the back door. Snickering at our daring escape, we jumped on our bikes and flew through the backyard. Caught up in the excitement, we pedaled down Fifth Street racing past the depot. Crossing the tracks, the circling lights of The Hollywood Cinema's marquee announced *The Brain That Wouldn't Die* as the afternoon matinee. It was the perfect hiding place. No one would find us in a dark theater.

"The movies," I yelled. "Head to the movies!"

Making the fatal mistake of parking our bikes in front of the theater, we scrounged our pockets for two quarters. With the movie well underway, we slid unnoticed down a side aisle past a handful of mesmerized moviegoers.

Splitting a cold drink with Bucky, I watched the black and white screen in fascination, forgetting my hellish life for a moment.

Suddenly a giant hand grabbed my arm! The viselike grip cut off all circulation. My crazed screams sent the theater into hysterics! At first, I thought the red glaring eyes belonged to Satan himself. Lifting me up out of my seat with one hand, I thought Mom was going to kill me right there. Bucky fled for his life.

Banned from riding my bike to piano lessons, Mom embarrassed me every Friday, picking me up right after school and depositing me at Mrs. Byrd's. Predictably the constant struggle between my mother and me continued its escalation. Destined for a defining battle to determine the outcome of the war, we both dug in, refusing to relent. Our Gettysburg took place fittingly on a Friday afternoon just before the end of the school day.

Desperate times called for desperate measures. Eagerly watching the clock above the blackboard, I waited for just the right moment. If I played this right, Miss Blanchard would chastise me, making me stay after school, saving me from piano lessons. Two minutes before the bell rang, I jumped up from my desk. Reaching over the aisle, I grabbed a handful of Mary Jane Dodson's brown hair and gave it a yank. Shocked by her painful screams, the entire class fell silent in disbelief. My reputation as classroom idiot had taken time to cultivate. While some weren't entirely convinced, this blatant display of sheer stupidity removed any doubt.

Miss Blanchard sprinted from behind her desk. Once again, I hadn't fully thought things through. Instead of making me stay after school as I had hoped, she paddled the snot out of me in front of my horrified class and a whimpering Mary Jane. Of course, my parents knew about the incident before I got home. Later that evening, with Mom cheering on, Dad, Mr. Belt, and I gathered in my bedroom for an intense conversation.

That did it. After months of agonizing resistance, I finally surrendered. Beaten, literally, and broken, I succumbed to the dull mindless routine. Reduced to an emotionless blob of jelly, I plodded off to Mrs. Byrd's like cattle being led to slaughter.

Feeling sorry for myself and with nowhere else to turn, I popped in at Bucky's house after school one day, hoping the visit would cheer me up. Bucky answered the door. Seeing me standing on his front porch, his eyes flashed a look of stark terror.

"What... what 'chu doin' here? Go away... I... I'm busy," he whispered, through the small crack in the door.

"What's wrong?"

"Git outta here will ya!"

"Who is it?" Mrs. Watkins interrupted, pulling open the door. "Bucky can't play right now, J.D. He has to go to piano lessons."

Blindsided by the punch, I stood on the porch in stunned silence. Speechless, Bucky looked at me as if painfully constipated. Recognizing the anguished eyes and premature age lines on his forehead, I knew he hated piano lessons as much as I did. Cold chills ran down my arms. I wasn't alone after all! There *were* others out there just like me. Kindred spirits yearning to be free. Pleadingly shaking his head, Bucky telegraphed the message loud and clear: *Please! For goodness' sake, don't tell anybody!*

The next day, Bucky showed up at my house after school.

"J.D., listen to me. Don't tell the guys... Please. I'll never be able to play Ambush again! Momma made me take the stupid lessons. Honest." With that, he slumped on the porch steps and broke into tears. It was simply pitiful.

Taking a seat beside him, I knew it was time to come clean. They say confession is good for the soul. Revealing my own dark secret for the first time relieved the burden, at least for the moment. That day, an inseparable bond formed between Bucky and me. Crossing our hearts and hoping to die, we pledged to support and defend our humiliation against all enemies foreign and domestic.

After that cataclysmic afternoon of admission, things got a little easier. Having someone to share and understand took a huge load off my mind. Covering for each other, our lies reached grand proportions. I began to think that we might be able to pull it off. Together, Bucky and I would fight to the end. Unfortunately, "the end" came sooner than we expected.

Our terrible secret remained safe until spring when Mrs. Byrd informed us of our participation in something called a "recital." I'd never heard the word before but quickly understood its hideous and wretched meaning. Of course, Mrs. Byrd portrayed the exhibition as a small concert for our parents to witness the fruits of our hard work. What it really meant was the end of the world for J.D. Harrison. The truth would finally be exposed. The reality of it all hit me when I got home from school one afternoon.

"Hey, honey," Mom said from the kitchen. She never called me "honey" unless something truly embarrassing awaited. "Your piano recital is just two weeks away," she said, setting the clothes basket on the couch. "It was in the paper today! Dad and I are so excited." My stomach rolled into a painful knot. "Here it is!" She smiled, presenting me the latest edition of the *Maybin Weekly News*.

Thankfully the small article had been mercifully relegated to the back page. No doubt Mom would cut the article out of the paper and have it bronzed.

PIANO RECITAL
Mrs. Penelope Byrd, wife of retired Rev. W.A. Byrd, will hold her annual spring piano recital at her home on Oakwood Street, Sunday afternoon, April 28th at 2pm. Seventeen of her students will perform musical selections for parents and friends.

PRAISE GOD, NO NAMES were mentioned in the obscure write up. Gazing down at the tiny blurb, I felt the tidal wave building in my stomach. It was really happening. My world was coming to an agonizing conclusion and there was absolutely nothing I could do to stop it.

Except for my trusted friend, Bucky, I had no idea who the other abused children were that would participate in this public display of humiliation. That all changed when Mrs. Byrd scheduled our recital's first dress rehearsal. All her performing students would be there.

Dropping me off at Mrs. Byrd's house that dreadful Saturday morning, Mom wished me good luck. Holding my songbook under my arm, I trudged along. The moment I walked through that frightful portal my horrible secret would be laid bare for the whole world to see. Walter Cronkite was probably standing there ready to shove a microphone in my face!

Mrs. Byrd escorted me to the den where the other students were sitting. Audible gasps ripped through the room as I stepped inside. Bucky waved pitifully from a corner. Linda Oaks, Karen Black, and Barbara Wallace, all Circle Drive girls, snickered in a group whisper. It was worse than I thought. The only other boy there besides me and Bucky was Aunt Shelby's twelve-year-old slug himself, Stanley, shaking with laughter. His chrome braces shined like the grill of a new Buick.

With clipboard in hand, Mrs. Byrd went through the details of our approaching concert. Introducing us one by one, we ran through the schedule. When it came my turn, I cringed at the faint giggles as I took my seat on the piano bench. Performing in front of the neighborhood kids was one of the worst moments of my life. Nervous and sweaty, I fumbled through the number.

As expected, my humiliation was on the lips of every child at South Maybin come Monday morning. When I walked through the classroom door, everyone stared at me as if I were engulfed in flames.

"Hey everybody, here comes Chopsticks," Billy Ray yelled.

The name stuck. Christened "Chopsticks Harrison," a horrible day of endless teasing quickly followed. Knowing a ruthless walk home with the guys waited after school, I hid in a broom closet for half an hour after the bell rang before summoning the courage to go home. The recital was less than a week away. Avoiding my friends at all costs, I quit Ambush, barricaded myself in the house, and refused all phone calls and visits.

After another excruciating rehearsal, the dreaded Sunday afternoon finally arrived. For my musical debut, Mom had my blue Sunday suit dry-cleaned. Along with a crisp white shirt and red bowtie, I was forced to wear my tan fedora that I wore to church at Christmas and Easter. Shamed and degraded, I sulked in the backseat while Dad backed out of the driveway. Cars lined both sides of Oakwood Street as we searched for a parking space.

Joining the other kids in the parlor, we listened while Mrs. Byrd welcomed the crowd. Slipping into the hall, I peeked through a crack in the door. The long-tasseled curtains were closed tight. Squinting into the darkness, I could barely make out vague outlines of proud parents sitting in rows of metal folding chairs. Light emanated from two spotlights above the piano. Burning candles in free-standing candelabras flanked each side of the black Baldwin. Marcus the monster was nowhere to be found.

Our nervous whispers ceased as Mrs. Byrd came into the parlor to address the condemned. Under no circumstances could we talk to each other or make a sound while waiting our turn. Glancing over at Bucky, I shook my head at the absurdity of the warning. What would Mrs. Byrd do if she caught me talking? Prevent me from performing? For a split second, I contemplated rushing through the crowded den screaming my head off. The only thing holding me back was the strong possibility of being publicly skinned by my parents in front of a live studio audience.

Returning to the den, Mrs. Byrd introduced our opening act, Alice Farrell, who received a pleasant round of applause. Listening to her methodical version of "When the Saints Go Marching In" echo through the house, I thought how much life had changed. Not so long ago, I'd been a brave soldier crawling through Ashley Woods, saving the world from Hitler. I thought of fond afternoons climbing the magnolia tree beside Knight's Furniture and racing bicycles around Circle Drive. What would become of me now?

Fittingly listed as number thirteen on the docket, my stomach counted off the performances with mounting anxiety. As I was introduced to the crowd I entered the dim room from a side hallway. Several "awes" drifted through the audience. Wonderful! They think I'm cute! Paraded like a mutt in a dog show for their petty amusement, I had officially reached the bottom of the barrel. Mortified, I plopped down on the bench. A scary silence took hold as I placed my hands on the keys. Slowly the notes from "Swanee River" filled the room.

Suddenly a bright flash distracted me for a split second. *Oh no! Not pictures!* Some impassioned photographer just preserved my degradation for all time. Perhaps the photo would be placed in a time capsule to be opened centuries later. Curious gawkers would ride by 209 Circle Drive and say, "Hey look! That's the house where old Chopsticks Harrison grew up!" Flustered by the interruption, I rushed through the number, thankfully missing only a few notes. Exiting the piano, I removed my hat, bowing to thunderous applause.

Collapsing on the parlor couch, I breathed a sigh of relief. OK, I didn't die. Not physically, anyway. Returning to the stage for my finale, I ripped through "Ode to Joy," then tipped my hat again to the crowd and skipped happily back to the living room. It was over!

With the recital behind me, I thought my embarrassment had mercifully ended. *Oh, hell no!* Wednesday afternoon I found my humiliation plastered on the front page of the *Maybin Weekly News*. A black and white photo of a young boy dressed smartly in a dark suit and fedora. I read my obituary below the picture.

J.D. Harrison, son of Will and Dottie Harrison of Circle Drive, impresses the crowd with an inspiring presentation of "Swanee River."

SOMETIMES IN THE MIDST of adversity's darkest moments, miracles spring from nowhere, surprising you in ways you never dreamed possible. Just when I thought life couldn't get any worse, God's mighty hand reached down and pulled me safely from the mire.

As far as anyone could recall, no child from the neighborhood had ever been featured in a newspaper article, much less had their picture displayed on the front page. How quickly my fortunes changed. Exasperated parents saw light at the end of an agonizing tunnel. If a godless heathen like J.D. Harrison, destined to spend his life in solitary confinement in a state institution, could turn his life around by simply playing the piano, there was hope for other rebellious brats.

Seen as a miracle worker, Mrs. Byrd became "Childhood Savior" of Maybin's wayward rebels. After the newspaper hit the stands, four more Circle Drive students joined her little troupe. The icing on the cake came when it was discovered that one of those new students was Satan himself—Billy Ray Satterfield.

Something else happened that I never would have imagined, taking up permanent residence inside my heart. A few weeks after the traumatic recital, I wandered into the living room one night after supper. The last rays of afternoon light filtered through the curtains, highlighting the piano's coppery finish. Sitting down on the bench, my hands reached for the keys.

"Ya miss it?" Mom's voice startled me.

"No, not really… maybe a little."

"Let me show you somethin'." She smiled, sliding onto the bench beside me. Taking the bass portion, she patiently walked me through the progression of notes and after several attempts, I got the hang of it. On that quiet spring night in our living room on Circle Drive, Mom taught me the classic piano duet "Heart and Soul." I had no idea playing the piano could be that much fun. With my sulky impression of the piano permanently changed, Mom and I would return again and again, most times after my pleading suggestion, taking our seats beside each other on the bench.

AFTER MY RATHER RAUCOUS embellishment, much to the delight of my family, I studied the vacant wall once more, remembering the pleasing sound of notes drifting through the house, brushed along by Mom's nimble fingers. Her piano had always been there. Relegated to a forgotten corner of her den, the once proud instrument now performed as an overlooked display for old photos and lonesome knickknacks. Another element of Dottie Harrison that had disappeared. I wondered when she'd last played. Knowing her response, I didn't ask.

Report Cards and the Bull

"Let's check out the rest of the house and see if it's a landfill too." Dad's voice strained as he rose from the planter. Taking Mom's hand, he led the way. The hinges to the door leading to the den begged for oil as he pushed it open. My heart skipped a beat, remembering the warm and comfortable room once bursting with noise and laughter. A safe haven and loving fortress where the world couldn't touch me.

Stained beige carpet blanketed what used to be hardwood floors. The rich grooved pine paneled walls had been exchanged for drab sheetrock painted a nauseating lime green. Oversized windows stretching the length of the far wall were still intact. Insulated replacements now. The massive glass wall, one of Mom's ideas when the house was constructed, offered her a panoramic view of her gardening creations that covered our backyard. Dusty pine bookshelves, another Dottie Harrison inspiration, ran beneath the giant windows.

"Damn if this house don't need a good fire," Dad opined, triggering another arm slap from Mom.

"I'm thinkin' a hot three-day shower is in my future," Suzie mumbled, stepping inside the room as if she were entering a minefield.

"Aw... it ain't that bad," I said, brushing against the filthy doorframe, contaminating my shirt. "Needs some paint, a little love... disinfectant... fumigation... maybe a wrecking ball..."

I pictured Dad relaxing in his recliner, reading a folded newspaper. Mom sitting barefooted on the couch, turning the pages of a magazine while Suzie and I laid on the den rug watching TV.

"Lordy, I used to iron right there," Mom blurted out, pointing to where our dappled gray couch once stood. I could almost hear the sharp metal shriek as Mom positioned the ironing board in front of the TV. Happy that his experiment finally showed signs of life, Dad moved closer, taking her hand in his.

"What else do ya remember?"

"I remember y'all runnin' in and out, slammin' doors." Dad didn't press. Thankful for the moment, he kissed the top of her head.

"Didn't our dinin' room table sit over there?" Suzie asked, pointing to the far end of the open room. I recalled gold Bourbon Street themed wallpaper covering the back wall above a thin chair rail.

"Shore did!" Dad chuckled. "J.D. used to sit there and pretend to do homework."

"Hold on now!"

A metal door at the far end of the windowed wall led outside to a flagstone patio. Like Mom said, I thought of the wooden screen door that I ran through at least a hundred times a day. A sweltering day in early September came to mind and I chuckled out loud at the recollection.

"Remember the School Summits we used to have?" At first Dad frowned at my question, trying to recall. Suddenly his face lit up.

THE SCREEN DOOR BARKED behind me, bouncing twice against the wooden frame. Hot and thirsty, I collapsed on the floor, reeking of sweat and grass. Our Labor Day cookout had just concluded, taking with it the last fleeting moments of summer freedom. Sitting there in the quiet, the pent-up pangs of denial descended into consciousness. Another school year began tomorrow morning.

A wildlife show that no one noticed played softly on the TV. Leaning my filthy back against the couch, I waited in silence for my accusers to assemble. The blur of summer vacation was over. It would be the simplest things that I'd miss the most. Lazy days spent with my friends. Feeling the warm breeze caress my face as I pedaled my bike around the block. The flicker of lightning bugs in backyard shadows. The smell of an approaching thunderstorm.

Hearing my dog Yankee's growling inflection in the distance, I could tell he was closing in on another passing car's spinning hubcaps. The steady hum of the window fan weighed heavy on my tired eyes, burning with sweat. Peering through the wall of windows, I saw the idle tip of Knight's Furniture's black smokestack in the distance, pointing into the afternoon sky. The clicking looms at Tarheel Textiles had gone silent. "CLOSED" signs hung on locked doors of downtown stores. Come to think of it, I hadn't heard but a couple of trains all day.

It seemed as if the whole world had taken the day off, enjoying one last sigh before summer unofficially ended. Resigned to my fate, I felt like a condemned prisoner waiting for the warden to come. Tomorrow morning I would resume another nine-month prison sentence at South Maybin Elementary. If only I had a harmonica.

Storming inside, Mom turned off the TV with authority, glaring at me as she rushed by. Her stern demonstration, of course, was to remove any potential distractions. That somehow sitting in total silence would stir embarrassing memories of the disaster that had been the third grade. Her message was clear. Parents forgave but didn't forget.

Smoke drifted from the grill's dying charcoal as Dad shuffled around the patio, straightening up after our last summer fling. Any minute now he'd come inside and our annual School Summit would come to order. Dishes rattled in the kitchen as Mom and Suzie darted about, putting away leftovers.

"J.D., ready for our little talk?"

"Yes ma'am."

I never understood why we held these stupid meetings every year. Before the session ever began I knew how it would end. No matter how loud Mom screamed and threatened, nothing ever changed. Although I had never received the coveted vowel on a report card myself, I had to give my parents an "A" for effort.

Toothless as a result from a great gnashing of teeth, my boundless mischief had pushed them well past the breaking point. My transgressions were so widely known that my parents were seen as abject failures at raising children. This school year something had to give and there was no doubt in my mind that I would be the one doing the giving.

The fourth grade awaited my dubious arrival, where my lawless reputation greatly preceded me. I was sure my new teacher, Miss Blanchard, already knew everything about me. I could just see those scheming teachers now, huddled in that smoky break room of theirs, carefully separating the good kids from the bad kids. Branded a "problem child" by the educational establishment, I didn't have a chance. Once a troublemaker, always a troublemaker.

Wiping his face on his shirtsleeve, Dad eased the screen door closed behind him.

"Glad that's done," he said, smelling of burnt charcoal.

"Hey pal," he winked. "Be back after I jump in the shower." The fact Dad referred to me as "pal" was encouraging. He dreaded the School Summit as much as I did. This was Mom's little horror show. Drying her hands on her apron, Mom gave me a half-hearted smile as she sat down on the couch.

"Ready for tomorrow?"

"Yes ma'am." And that was it. A difficult silence set in as defendant and prosecutor waited for Dad to join the dais. When it came to our annual meeting, there was no official call to order or playing of the National Anthem, although I felt a solemn invocation would be nice.

Taking a seat beside Mom on the couch, Dad glanced at his watch. Almost time for *I've Got A Secret.* Heaven forbid he might miss that one contestant that went over Niagara Falls in a barrel and lived to tell about it. With his favorite show just minutes away, Dad breached standard decorum, hastily initiating the meeting before Mom got started. Glaring at the obvious infringement, Mom simmered, waiting her turn.

"Son." I liked it when he called me "Son" too. "Another school year starts tomorrow. Big fourth grader!" He winked. His voice soft and supportive, Dad opened with the standard "new beginning and a fresh start" narrative.

"We know you're smart and can do well in school if ya just try." Recapping last year's escapades that under no circumstances were to be repeated, Dad switched gears much too fast. Obviously uncomfortable, Dad bumbled along. Citing the nine paddlings I received last year, Dad's halfhearted reprimand didn't possess quite the degree of fire and brimstone as far as Mom was concerned.

Realizing the mistake of allowing Dad to lead off the meeting, Mom interrupted him in mid-sentence. An unpolished negotiator, Mom's forte was screaming and she wasted no time.

"J.D.! What in the world are we gonna do with you? When are you gonna straighten up? Just look at Patsy's boy, Jerry. That boy is so smart! Why can't 'chu be more like him? And what about Freddie Dodson? 'Member him winnin' the spellin' bee over at the high school? Why can't 'chu be like that?" Left with no choice but to let Mom take the floor, Dad peeked again at his watch.

Quite the motivational speaker, Mom scrutinized my questionable tendencies in great detail, comparing me with every single child at South Maybin Elementary. Convinced that the louder she spoke the better chance I had of remembering, she began with a slight roar. When her voice reached thunderous heights, she quickly segued from the frustrated "Why can't yous" into the always regrettable "I wishes."

"I wish we'd put you in private school like Larry's parents did. Look how *that* boy turned out. Smart as a whip! He's the only friend you got with a lick of sense!"

While Mom "wished" the meeting away, I fully expected her to announce at any moment her remorse at having sex with Dad and conceiving a loser like me. Like a fiery preacher at a summer tent revival, Mom let me have it. Speaking in tongues, she skipped over most of her sermon, jumping into the conclusion and recommendation portion.

"Let me tell you somethin' else, Buddy Roe! This school year, things are gonna be a lot different 'round here. You hear me?" Among the myriad of name references I received when I was in trouble, the designation of "Buddy Roe" meant Mom was at the end of her rope and was in no way responsible for her actions.

"You come home with anything less than a 'B' on your report card, the only army you'll be playin' is when you enlist when you're eighteen! You hear me?"

Big deal. A carbon copy of the same crap she spewed every year. Like every School Summit I'd ever experienced, Mom's screaming oration offered nothing new. While Mom rambled on, the heat and sweat of the afternoon set in and I began to fade. It happened during a rather boring and repetitious point she was making for the third time. I tried to hold it back but couldn't.

"And another thing, you're always playin' outside when ya should be—"

The disinterested yawn, long and weary, expressed not only exhaustion but my outright boredom. To top it off, I stretched my arms a little. The screaming stopped. Mom's face transformed from an angry sea to a flat lake in a split second, followed by absolute silence. Scary, unholy, terrifying silence. Slowly, the corners of her mouth turned up into a terrifying grin that scared the hell out of me. I could take the yelling and screaming, but when Mom got quiet, the world as I knew it was about to end.

"Let me put it this way," she continued in a calm eerie voice. "Come home with anything lower than a 'B' on your report card and you can fergit about watchin' *Combat* or playin' with your friends. You understand me?" *My Goodness! Don't I get a minute for rebuttal?*

Seeing his chance, Dad jumped in.

"OK. What 'cha think?" he asked, like an anxious real estate agent. "Oh look! Time for *I've Got A Secret!*" Jumping from the couch, Dad sprinted across the room and turned on the TV.

After a few shows and a quick bath, I crawled into bed to a distant rumble of thunder. A sudden gust of wind hissed through the trees while opening volleys of rain slapped against the window.

"Hey buddy," Mom said, knocking on my open door. Sitting down on the bed, she softly rubbed my arm.

"Excited about tomorrow?"

"I guess." A silent flash of lightning bled through the window blinds followed by a slow roll of thunder.

"J.D., I just don't know what to do with you sometimes. All we're askin' is that you do better in school. What's so hard about that?" Now *this* is a School Summit. Tender voice. Sensible questions. No enraged Nikita Khrushchev slamming his shoe on the table. Dr. Jekyll had become the lovable Mrs. Hyde. I shrugged at her question.

"Meant what I said, J.D.," she repeated with a stern face. "You come home with a bad report card and you're grounded. Understand?"

"Yes ma'am."

"Promise me you'll do your best."

"OK… I promise," I said, like a budding politician.

"Git a good night's sleep. I'll make ya pancakes tomorrow." She winked.

Laying there, listening to the storm outside, I contemplated the harsh threats laid out during the Summit. The idea of Mr. Belt carving up my legs like a Thanksgiving turkey was bad enough, but no *Combat* for a whole six weeks was out and out blasphemy! No Sergeant Saunders? My hero? Never had such sinister intimidations been employed at the Summit before.

Searching the trusty ceiling tiles for confirmation, I honestly believed Mom was serious. OK…This was it. No more fooling around. Lying in bed that stormy night, I made a solemn pledge, to bear all sacrifices, to complete my homework assignments, and, swallowing hard, to study for tests. It would only be for six weeks anyway. Long enough to get Mom off my back. While the rain pounded outside, the last thing I remember before drifting off to sleep was thinking *OK, here we go. It's Straight As or bust!*

It was bust. Honestly, Mom's unholy threats were categorically seared into my brain when I went to bed that night. I fully understood the consequences of another school year filled with bad decisions. I guess Mom was right about one thing. Things she said to me went in one ear and out the other.

A thin layer of fog hung ghostly white from last night's rain. Lost in the anticipation of seeing everyone on the first day of school, the recollections of the School Summit floated aimlessly into the mist that drifted over the hood of the Pontiac. Turning onto South Drive, we joined the train of cars waiting in line. A one level nondescript building, the dirty brick exterior of South Maybin Elementary reminded me of a creepy prison. The only things missing were guard towers and razor wire. The car crept forward, making its slow turn around the traffic circle.

"Remember our talk last night?"

"Yes ma'am."

"Gotcha lunch money?"

"Yes ma'am."

"Walkin' home this afternoon?"

"Yes ma'am."

"Good luck today. Love ya!"

"Yes ma'am."

Throwing a quick wave, I jumped out of the car, merging quickly into a jittery crowd of kids. Excited chatter and nervous laughter followed me up the walk. Shy first graders held tight to their moms' comforting hands as they faced the unknown for the first time. Older kids, veterans of past campaigns, skipped up the walk, searching for their friends.

"Hey buttface!" I knew Billy Ray's squeaky voice anywhere. Looking back, I waited as both he and Skeeter crossed the street.

"Know what I heard?" he continued, out of breath. "I heard Miss Blanchard used to be a prison guard!"

"Miss Blanchard? Our new teacher?"

"Jimmy Hardy told me," he rambled as we hurried up the walk. "Said she killed two prisoners one time who were tryin' to escape. 'Cept they weren't really escapin'! Shot 'em both dead. Just for the hell of it! Gotta tattoo of a skull on her left shoulder. Smokes two packs of Camels a day… no filters. Principal Kincaid brought her in to keep us in line." A natural born liar, anything Billy Ray said had to be taken with a shovel full of salt. Last year he swore that our teacher, Miss White, was a witch who boiled children in oil on the weekends.

Out of the blue, Billy Ray caught everyone off-guard with a high-pitched scream.

"Wyatt *EAAAAAAARP*!" The thunderous belch, deep and resonant and possessing the depth and range of a kid twice his age, took everyone by surprise. A gastric triumph! A master at abdominal explosions, Billy Ray spent hours perfecting digestive blasts. His unexpected and raunchy presentation of Wyatt Earp was simply breathtaking. Skeeter and I nodded out of respect.

As much as I hated returning to school, I had to admit there was something exciting about the first day. Friends I hadn't seen over the summer certainly contributed to the exhilaration. But what attracted me most was the challenge the new year presented. I don't mean that in an academic sense. The first day of school meant "The Game" officially began. Round One of a championship bout as students and teachers sized each other up for the first time. Every year on that first day, I examined every detail of my new teacher, searching for potential weaknesses that could be easily exploited. However, the one important feature that I paid the most attention to was the size of my teacher's arms. Last year, Miss White was blessed with woefully thin arms possessing extremely poor strength and limited wrist action. Paddlings were no big deal.

Playfully pushing each other, we charged up the sidewalk. In front of us, Linda Sue Hunsucker, Sissy Ledbetter, and Brenda Gail Breedlove sashayed along, caressing their notebooks like precious dolls. Seeing an opportunity, Billy Ray's eyes lit up. Following his lead, our pace quickened.

Tiptoeing behind the clueless trio, Billy Ray gave Skeeter a hard shove. As if walking a tightrope, Skeeter's arms flailed wildly like an airplane turning a hard bank. Losing his balance, he slammed into Linda Sue, who bounced off the other two girls like a prissy pinball. Notebooks went flying.

"You stupid pig," Linda Sue screamed, sticking out her tongue. The three of us took off running. Yep. No doubt about it, this was going to be the best school year ever!

Standing just outside the double front door, Principal Kincaid welcomed new arrivals with a broad smile. His black suit strained, attempting to hold back his overlapping potbelly. The helpless middle button of his bulging coat resembled a dam about to break. Seeing the three of us marching up the walk, his warm expression quickly disappeared. Squinting at us over glasses that hung snugly on his banana-sized nose, Mr. Kincaid frowned as we slipped inside.

PUNCH!

The fist in my left shoulder belonged to Brodie Fitch. One of my pals who I hadn't seen since school ended.

"Come back here!" I chuckled. Whirling around, I took off after him. Dodging oncoming children, Brodie laughed as he fled down the hall.

"No running!"

Recognizing the insidious growl without turning around, Brodie and I slowed to a crawl. The snarl belonged to Snyder the Spider! Like an angry troll guarding a bridge, Miss Snyder leaned on an open doorway. Three hundred years old and single, the Spider didn't have kids of her own to beat, so she became a teacher. A silver bun resembling a small rodent crowned the top of her head. Over the years, her dried prune face had congealed into a permanent scowl.

Miss Blanchard's classroom was the last door on the left at the end of the hall. Making our grand entrance to welcoming waves and a few snickers, I joined the other members of my dopey fraternity. Thoroughly hypnotized by the booger he'd just harvested, Junior deposited the golden nugget under his chair. Billy Ray winked at me and nodded toward the front of the room as I took my seat. There she was. Miss Blanchard. Well one thing was certain: her blazing red hair made her easy to spot in a crowd.

At precisely eight o'clock, the high-pitched bell officially announced the new school year. Low level chatter ceased as all eyes turned towards the teacher's desk. Time to check out this year's pathetic target. Showing no emotion, Miss Blanchard rose from her chair. The sharp clicking of high heels followed as she made her way to an oak podium.

My heart stopped beating! Bulging from the short sleeves of her flowery dress were two biceps the size of my thighs. One smack from a paddle powered by those burly arms would send me crashing through the wall! I didn't see the tattoo. Exchanging fearful glances, the class sat frozen in their seats, too scared to move. The guys agreed later she looked strong as a bull and the name stuck. On the first day of school, Miss Blanchard officially became "The Bull."

"Good morning class."

"Good morning, Miss Blanchard," came the collective response.

Smiling at the dutiful reply, The Bull opened a green spiraled notebook and began calling the roll. Waiting patiently, I was ready when she got to the H's.

"J.D. Harrison?"

"Here," I shouted enthusiastically. Waving my arms as if hailing a cab, I offered her one of my patented smiles, revealing the cute gap in my front teeth. Gazing up from her notebook, her steely eyes narrowed as if she were staring at me through the scope of a sniper rifle.

And so it began. For weeks I observed The Bull's every move, trying to figure out what made her tick. I had to hand it to her. She was one tough nut to crack. Like a poker player in a smoky casino, The Bull played it close to the vest, never tipping her hand. Hiding behind the mask, revealing only what she wanted us to see.

By the end of September, The Bull hadn't killed anyone. In fact, she'd been downright pleasant. Nothing I did seemed to rattle her in the least. At times, she appeared almost human. But so does Frankenstein. Constantly on pins and needles, days became ticking time bombs. The whole class watched and waited, wondering how The Bull would react when faced with confrontation. Like the opening volleys of a major battle, I pressed to see how far I could push her. My initial infractions were strictly frivolous of course. But escalation was inevitable.

Things came to a head one morning during spelling period. With a sheepish grin, Skeeter leaned over in his desk. Raising his left cheek off his seat, he let one fly. Billy Ray and I dissolved into uncontrollable laughter. Calling us down several times, it was clear The Bull was losing patience. After another stern warning, she turned to write on the blackboard. Taking advantage of the momentary distraction, I playfully threw a balled-up piece of paper at Billy Ray.

Just as the crumpled wad left my hand, The Bull spun around, catching me in the act. Strolling calmly to her desk, she opened the top drawer, retrieving a yellow wooden ruler. Gasps hissed through the room. Allowing the suspense to build, The Bull strolled to my desk as if she were lingering on a produce aisle.

"Give me your hand, please," she said calmly.

Grinning, she grabbed the four fingers of my right hand, exposing the soft white tissue of my palm. Petrified, my classmates watched in horror as The Bull raised her muscular arm. Closing my eyes, I gritted my teeth, bracing for impact!

WHAP!

Sharp and crisp, the sound of the ruler striking my hand reminded me of the cracking whip from the opening theme to the TV show *Rawhide*. Which also perfectly described the condition of my hand. Peeking with one eye, I was relieved to see the scarlet appendage was still attached to my arm.

No words were needed. The effective demonstration conveyed the orchestrated message: Don't mess with The Bull! With a four-alarm fire raging in my palm, I felt a strange sense of relief. After weeks of goading, daring her to charge, I'd done it. I'd successfully pushed The Bull over the edge and lived to tell about it! Battles between The Bull and I accelerated after the infamous ruler incident, but nothing serious. I spent so much time standing in the corner of the classroom for misbehaving, I began to worry that my nose might be taking on a distinctive pointed quality.

Then came that fateful Thursday afternoon in mid-October when my wonderful little world came crashing down. Just before the bell rang to end the school day, The Bull stepped to the blackboard.

"Class, I want to let you know that our first report cards of the year come out tomorrow." A collective groan rippled through the room. Billy Ray rested his head on his desk while Junior closed his eyes, his lips quivering in silent prayer.

"Most of you have done very well and I am extremely proud of you."

The Bull's beady eyes swept the room like a searchlight, stopping on me and my shady friends. At that moment, something clicked in the sleepy cobwebs of my brain. A faint memory emerged: The School Summit! Mom's unholy threats came rushing back! Dismissed, forgotten, buried by weeks of disobedience and mischief, the exhumed monster rose from the grave! Mom's warning echoed as I closed my eyes.

"Nothing below a B! Or no playing army or watching *Combat!*"

The piercing bell sent me jumping. In shock, the four of us sat glued in our seats while others scrambled past The Bull who stood at the door.

"See you in the morning," she beamed. Taking the biting cue, we gathered our books and filed quickly past her.

Waiting cars stretched around the school's traffic circle. Anxious little ones stood nervously by the curb looking for their moms' comforting faces. Most afternoons our playful troupe were among the first to leave, punching each other, laughing our way through the busy throng of kids on our way to another exciting afternoon of Ambush.

But today's walk was anything but amusing. Grim faces stared down at the sidewalk; our feet on autopilot.

Why? Why for goodness' sake did I do this every year? I always vowed to do better, but nothing ever changed.

"Y'all worried?" Junior wondered.

"What do you think butt breath?" Billy Ray snorted.

"Look y'all. We ain't seen the report cards. How do we know they're that bad?" Skeeter asked.

"You stupid doofus! You saw The Bull grinnin' like a possum when we was leavin'. She knows our grades stink," Billy Ray yelled, taking his frustrations out on an empty beer can, kicking the crumpled tin across the street. Turning onto Circle Drive, we planned to meet back at Ashley Woods.

Climbing the front porch steps, I paused at the door. Slowly turning the doorknob, I stepped inside. Mom's muffled voice came from the kitchen. Oh my Lord, she's on the phone! I was dead meat! Lost in another gossip marathon, the topic of tomorrow's report cards was bound to come up.

Tiptoeing through the den, I put my books down on the couch. Stretching the phone cord, Mom gave me a wink and a quick wave. Sprinting to my room, I quickly changed into my fighting fatigues. Charging out the door, I didn't slow down until I reached Ashley Woods. When Mom's voice called me home for supper, panic returned to my churning stomach as I shuffled home.

Suppertime at our house offered the same standard menu week after week. Thursdays meant liver and onions and sometimes, when Mom was in a good mood, we got spaghetti. The sharp aroma of marinara sauce met me at the door. Mom stood over the stove whose overhead exhaust fan roared like a 707.

"That makes me hungry."

"Almost ready!" Timing it perfectly as always, Mom had supper waiting on the table when Dad walked through the door. Taking our seats, Mom nodded at Suzie.

"God is great. God is good. Let us thank Him for our food. Amen."

Avoiding all conversation, I ate as fast as I could. Taking a sip of tea, Dad paused.

"Ready for tomorrow?" he asked, staring at me with curious blue eyes. My face heated up like a toaster. I wasn't sure Dad knew what grade I was in, much less about report cards!

"Uh... Uh... I..."

"You mean ya don't remember what tomorrow is?" Dad said, setting his glass down in amazement. "*The* game is tomorrow night. The Haw River game!"

"*Oooohhhh* yeah!" I exhaled a long breathy sigh. "I forgot! We goin' early ain't we?"

"You bet! Homecomin' too!"

Ever since The Bull dropped the report card bombshell that afternoon, my tormented mind couldn't comprehend anything else. I'd forgotten all about the game. A ray of hope burst through the clouds.

Every man, woman, and child in town lived for Friday night football and everyone marked the Haw River game on their calendars. When Maybin and Haw River settled things on the gridiron, proving which mill town was the toughest. Hometown destinies riding the prideful backs of young boys playing a simple game. There'd be fights on and off the field. Nothing else mattered during those magical hours, sending worries and cares drifting into the crisp night air.

Thankfully, our dinner conversation turned to the approaching matchup. After supper, I sat down at the dining room table in a failed attempt at homework. The sound of rattling dishes and running water echoed from the kitchen. With his feet propped up in his recliner, Dad thumbed through the afternoon paper.

Plucking the frayed edges of my arithmetic book, I knew it was only a matter of time until my parents found out about report cards. Wait a second, The Bull wouldn't hand out my death sentence until the end of the day. I still have time to think of something. But what? As daylight faded, I laid on the floor with Suzie, pretending to watch TV while my dilemma tumbled around in my head. After a bath, I crawled into bed.

Slowly, a faint glimmer of light flickered in my sleepy brain. The more I pondered the idea, the brighter the beacon became. It was certainly a long shot, but that's about all I had left. Without a doubt it would have to be my greatest performance ever! Mom startled me when she came in and sat down on the side of the bed.

"Lookin' forward to tomorrow night's game?"

"Yes ma'am."

"Somethin' botherin' you, J.D.? You ain't hardly said nothin' all night."

"Oh no ma'am! Just tired." Cutting her off, I jumped into my standard nighttime prayer, thanking God for everyone in the free world in less than ten seconds. Kissing me goodnight, Mom smiled and turned off the light.

Seeking inspiration from the trusty ceiling tiles, I put the finishing touches on my plan. If I figured this right, I'd have close to six hours to convince The Bull that underneath this dirty blonde crewcut, burned, somewhat dimly, a spark of basic intelligence. Gushing with innocent childhood charm, I'd impress her at every turn. Overcome by sympathy and compassion, she'd realize she'd misjudged me. All I needed to succeed was a little praise and encouragement. And what better way to show me that praise and encouragement than to take my report card aside and change my grades! It could work. Couldn't it?

Obsessed with the football game, Mom spared me the usual cross-examinations on a quiet ride to school. When the cafeteria's tall square chimney appeared in the distance, a swarm of nervous butter-flies gathered for a rousing party using my stomach as a dance floor. The bold plan that sounded pretty good last night to a desperate fourth grader now appeared stupid and silly. Too late to chicken out now. Besides, I had nothing to lose, except the skin on my backside. Making the slow turn, Mom stopped the car in the traffic circle.

"Now listen. Don't be all day gettin' home. No playin' around. We need to go early. Love ya!"

"OK. Love ya too, Ma!"

Hurrying down the hall toward my classroom, I deliberated on which "southern gentlemen" would attract The Bull's attention. Per-haps a prim and proper fourth grade version of Ashley Wilkes would make an impression or maybe a dashing Rhett Butler would do the trick. Surprisingly, I received a golden opportunity to unveil the "new me" before I ever got to class.

Seeing Elaine Dickerson walking down the hall behind me, I wait-ed. Holding the classroom door open, I swept my hand along.

"Please. After you."

Frowning as if I'd just handed her a fresh booger, Elaine rushed by me, careful not to get too close. Excitement and apprehension ampli-fied the usual pre-bell babble. Giddy anticipation and horrible dread of report card day painted the faces of my classmates, making it easy to distinguish the gifted from the goofy and the pets from the pathetic.

Glancing up from her desk, The Bull gave me one of those nasty looks of hers reserved for classroom losers.

"Good morning, Miss Blanchard." As if someone lifted the tone-arm from a blaring record player in mid-song, nervous chatter abruptly ceased. It was the first time I'd ever greeted a teacher in four years of school. A crack in the universe had opened to another dimension.

"Good... morning J.D.," she stammered in surprise. Sensing a chink in the armor, I charged up the hill with fixed bayonets. Class snob Betty Lou Sampson, a girl born with a tray of silver spoons crammed in her mouth, glared down her pudgy nose at me as I took my seat. Destined to marry the quarterback, move to the country club, and spend the rest of her life drinking wine and playing canasta, Betty Lou was despised by everyone in class. Even the girls hated her.

"Hey Betty Lou! Your hair looks really nice with that big red bow," I said, loud enough for The Bull to hear.

"Oh, shut up J.D.!"

The clanging morning bell got our attention. Rising from her desk, The Bull could hardly contain her excitement. Eager to get the show on the road, she skipped across the floor to the blackboard. Before the day was over, she would gleefully extract her revenge on classroom troublemakers like me.

"Good morning class," she beamed.

"Good morning, Miss Blanchard."

OK. Here goes nothin'. Time for the "new me" to take the stage!

"Miss Blanchard! Would you like for me to wipe down the chalk-board before we start?"

An eerie silence followed as the entire class sat stunned at my suggestion. The Bull's eyes narrowed as she cocked her head in amazement. Slowly the corners of her mouth turned up into a sarcastic smirk.

"Why yes J.D., that would be nice." Gritting my teeth, I grabbed the sour damp rag from the coffee can below the blackboard. Amused, The Bull watched my every move, never taking her eyes off me. After cleaning the board, I forced a smile and took my seat.

"Psst," Billy Ray snorted. Burying his nose into a turning fist, he shook his head in disgust. Whispers floated through the room and fingers pointed. I wasn't fooling anyone. My classmates knew a pathetic suck up when they saw one.

Ignoring the teasing, I stayed the course, hanging on The Bull's every word. Paying attention for the first time in my school career felt odd and strange as if I were coming down with a nasty cold. By lunchtime I had developed a splitting headache. With the needle on my patience tank sitting firmly on "E," things began to unravel. Scrambling to the front of the room at lunchtime, the real J.D. Harrison surfaced and I was immediately sent to the back of the line for pulling out Skeeter's shirttail.

The steady buzz of conversation greeted us as we pushed and shoved our way through the cafeteria door. Overcome by the warm scent of yeast rolls drifting by in a seductive cloud, I ambled along under the influence. Considered legal tender, the coveted biscuits were exchanged for just about anything from chewing gum to ice cream. Kids honed their negotiating skills, posturing for the rolls in clandestine transactions. Fights were commonplace if some shameful soul was caught stealing another's roll.

Pushing my tray along the silver glide, I peeked through the clear plastic panel at the day's nauseous creation; a radioactive looking orange meat bathed in a cesspool of brown water gravy. Mrs. Cantrell, her hair in a fishnet, splashed a ladle of the concoction into a glob of instant mashed potatoes. A sliced pear cradling a dab of mayonnaise topped off the repulsive entrée. The soft yeast roll waiting at the end of the serving line would be the only redeeming factor.

Thanks to Harvey Thompson, I'd have an extra one waiting for me. A tall skinny kid who never ate anything, Harvey and I had developed an understanding since third grade. Every day at lunch, he willingly presented me his yeast roll, most times without me asking. Holding my tray high, I weaved between packed tables. I was about to sit down when I noticed Harvey's roll was missing.

"Hey Harvey! What gives? Where's ya roll?"

"Too late J.D.," interrupted Arlie. "I got it today!" Pressing the masking-taped bridge of his glasses against his nose with one finger, Arlie grinned back at me, revealing a mouthful of silver braces.

Embarrassed, Harvey looked up at me like a sad puppy. It was the last straw. Report cards, my failing acting debut, and now this senseless violation sent me over the edge. I snapped. Balancing my tray with one hand, I snatched both rolls off Arlie's plate. Laughing hysterically, I squeezed the rolls into a ball of dough. If I couldn't have Harvey's roll, nobody would!

Suddenly the contents of my tray shifted! Trying to right the ship, I overcorrected, sending my milk bottle crashing into a million pieces on the floor. All eyes turned toward me in a nervous silence. The Bull sprang from her seat.

"Get yourself against the wall right now young man!"

The Wall. The isolated span of cinderblock between two large windows of the cafeteria served as South Maybin's version of medieval stocks and pillory. Where troublemakers were placed on public display for a giggling audience. Slumping between the two windows, I stared at the room full of snickering faces. It was over. Finished. I knew exactly what was coming next. For those of us on the dark side, justice was swift and painful. Punishment took many sadistic forms at South Maybin, directly correlating to the accused, and career troublemakers like myself received the harshest of penalties.

Leaning against The Wall, I saw the look of satisfaction on The Bull's face. She'd longed for this moment ever since she'd laid eyes on me the first day of school. All she needed was an excuse to beat the ever-living daylights out of me and now she finally had her chance.

When lunch was over, I was ashamedly paraded once more in front of the cafeteria crowd as village idiot. Sending the rest of the class back to the room with Miss Hartsell, The Bull escorted me down the hall to a destination I knew all too well. Pausing at the supply closet door, The Bull retrieved a silver key from her dress pocket, unlocking the deadbolt.

Reaching for the light switch, she ushered me inside, slamming the door behind her for effect. Reeking of chalk dust, I knew this little torture chamber like the back of my hand. I'd visited the room so many times in my school career that I fully expected a bronze plaque to be placed on the door, declaring the closet to be the J.D. Harrison Memorial Beating Room.

The chemical smell of purple ink meant someone had recently used the mimeograph machine. With measured breaths, I concentrated on the windowless room's cluttered details, momentarily diverting my attention from the forthcoming pain. Unruly shelves, packed with Crayola boxes and bundles of unsharpened yellow No. 2 pencils reminded me of my messy bedroom. Stacks of multicolored construction paper and several jars of clay set next to stacks of worn books. A neglected reel-to-reel projector hid in a corner.

Suddenly, my body went numb. On a table next to an open file cabinet rested the South Maybin Guillotine! The lethal paper cutter's sharp angled blade looked like something out of a horror movie. I'd heard the stories surrounding the deadly machine, figuring it was all a joke. A horrifying story fifth graders concocted to scare younger kids. From our earliest school days, tales floated around the playground of sadistic teachers employing the Guillotine to sever fingers and toes of misbehaving thugs. One boy was supposedly relieved of both little fingers and an ear the same day. Had the establishment finally had enough of J.D. Harrison? Had I been sentenced to the South Maybin Guillotine? *Please Lord! Don't let her cut off my trigger finger!*

Before a directive could be given, I assumed "the position" at the end of the table, praying for just a beating. Producing a long paddle from somewhere in the darkness, The Bull clinched the lumber in her fists, digging in at the plate like Mickey Mantle. Closing my eyes, I sensed the paddle being raised high above her broad shoulders.

Positive that every child at South Maybin cowered in their seats the moment three powerful blows echoed through the school, I wondered if they observed a moment of silence. Limping through the classroom door, I eased my flaming behind into my desk. With my plan blown to smithereens and my butt cooking on high broil, I had no choice but to face the inevitable. Squirming nervously in my desk, I watched while The Bull gleefully handed out the report cards. A few *ooohs* and *ahhhs* blended together with solemn whimpers. Making it a point to drool over her favorites, The Bull smothered them with sickening compliments. Ignoring my pitiful expression, she tossed the card on my desk like a stained menu at a greasy truck stop.

Taking a deep breath, I eased the report card out of its yellow sleeve as if it were wired to explode. Peeking at my grades, I was pleased to discover my Reading and Writing grades were both Cs. Passing grades! Noticing the subsequent Ds and Fs immediately quelled any budding interest. Below the messy collection of consonants, I cringed at my Conduct grade—D. Next to the grade a comment appeared in red ink!

"I am very disappointed in J.D. He could be a bright student if he applied himself." Unfortunately, the only object that would be "applied" in this instance would be "Mr. Belt!"

When the bell rang to end the day, excited kids scrambled to their feet, grabbing books and jackets. The Bull stood at the door while everyone filed out. She wouldn't see me again until the funeral.

Parading silently down the sidewalk, we pondered our last hours we had left among the living. There was no way on God's green earth I could show my parents this pathetic excuse of a report card. My only chance of survival hinged on my parents' preoccupation with tonight's football game.

Making the somber turn onto Circle Drive, I made a quick and hasty decision, throwing my report card into a group of overgrown bushes. Although the desperate act drew laughter from my fellow condemned, no one followed suit.

Waving goodbye to my friends, possibly for the last time, I lumbered slowly through the yard. Reaching the front steps of our house, I knew something was horribly wrong. I'd gotten my first beating of the school year and my fuming mother wasn't waiting on the front porch to skin me alive. Normally on these occasions, Mom already knew the juicy details of my escapades well before I got home. Slowly opening the door, I wondered if she were lying in wait somewhere inside to ambush me. Thankfully I found her sitting on the couch holding the Lucky Quilt in her lap.

"I forgot we tore the quilt," she admitted, repairing the latest gash inflicted by Tiger Field's notorious bleacher splinters that could penetrate solid concrete. On its last leg, the Lucky Quilt had faded into a blue and gold collage of yarn and patches. Convinced the Maybin Tigers didn't have a chance to win if she didn't bring the Lucky Quilt, Mom carried the pathetic rag to every game.

The fact that I remained a living breathing creation assured me that she was unaware of the day's fiasco. Leaving nothing to chance, I offered a cursory wave and raced down the hall to my room. Throwing on my army gear, I dashed out the door.

"Be home by five and no later! Ya hear me?"

"Yes ma'am!"

Counting my lucky stars, I sprinted to Ashley Woods. In no time the worries of the day vanished in the heat of battle. After a few hours of glorious combat, I heard my name echo through the woods.

"J.D.! Time to come home!" My heart skipped into overdrive.

"See y'all tonight," I yelled at the squad, hoping to keep my promise.

Friday night football meant Brunswick stew for supper. A quick and easy meal before the game. Every church in the county held their annual stew sales in the fall and Mom bought the meaty concoction by the case. Quite an authority on fine Brunswick stews, I preferred the Methodist recipe over other denominations. Somehow the Baptists' mediocre attempts didn't quite measure up. Dad explained that Methodists prepared such good Brunswick stew because they spent most of the time drinking while cooking the southern staple.

A steaming bowl of stew and a grilled cheese sandwich along with gridiron-obsessed parents made for a delightful supper. The Game was all they talked about. Then out of the blue, panic struck again. Stirring my spoon through my bowl, I suddenly remembered seeing The Bull at the last football game. *Oh, no! Would she be there tonight? What if she runs into Mom?*

"J.D.," Mom chuckled. "You look like you just saw a ghost. What's wrong?"

"Oh… uh… nothing," I muttered.

"J.D.! Elbows off the table. What's bothering you? You seem to be out in space somewhere," Mom frowned.

"Sorry Mom. I'm just worried… about the game."

"Both are undefeated," Dad said. "Hey! I might even suit up myself, score the winnin' touchdown." He winked, poking Suzie in the side with a finger.

Leaving an unruly pile of dirty dishes in the sink, we rushed to get ready. Grabbing a light jacket and my tattered New York Yankee baseball cap, I joined Dad and Suzie in the garage.

"Hurry up Dottie! We're never gonna find a parkin' place," Dad yelled, while Suzie and I piled into the backseat. After a few minutes, Mom stumbled out the back door carrying the refurbished Lucky Quilt.

Staring out the window, I couldn't shake the thought of The Bull and Mom running into each other at the game. Somehow I had to make sure that didn't happen. Perhaps the elation of beating the snot out of me had been enough excitement for one day. Maybe she'd retire to her favorite chair celebrating the momentous occasion with a carton of cigarettes and a case of beer.

Making a snail's turn onto Second Street, we trailed behind an endless line of brake lights towards the ballpark. Cars and trucks lined the edges of the street, spilling into yards and driveways. Finding a spot in Mr. Wallace's front yard, Dad squeezed the Pontiac between a Chevy pickup and a large oak tree. In the distance, the giant light poles of Tiger Field rose above the tree line, burning in the late day sun. Yellow beacons summoning the Tiger faithful to worship.

Breezy fumes of hot dog chili, popcorn, and cigarette smoke drifted through the air as we merged with the masses at the front gate. As expected, the whole town turned out. Cautious moms handed out last minute instructions to fidgety kids while zealous fans exchanged friendly threats and wagers.

"J.D., you and Suzie find Grace and Shelby. They're savin' us a seat." Her voice trailed off as she joined an exodus of women for one last restroom seating before the game. Marching behind Dad, we joined a lively stream of fans passing packed bleachers and a nervous Tiger bench. Locked in pregame jitters, our hometown warriors paced the sidelines, yelling encouragement as they pounded each other's shoulder pads. Weaving through the crowd, I could almost feel The Bull's beady eyes following me.

Giving us a wink, Dad joined a group of men huddled under a light pole. Reaching the smiling party, he playfully punched one of them on the shoulder. For the rest of the night these men, who once upon a time played Tiger football, stood together under a hazy dome of cigarette smoke, reliving their glory days.

Somewhere in the garbled noise, I heard someone call my name. Glancing at faces in the massive crowd I spotted Aunt Grace waving at us from the bleachers.

"Here's Suzie," I yelled back.

Taking her cue, Suzie twisted through shoulder-to-shoulder spectators, weaving her way up the rows. Of course, I wouldn't be caught dead sitting in the stands and neither would any other self-respecting nine-year-old. Bleachers were for mommies, little kids, and geezers.

My destination lay waiting near the end zone, where kids gathered for spirited games of football using a crumpled paper cup. Dodging past sluggish walkers, I was suddenly blinded by a flaming mass of red hair from the third row of a crowded bleacher. Dressed in a bright gold scarf and blue sweater, The Bull sat talking with fellow teachers, Miss Andrews and Mrs. Heath.

Doing a quick about face, I fought a tidal wave of oncoming fans. Discovering an empty front row seat, I plopped down beside a kid eating a popsicle. What do I do now? Another nervous squirm sent a sharp pain ripping through my jeans, rekindling the burn from the lunchtime paddling. I'd become the latest victim of Tiger Field's unforgiving bleachers.

"*OOOUCH!*"

"*Ha*! Look Momma! He got a splinter in his behind," observed the popsicle brat. To the amusement of those around me, I pulled a spike out of my backside that would have made Captain Ahab proud. Realizing the scene I was making, my head whipped around. There, in the next set of bleachers, Miss Andrews and Mrs. Heath shared a look of concern at my painful circumstances while The Bull just shook her head.

She knows I'm here! That Mom's here! She'll comb every inch of the ballpark until she finds her and tells her about my horrible grades and the paddling! Panicked, I lost myself in the crowd, determined to find Mom first before The Bull got the chance.

Echoing feedback from the ballpark's loudspeakers muted the anxious crowd. With Mom nowhere in sight, I limped over to the end zone. My coarse jeans rubbing hard against my wounded butt with every painful step.

"All rise," blared from two pitiful speakers hanging precariously from leaning light poles. It would be the only audible words spoken all night. Tiger Field's archaic sound system made Mr. Evans, who announced the games, sound like he was talking through a kazoo.

With hands over hearts and hats dutifully removed, the crowd cringed while the Fighting Tiger Band butchered the National Anthem. Playing dented artifacts that resembled instruments, the twenty or so band members, dressed in ill-fitting hand me down uniforms, never left the bleachers. The tune sounded somewhat familiar. The six-piece horn section was all over the place, sounding like a herd of bellowing cattle at feeding time. After an excruciating minute of noise, the band received a polite round of applause.

Cheers erupted when both team captains marched to midfield along with the referees and principals from both schools. Leading the way was our quarterback Frankie Holt, number twelve. Tall with sandy blond hair, Frankie could throw a football a country mile and every little boy in town wanted to be just like him. Haw River's captain, big Eddie Wilkins, wore number thirty-two. The bruising running back scored three touchdowns last year as Haw River thumped our beloved Tigers.

Short and balding in his dark blue suit and gold tie, the principal of Maybin High School, Mr. D.L. Shambley, kindly referred to by the students as "Mr. Shambles," had more hair growing out of his nose and ears than the top of his head.

While the crowd rose for kickoff, I wandered over and stood in the shadows near the women's restroom. When Mom exited, I rushed up behind her.

"Hey!"

"Hey there! Well, I swanee. Did I miss kick off? There's fifty women in there waitin' on two stalls," she growled.

"Listen, Ma. Aunt Shelby saved ya a seat, but you and Suzie need to find another one."

Her pace quickened as she rushed towards the stands with me hot on her heels.

"What?" she mumbled, craning her neck at the action.

"Them seats Aunt Grace saved. They're just awful. Ya'll need to move."

"Honey, look at the bleachers. They're packed! Where we gonna move to...? Who's got the ball now?" she wondered.

Suddenly, my heart stopped. Emerging from the crowd and heading straight toward us was a bright gold scarf, blue sweater, and blazing red hair! Fumbling with words, I tried to think of something.

"Uh! Momma! Uh... I think I'm gittin' sick!"

"What?"

"Uh... my stomach! It's all that stew I ate... I...I... think I got diarrhea!" I had officially reached the bottom of the barrel. Blatantly pathetic, but it was all I could think of at the moment.

"*Diarrhea!*" She screamed, sharing the condition of my bowels with the rest of the ballpark.

"J.D. You ain't messed up your britches, have ya?"

"*No,*" I yelled, mortified.

Grabbing her hand, I dragged my mother through the multitude. If my friends saw me clutching my mommy's hand, sprinting for the restroom, I'd never be able to show my face again. At the last minute, The Bull veered off toward the concession stand. I still couldn't risk it. If The Bull ever caught up with Mom, the half-time show would feature a screaming fourth grader as human sacrifice.

Where does this all end? I thought, tugging Mom's hand. Report cards, paddlings, lies, deception, an impaled butt, and now, a giggling crowd imagining the volatile condition of my stomach. I didn't slow down till we reached the entrance to the men's restroom.

"For heaven's sake, J.D., I can't go in there with you!"

"I know... uh... just... wait right here. Don't leave me Momma! Promise ya won't leave."

"OK, I'll wait right here."

Brushing past a man combing his hair on his way out, I rushed inside. What the heck do I do now? A glorified outhouse, the one-seater, two urinal sewer was no place to formulate a successful strategy.

Maintaining a safe distance from a toxic pool puddling under the urinals, men aimed at their target from three feet away. In a back corner, a couple of junior high boys passed each other a cigarette. Two rust-stained porcelain sinks hung from the wall. Dodging a floor full of spent paper towels, I stood against the wall plotting my next move.

They appeared out of nowhere, hidden by the line at the urinal. I couldn't have dreamed up this nightmare if I tried.

"Well, hey butthead! Where ya been?" Billy Ray asked, wiping his wet hands on his pants.

"Uh... uh... We just got here."

"We got a game goin' behind the far end zone," Skeeter said, wanting to leave.

"J.D.! J.D.!" Mom's voice echoed through the open door. I closed my eyes. "Are you all right?"

"*Yes!*"

Billy Ray's eyes became wide as saucers. Falling against the wall, both of them busted out laughing.

"What's wrong? Poor little J.D. need his butt wiped?" Billy Ray cried.

"J.D.? Everything OK?"

"It's OK Ma. I'm better now," I yelled.

"Has J.D. stunk up his britches?" Billy Ray snickered, elbowing Skeeter.

"Billy Ray! Is that you?"

"Yes Mrs. Harrison," he yelled, holding his stomach in laughter.

"Is J.D. all right?"

"Oh, he's just fine!"

"See ya later J.D.," he said, heading out the door. "Come play football after you've had ya diaper changed!"

I… was a dead man. The only honorable thing left for me to do was drown myself in the brown water of the clogged-up toilet. When word spread around school that my mommy waited for me outside the men's room, I'd have to run away and join the circus!

Turning towards the door I slipped on a puddle of water. Both feet shot out from under me. My pierced rear end took the brunt as I slammed into the wet cement floor. Soaked, I limped to the door.

"Oh my goodness, J.D.! You done wet yourself somethin' fierce!" Mom said, grabbing my arm. Piercing eyes fell on me from every direction. I fully expected the highlights of my restroom disaster to be covered in gory detail by the newspaper.

Although I was a wet stinking mess, there was no way my parents would leave the Haw River game unless I'd lost a limb. For the remainder of the night, I shivered in the dark recesses of the tall grandstand, oddly enough, wrapped in the Lucky Quilt. By the grace of God, Mom and The Bull never crossed paths. Mercifully, Maybin High School won the game. A Tiger loss combined with my antics and they may have never found my body.

As the last few seconds of the game clock ticked away, so did my chances for survival. With the game out of the way, there were no more distractions. But I was in too deep. I didn't mop up the floor of an outhouse to give up now. The only thing left to do was lie, lie, and keep on lying!

By some strange miracle I was still alive Sunday morning. Sitting in church, I had a horrible feeling something terrible was about to happen. Like she did every Sunday, Mom prepared our standard lunch of broiled roast, green beans, and mashed potatoes. I didn't say anything as we sat down at the table. Of course, Mom was way ahead of me. Her fangs came out right after the blessing.

"Where's your report card? I didn't see it in ya backpack." Ignoring the obvious invasion of privacy, I slipped quickly into lying mode.

"It ain't in my backpack? Hmm. Maybe I left it at school."

"Listen here Buddy Roe. You better *not* have left it at school! You're cruisin' for a bruisin'!"

"Momma honest, cross my heart and hope to die I'll bring it home tomorrow!"

"You come home with a bad report card and I'll jerk a knot in you. You hear me? What did we tell ya when school started? You bring back bad grades and you ain't gonna be watchin' *Combat* or playing army with your friends!"

Staring down at my plate, I didn't respond.

"Look at me! Do I need to come pick you up at school tomorrow?"

"*No*! No ma'am…"

"Don't stop nowhere. You come home straight home and you better have that report card!"

As expected, I caught hell the moment I set foot into class the next morning. Everyone, including The Bull, knew about my restroom fiasco. A neatly folded diaper laid in my seat, courtesy of Billy Ray. Busy at her desk, The Bull examined the stack of cards.

"J.D.? Where's your report card?"

"I guess I left it at home," I sighed. *First Mom, now The Bull! Where does this all end?*

"You mean your parents haven't signed your card?"

"Oh yes ma'am! They… signed it all right… I think. I left it on the dinin' room table. I'll bring it back tomorrow."

"Want me to send a reminder home with you?"

"No ma'am! I'll remember!" *If I can find the damn thing buried in the bushes.* With my luck, the card was part of a squirrel nest by now. After school, we weren't out the door before the discussion began.

"I can't play Ambush anymore y'all," Skeeter mumbled. "Ma had a full-blown hissy fit 'bout my grades. Sent me to bed with no supper and guess what? I can't watch *Combat* for a month!"

"I'm grounded till next report card too and no TV neither," admitted Junior.

Detailing our stern jail sentences, we moped along. When our caravan reached Circle Drive, I fumbled through the bushes and unfortunately found my report card.

This time Mom was waiting for me on the front porch, her arms dutifully folded. Without saying a word, I handed her the yellow card. For a moment, I thought Mom was going to explode right there on the steps.

"Git yourself in your room and stay there!" Like an angry town crier, her screeching voice echoed through the trees, announcing my pending execution to the entire neighborhood.

Closing the door to my room, I laid down on the bed and waited. Figuring there was more to the story, Mom reached for the telephone. After a quick call to The Bull, it was over. Slamming the receiver down so hard the bell resounded down the hallway, Mom's heavy footsteps bounded through the house. Bursting into my room, she let me have it. As promised, no watching TV or playing army till next report card. No chance for parole.

Later that evening with Dad's assistance, Mr. Belt and I held a lengthy post report card conference. Before the beating, he explained that I was getting a whipping, not because of my grades, but because I had lied. I didn't dare ask him which one!

Life as I knew it ceased to exist. With nowhere to turn, I convinced Bucky to help with my academic rehabilitation. One afternoon, we were sitting in my room, going over multiplication tables.

"J.D., when ya goin' back to playin' Ambush?"

"When my grades get better, I reckon."

"Well, what if your grades don't get no better?"

"What 'cha mean?"

"Well, if your grades keep stinkin', ya might fail the fourth grade."

What! I'd never considered the prospect of failing a grade! I fully expected to be passed on to the next grade like every other stupid doofus! If I failed a grade, I wouldn't go on to the fifth grade with the rest of my buddies. Holy smokes! I might even get stuck with The Bull again!

On that beautiful October afternoon, sitting in my room with Bucky, I experienced my first mid-childhood crisis. My parents finally got their wish as I magically transformed into a completely different kid. Someone I wasn't sure I knew. A student who religiously completed his homework assignments and studied for tests. Somehow some way, I made it through the torturous six weeks.

When report card day rolled around again, I sat nervously in my seat as The Bull strolled down the rows of desks carrying the stack of declarations. Swallowing hard as she approached, I looked up, hoping for the best.

"Very good J.D. Your grades have improved tremendously. I'm very proud of you."

For the first time ever, The Bull smiled at me. Not that evil looking smirk of hers, but a pleasant sincere smile.

"Thank you, Miss Blanchard," I said, returning a smile of my own.

Tearing open the cover, I pulled the card from its yellow sleeve. I was pretty sure of the results but still I couldn't believe my eyes. All As and Bs! Mom made such a fuss that I fully expected her to have my report card framed and placed on a neon billboard in our front yard. With parole proudly granted, I was released back into society. Free to fight once again in the trenches of Ashley Woods.

The following Tuesday night, I settled back on the couch with an ice-cold cup of Hawaiian Punch and gleefully watched *Combat* for the first time in over a month. I thought about the six long weeks of working my butt off. The sacrifices, the endless studying. Then it hit me. *What in the world was I so happy about? This wasn't the end of anything!* I'd have to do it all over again the next six weeks! And the one after that and the one after that! My bottom lip quivered at the revelation.

Gazing at the black and white TV screen, I saw the lonely eyes of my hero, Sergeant Saunders. Crouching behind a fallen tree, his machine gun at the ready, he seemed so sad. He'd signed on. Made the commitment to his country. Still deep down inside, all he wanted to do was go home. Return to the life he once knew. Time for me to do the same thing.

For the first time in my life, I understood that everything had a price. I just wasn't sure I wanted to pay the toll right now. What I needed was a vacation. It was high time I became J.D. Harrison again. My parents would get mad but that was six weeks away. A whole lifetime in the mind of a nine-year-old. Hey, I'd figure out something by then. I always did.

An Unlikely Bookworm

"You weren't exactly an Einstein, were you?" Suzie laughed, fittingly punctuating my adventures in the classroom.

"I remember that report card mess. Your momma was fit to be tied!" Dad grinned. Offering a pleasing expression of her own, Mom listened politely to my recollection.

"I was a late bloomer," I conceded with a wink.

Arm in arm they stood with their backs pressed against the dusty bookshelves, taking it all in.

"There's no place to sit. Y'all OK?" Suzie asked, stepping to the center of the room.

"I'm all right," Mom said.

"If there was a place to sit down, I'm not sure I'd want to chance it," Dad chuckled. "Momma… we never did fill up these bookcases like we hoped to, did we?" he sighed, running his hand lightly over the flaxen shelf top, thick with prehistoric varnish.

"No, I reckon we didn't."

Peering into the bookcase's grimy ledges, I remembered Suzie curled up in a motionless ball during a feisty game of hide-and-seek. A russet baseball glove and jump rope crammed next to her along with stacks of magazines that Mom refused to throw away. I imagined the glossy white bindings of *World Book* encyclopedias leaning on each other for support. An ancient search engine that opened my eyes to the outside world.

"Y'all remember the encyclopedias that used to sit there?" I asked, pointing to the second shelf.

"That's right! I remember them!" Suzie laughed.

"We bought them one night from a door-to-door salesman," Dad recalled.

AMONG THE CONSTANT BATTLES I encountered as a child, the elusive spoken word went straight in one ear and out the other. This rather disturbing trait prompted my mother to often employ the necessary yet rarely effective screaming word, frequently accompanied by hand-held props such as a hairbrush or flyswatter. When necessary, the heavy artillery of Mr. Belt joined the fray.

But those turned out to be only minor skirmishes compared to my constant battle with the puzzling and often misunderstood written word. Reading required two important traits that I had no intention of ever acquiring: attention and concentration. Comic books and cereal boxes pushed my woeful literary skills to the limit. Of course, Mom was determined to change all that.

People were always dropping by our house unannounced, selling stuff. Regulars like Mr. Sherwood, the Fuller Brush Man, gave our front doorbell a workout. Wearing the same worn blue suit, coffee-stained white shirt, and loosened yellow tie, Mr. Sherwood showed up at our doorstep like clockwork on the first Tuesday of every month.

Things got interesting when Miss Darla, the Avon Lady, came calling. Petite with dark brown hair, Miss Darla's brilliant smile shined like new money. Her pretty round face and short skirts were something to behold. But one night the appearance of an unexpected visitor changed everything.

Reluctantly taking my seat at the dining room table, I engaged in another exasperated attempt at homework. Mom and Suzie were busy cleaning up the supper dishes while Dad settled back in his recliner when the doorbell rang. Running through the living room, I peeked through the curtains. Standing on the front porch was a stranger flanked by two large suitcases. Dressed in a black suit and matching fedora, he reminded me of Mr. Landis down at the funeral home. Straightening the knot in his red tie, he lifted his hat briefly and placed it back on his head.

"Ma! It's some man!" Coming up behind me, Mom eyed him through the curtains.

Annoyed, she opened the door. With a broad smile, the man removed his hat with one hand and held out a business card with the other.

"Good evening, ma'am. My name is Franklin Winters and I represent the *World Book Encyclopedia*. Do you have the *World Book*?" Before Mom could answer, Suzie and I peeked at the stranger from the partially opened door. "Well, I see we have a couple of inquisitive little folks here! How old are you son, twelve?" I liked this guy already.

"No sir, I'm nine."

"Boy's big for his age. And you, cutie pie. How old are you?"

"Five," Suzie answered, barely audible, twisting strands of her hair with a fidgety finger.

"You're just a doll baby!" Very smooth.

"Well, Mrs....?"

"Harrison, Dottie Harrison."

"Nice to meet you Mrs. Harrison. I'm sure you know that the Tates, the Watkins and the Satterfields recently purchased the *World Book* from me and of course ordered a set of *Childcraft* as well. Are you familiar with *Childcraft*?" I could hear the wheels turning as Mom cut her eyes at me.

"Yes, I know all about *Childcraft*. Barbara Tate showed them to me. Please come in Mr. Winters."

Glancing at his watch, Dad gave Mr. Winters a halfhearted hand-shake. Almost time for one of his favorite westerns, *Wagon Train*.

"Mind if I sit down?"

"Oh yes, please." Mom gestured. "J.D., clear off the dinin' room table." Mom didn't have to tell me twice. Seizing the opportunity to avoid homework, I eagerly put my books away.

"Would you like some coffee, Mr. Winters?" Dad glared at Mom's question.

"That would be nice. Black please."

Flashing a corny grin, he set his suitcases on the table. Delivering a well-rehearsed script of the educational advantages of the famous *World Book,* the polished salesman never missed a beat. Peering at the open suitcases, I noticed different colored bookmarks protruding from the tops of several books.

"Here honey, sit in Uncle Franklin's lap." Opening a volume, he turned to a pink bookmarked page and placed the book in front of Suzie.

"Honey, what do you see?" he asked, winking at me.

"*Puppies!*" Pawing at a full page of cute collie pups, Suzie squealed with delight.

"Yes sweetheart. Puppies!" Never rushing the moment, Mr. Winters played it perfectly, allowing Suzie to take it all in.

"Look Momma! They're so cute!" Resigned to his fate, Dad wandered off in search of his checkbook.

"Here little lady. Sit down in that chair and look all you want while I talk to your brother." With Suzie eagerly eating out of his hand, Mr. Winters turned to me and smiled. Selecting the encyclopedia with an embossed "W" on the spine, he opened the book to a predetermined page.

"What do you think of that?"

I couldn't believe my eyes. In front of me was page after page of World War II in glorious pictures!

"There's a B-17," I yelled. "It's the Memphis Belle. Look Dad! A P-51 Mustang! A B-29! Gosh! It's the Enola Gay!"

Fascinated, I placed the book on the table, examining each glossy page, brimming with ships, tanks, and fighting gear of every description. Paratroopers fell from the sky in clouds of white chutes while bombs dropped from open bellies of planes on another. Massive guns draped in smoke fired from mighty warships.

"He's a lieutenant," I said, pointing to the white vertical stripe on the back of a soldier's helmet.

"Well done young man! I only made it to First Sergeant."

"You were in the war?"

"First Infantry Division."

"You were in the Big Red One?"

"My goodness. How did you know about the Big Red One?"

"I read a lot." I lied.

At that moment Mr. Winters could have been peddling a suitcase full of nuclear waste and my parents would have gladly bought every radioactive ounce. There was no way they could refuse with Suzie and me firmly on the hook. Without saying a word, Mom flicked the end of a ballpoint and handed it to Dad while Franklin and I shared war stories. After the paperwork, Mr. Winters explained that our set of encyclopedias and *Childcraft* would be delivered in a few weeks.

Time crept by like the last sluggish days before Christmas. Every afternoon I rushed home from school hoping the encyclopedias had arrived. When the books finally came, I sat on the couch for hours, beholding every volume in all its literary splendor. In no time I had the whole world from "A" to "Z" neatly arranged on the long bookshelf under the windows of our den. To my surprise, exploring the pages of these marvelous books took the edge off schoolwork. Things came easier in class. It wasn't long before my newfound thirst for literature opened new doors I never imagined.

MARCHING IN SINGLE FILE, the sound of busy shoes echoed down the hall for our standard Tuesday morning trip to the school library. A dark dismal place in the bowels of South Maybin Elementary, where the slightest whisper sent Miss Dillon, our fussy librarian, into frenzied delirium.

Happy to get out of class, our squad playfully pushed each other while we skipped along. With one finger pressed tightly over her lips, The Bull held the library door open as we filed inside. Standing behind the front desk, Miss Dillon who possessed the personality of a coffee table, sneered her disapproval. Thin and frail with graying hair, she reminded me of Granny from *The Beverly Hillbillies.* The only words I ever heard Miss Dillon utter in four years of school were "Be quiet" and "Look it up in the card catalog."

No directives were needed. Excited for another morning of literary stimulation, the girls in class scattered to the inviting bookshelves while boys, bored out of their minds, slumped down at the tables like sloths ready for a nap. Elbowing each other, Skeeter and I fought for the coveted end seat.

After successfully mining a nostril, Billy Ray picked up a ruffled copy of *National Geographic* someone had left on the table. Pressing the slimy glob between two pages, he tossed the defiled magazine at Junior who batted it down. Glancing at the open pages, Junior's eyes flew open.

"*Oh my gosh*," he whispered. "Look y'all! She's neked as a jaybird!"

Scampering to our feet, we fanned out, peering over Junior's shoulder. Giggling in little boy amazement, we gawked at a full-page picture of a tall black woman with a basket on her head wearing nothing but a grass skirt! Naked! Right there in front of God and everybody! Huddled at her feet were two small children playing in a rut-filled road.

With gaping mouths, we took it all in, examining every minute detail. Minutes flew by as we immersed ourselves in the rural culture of Central Africa. When The Bull signaled time to go back to class, Junior quickly folded down the top corner of the sultry page, marking our discovery for future reference.

For the rest of the week, we relived our exciting discovery, whispering silly particulars to each other. By the time the following Tuesday rolled around, we were fired up and ready for another morning of intense study.

Rushing through the library door like hungry hyenas, the four of us sprinted to the magazine rack. Tearing through the shelves as if it were a sock drawer, we searched for *National Geographic's* seductive golden cover.

"It ain't here," Billy Ray whispered, leaving the shelves in disarray. The sexiest thing we found was the September edition of *Highlights*. Smirking from behind the front desk, Miss Dillon reveled in her little surprise. Obviously, she'd taken great delight in removing the sought-after magazine.

Oh, that's just great! I finally discover something at this neighborhood penal colony that holds my interest for more than five minutes and the powers that be take it away. Under no circumstances would fun be tolerated in this establishment. The library quickly became its boring self again. Still, a small seed had been planted in my small, infantile brain. A few weeks later, that seed was watered and fertilized.

A heavy downpour forced cancellation of Ambush. Everyone scurried home while Skeeter and I ended up at Billy Ray's house. Leaving our mud-caked tennis shoes in the carport, we stepped inside.

"Mom's gone shoppin'!" He grinned, locking the door behind us. Running to the living room, he ruffled the curtains, making sure they were closed all the way.

"What 'cha doin'?" I asked.

"You'll see. Follow me!"

Scampering down the hall, we burst through the door to his parents' bedroom. Opening the closet door, Billy Ray climbed on a small chair. Standing on his tiptoes, his outstretched arm felt along the top shelf.

"Get a load of this!"

There, in Billy Ray's grubby little hands, a pretty girl with jet-black hair smiled back at us from the glossy cover of a *Playboy* magazine!

"Holy crap!" Skeeter marveled.

Laying several issues side by side on the bed, we fidgeted with excitement as Billy Ray selected the June edition. With a sly grin, he opened the magazine to a section entitled, "A Toast to Bikinis." Unlike my first encounter with nudity that tantalizing day in the school library, none of these naked beauties wore baskets on their heads or seemed ticked off like the woman in *National Geographic*. In fact, every gorgeous one seemed pretty darn happy about the whole thing, except for a few who appeared sweaty and sleepy looking.

"Sure beats the hell outta National Geographic, don't it?" Billy Ray smirked.

Lost in giddy prepubescent wonder, we stared at the enticing pictures while Billy Ray slowly turned the pages. Then on page 37, the world as I knew it changed forever. Perched on bent knees atop a beach towel, a striking blonde with mint-green eyes looked longingly into mine. With dark red lips pursed in a playful grin, she sported a small red bikini bottom, holding the other half of her swimsuit around her neck with both hands. My wide eyes bounced up and down the page like an out-of-control rollercoaster!

"Who is she? Who is she?" I begged.

"Uh… says here she's Bonnie Sue Mitchell… twenty-three-years-old from Fay… ette… ville, Arkansas… 36-24-36."

"What them numbers for?"

"Her phone number!" Skeeter grinned.

"Naw stupid, ain't enough numbers."

"What they mean then?"

"How would I know? Say's here she's a hog fan."

"A hog fan?" I laughed. "She grow up on a farm?"

"Don't say."

"Why would she like pigs for?"

"Says she goes to all their home football games."

Since when did pigs play football? Probably some coded grownup stuff like the 36-24-36 numbers. A teasing mystery for us to figure out. What was *Playboy* trying to tell us? Honestly, I didn't care!

Over the course of that rainy afternoon, we painstakingly examined every page of all five issues. With so many amazing poses available for our viewing pleasure, a strange indescribable force drew us back to page 37 of the June issue.

I'd once had a thing for Hayley Mills, after seeing the movie *The Parent Trap*, and there was that short-lived bread obsession I had for Little Miss Sunbeam, but none of them could hold a candle to the lovely Bonnie Sue. The sound of car tires crunching on the gravel driveway broke the spell.

"Mom's home!"

Like fireman summoned to a four-alarm blaze, we handed the magazines to Billy Ray who quickly returned them to their hiding place.

For the next week, Skeeter and I met at Billy Ray's house every afternoon while his mother was out running errands. We considered sharing this once in a lifetime experience with the rest of the squad but thought it best to keep the sultry secret between the three of us. Our clandestine rendezvous quickly became delicate operations. Still, there was something about our alluring discovery that seemed too good to be true. Although everything always went smoothly, I had an uneasy feeling that somebody might be watching us.

Waiting for the "All Clear" signal one afternoon, I stood nervously by the phone. When the call came, I tore out of our garage on my bike.

Just as I turned the corner, I was surprised by Mrs. Eastman picking weeds out of her flower bed.

"Hey J.D.! Where're you goin' in such a hurry?" she chuckled. I almost fell off my bike! Did she know? I'd never seen Mrs. Eastman gardening this time of the day. Had she watched me ride to Billy Ray's every afternoon?

"Uh… nowhere Mrs. Eastman. I ain't goin' nowhere! I ain't goin' to Billy Ray's house to look at nothin'. Honest I ain't!" Scared out of my mind, I blew past Billy Ray's, circled the block, and went home.

Later that week, Billy Ray clued us in that his mom planned to spend the entire afternoon shopping in Burlington. We'd have hours alone with Bonnie Sue! Anxiously pacing the floor, I waited for the call. Leaning on the kitchen counter next to the phone, I prayed Aunt Shelby wouldn't call Mom. Not today. If they ever got going, they'd tie up the phone till supper! The sudden ring startled me.

"I'll git it!"

"Hello."

"Come on over." Click. Speeding out the driveway, I met Junior pedaling his bike down the street.

"Hey! I was comin' over. Where ya been? You missed Ambush all week. So's Skeeter and Billy Ray. The guys been askin' about 'cha."

"Yeah… Uh… been busy."

Staring into Junior's youthful eyes, so innocent and childlike, I felt guilty lying to one of my best friends. My naïve little buddy had no idea that an enticing world full of adventure waited out there for him to discover. Maybe it was time I helped him along. Billy Ray would get mad, but he'd get over it.

"I'm goin' to Billy Ray's. Wanna go?"

"Sure!"

Laying our bikes down in Billy Ray's front yard, we scampered up the steps and rang the doorbell. Standing on the front porch peeking over my shoulder, I felt like some thug at a speakeasy. The curtain in the large bay window peeled back. An angry Billy Ray quickly opened the door.

"What the hell ya doin'?"

"Let us in 'fore somebody sees us!"

"You promised! Crossed your heart and everything," he yelled, slamming the door behind us.

"Junior's OK. Let 'im see it."

"See what?"

"How ya know he ain't gonna tell everybody?"

"Tell everybody *what*?"

"Just watch!" I winked. "Come on. Let 'im see it." Disgusted, Billy Ray relented.

"OK! I'll let 'im see it all right!"

Escorting our ever-expanding literary group to his parents' bedroom, he reached for the top shelf, grabbing the June issue. *What's he doing?* I thought. Flashing a nasty smirk, he quickly flipped through the pages. Then it hit me. *Oh my gosh! He's going straight to page 37!* No warmup or nothing. This wasn't *National Geographic* Billy Ray was toying with. This was lethal! The atomic bomb of naked women! Thrusting the sexiest picture in the entire history of *Playboy* into the face of an innocent little boy like Junior just might kill him!

Without warning, Billy Ray held the magazine open with both hands, giving the centerfold a certain Panavision quality. Giggling, he shoved the picture in Junior's timid face. There she was, Bonnie Sue Mitchell in all her glory!

It took a moment for the potent imagery to pierce Junior's dim-witted brain. The trembling began at his knees. Like an 8.9 magnitude earthquake, Junior shook violently, struggling to stand. Like a drowning man grasping for a float, Junior's quivering hand stretched out for Bonnie Sue. Latching on, he gripped tightly to the top right corner of the page.

"Hey! Let go!" Billy Ray frowned. Stunned into a catatonic state, Junior held firm.

Suddenly the boy collapsed to his knees, pulling Bonnie Sue down with him! Our mouths flew open at the sound of ripping paper. The jagged gash cut Bonnie Sue in half! Somehow Skeeter wrestled what was left of the goddess from Junior's trembling hands. Helplessly we stared in disbelief at Bonnie Sue's lifeless picture. Cradling the wounded deity like a newborn, Billy Ray was about to cry.

"I'll get some tape," he whined, fighting back tears.

"No, ya can't! Somebody'll see it," I yelled. Regaining consciousness, Junior mumbled he was sorry while the rest of us shared a desperate look of indecision.

"We got to," Billy Ray conceded. With shaking hands, he carefully lined up the ragged edges. Making sure the tape blended smoothly with the shiny page, Billy Ray covered the tear with the tape. It was no use. The damage was done. Bonnie Sue just wasn't the same anymore. Wrinkled and folded with a glaring piece of tape stuck across her chest, page 37 soon became a tainted memory of things that used to be. A few days later, our wonderful world came tumbling down.

On the way home from school, Billy Ray whispered to wait for the usual "All Clear." When the call came, it wasn't what I expected.

"Hello."

"Bonnie's gone! They're all gone! All of 'em... gone!" he sniffed.

Blinking back the tears, I tore out the back door. Consumed with grief, I climbed on my bike and pulled out of the driveway into the path of an oncoming car whose blaring horn sent me swerving into the ditch. Rounding the block, I saw Billy Ray slumped on his front porch steps. Jumping off my bike, I sprinted across the yard.

"She's gone J.D. Bonnie Sue! Gone!" Overwhelmed with sorrow, Billy Ray sobbed like a baby.

"So, THAT'S WHAT HAPPENED to you! Perverted at age nine!" Suzie laughed.

"Just curious. Mom insisted that I read. Just followin' orders. Quite riveting as I recall!"

Suzie chimed in with the story of an afternoon giving life and color to several pages of our new encyclopedias with a box of crayons, forever ruining volume E.

"Speakin' of reading," I chuckled. "Mom? Remember you'd make me go to the library to pick out books for the summer?"

"I did?"

"Yep, every year! Right after school ended. I'll never forget the time Billy Ray tagged along."

WHY IN THE WORLD did Mom do this to me every summer? Here I was, free from the sinister shackles of school for three whole months and Mom expected me to waste these precious days with my nose stuck in a book. Of all the ruthless punishments available at her disposal, reading was by far the worst.

Another glorious summer vacation had begun. I'd just finished mowing the yard when Billy Ray stopped by. Running across the yard, we were almost at my tire swing when Mom yelled at me from the patio.

"J.D.! Come here a minute." Adding "a minute" to her summons was never a good sign.

"Time ya went down to the library and got some books for the summer."

"Ma! Billy Ray just came over. Can't I go tomorrow?"

"Take him with ya if ya want."

Maybe the early summer heat had gotten to her. Perhaps the sudden realization of having me home for three months clouded her reasoning. Whatever the case, Mom knew good and well that Billy Ray Satterfield was the last person on the planet that should accompany me anywhere unsupervised. As usual, the Clown Prince didn't disappoint.

A warm afternoon breeze brushed past as our bikes bounced over the tracks at the depot. Making our way to Clay Street, we parked on the sidewalk next to the three-story, once upon a time bank building, now the stately home of the Maybin Public Library. Judging by the other bikes left outside the cellblock, there were other poor souls whose summer had been laid to waste.

A few heads turned at the front door's rusty cry. The sleepy hum of an aging window air-conditioner welcomed us inside. Water dripped from the corroded unit into a blue coffee can. Brilliant sunshine poured through tall glass windows, cutting angled shadows across worn hardwood floors that announced our every step.

Waddling down the center aisle, Mrs. Langley, the librarian from hell, glared at us as we shuffled inside. Four feet tall and as wide as my grandmother's Kelvinator, she reminded me of a Volkswagen in a dress. Mrs. Langley made no bones about it. The stern librarian adored obedient little girls whose innate thirst for reading led to the creation of libraries in the first place. Boys, on the other hand, were illiterate scum spawned in the bowels of the netherworld. The lowest of all lifeforms who replaced books on the wrong shelves and only returned overdue books after receiving a federal summons. Determined to get this torture session over with as quickly as possible, I hurried to the bookshelves.

Suddenly a loud bang broke the silence. Everyone turned to see a young boy who accidentally dropped a book on the floor. Shushing him with one of her crooked fingers, the annoyed librarian scowled at the frightened child through her thick glasses. Embarrassed, the boy's mother grabbed her son's hand. Terrified, the poor little kid began to cry. Moving out from behind the front desk, Mrs. Langley pointed to the front door.

"*Out,*" she mouthed. The flustered mother and her wailing child were barely out the door when a chorus of excited giggles echoed through the room from a table full of girls, worshipping their newly found hardbacks. It was obvious Mrs. Langley heard the laughter. Everyone did! Of course, nothing happened. Girls always got a pass.

Shaking our heads in disgust, Billy Ray and I stared at each other in disbelief. A crime had been committed and it was obvious Mrs. Langley would let it ride. Time for a little dose of vigilante justice. Prepared for every possible scenario, Billy Ray retrieved a whoopee cushion from his shorts' pocket. Lurking behind a bookshelf, he waited patiently, studying his prey.

When the cackling girls left their seats to find another riveting volume, Billy Ray made his move. With the stealth and cunning of a lynx, he strolled quietly past the table. Bending down on one knee, pretending to tie his shoe, he gently placed the inflated cushion onto one of the empty seats. The trap was set. Snickering from the fiction section, we waited. A few minutes passed when the girls came skipping back to the table, engrossed in their latest find. The syrupy quartet never saw it coming.

PBPBPBPBPP! All eyes turned at the disgusting reverberation. The surprised victim melted into a red bundle of humiliation, her face buried in her hands. Unable to contain their mischievous snickers, the few boys in the room laughed uncontrollably, reveling in a soothing language they understood.

Knowing the prank would draw Mrs. Langley from her lair, Billy Ray grabbed a book from a shelf and stuffed it under his shirt. Walking nonchalantly to the bathroom, he walked right past the fuming librarian. Billy Ray told me later he threw the book in the toilet.

"Who did that?" Mrs. Langley screamed. "Who dared make such a horrible sound in my library?" Children cowered in submitted silence. Scowling, Mrs. Langley examined every young boy, searching for signs of guilt. The sound of the opening bathroom door broke the tension. A girl stepped forward.

"Mrs. Langley? That boy right there did it. I saw him," she said, pointing at Billy Ray.

Stopping dead in his tracks, Billy Ray's face flooded red with blame. Realizing what was about to unfold, I ambled down the aisle, ignoring the pending showdown. Obsessed with killing my friend, Mrs. Langley staggered right past me. Slick foam covered her lips as she growled through clinched teeth.

"Get out of here and never come back," she screamed. Sprinting to the door, Billy Ray paused, turned around, and shot Mrs. Langley double middle fingers! Girls and mothers gasped in horror at the gesture. On the verge of a stroke, Mrs. Langley retreated to the front desk. It was the funniest thing I'd ever seen!

Waiting for the smoke to clear, I fumbled around for a couple of books to take home when a collection of North Carolina ghost stories caught my eye. The ghostly image of a young woman appeared on the glossy jacket. Attired in a flowing white dress, she stood by a dark roadside on a stormy night. Thumbing through the pages, I was happy to discover the tales were short with plenty of spooky pictures.

Making my way to the checkout desk, I randomly selected several other books for Mom's approval. Surely, she'd send me back to the library if I didn't show up with at least five books to read for the summer. With my head bowed, I placed my selections on the desk. Angered by the interruption, Mrs. Langley stamped my books as if she were swinging a meat cleaver.

"Bring 'em back on time," she hissed.

Tossing the books in the wire basket of my bike, I headed for home, unaware that in just a few hours, I would discover firsthand the overwhelming and frightening power of literature.

Giving my summer choices a satisfactory nod, Mom continued ironing while I scampered off to my room. Opening the book of ghost stories, I leaned back on my bed. Every spooky page offered terrifying stories accompanied by dark menacing pictures. The tale of Joe Baldwin swinging his lantern on dark nights along the railroad tracks, searching for his head, sent cold chills down my arms.

Fascinated, I turned back to the scary front cover. The apparition's name was Lydia, a young girl who was killed in a car wreck back in the

1920s. On dark rainy nights, she appears at the scene of the accident, dressed in the same white gown, flagging down unsuspecting motorists for a ride home.

Sitting there with my back against the headboard, I suddenly felt the strange sensation that I was being watched. Peeking over the top of the book, my body went numb. The red fiendish eyes of my plastic Wolfman model glared back at me from my desk! Beside him, the outstretched arms of a gruesome Frankenstein replica reached out for me!

Mom's stern voice drifted down the hall as she angrily chastised one of her stupid soap opera characters. Slamming the book shut, I hopped off the bed and ran out of my room.

With Mom only a few feet away, I settled back in Dad's recliner, returning to the chilling stories. For the rest of the afternoon, I studied each black and white photo as I read and reread the book. At supper, I hadn't said much, still obsessed with the ghostly tales.

"J.D., you OK?" Dad wondered.

"Huh? Oh yes sir, I'm fine."

"Tired of readin'?" Mom grinned as she passed around a bowl of squash and onions.

"Oh no ma'am!"

"Will, ya won't believe it. After he came home from the library, J.D. sat down right there in your chair and read all afternoon," she announced proudly, as if I had just discovered the cure for midriff bulge.

That night, television took a backseat to my supercharged thoughts. Returning again to the book, I imagined myself standing in the circle of the Devil's Tramping Ground, wondering if Lucifer himself would jump out from behind a tree. Then it happened. Glancing out the window into a pitch-black night, my heart stopped beating. Swallowing hard, I knew that in a few minutes, I'd be going to bed… in a dark room… all by myself!

"J.D.?" Mom's voice sent me jumping. "I scare ya?" she laughed. "It's almost ten. Ain't 'cha tired?"

"Uh… I guess… You goin' to bed now?"

"In a little bit… You head on… night!"

"Night," came my wimpy response as I sat paralyzed on the couch.

In no hurry whatsoever, I crept toward the abyss of terror waiting for me at the end of the hall. Pausing at my doorway, I ran my hand across the wall, flipping on the light switch. At first, the comforting brightness revealed nothing out of the ordinary. Then I saw it! A small crack appeared in the closed blinds. Somebody, or some *thing*, could be standing right outside my window, watching my every move! Sprinting to the window, I stuffed a pair of underwear in the small opening.

Standing in the doorway, I examined the four corners of my room one last time. Taking a deep breath, I switched off the light. Sprinting through the dark, I dived into bed! Panting like a greyhound, I pulled the covers over my head.

Summoning the courage to peek out from underneath, I pulled the sheet halfway down to the trembling bridge of my nose. Slowly my eyes adjusted to the cold black room. Menacing shadows cast by the orange nightlight formed eerie shapes on the walls. Contorted faces stared back at me from folded clothes stacked on a corner chair.

On the verge of wetting the bed, I shut my eyes tight as the ghostly images of Joe and Lydia filled my head. Did they know that I was thinking about them? Could my frenzied fear mysteriously summon these restless spirits to my bedroom?

Somewhere in the crazed delirium of the moment, a rational thought penetrated my paralyzed brain. Wait a minute! *It's the stinkin' book! The damn thing's haunted!* What other explanation could there be? All those years I'd been told repeatedly that reading was good for you. Another bald-faced lie!

With my mind racing a hundred miles an hour, I feverishly twisted under the bedcovers. For the life of me, I couldn't remember what I did with the fiendish book when I came to bed. Did I leave it in the den? Oh Lord, please! If by some chance You let me live through the night, I promise I'll take that possessed book back to the library first thing in the morning!

And that's the way it went all night. Every time I rolled over, I expected to see the scalding red eyes and bright shiny teeth of some slobbering creature crouched beside my bed. Sleepless hours slogged by as I tossed and turned. Somewhere in a fog of consciousness, a reassuring hint of early sunlight filtered through the blinds, sending ferocious monsters scampering back to their caves. I was safe.

Waking the next morning, my foot kicked against something on the bed. Looking above the covers, I went numb. To my horror, the ghost book laid at the foot of my bed. I knew it! Sensing my fear, the book had floated down the hall during the night, landing right on my bed. Hearing Mom in the kitchen, I fled for my life!

"Hey sleepyhead," she said, reaching inside a cabinet. "It's almost nine o'clock! Oh. Ya left ya book on the couch, so I laid it on your bed. You were sound asleep."

Praise God from whom all blessings flow! I didn't care how the book found its way to my room; I wasn't taking any chances. Wolfing down the last of my Cocoa Krispies, I grabbed the evil hardback and pedaled back to the library. Staring one last time at Lydia's pale figure on the front cover, I laid the possessed book on the desk. Smiling at Mrs. Langley, I headed for the door.

Church Pews and Mountain Lions

"**Y**ou were a scaredy-cat back then, weren't you?" Suzie laughed.

"You bet I was! The Wicked Witch of the West scarred me for life!" Gazing again at the dusty shelves triggered another precious memory.

"Remember your Bible, Mom? You used to keep it right here." I said, placing my hand on the top shelf.

"Still got it," she responded.

"Really? The same one?"

"Four hundred years old and limp as a dishrag! Belongs in a museum," Dad chimed in. "The gold letters on the front are all worn off. All kinds of handwritten notes in the margins and plenty of underlined verses. I got her a couple of new ones over the years, but she never even opened 'em."

"One I got's just fine. God's word ain't changed none. Don't need no new Bible."

Contemplating the leather-bound King James Version's exclusive place on the shelf, I recalled the book in its younger days. Its gilded edged paper gave the book the appearance of a gold bar wrapped in a black covering.

A consummate child hellion, I was quite accustomed to the constant battle between good and evil. Flowing back and forth like a shifting tide, I could assume the sweet disposition of an angel one minute and become an unholy demon the next. The fact that my parents taught Sunday School for as long as I could remember only magnified my crimes in the eyes of other churchgoers. Struggling to stay one step ahead of my childhood mischief, I never imagined Mom having time to read anything back then. Come to find out she began every morning with her Bible and a cup of coffee in the momentary quiet while everyone else was still asleep. A daily ritual she still practiced.

"We never missed church back then, did we?" Suzie noted, remembering hot summer mornings attending Vacation Bible School. Smiling to myself, I thought about those early days: Sunday School class, church picnics, children's choir and of course, Sunday morning worship. You best believe, if there was a kid's program at Maybin Baptist Church, Dottie Harrison's children would be there. And, of course, Mom remained a permanent fixture on the front row, fifth seat from the end in the choir loft every Sunday.

"Sunday mornings were always wild. Remember?" I laughed, recalling the chaos of getting ready for church that resembled a frantic Marx Brothers movie. Where the slightest disruption sent events spiraling out of control, leading to eventual panic and raised voices. "I think we spent more time getting dressed than we ever did sitting on those torturous pews!"

Dad grinned at my recollection and again a treasured Sunday morning long ago came into view. A classic memory shared countless times through the years at Sunday lunches and Christmases, each time with affectionate embellishment. Before I opened my mouth to relive the tale, everyone knew what was coming.

WOLFING DOWN A HURRIED breakfast, we shifted into high gear. With her foot firmly on the accelerator, Mom orchestrated our standard Sunday morning ritual; dressing Suzie, helping Dad find just the right tie, and ensuring my clothes matched. All this while keeping an eye on a roast in the oven.

Attired in my standard blue suit, white shirt, and clip-on plaid bowtie, I stood for inspection. Taking a cue from Mom's twirling finger, I turned in place while she studied every detail. Surprisingly ahead of schedule, Mom had Suzie dressed and ready in record time, leaving my younger sister to her own devices. Ever mindful of the clock, the rest of us scurried around, trying to stay on schedule.

Then it happened. An unexpected series of events sent our Sunday morning express careening off the tracks in a fiery derailment. Bouncing into the den singing "Jesus Loves Me," Suzie tripped over the oval rug, sending her face first into the coffee table. Rushing to the scene barefooted, Mom savagely kicked the leg of an end table. Falling backwards, she landed on the couch.

Hearing Suzie's shrieks, I ran to the den and discovered Mom sitting in a very unladylike pose, squeezing her foot in agony. Bloody polka dots speckled the front of Suzie's green dress creating a gruesome Christmassy effect as she squirmed in pain on the den rug. Bending over to help, I heard the unmistakable sound of ripping cloth. Reaching back, I felt the open tear in my pants.

With the apple cart fully overturned, there was no way we would make it to Sunday School on time. Instead of arriving late, an unforgivable offense, we decided to skip Sunday School altogether, ensuring the congregation's whispered speculation of our absence. Growing up in a small town, church attendance became the lengthy community yardstick used to sort out the heathens from the pious. The only way to redeem our now questionable reputation was to make it to the eleven o'clock preaching or else the Harrisons would be on the lips of every gossip in town.

After a minor surgical procedure to Suzie's wounded face, Mom hobbled to my sister's closet to grab another dress. Selecting a replacement pair of plaid pants that didn't match my coat, I stood for another inspection. Any other Sunday Mom wouldn't dare let me leave the house looking like a used car salesman, but given the morning trauma she nodded a painful approval.

Limping down the hall to her bedroom, Mom slammed the door behind her. The crazed bedlam of the morning had severely delayed a crucial component of her Sunday morning routine: Mom's precious time in front of the makeup mirror. Holding her face inches away from a round magnifying reflector that enlarged the pores of her skin to the size of small craters, Mom meticulously applied several layers of paint. Michelangelo had nothing on my mother. This final, yet tedious stage of the ritual was by far the most challenging.

Although missing Sunday School gave Mom a few extra minutes in front of the mirror, Dad knew if she were granted four hours, she'd drain every last second. With the three of us ready and waiting in the den, Dad paced the floor, glancing at his watch.

"What could she possibly be doin' that takes this long?" he mumbled.

Hobbling from the bedroom carrying Dad's shoehorn, Mom plopped down on the couch. Grimacing, she took the metal device and painfully wedged her wounded foot inside a shiny pair of high heels. If it had been me, I would have put my pajamas back on and went back to bed. Oh no! Not Dottie Harrison. We were going to church if it killed us, which was becoming a very distinct possibility.

We were almost there. Rounding the clubhouse turn, headed down the home stretch. The finish line in sight. Suddenly Mom's nose shot into the air like a bird dog probing for a scent.

"*No… No!*" In a hobbling sprint, she raced to the kitchen. "*Will!* Get in here!" Snatching two potholders from a drawer, she bent over, opening the canary yellow oven door.

"This stupid stove's been actin' up all week. Now it ain't workin' at all!"

What happened next still lives in infamy at the Harrison household to this day. Trembling in anger, Mom yanked the lukewarm pan from the useless oven. This was it. The last straw. The coup de grâce. Glaring at the rebellious stove, Mom erupted, sending molten rage spewing into the air. With the pan quivering in her hands and numbed by anger, she viciously punted the oven door closed with her throbbing foot!

"*AAAHHHHHHH!*" With the pan jostling in her hands, Mom painfully twirled through the kitchen in an agonizing ballet. Bouncing up and down on her good foot, she slammed into the refrigerator sending the foil-wrapped feast ricocheting off her cobalt blue dress and tumbling to the floor.

"Damn… magummit!"

Damnmagummit? Did my mother just say "Damnmagummit?" Her redirected expletive fooled no one. Dad's frightened eyes met mine, then shot back to his dying wife. Was this the same virtuous woman who'd given birth to me? Did the righteously divine matriarch of the Harrison family, queen of the straight and narrow, just utter… *a cuss word?*

Something gloriously wicked emerged from that fateful day. "Damnmagummit" became the premier exclamation of dissatisfaction in the Harrison household. A splendid, never forgotten albatross lovingly flung around Mom's neck at every turn. Something she would never live down. Dad swore he'd have the word engraved on her tombstone.

Undeterred, Dottie Harrison wasn't about to quit. After a quick rush to change into another dress, we stampeded to the car. Anxious that he wouldn't get his favorite parking spot, Dad jerked the car in gear. Slamming the accelerator to the floor, the swerving car threw gravel everywhere as he sped out of the driveway. Sure enough, our usual parking space under the corner maple was taken.

"I bet we won't get our pew either," he snarled. Speeding down the street, Dad careened into another parking spot a block away. Slamming his door with authority, Dad marched up the sidewalk, prepared to fight to the death to get his pew. Obviously, our Sunday morning fiasco had placed us in the perfect and reverent frame of mind for worship.

The silver steeple of Maybin Baptist Church rose high above the shady corner of Jackson and Third Street. The aging white frame exterior set peacefully in a grove of tall maples, alive with fall color. Its melodic bells summoning worshipers inside.

Running to catch up with Dad's hurried steps, I knew we were cutting it close. Men in dark suits finished their last cigarette while exasperated ladies hurried up the front steps with children in tow. Mom hobbled off to the choir room while we sprinted inside.

The massive stained-glass windows, lit by the bright morning sun, painted the sanctuary in a sparkling rainbow of colors. Light fixtures resembling medieval castle lanterns hung from the angled wooden beams on the high ceiling. Burgundy carpet flowed down the double aisles ending at the raised pulpit. The dark oak pews were filling fast.

Finding our seats surprisingly unoccupied, Dad smiled for the first time all morning. As I turned to go into our pew, Billy Ray met me in the aisle.

"Hey! Where ya been? Missed a good time at Sunday School."

"Couldn't get here on time."

"Give this to your momma," he said, handing me a folded note. "Mr. Monroe's having our Sunday School class over to his house next Saturday night for a weenie roast. Says we're going hikin'."

"OK," I said, cramming the note in my pocket. "Playin' Ambush after church?"

"Yeah. See ya then!"

Taking his seat on the wooden pew between Suzie and me, Dad studied the morning bulletin in the first moments of peace we'd had all day. Settling in, I quickly realized something was terribly wrong. Although we managed to claim our precious pew, the Nelsons, who sat in front of us every Sunday, weren't so lucky. Two complete strangers had blatantly stolen Mr. and Mrs. Nelson's seats! Surely these misguided folks were visitors. Everyone at First Baptist knew the Nelsons sat in the sixth pew from the back every Sunday. Claiming someone else's rightful pew was worse than chugging a shot of nasty whiskey, sending offending Baptists straight to hell. I spotted the Nelsons in the center pew section, glaring at the heathens as if Lucifer himself had plopped down on their pew.

A surge of people streamed into the front of the sanctuary through a large oak door. Among the throng, wearing his standard red bowtie, white shirt, and black suit, Mr. Elliot Monroe shook hands with others as he made his way to his seat. Watching him weave through the crowd, I thought how quiet and soft-spoken he was. Almost shy, never the center of attention, it was hard to believe he'd been a Marine during the war.

Short and stocky with dark black hair, Mr. Monroe looked nothing like those brazen tough soldiers I saw on TV. A local farmer, he was always helping out at church. Most Saturdays you'd see him mowing the yard and raking leaves, getting things presentable for Sunday service.

Billy Ray, Skeeter, and I had just moved up to his Sunday School class a few weeks earlier and the jury was still out on whether this would be another boring year. My previous teachers seemed to be cursed with the same terminal case of The Dulls, possessing the uncanny ability to turn a simple Bible story into a laborious funeral wake. All they ever did was recite in tedious detail the same stories that I'd heard a thousand times. I knew Adam and Eve got kicked out of the Garden of Eden for eating apples, which was a little strong if you ask me. Of course, David killed Goliath with a slingshot, Noah built an ark and Moses parted the Red Sea. Boring.

I hoped Mr. Monroe would be different. I had to hand it to him though. None of those other stuffy old codgers we had for teachers had ever invited us hellions anywhere. The thought of a weenie roast and a hike sounded like fun.

Suddenly the mood in the sanctuary took a horrible turn. Like the opening soundtrack to a B-grade horror movie, gloomy organ music blanketed the room in a woeful shroud. Cheerful morning greetings abruptly ended. Time to get serious. The congregation rose while the choir, adorned in black robes, filed solemnly through the side door of the choir loft.

Mom hobbled to her seat on the front row. Our eyes met. The corners of her mouth turned up in a tiny smile, but quickly faded. Open displays of emotion bordered on fun, which was absolutely frowned upon.

Wearing his standard black suit, white shirt, and thin black necktie, Pastor Larkin glared at the congregation as he entered the sanctuary. Incapable of smiling, his gaunt face and thinning gray hair gave him a sinister look like an evil undertaker. Our ancient organist, Mrs. Boone, held the last dismal note of the intro for a full agonizing minute.

Taking hymnals from the racks in front of them, the congregation sang the opening hymn with all the reverent countenance as if they were cleaning toilets. After enduring another sad song, the ushers passed the plate. When the notes died from the last refrain, the crowded room buzzed in a noisy shuffle as everyone took their seats. Slouching down on the wooden bench, I prepared myself for an hour of sheer torture. Thank God we were Baptist and worship service would end precisely at twelve o'clock, no matter who got saved.

Pastor Larkin ambled over to the large oak pulpit, opened his Bible, and began to read. With the formalities out of the way, things became dreadfully dull. As the numbing sermon wore on, the standard cast of restless actors assembled for the traditional Sunday morning battle between squirmy children and frustrated parents. As usual, the fidgety show began slowly at first, then like a swelling tidal surge, a sea of little heads bobbed up and down all over the sanctuary.

Although I'd witnessed this Sunday performance countless times, there was always something new, providing raucous entertainment for the distracted. On cue, Mrs. Sanderson's newborn, whom she refused to take to the nursery, opened the show. Little Sarah, the newest and youngest member in the troupe, quickly grabbed the audience's attention with a slow unnerving moan. Folks cut their eyes at each other in a standard "here we go again" look they exchanged every Sunday.

Destined for sanctuary stardom, little Sarah never rushed her delivery, allowing the suspense to build. With the passion and stage presence of a baby twice her age, Sarah played it perfectly. Catching the audience totally off guard, the infant suddenly burst into a bloodcurdling cry. The chilling scream surprised Pastor Larkin, who lost his train of thought. Unable to control her shrieking child, Mrs. Sanderson took little Sarah in her arms and hurried up the aisle and out the door, taking with her any hope for a quiet and peaceful worship service.

The congregation had barely recovered from Sarah's stunning rendition of an air raid siren when the evil duo of Earl and Burl Gardner took the stage. Struck with an incurable case of the terrible twos, the Gardner twins were so bad the nursery refused to keep them. Mr. Gardner was so embarrassed by their behavior that he never accompanied his family to church.

The pathetic victim in this horrible tragedy remained the lovable Mrs. Katherine Gardner, a crowd favorite. Sunday after heartbreaking Sunday, the audience rooted in silent anguish, praying God would give Mrs. Gardner strength as the twins unleashed themselves on their hapless mother. That somehow this would be the Sunday that good would finally triumph over evil. Before her two devilish trolls came along, Mrs. Gardner had been another happy and smiling member of the congregation, thankful for each Sunday morning. With her fuse worn to a short frazzle, her expression now took on an air of painful sorrow.

Her weary eyes darted nervously at Pastor Larkin then back to the twins. Sitting between the two, she kept her arms spread over both boys' shoulders in anticipation of a sudden outburst. Jumping quickly into action, the twins crawled into their mother's lap, performing a twisting tag team squirm. All eyes turned as our ill-fated heroine discretely attempted to restore order.

Suddenly Earl grabbed his mother's black beehive, twisting the small shrub into total disarray, destroying hours of teasing in a split second. Out of sheer desperation, Mrs. Gardner reached up and popped Earl's hand!

A gasp ripped through the sanctuary. Earl slumped back in disbelief. With her beehive in shambles, she snatched the two monsters off the pew and stormed up the aisle to a sanctuary of smiles. She'd done it! The unexpected plot twist took the audience by surprise, enduring her in their hearts forever. For a moment I thought Mrs. Gardner would get a standing O!

Just when I didn't think the show could get any better, I glanced across the aisle at four-year-old Willie Howell who sat calmly beside his mother. His deceptive sweet innocence, a standard part of his fiendish act, didn't fool anyone. Behind the brown freckles and sandy flattop churned the soul of a devil. Willie had topped the bill at Sunday morning worship service since he was old enough to walk. Destined for solitary confinement somewhere in a maximum security cell block, his performances were legendary. Observing his standard warmup fidget, I knew the show's raucous finale was about to begin.

Without warning, Willie slumped down in his pew, sliding onto the carpeted floor. Never taking her eyes off Pastor Larkin, Mrs. Howell nudged little Willie with the tip of her high heel. Like a fish toying with a lure, Willie poked at the dangling shoe. Flashing a sinister grin, he slipped the red high heel off his mother's foot. Crawling under the pew, Willie waited for just the right moment. When his mother's silk-wrapped toes came to rest, Willie reached down and bit the fire out of his mother's ankle!

Unable to mask the pain, Mrs. Howell lunged forward. Dropping her hand below the pew she searched for the giggling brat who rolled and squirmed just out of her reach. Hitting pay dirt, Mrs. Howell gripped her son's arm as only superhuman moms can do, yanking the little snot up onto the pew.

With his mother's high heel still clutched in his hand, Willie closed his performance with his signature yell, hitting full tantrum mode. The sound of his loafers pounding the pew reverberated through the sanctuary. Humiliated, Mrs. Howell hauled the whiny imp up the aisle towards the door as if she were pulling a lawnmower. It was without a doubt one of the troupe's greatest performances of the year. Worthy of every single tithe!

At precisely 11:55 throats began to clear as folks impatiently glanced at their watches. When the service mercifully ended, weary parents and children staggered to their feet for the closing hymn. Nothing like hand-to-hand combat with a restless child, accompanied by a boring sermon to suck the life right out of you.

The upcoming Sunday School picnic quickly faded from memory like most important things have a tendency to do, until Skeeter mentioned it during Saturday morning war games. Later that afternoon, Dad drove me out to the Monroe farm north of town. Turning off the main highway onto a gravel road, the DeSoto bounced over ruts and potholes leaving a dusty contrail. Dad pulled over and I exited the car near a row of tattered mailboxes.

Holding my light jacket over one shoulder, I hurried down a long gravel driveway flanked on each side by a rambling barbed wire fence. A quick shower of golden leaves fell from colorful hardwoods as I joined the others standing with Mr. Monroe near a metal gate.

"OK. We're goin' on a tour of the place, so watch ya step boys."

Poor Carl Wayne didn't fully understand the directive. Moping along, his P.F. Flyers suddenly disappeared in the brown slush of a fresh cow pie. From Carl Wayne's horrible scream, you'd have thought his foot had just been amputated. Spinning with laughter, we watched Carl Wayne stagger to a patch of tall grass where he spent the next half hour wiping his nasty shoe.

Hiking through an open pasture, we entered the double doors of a spacious red barn reeking of hay and manure. Chewing on a piece of grass, Mr. Monroe asked for volunteers to throw down a few bales of hay from the hayloft. All nine of us scurried up a makeshift wooden ladder on the barn wall.

Circling back to the main house, we stood on the bottom rung of an old wooden fence while Mr. Monroe pointed to a large field where he would plant tobacco next spring. Somewhere in the mixture of strange odors accompanying our tour I caught the unmistakable aroma of hotdog chili. I turned to see Mrs. Monroe step off the back porch carrying a large bowl of potato salad.

"Y'all gettin' hungry?" she asked.

"Yes ma'am," came the excited reply.

"Well come on!" Racing to the backyard, we jockeyed for position around a blazing campfire. After prayer, Mr. Monroe nodded towards a large folding table loaded with goodies.

"OK… looks like we got everything set. Let's eat!" Skewering hotdog weenies with coat hangers, we playfully parried each other as we roasted them over the twitching fire. Gorging ourselves on dogs, baked beans, and potato salad, we washed it all down with bottles of cold Pepsi. Just when I thought I couldn't eat any more, Mrs. Monroe presented us with a fresh tray of Rice Krispie treats.

Munching on our dessert we listened while Mr. Monroe hit a few standard Bible stories. Maybe it was the calm of the crackling fire or the darkening shadows from the setting sun. Whatever the reasons Mr. Monroe's version of those tiresome tales seemed different than they did at church, holding my attention for a change.

A cool draft rushed in when the sun disappeared. The shifting flames of the fire felt good. Whispers floated around about the hike we were supposed to take. Maybe Mr. Monroe would share stories about his time in the war. Sometimes we'd quiz him during Sunday School, but he always changed the subject. Watching the firelight shadows dance across his face, I wondered how in the world this kind and gentle man could have ever fought in the war. He didn't look like a Marine. He looked... well... like a Sunday School teacher.

"Listen," Mr. Monroe said suddenly, holding his arm high in the air. Everyone got quiet.

"Y'all hear that? That deep howlin'?" Standing up, he squinted into the dark woods. "It's him. I know it's him!" Hurriedly, he retrieved a brown leather pouch from underneath the folding table. Reaching inside, he produced a silver .45 caliber pistol. Spellbound, we watched Mr. Monroe wrap a leather holster around his waist.

"OK men, listen up." he continued, securing the buckle as he talked. "The reason ya'll are here tonight is 'cause you been chosen for a special mission. A very dangerous mission." Spellbound, we sat wide-eyed as Mr. Monroe spoke. "Over the past two weeks, I've lost almost a dozen chickens to a mountain lion. Big, yellow lookin' thing with a black streak runnin' down his back. Big green eyes. Comes in, grabs a few chickens, then disappears back in the woods. I've tried everything.

Traps, poison, even tried huntin' him down myself." Taking a knee, Mr. Monroe lowered his voice. We huddled closer. "Last week, he ambushed me… almost took my arm off!" Stunned faces stared back in disbelief. "It's too dangerous for me to go it alone. I need a squad of fearless men to go with me."

Hey! I'll be happy to go back to town and find some! I almost blurted out.

"Listen," he whispered. "There he goes again! He's on the prowl," he said, tightening the buckle of his holster. "Tonight's the night. We're goin' to track down the enemy and destroy 'im. Stay close, listen to me, and you'll make it back alive."

Excuse me, but what did he just say?

"You survive by stayin' alert and followin' orders. I'll take point and I don't want any talkin' in the ranks. Is that understood?"

"Yes sir," we mumbled in frightened unison.

Stark terror appeared on the faces of my friends, whose mouths hung open like a nest of hungry birds. Traipsing through Ashley Woods in the spirited throes of Ambush with our trusty plastic guns was one thing, but it was clear that Mr. Monroe wasn't playing!

"When I say, 'hit the dirt,' dive to the ground and don't look up till I tell ya the coast is clear. Stay behind me, single file. Keep ya eyes and ears peeled. Any questions?"

Questions? Hell yeah, I got questions! A few minutes ago, I was feeding horses and jumpin' around in a hayloft, having the time of my life. Now I stand a good chance of being eaten alive!

Anxiously, our troupe of cowardly lions fell into single file behind Mr. Monroe as he navigated a narrow dirt path leading into the murky woods. The crunch of dried leaves matched every timid step. The side-to-side motion of his flashlight cast eerie shadows on trees and bushes.

With a halfhearted moan, Carl Wayne looked over his shoulder at me with the eyes of a fearful toddler.

"J.D.? Reckon… there's… snakes out here?"

"I… I don't know," I replied, taking a sudden interest in the dim underbrush.

Grabbing tree limbs and tangled bushes, we moved deeper into the dark forest that seemed to swallow us whole. Suddenly Mr. Monroe raised his hand and took a knee. Without warning he turned off the flashlight! Quivering in the darkness, I listened as crickets sang harmony with my thumping chest. The flashlight's sudden return sent a second wave of panic through the ranks. Kneeling in front of me with fingers in his ears, Carl Wayne trembled like a wet dog.

"False alarm," Mr. Monroe whispered. Popping the strap on the holster, he eased out the silver .45. Pulling back the metal glide and chambering a round, Mr. Monroe continued the march. The annoying sound of nervous voices behind me grew louder with every step. Anxious and on edge, I lost it.

"Shut up, ya idiots! You're gonna get us all killed!" Pausing at a meandering creek we squinted at the flashlight's reflection in the trickling water.

"Look!" Mr. Monroe pointed. "There's his footprints. I'd recognize 'em anywhere!" Gouged shapes appeared in the shallows of a miniature beach. Deep paw tracks of something. Something big! "See that hick'ry over there?" he said, shining light on the slanted tree. "That's where it happened. He jumped me right there. Almost took my arm off."

Steadying ourselves on low hanging branches, we crossed the shallow creek, stumbling into a small clearing at the base of a hill.

"*Hit the dirt!*"

Falling over each other, we dove for the ground. The panicked flashlight seemed to shine in fifty directions at once! Suddenly the forest exploded!

BAM! BAM! BAM! The deafening shots from the .45 echoed through the woods, pulsating in my chest!

"Follow me!"

Locked in adrenaline overdrive, we jumped to our feet. Screaming at the top of our lungs, we charged up the hill behind our intrepid leader. The sharp stench of gunpowder filled the cool air. My ears rang like a telephone.

"I'm hit! I'm hit!" came a tearful voice.

"Carl Wayne?" Mr. Monroe yelled.

Following the sobbing whimpers with his flashlight, Mr. Monroe found Carl Wayne's frightened face squinting into the light's glare. Lying in a clump of bushes, Carl Wayne held his right side. Retreating down the incline, Mr. Monroe bent down and pushed the brush aside.

"You're OK, son," he said, checking the wound. "You just fell in a bunch of old briars, that's all." Smiling sheepishly, Carl Wayne pulled himself out from the maze of thorns.

"I think I got 'im. Spread out. Look for blood!" Peering into the shadows we combed the hillside, searching for mountain lion blood.

"Over here! I found some!" Richie yelled. Sprinting through the trees, Billy Ray let go of a bent branch that whipped back, slashing across Skeeter's face.

"Dadgummit, Billy Ray!"

"You OK, son?" Mr. Monroe asked.

"Busted lip," he answered, wiping his bloody mouth on his sleeve. "I'll make it." Excitedly, we huddled around Richie, who pointed at a red blotch floating in a sea of dried leaves.

"There! Right there! Look!"

"That ain't blood, ya dummy, that's an empty cigarette pack," Billy Ray yelled. Raising his hand, Mr. Monroe dropped to one knee.

"On me," he ordered, holstering his pistol. Scared out of our minds, we bunched together. "Boys, I guess I missed 'im. He was right there. I was sure I had 'im." Shining the light on his wristwatch, he looked up. "Gettin' late. We'd better head back. We'll get 'im next time."

What? Are you kidding? We can't go back in the middle of the greatest adventure of my entire life!

"Can't we look awhile longer Mr. Monroe?" I managed, prompting a few begging "Pleases."

"Men, we got casualties in Skeeter and Carl Wayne. Purdy soon your parents will be by to pick ya'll up." One last time he shined the flashlight in all directions. I prayed with all my might he'd change his mind. "He knows we're after 'im. I'll bet the farm he'll circle around and strike back."

Strike back? Well… in that case, maybe we should call it a night. Dad's probably sitting in the driveway waiting to take me home right now!

"Mountain lions like to surprise their prey," he warned, rising to his feet. "Keep ya eyes peeled. He'll try and flank us. They always go for ya ankles when ya ain't lookin'. This fight ain't over boys!"

Terrified that somewhere in the darkness lurked a steely-eyed monster with a hankering for nine-year-old boys, our fearful band began the trip back to camp. Making a point to stay close to Mr. Monroe, I prayed that he brought more than one clip. Sounds I'd never heard before echoed through the woods. A sudden breeze sent chills rippling through my sweat-logged flannel shirt. My mouth became a thirsty desert. The sluggish trek back to camp seemed to take forever. Looking for anything familiar, I wondered if somehow we'd gotten lost.

The faint light of a campfire flickering through the trees quickened our pace. The frightening ride was almost over and by the grace of God we were still alive. Overcome with relief, the troop sprinted past Mr. Monroe the last few steps.

Mrs. Monroe greeted us with milk and cookies.

"Y'all git him?" she asked.

"Naw," Mr. Monroe said, shaking his head. "But Lois I gotta tell ya, I had the best squad with me tonight." Smiling at each other, we exchanged tough guy glances like a group of hardened veterans who'd seen it all.

"I can't go in those woods alone. It's too dangerous. I won't go on another mission unless I have these brave men with me." The hairs on my arms stood at attention. At that moment, I wanted to be just like Mr. Monroe when I grew up. A tough Marine, leading men into battle.

Unable to shut up, I shared every thrilling detail with Dad on the ride home. That amazing night at Mr. Monroe's farm changed everything. Baptized in the churning waters of fearful imaginations, we became part of something bigger than ourselves. Those who'd never experienced the rush of battle wouldn't understand. For the first time in my life, I'd walked to the edge of a jagged cliff and dared to look down. I wanted to feel it again. The thrill of the hunt. The sound and smell of gunfire.

Action-charged dreams filled my sleep. Sunday School quickly became a new and exciting place filled with wonder and adventure. In his own quiet style, Mr. Monroe transformed those tired old Bible stories into thrilling life or death missions. Never again did I require the slightest parental warning on Sunday mornings. First to be dressed and ready for church, I assisted Mom in every way I could to get us out the door on time. Taking the stairsteps two at a time, I raced to Sunday School class just to get a seat next to Mr. Monroe.

Anxiously, I waited for the call. To experience again the excitement of another daring mission that Mr. Monroe promised would happen. Unfortunately, that day never came. It took a while for me to figure it out, but I came to the sad realization that there had never been a mountain lion prowling through the forest that night. That the only thing lurking in the dark corners of those spooky woods were the wild impressions fashioned by supercharged imaginations. True to his vocation, Mr. Monroe had carefully and lovingly planted the thrilling seeds of fantasy in the minds and hearts of nine little boys on a dark November night long ago. Something that has lived inside me all my life, forever enticing me to dream.

"You know if Mr. Monroe did that today, he'd be under the jail," Suzie quipped.

"No doubt about that! A shame really," I sighed, realizing the innocent world I knew as a young boy no longer existed. "I didn't understand it then, but maybe the lesson Mr. Monroe was trying to teach us that night was that one's fear is often worse than what is really out there." Surprised by my comment, Dad's eyes met mine. Listening intently, he hung on every word. "That you might start out searching for one thing and end up finding something completely different, or in our case, finding nothing at all. That the pursuit, as unpredictable as it might be, is just as important as the prize. It's something I've never forgotten. I thought about it again a few years ago when I found out Mr. Monroe had passed away."

A devilish grin quickly stretched across Dad's face.

"Well, damnmagummit!" he shouted.

Our laugher resounded through the empty house. All eyes fell on Mom as her worn face stretched into a naughty smile.

Miss America, Rasslin' and Annette Funicello

Each story, lovingly dramatized, segued into another. Listening to our heartfelt exaggerations, Mom wanted to contribute but couldn't. The stories sounded familiar to her, but important pages were missing. Her eyes searched the room for a spark. There was something about this house. She'd lived here. Raised her children within these walls.

Circle Drive had been their first home. The starting line. Where Will and Dottie Harrison began life together. The place where their three children had taken their first steps along with a million other "firsts," laying the foundation of who we became as a family. Exciting birthdays and hectic Christmases along with the mundane she'd once vividly recalled, now rang hollow like our voices in the empty room. A life lived and forgotten, like a pleasant dream glowing brightly in the night, suddenly lost at morning's first light.

Helplessly, I studied her puzzled face, wishing she could have known a tiny portion of the thrill I experienced the moment I stepped through the front door. Like an old soldier returning to a long-ago battlefield, my childhood burst into consciousness. Suddenly thirsty, I wondered if somehow I were shadowing her. Just a curve or two behind, following the same labored path. That one day, these precious memories, stirred from their slumber, would disappear for me as well.

Staring past the room's filth, I imagined our gray upholstered couch, marred with splotches of a thousand spills. A matching loveseat against the interior pine paneled wall, flanked by a triangular end table. At the other end of the loveseat sat a metal magazine rack shaped like a music staff, crammed with issues of *Life, Vogue,* and *Cosmopolitan*. On the wall hung three gold-framed baby portraits of Suzie, Eddie, and me. I imagined Dad's weathered hunting boots sitting just inside the back door.

Both of them stared through the picture window as if looking at a movie screen. Mom's age-splotched hands rested on the shelf in front of her. In an instant, I could see her again, just a few feet away. Laid back on the couch, her bare feet crossed at her ankles. A bowl of popcorn resting in her lap. To her left, Dad's socked toes propped on the extended footrest of his recliner, while Suzie and I sprawled atop an oval rug. All eyes glued to the TV screen.

A curled black cable protruding from the scarred baseboard caught my eye. A sudden reminder of the here and now. There was no cable TV in those days. No flat screens, satellite dishes, high definition, or remotes. Not even color TV in our house.

"Remember our TV sat right there?" I pointed. One small prompt was all it took, sending stories flowing once more.

BESIDES SERVING AS A loving home, our house on Circle Drive functioned as battle headquarters for a rambunctious nine-year-old. Household furnishings of any value stood a good chance of being destroyed. Purchased at an after Christmas sale, the twenty-eight-inch RCA console replaced our old TV whose fragile picture tube caught a baseball that slipped out of my hand.

The new set's angled legs jutting from the bottom of the glossy silver cabinet gave the TV the futurist appearance of a flying saucer. Tangled wires snaked from the back of the set through the wall, reaching a rooftop rotary antenna. Speaking its own language through grainy black and white pictures, the omnipotent screen gazed out over the den like a king surveying his subjects. Furniture was arranged just so, giving optimum viewing pleasure.

Television's tantalizing spell quickly captured my heart and mind, revealing a neat and tidy world. Wrapped in sheltered innocence, where good always won out in the end, TV revealed the way life was supposed to be if we would just pay attention. In the vastness of its luminous screen, the answers to life's toughest questions lay waiting for me to discover. Where the worst of problems, no matter how complex, were neatly solved in thirty minutes and everyone lived happily ever after.

An orderly disciplined world where TV Dads hurried off to TV work, leaving behind joyful TV Moms, giddy at the prospect of spending another glorious day dusting and vacuuming. With jubilant smiles plastered on perfectly made-up faces, Moms attired in fitted dresses and shiny high heels gleefully cleaned TV homes without a care in the world.

It saddened me to think that our house on Circle Drive never quite matched the high bar set by prim and proper TV Moms. With her dark hair wrapped in large curlers the size of empty toilet paper tubes, Mom slogged through housework, usually barefooted, wearing a plain pair of slacks and mismatched top. No makeup, no smile.

I imagined myself sitting cross-legged on the den rug, fixated on the screen. Fighting alongside my hero Sergeant Saunders in the fields of France or following Rowdy Yates on horseback, driving cattle across the grassy prairies of Texas. Riding through crime-ridden Chicago with Eliot Ness or facing down dangerous gunfighters alongside Matt Dillon in the dusty streets of Dodge City.

By watching TV's magic screen I discovered The Beatles and marveled at Neil Armstrong's giant leap. Then there were the images TV shoved in my face that I wished I'd never seen but couldn't dare look away. A black limousine convertible surrounded by tall buildings crawling slowly through the crowded streets of Dallas on a sunny November day. A flag-draped coffin pulled by a horse-drawn carriage. Angry police dogs and water hoses chasing people from chaotic streets. Riots and burning cities. Soldiers jumping from open helicopter doors into swirling grassy fields that bent under the tornado of thumping blades.

Daytime television belonged to my mother. With amazing efficiency, Mom could mend clothes, snap beans, peel potatoes, and iron endless dress shirts while never missing a minute of her soap operas. I learned early on that nothing short of nuclear holocaust would drag her away from the pitiful characters who'd stolen her heart. It didn't matter what horrible disaster had befallen these poor souls; Mom got down in the mud and wallowed right there with them.

Whatever dire situation arose in our lives, Suzie and I knew better than to interrupt her during a tense episode, waiting instead until the safety of a commercial.

Leaning on the bookshelf, Mom grinned as I recalled the time I came inside after playing one afternoon to find her sitting on the edge of the couch crying like a baby, a box of tissues in her lap.

"Momma! What's wrong?"

"Oh nothin'," she said, blushing at my discovery. Turning towards the TV, I watched the camera move in for a close up of a forlorn Lisa from *As the World Turns,* which explained everything. Taking every pathetic step alongside these blundering characters, Mom constantly yelled at the TV, warning the hapless buffoons of some stupid mistake they were about to make.

Although her addiction to her afternoon stories became legendary, Mom's passion for TV spread up and down the dial covering a variety of genres. Standing at the top of her favorites list were the live telecasts of the *Miss North Carolina Pageant;* and of course, the embodiment of womanhood, *The Miss America Pageant.* On those sleepy Saturday nights, Mom and her sisters Grace and Shelby, the Andrews Sisters as Dad called them, commandeered our TV, critiquing each contestant down to the last detail.

When *The Miss America Pageant* aired the earth stood still. North Carolina's lovely contestant represented the sanctity and purity of every woman from the Tar Heel state, and the Andrews Sisters were determined to pull her through to victory. Still, no matter how hard they pleaded, prayed, and shouted at the TV, Miss North Carolina rarely made the Top Ten finalists. Their hopes and dreams were painfully dashed every year. Then came that amazing Saturday night in September 1962.

Hours before the show, Dad grilled hamburgers on the patio while Mom, Grace, and Shelby plotted their strategy for the pageant. After supper, Dad disappeared, barricading himself in his room for the rest of the evening, leaving me to endure the emotional rollercoaster with the obsessed Andrews Sisters. Moments before the show, the three of them huddled in the den for a moment of prayer and guidance. Holding hands and bowing their heads, they asked for God's divine blessing on Asheville's Maria Fletcher, North Carolina's worthy contestant.

As usual, the pageant dragged on mercilessly until the long awaited moment when host Bert Parks stood on the stage holding a white envelope containing the names of the Top Ten finalists. Barely able to watch, the Andrews Sisters anxiously rocked back and forth on the couch.

Wearing a cheesy white tuxedo with a black bow tie, Bert flashed his signature corny smile as he opened the envelope. A tense drum roll added to the torturous agony. As if they were facing a firing squad, the pageant's nervous contestants crowded together on the stage.

"Our first Top Ten finalist is… Miss Texas!"

"Crap," Shelby mumbled.

"Our next finalist is… Miss Alabama!"

And so, it went. With each name, hope faded like it did every year. Then, a miracle happened.

"Our next Top Ten finalist is… *Miss North Carolina!*"

Mom threw a plastic bucket of popcorn into the air, raining down buttered confetti on their celebration. After years of agonizing disappointment, a glimmer of hope emerged! A light at the end of a long and frustrating tunnel. Maria Fletcher was one step away from becoming Miss America and it was up to the Andrews Sisters to pull her successfully across the finish line.

Regaining their composure, the three of them settled in. Time to get serious. From evening gown, talent, and swimsuit competition, the stalwart sisters sweated through each exhausting segment. Shouting encouragement and advice, they fretfully walked the narrow tightrope alongside young Maria.

Fighting drooping eyelids, I began to fade. Spellbound by the unfolding events, the Andrews Sisters never acknowledged my sleepy "night y'all" as I shuffled down the hall. Lying in bed I listened to the barks of nervous voices, eventually drifting off to sleep.

Somewhere in the dense fog of slumber, panicked screams shook me awake. Jumping out of bed, I scampered down the hall. Standing in the doorway, I gazed at our disheveled den that appeared as if it had just hosted a hobo festival. Overturned glasses, popcorn, tissues, and candy wrappers littered the floor. Hopping up and down in a group embrace, the Andrews Sisters reveled in the moment.

"There she is… Miss America!" Bert crooned while Miss North Carolina, now the newly crowned Miss America, smiled tearfully as she strolled down the runway to rapid fire flashbulbs. They'd done it! The Andrews Sisters' pleading prayers magically traveled through the airwaves, all the way to Atlantic City. And Maria Fletcher heard them.

MOM GRINNED AND SHOOK her head at my lively description of that incredible night long ago. Despite her quiet admission, I wasn't sure if she truly remembered that night or not.

Still in its infancy, this strange space age technology wielded its seductive power over helpless viewers, luring them into believing almost anything. Television was like that. Even Grandma Harrison fell under its intoxicating spell.

HAVING GROWN UP LISTENING to radio programs, my grandparents' imaginations were ignited by the spoken word. Television was a totally new concept that took a while for them to fully grasp. Dad purchased their first TV for Grandma's sixty-fifth birthday and their lives were never the same.

Accustomed to having folks come over for sit-down visits, Grandma regarded TV the same way. She figured that if she could see people on the screen, it stood to reason folks appearing on TV could see her as well, sitting comfortably in her padded rocking chair. Before the TV could be turned on, Grandma scurried around the house making sure the place was neat and presentable as if she were entertaining a room full of guests.

One night after one of Grandma's fabulous suppers, we were sitting in the den watching TV, when I accidentally interrupted our viewing pleasure with a rather thunderous belch. Sprinting to the TV, Grandma turned the volume down.

"J.D. Harrison, that was the nastiest thing I ever heard in my life!"

"I'm sorry Grandma. It slipped out."

"I can't believe you'd do such a thing! Listen here, when I turn the sound back up, you tell 'em how sorry ya are! Then go stand in that corner over there till I tell ya to come out!" Glaring at me, she turned the sound back on.

"I'm sorry for burpin' y'all," I mumbled. At that moment, Earl Scruggs feverishly picked a lively rendition of "Foggy Mountain Breakdown" on his banjo. My heartfelt apology never fazed him.

Although Grandma remained very particular about television etiquette, there was one show where I could hoot and holler all I wanted. Whenever *Championship Wrestling* came on TV the only person screaming louder than me was Grandma.

Grandpa assured me that "rasslin'" was fake. That the wrestlers knew before they ever stepped into the ring who was going to win. But you could never convince Grandma of that.

Strangely, she never believed for a minute that John Glenn had blasted into space aboard a rocket. "It was all made up," she said. "A movie filmed out in Hollywood." But ugly fat men jumping around a ring in wrestling tights was as real to her as rain.

One weekend Suzie and I were staying with my grandparents while Mom and Dad went to the beach for their anniversary. It just so happened that on Saturday night, Grandma's favorite tag team of Johnny Weaver and George Becker would battle their archrivals, Rip Hawk and Swede Hanson, for the wrestling championship of the universe. The upcoming match was all Grandma talked about. In a tizzy, she spent the entire afternoon darting around the house, making sure everything was presentable while Suzie and I swept the floors and dusted the furniture.

After an early supper, Grandma disappeared into her bedroom. I could hear the sound of rushing water filling the bathtub. After a bit, the bedroom door slowly opened. Like a celebrity parading to a ringside seat at Caesars Palace, Grandma made her stunning entrance. In shock, Grandpa laid his Bible down beside him in his recliner. Sporting a brand new blue dress and ankle hose, Grandma paraded through the den in the only pair of high heels she owned. Her hair neatly rolled in a tight bun. She even had on lipstick!

"Grandma! You look purdy!" Suzie grinned. Taking a seat in her rocker, she smiled at her curious audience.

"Land sakes Sally Harrison! What in the world's come over you? A new dress?"

"On sale at Katheryn's!" she snapped. "Bought it with my coffee can money!" Grandma squirreled away loose change in a blue coffee can she kept in the pantry for just such emergencies. The fact that she had never sat behind the steering wheel of a car her entire life meant she'd walked downtown to Katheryn's Dress Shop to purchase the dress. Nothing was going to spoil the night. Not even Grandpa's cutting eyes and sneaky grins.

Wringing her hands, Grandma took a deep breath as I turned the TV to Channel Five. After a Martha White Flour commercial, the familiar music blasted over the TV. Then came those magic words.

"*Live*! From the state capital! It's time for *Championship Wrestling*!"

Unfortunately, the main event we'd waited for all day didn't take place until the second half of the show. I thought Grandma was going to rock the legs off her rocker while we endured two preliminary matches. Munching chocolate chip cookies, I settled back on the couch, watching and waiting. By the time Johnny and George were announced, Grandma was a nervous wreck. Smoke from Grandpa's cigarette drifted lazily toward the pale yellow ceiling. Watching her every move, he shot me a wink and chuckled under his breath.

With all the fanfare and splendor of the Kentucky Derby, our heroes, Johnny and George, were announced to a wild ovation, while Rip and Swede were booed by the studio crowd. When the bell sounded, the evil duo wasted no time. Like a well-oiled machine, Rip and Swede kept our heroes off balance. Catching George off-guard with a cheap shot to the head, Swede slammed the dazed wrestler's face into one of the ring's corner posts. George's wobbly knees swayed as he staggered backward.

"Come on George! Tag Johnny! Go tag Johnny," Grandma screamed, sliding to the edge of her rocker.

Grandpa snorted, shaking in his chair.

"You hush up!" Grandma snapped, pointing a trembling finger.

No one gave an inch as the match's momentum swung back and forth. A suddenly revived George sprinted hard into the ropes that stretched towards the stunned audience like rubber bands. As if hurled from a slingshot, the ropes threw the burly wrestler straight for Swede. At the last second the blonde-haired devil ducked. Unable to stop his momentum, George's face plowed into the cocked forearm of Rip Hawk who stood just outside the ring.

"*No*! Heavens *no*!" Grandma's right hand covered her mouth.

George's reaction to the blow was certainly Oscar worthy. Staggering dramatically, the dazed wrestler collapsed in the center of the ring. Grinning from ear to ear, Swede took his time parading in circles around his woozy prey, mocking the angry crowd. Dropping to his knees, Swede wrapped his burly arms around George's neck, jamming the knuckles of his right hand into George's sweaty temple and twisting them like a corkscrew!

"*Oh no*! Not the Sleeper!" Grandma screamed.

The dreaded "Sleeper!" The deadly Kryptonite wrestling hold every wrestler feared. George was a goner for sure! Flapping his arms like a wounded duck, George struggled helplessly in Swede's powerful grip.

Sliding out of her rocker, Grandma's knees hit the floor.

"*Git up George! Please George! Git up!*"

"Hush up Sally! The neighbors'll think ya lost your mind," Grandpa snorted.

Grandma's body trembled as she clasped her hands under her chin and began to pray. Cocking her head, she peeked at the TV with one eye while her lips quivered in a silent plea.

Tears dribbled down Grandpa's wrinkled cheeks as he shook with laughter.

Seeing his partner slipping away, Johnny jumped into the ring to wild cheers from the crazed crowd. Dropping to the mat behind Swede, Johnny wrapped his burly arms around Swede's thick neck, applying a Sleeper of his own! Grandma's zealous screams blocked out the sound from the TV.

"Give it to 'im, Johnny! Kill 'im Johnny! Kill 'im!" All this from a woman who most times barely spoke above a whisper. Clutching a metal folding chair, Rip jumped into the ring. In a riotous frenzy, the crowd screamed warnings to Johnny as Rip snuck up behind the clueless wrestler. Raising the chair above his head, Rip stood poised to take Johnny's head off when suddenly Grandma yelled!

"Look out behind ya, Johnny!"

At the very second Grandma screamed her warning, Johnny jerked his head out of the way. Unable to stop, Rip brought the chair crashing down on his partner's head! Swede collapsed into a crumpled heap. Bedlam ensued as wrestlers from earlier matches piled into the ring for a bloodthirsty free-for-all finale.

"I done it! Yes siree! Sure, as the world, I done it! You seen old Johnny duck when I yelled at 'im!" Convinced her voice had traveled through the TV screen, transcending both time and space, Grandma had saved the day. It became a known fact that Grandma Harrison's

split-second thinking had saved the life of wrestler Johnny Weaver. Nothing like an evening of refined southern culture at Grandma's!

The unimaginable power television wielded on its first generation of viewers captured my emotions as well, and just like Grandma, I was helpless to stop it. By simply looking at a TV screen, I fell in love for the very first time.

EXHAUSTED FROM ANOTHER GLORIOUS day of battle, I stumbled through the screen door. Ignoring my entrance, Suzie sat spellbound on the oval rug watching *The Mickey Mouse Club*. Giving the TV a fleeting glance, I stopped dead in my tracks. There on the black and white screen, wearing a pair of Mouse Ears, was the most beautiful girl I'd ever seen! Flanked by a lively bunch of dancing kids, a lovely dark-haired Mouseketeer dressed in a cute sweater floated gracefully across the stage. Her dark eyes and dazzling smile grabbed me by the heart! At that moment I fell in love with Annette Funicello.

With my eyes glued to the TV, I fell to my knees. By the time a commercial appeared on the screen, my life had changed forever. From that day on, I never missed a single episode. Coming up with a variety of excuses to quit Ambush early, I rushed home, taking a seat beside Suzie, immersing myself in *The Mickey Mouse Club* and lovely Annette.

One Friday afternoon after another riveting show, I sat there dejected while the ending credits flashed across the screen. I wouldn't see Annette again until Monday afternoon. An entire weekend alone, without the love of my life. Suddenly I remembered Suzie received a pair of Mickey Mouse ears for her birthday. Sprinting down the hall,

I made a quick right turn into Suzie's bedroom. Rummaging through her toy-littered closet, I retrieved the pair of black mouse ears.

Locking my bedroom door, I put them on and began twirling around the room, imagining myself dancing on TV with Annette. If the guys ever got wind of this pathetic scene I wouldn't be able to show my face in Ashley Woods ever again. Cootie-infested, girls were strictly off limits. But Annette wasn't just another girl. She was a TV star!

Catching my gyrating reflection in the mirror, I pulled the mouse ears off my head and slumped down on my bed. Who was I kidding? Kids like me never got the chance to meet famous people like Annette. The ultimate "in" crowd, TV stars didn't have time to pal around with normal kids. I guess if I ever wanted to meet Annette, I'd have to become a TV star too.

And just like that, a door opened. Well, almost.

When school began back in the fall, Billy Ray, Skeeter, and Junior roped me into becoming a member of Cub Scout Troop 39. Every Wednesday after school, I'd don my blue Cub Scout uniform, including a stupid looking beanie. Tying a sissified yellow scarf around my neck, I'd join the other members of my scout troop for our weekly meeting in the basement of the Methodist church.

I'll admit being a scout was kinda fun at first but quickly became boring. All we did was recite a bunch of dumb pledges and craft trash cans out of old wooden pallets that weighed three tons. Our den mother and keeper of the flame, Rusty Bradley's mother, took her sacred role very seriously. She and she alone held the futures of eleven little boys in her controlling little hands. Standing squarely on the thin line between decency and debauchery, it was up to her to mold heathens like us into fine upstanding young men.

We'd just gathered in the church basement for what I thought would be another dull weekly meeting when Mrs. Bradley made the stunning announcement.

"Boys, I have a wonderful surprise for you. Next Wednesday afternoon our Cub Scout troop is goin' to be on *Uncle Jubal's Playhouse!*" Everyone went nuts! Jumping up and down and hollering with everyone else, I couldn't believe it. Every kid in town watched Uncle Jubal and his pal Rascal Joe live on Channel 2 every afternoon at five o'clock. Somewhere in the crazed celebration, the thought hit me like a sledgehammer.

Wait a minute! Being on Uncle Jubal's meant that I'd be on TV! Being on TV would... make me... a TV star! Just like Annette! Holy smokes! Could this really be happening? Suddenly dizzy, I sat down on the edge of a chair. While the guys slapped each other on the back and cheered, my mind raced ninety miles an hour.

This was it! My big break. I could see it now! First, *Uncle Jubal's Playhouse!* Next *Captain Kangaroo!* Then Hollywood! *The Mickey Mouse Club!* Movie contracts! Cigarette commercials! Annette and I would get married and raise a house full of little Mouseketeers!

Of course, our raucous display of emotion shook Mrs. Bradley to the core.

"OK! OK! Calm down! Here's a list of rules for our trip." For the next half hour, Mrs. Bradley outlined in boring detail our trip's agenda that covered two typed pages. Single spaced. Each scout was responsible for having their uniform pressed and starched before the trip. Examining the list, the troop yelled its approval that we planned to stop and eat an early supper at the new Burger King!

Wednesday couldn't get here fast enough. Lying in bed the night before the trip, I stared up at the trusty ceiling tiles, trying to comprehend it all. A mouthwatering trip to Burger King, then on to the studio for my television debut. Life would never be the same.

When the final school bell rang that fateful afternoon, our troop dashed to the restroom, quickly changing into our scout uniforms. Gathering in the hallway, we stood bored to tears, enduring another one of Mrs. Bradley's patented lectures, stressing the importance to be on our very best behavior. We represented not only Troop 39, but also South Maybin Elementary and every kid in town. It was our responsibility to demonstrate through the power of television what it was like to be a good Cub Scout.

As expected, Mrs. Bradley's passionate sermon fell on deaf ears. She'd barely finished when our rowdy troupe stormed out the double doors to the waiting motorcade idling in the traffic circle. Junior, Billy Ray, Skeeter, and I jumped in the backseat of Mrs. Bradley's Buick while the rest of the scouts piled into the cars behind us.

The soft playful voices of my friends filled the car as we rode along, inducing an unexpected pall of sadness. Once I moved to Hollywood, I'd be hanging around with other TV stars, like Opie, the Beaver, and of course, Annette. I'd never get a chance to see these guys again. At that moment, I made a solemn promise not to forget the "little people" who had meant so much to me growing up.

Although cautioned to be on our best behavior, our car full of lively boys couldn't resist a collective yell as our procession passed a brown and white "Welcome to Greensboro" sign. Another round of cheers went up when we turned into the crowded Burger King parking lot. Stepping out of the car was like walking into the best dream of my life! The warm siren song of flame-broiled burgers pulled me toward the door. Reaching in my pocket, I felt the crisp dollar bill Mom gave me that morning before I left for school, and I planned to spend every last dime.

Garbled voices and screeching chairs welcomed us inside. Ordering a Whopper, fries, and a drink, I crowded inside a booth with the guys. The four of us tore into the wrappers like hungry jackals on the savannah. Glancing around at the naïve minions pounding down fries like there was no tomorrow, I caught myself smiling. None of them had the faintest idea they were dining with America's next great child star!

Trying to stay on schedule, Mrs. Bradley glanced nervously again at her watch.

"OK everyone, line up at the door," she shouted over the mayhem. In noisy unison, our troop slid out from our trashed booths. The excitement of our first ever television debut was just too much, sending any semblance of manners out the window. Looking as if each of us had eaten a meal out of a trash can, our neatly pressed uniforms were unceremoniously pinned with messy scout badges of ketchup, burger sauce, and mustard. Shirtsleeves striped with food stains highlighted the messy ensemble. I thought Mrs. Bradley was going to have a stroke.

"What! Look at your shirts! You can't go on TV lookin' like that!" Herding us to the restroom, we washed our uniforms the best we could using wet paper towels. Looking as if we'd just returned from a harrowing scout jamboree, Mrs. Bradley ushered her unkempt crew out the door. Hopelessly behind schedule, we sprinted to the waiting cars. Leading the way, Mrs. Bradley sped through Greensboro. Blowing her horn and running two red lights, she careened into the TV station parking lot like Richard Petty crossing the finish line.

Exhausted, Mrs. Bradley and the other parents assembled the troops. I nearly fell over backwards staring up at the enormous TV tower. The narrowing pyramid of steel girders rose hundreds of feet in the afternoon sky. Small red lights blinked on the massive structure, reminding me of the Mercury launch pad at Cape Canaveral.

Approaching the station's ornate front door, the wild emotions churning inside me finally came to a head. In just a few minutes, my adoring face would be plastered across every television screen in America. A giant stepping stone to a life of fame and fortune alongside my true love, Annette. The enormity of the moment took over. Staring into the afternoon sky, I could see it all unfolding before my eyes.

White beams from powerful searchlights, crisscrossed, lighting the dark Hollywood sky. Our driver slowed the limo to a stop under a curtained awning. Lit up like a Christmas tree, Grauman's Chinese Theatre beckoned us. Thunderous screams blasted from a shoulder-to-shoulder crowd as the attendant opened the door.

Wearing my favorite black tux with light blue bowtie, I stepped onto the red carpet. Overcome by my steely handsomeness, fans fainted by the dozens. Reaching back inside the limo, I gently took her hand. Placing one high heel on the carpet then the other, Annette stepped gracefully from the car, flaunting her signature smile. Her white diamond sequined gown glistened in a storm of lightning bolt camera flashes. With her arm wrapped firmly in mine, we strolled through the bedlam, held in check by the locked arms of LA's finest. Uncontrolled tears flowed from adoring faces. Desperate outstretched hands groped wildly for a fleeting touch of my garment.

Following our handler's lead, we bent down, placing our knees on a small velvet bench. Scrambling to be the first, the paparazzi surrounded us, firing off pictures. Blowing a kiss, Annette squeezed my arm. Sharing a loving glance, we pushed our hands into the wet cement.

"J.D.! J.D.! Autograph! Please J.D.! An autograph!"

"J.D.! J.D.!"

"Huh?"

"J.D.! Git yourself in line right now young man or you'll be spendin' the rest of the day in the car!" Mrs. Bradley snapped. Shaken back to reality, I fell in line behind Skeeter. Mrs. Bradley had barely opened the door to the lobby when our excited troop sprinted past her, jockeying for a seat on a leather couch.

"Stop it! Stop it! Git up this instant!" Nearing the end of a very short rope, Mrs. Bradley announced our arrival to a young woman behind a sliding glass window. Photos of TV stars lined the walls of the dark paneled lobby. An oversized picture of Uncle Jubal and Rascal Joe hung above a humming water fountain. Beside a double door, Lee Gibbons, host of *Sunrise Carolina*, smiled for the camera. A golden framed portrait of Matt Dillon, Chester, Doc, and Miss Kitty from *Gunsmoke* decorated a space between two large windows. And of course, I couldn't miss the collection of pitiful characters from Mom's afternoon soap operas.

A huge photo of the entire cast from *The Andy Griffith Show* hung prominently on the back wall. Front and center in the color shot, Opie grinned at the camera. His sandy hair cutely mussed. A thin band of freckles climbed the bridge of his nose, riding from one cheek to the other. Smiling back at the picture, I knew that if I played my cards right, there just might be a golden framed picture of yours truly hanging on that wall next week.

A set of double doors clicked open and out stepped a pretty young lady with a blinding white smile. Her platinum blonde bouffant reminded me of a huge swirl of vanilla ice cream. A tight-fitting scarlet dress allowed only short baby steps in a pair of matching red high heels. Her cartoonish voice reminded me of Rocky the Flying Squirrel. With stilettos clicking like a typewriter, the young lady led us on a tour of the station. After visiting the Control Room, we approached another set of double doors marked "Studio B."

The doors opened into a gigantic studio. Heat from row after row of bright spotlights blazed from the elevated ceiling. A maze of black cables ran along the floor like a giant spiderweb, connecting four huge TV cameras. I recognized the familiar sagging front porch and rickety steps of Uncle Jubal's playhouse at the far end of the corridor. Two high back rocking chairs sat prominently under the awning.

The prissy blonde handed us off to a tall familiar looking man with a clipboard. When he spoke, I recognized the deep baritone voice of Benny Wright, The Atlantic Weatherman! Sporting a white dress shirt and black trousers, Benny was a lot shorter than I expected.

Thrilled to see a fellow TV personality, I figured the two of us could get in a little backstage chitchat before we went on the air. Getting a few pointers from a local legend couldn't hurt. But what could I say to break the ice? Then it came to me. I knew the perfect question! Reaching out, I tapped him on the arm. Having been in show business forever, Benny easily recognized the handsome countenance of an aspiring young actor. Shifting his clipboard, he bent down.

"Hey there young man. Excited about seeing Uncle Jubal?"

"Sure! Hey… Mr. Wright. Can I ask you a question?"

"Sure, you can!"

"How much money do you make?"

Benny's broad smile quickly morphed into an annoyed frown. Shaking his head, he turned and walked away without as much as a "break a leg" or nothing! OK Benny. I'll remember this little snub when I get to Tinsel Town!

Another man with a clipboard ushered our troop onto the top row of a large set of metal bleachers. Other excited kids hustled into the studio, filling in the seats below. I had to admit there was something magical about sitting under those steamy bright lights. Something I could get used to.

Two television monitors stared back at us from the base of the bleachers. Then I remembered. At the end of every Uncle Jubal show, a camera panned across each row, showing close-ups of every kid's face while they watched themselves on the TV. That's it! Of course! When the camera panned the top row, my cute little face would be broadcast live around the world. It was my big chance! My shining moment! But what could I do to get noticed?

A commotion from across the studio quieted the audience of snickering kids. There he was. Uncle Jubal himself! Attired in his customary brown outfit with fringe running the length of his sleeves and coonskin cap, he resembled a chubby Daniel Boone. Applause filled the cavernous room. Smiling back, Uncle Jubal held his musket high in the air. Behind him marched a barefooted Rascal Joe in his standard straw hat and overalls, chewing on a long piece of grass like he did every show. Shielding his eyes from the lights, Joe squinted into the glare.

"Hey y'all! Ready for some fun?"

"Yeah!" came the collective response.

Leaning his musket against the front porch, Uncle Jubal joined Benny and his clipboard for a quick meeting. No doubt Benny pointed out the handsome Cub Scout with the blonde crewcut and cute gap in his front teeth. Top row. Fourth kid down. Of the thousands of children who had been on the show, *he's* the one. A future superstar!

Taking their seats in the rocking chairs, Uncle Jubal raised his head high while someone shoved a small mirror in his face one last time. Standing off camera, Benny glanced back and forth from his wristwatch to another man wearing a headset. Suddenly Benny raised the clipboard over his head.

"Quiet on the set!" The familiar music that I'd heard a thousand times blared from somewhere off stage. Like an orchestra leader, Benny raised his hands.

"Hey there boys and girls! It's time for…" The bleachers erupted on Benny's cue, shouting the show's opening words.

"UNCLE… JUBAL'S… PLAYHOUSE! YEAH!"

Spellbound, I sat there, taking it all in. Jumping quickly into entertainment mode, Uncle Jubal recalled thrilling stories of his dangerous days in the wilderness. Cartoons followed a quick magic show from Coco the Hobo. When they broke for another commercial, I knew the end of the show was approaching. I'd have only a few seconds to reveal my talented face to the world.

Out of nowhere, a lightning bolt struck me. What if Annette was watching? A huge knot rose in my stomach. Oh my gosh! What if I boogered it all up? As another exciting episode of *Clutch Cargo* wound down, one of the large cameras turned and moved closer to the bleachers. Here we go! Time for the close-ups. *It's your one and only chance. Don't blow it!* I thought to myself.

Beginning with the first row, the camera began its measured pan. Nervously, I stared at the monitor as doofus kids grinned like a bunch of dumb hillbillies. Great! I'm surrounded by a room full of amateurs! Angling up the bleachers, the camera reached the back row as Junior's goofy mug lit up the screen. Ever the live wire, he dropped his head, taking a sudden interest in his shoes. Skeeter's mouth flew open when his face appeared and he managed a silly grin.

OK. Get ready. Billy Ray was next, then me! My chest pounded like a jackhammer. Everyone in the civilized world was watching this historic moment unfold on live TV. The day J.D. Harrison, star of stage and screen, was discovered. But what was I going to do to make an impression? Stand up and recite a scene from *Hamlet*? Incredibly the idea came to me out of the blue. It was the perfect hook. Why had I been so worried? I'll show Hollywood the true meaning of improvisation!

Billy Ray's freckled face suddenly appeared on the black and white monitor. The unflappable clown prince who lived for the spotlight turned white as a sheet. Scared out of his mind, he grinned at the camera like a drunken mule. OK! Time to separate myself from the pathetically stupid! "Here we go," I whispered.

Time stood still. In a moment of sheer comedic genius, I shoved my thumbs in both ears, wiggled my fingers, stuck out my tongue and wagged my head like a crazed dog! My adorable features crawled across the screen as the camera inched its way down the row.

Here I am Walt Disney! Your next Mouseketeer! Next time, I'll be sticking my thumbs inside a velvety pair of mouse ears. I could hardly breathe. My cutely freckled face was simply breathtaking. What an amazing move. Bold and daring. Wherever she was, Annette had to be smitten by the handsome kid with the wagging tongue!

It was over in a couple of seconds. A wild unexplainable rush washed over me. Not only did my troop burst into hysterics at my stunning performance, but so did the entire studio audience. Here I was. My television debut and I already had the crowd in stitches!

Like they did at the close of every show, Uncle Jubal and Rascal Joe stood on the front porch, waving at the camera.

"Join us again tomorrow boys and girls for another exciting afternoon of fun and adventure on…"

"UNCLE… JUBAL'S… PLAYHOUSE! YEAH!"

Starstruck kids turned and laughed, parting as I descended the bleachers. An unforgettable moment they could tell their grandchildren. The day they saw J.D. Harrison. In person! If only I had a pen, I could have signed a few autographs. They'd be worth millions one day.

Mrs. Bradley, however, was not the least bit amused. Everyone in the free world had witnessed my performance. It had happened on her watch. She was responsible somehow. If I turned out to be a loser one day, it would be her fault.

"J.D. Harrison! That was the nastiest thing I ever seen in my life! Lorda mercy! You outta be ashamed of yourself. Do you know that every child in Maybin saw what you just did?"

Well… Yes, I started to say. *That was the whole idea!*

"How embarrassin'! How could you show such disrespect for Uncle Jubal! How could you disrespect the Cub Scouts like that! I have half a mind to make you walk home," she screamed, her voice trembling with rage. "Listen to me, young man. You ain't never goin' nowhere with this troop again. Is that understood?" Groping for words, she finally lost it.

"Let me tell you somethin' else! You ain't a member of Troop 39 no more! You're out! Finished! Wait till I tell your momma and daddy! Now git yourself over there and stand in that corner while I git everyone together," she said, turning me around by the shoulders and shoving me toward the wall.

At that moment, I officially became the first juvenile delinquent in the history of Troop 39. My name would be forever purged from Cub Scout records. I never existed. As the familiar aroma of another dusty corner filled my senses, I laughed. No big deal. Why should I care about silly Troop 39 when I was standing on the doorstep of fame?

For my TV debut, I was generously compensated with an entire loaf of Sunbeam bread along with an unopened twelve ounce bottle of warm Coke. OK. It's a start. Next time though, I'm thinking of something more in the six-figure range.

On the way home I sat in the backseat, listening to the guys imitate my award-winning performance. As expected, Mrs. Bradley gave me the silent treatment. Steaming like a simmering tea kettle, she hit full boil by the time we reached my house.

Pulling into our driveway at ninety miles an hour, Mrs. Bradley hit the brakes, sending gravel flying. Slamming the car door behind her, she marched towards the house. With her head bowed in shame, Mom waited on the porch steps. Dad stood behind her, his hands on her shoulders. Foaming at the mouth, Mrs. Bradley gave a blow-by-blow description of my deplorable antics. Embarrassed, Mom said they'd seen it all on TV and that she would take care of it.

Continuing her rant, Mrs. Bradley ignored me as I slithered past. Mom's steely glare said in no uncertain terms that I was about to receive the beating of a lifetime. OK. So, Mom was upset. I bet she'll change her tune when Walt sends me that first fat paycheck.

When Mrs. Bradley left, Mom explained to me in a lengthy tirade that I had not only shamed past and present generations of the Harrison family, but I had disgraced future generations as well. The fact that I had been expelled from the Cub Scouts surely meant that I was destined for a life of sin and degradation. Years from now, my grandchildren wouldn't be able to walk the streets of Maybin or show their faces in public. How would she ever explain this humiliation to her friends? Dad stood there, knowing better than to interrupt one of Mom's meltdowns.

At school the next morning, admiring fans mobbed me the moment I hit the door. The whole school had witnessed my debut. When everyone found out I got kicked out of the Cub Scouts, I became the

James Dean of the fourth grade: a rebel without intelligence. Fussed over at every turn, kids insisted I go to the front of the lunch line and followed me around during recess.

And just like that, it was over. No phone calls from Walt and not so much as a postcard from Annette. My doting fan club quickly disappeared. The next thing I knew I was standing in the lunch line like everyone else. Kids, who just a few days earlier, smiled and called my name, stared past me like I wasn't there. The *Mickey Mouse Club* quickly lost its luster. Wounded and rejected, I couldn't handle gazing at Annette's beautiful face anymore and quit watching the show altogether.

"So your first love was Annette Funicello." Suzie chuckled.

"Of course! Along with every other little boy in America!"

"Now there's what, five hundred channels on my TV?" Dad chuckled. "And I don't watch but a handful of them. Momma, let's get some fresh air and check out the patio," Dad said, taking Mom's hand.

The Calling

Exiting through a metal door, we stepped into the warmth of the exposed terrace. A curved brick wall, much shorter than I remembered, wrapped the kidney-shaped patio in a daunting fortress where I had been among the many young soldiers who bravely defended its ramparts in long ago battles. The once smooth flagstone floor, ravaged by time and weather, was now a moonscape of broken slabs and mismatched mortar joints. Home to countless cookouts and neighborhood parties, the spacious expanse functioned as Mom's gardening headquarters where she planned the location of every flower, shrub, and tree while potting endless containers and hanging baskets.

"Where's my azaleas?" she frowned, peering over the wall. Gone were the colorful masses of Hershey Reds that flanked the patio in a dark red background every April. In their place laid a dirty blanket of aging mulch. Island chains of Pink Ruffles, Delaware Valley Whites, and bourgeoning perennials that once spread across our backyard in a sea of color were left to drown in mounds of weeds and patchy grass.

"Looks like somebody didn't appreciate gardenin' like you did," Dad sighed, retrieving his sunglasses from his shirt pocket.

"Why would somebody do such a thing?" she asked, her voice quivering.

"I don't know," Dad sighed. "Shame ain't it?"

Of all the plants and shrubs she'd painstakingly nurtured over the years, nothing matched her passion for azaleas. She lovingly planted, watered, and groomed each plant as if she were dressing a child for school. All of them gone.

"Mom? You remember the Azalea Festival, don't 'cha?" Suzie asked.

"Spring wasn't spring without the Azalea Festival." Dad chuckled.

"Oh, I remember." She smiled.

"What do you remember about it, Mom?" Suzie asked, moving closer. Mom paused, searching.

"We had to get there in time for the parade, didn't we? Didn't I make spaghetti?"

"We always had to have your spaghetti!" I grinned. Mom's head tilted as the memory pushed through.

"Ya got sick once, didn't ya J.D.?"

"I sure did," I said, shaking my head at the recollection.

WHY MY PARENTS INSISTED on crushing the tender spirits of their young children was something I never fully understood. Soon after mastering my first baby steps, I was immediately forced into obedient servitude where my attendance was required on boorish outings that had absolutely no value whatsoever. Another nameless face of the "seen and not heard generation," I reluctantly answered to my parents' every whim, regardless of the blatant stupidity of the directive. One of those torturous trips involved my accompanying the Andrews Sisters on their annual pilgrimage to Wilmington's Azalea Festival.

Like tiny hummingbirds braving their annual migration covering thousands of miles, an inborn instinct drew Mom and her sisters south to Wilmington's Arlie Gardens, center of the azalea universe. When the gloomy skies of winter gave way to warm sunshine, voices whispered to them in a language only they understood.

Immune to this specially coded song, I never caught the smallest of sounds. What possible significance could there be in the life of a nine-year-old boy to endure a women's only weekend spent gazing at stupid bushes? It was her calling, not mine! Suzie's presence on the excursion, a crucial element of the Master Plan, ensured her early indoctrination into the world of gardening, guaranteeing "the calling" would be passed on to future generations.

Why couldn't I just stay home with Dad? Everyone would be happy. Of course, Mom tried her best to schmooze me into believing I'd have a good time. What she really desired was a personal valet to lug her three hundred pounds of luggage she packed to stay one night.

Founding members of the Beautiful Blossoms Garden Club, the Andrews Sisters felt it was their solemn duty to attend the annual soiree. After returning each year from the sacred trip, the three of them presented a much-anticipated program to a standing room only crowd. Fussed over by the rest of the club, they rose through the ranks achieving the moniker of all-knowing garden queens. Experts on all things floral.

Constantly searching for sources of inspiration, Mom's entire human experience was dedicated to creating the best-looking yard in Maybin. Once following a trip to the Biltmore House, she spent more money on tulips that year than on groceries. When Mom's springtime flowering creations were at their peak, cars cruised slowly past our house, admiring her amazing handiwork.

Besides serving as the Andrews Sisters' personal pack mule, I figured the real reason I was forced to attend the stupid quest was some form of sinister payback for my oftentimes questionable behavior. Unlike Suzie, any hopes this gardening crap would rub off on me was a huge waste of time. Besides, it was widely known that I was downright destructive when it came to yard work.

Examples of my tornadic gardening prowess were legendary. Once when Mom was to receive her latest Yard of the Month Award from the Maybin Beautification Committee, I was conscripted to help her get the yard in tiptop shape. Cruising along on the riding lawnmower near a neatly arranged flower bed, I was suddenly attacked by an angry yellow jacket. Flailing my arms in attempts to ward off my attacker, the out-of-control lawnmower veered off course, transforming several rows of Mom's prized irises into fresh mulch.

Then there was the time Skeeter and I drew inspiration from a TV show about lumberjacks. Both of us watched in awe as two burly men with thick beards, wielding long shiny axes, stood on opposite sides of a huge tree. Rolled-up shirtsleeves revealed enormous arms bulging under plaid flannel shirts. Raising their shiny axes high, the men laid powerful strokes to the base of a massive oak.

Inspired by the amazing demonstration, Skeeter and I searched the backyard for something to chop down. Unable to find axes, we grabbed two croquet mallets from the garage. Like the two lumberjacks on TV, we stood on both sides of Mom's favorite peach tree and whacked away. Discovering the bark had been mercilessly stripped from her prized sapling, Mom cut a switch and viciously created a similar result on my legs.

The night before our trip, I tried my best to convince Mom to let me stay home to no avail. Resigned to my fate, I reluctantly packed my clothes in one of Dad's small suitcases and was ready in five minutes. Lugging the suitcase into Mom's bedroom, I found her standing in front of her open closet, deciding what to pack. It was the first time I'd taken a good look at my pregnant mother. Officially the size of an Oldsmobile, her floral-patterned dress resembled a festive funeral tent.

Given her somewhat tender condition, I thought for once in her life she might forego the senseless trip. Wishful thinking. It'd take a lot more than simple childbirth to keep Dottie Harrison from attending the Azalea Festival. Should labor pains ensue, Mom was the type who'd crawl up in a corner of Arlie Gardens, have her baby, hop up, and continue the tour.

"Momma, I'm packed."

"Oh good. Sit it over there."

Covered with every form of luggage known to woman, Mom's bedroom resembled a baggage warehouse. I thought for a moment she was contemplating leaving home. Prepared for any situation, Mom packed enough matching outfits to last a month. Searching for floor space, I set my suitcase beside a small cedar chest.

Like a kid at Christmas, Mom hardly slept that night. Pacing the floor, she combed the house, making sure she hadn't forgot anything. At 4:30 a.m. we were up and dressed. Sitting on the couch in a semi-conscious state, I'd almost drifted back to sleep when Grace and Shelby came bouncing through the door like a couple of perky airline stewardesses.

Rubbing the sleep from my eyes, I thought about my friends who were resting comfortably in their nice warm beds. In a few hours they would gather in Ashley Woods for a glorious day of Ambush while I endured a grueling four-hour car ride with a bunch of cackling hens!

As she did every trip, Mom prepared her traditional, pre-quest meal that could satisfy an entire Army division. Platters of scrambled eggs, waffles, country ham, grits, biscuits, and gravy covered the entire breakfast table. While the Andrews Sisters discussed the day's game plan, I ate like there was no tomorrow. After consuming my third help-ing, I was positive I could go the rest of the year without food. Seeing I was finished eating, Mom gave me a nod. Glumly, I headed out to the garage.

Risking a double hernia at age nine, I loaded the Andrews Sisters' entire worldly possessions into the back of our station wagon. Wip-ing my sweaty face on my shirtsleeve, I sat down on the rear bumper. My labored breaths misted in the cool morning air as Circle Drive slept dark and still. Corner streetlights stood like tall sentries, illumi-nating the pavement below. It wouldn't be long before Mr. Carpenter the milkman made his rounds along with Chucky Freeman, lobbing morning papers from his swerving bicycle. Enjoying the quiet, I knew full well that this would be the last moment of sanity I'd have for the next two days.

On cue, the Andrews Sisters skipped gleefully through the garage. Behind them marched Suzie clutching two naked Barbies. Placing two picnic baskets containing our standard afternoon lunch into the car, Mom pushed the tailgate closed. Reluctantly, I slid in the backseat with Suzie and Aunt Grace while Shelby sat up front. Checking everything one last time, Mom wedged her pregnant self behind the wheel. After a quick prayer, Mom threw the car into reverse.

What happened next became a horrible omen of things to come. Blindly backing out the driveway, Mom knocked over two metal trash cans. Of course, yours truly had the malodorous dishonor of retrieving the strewn contents that smelled like rotting fish.

Ten minutes into our journey, Mom realized she'd forgotten her sunglasses along with a fifty-pound bag of cosmetics. Making a U-turn, we sped back home. Part of this cryptic calling must trigger the need for just the right amount of mascara so as not to anger the Azalea gods.

Back on the road, the Pontiac bounced along the dark countryside. A black and white highway sign appeared in the car's high beam headlights. Highway 87: The Road to the Promised Land. The twisting, turning two lane ribbon of asphalt would pilot us through every small town in eastern North Carolina. No map was needed. Pure instinct beckoned Mom faithfully toward the horizon.

Another prophetic moment occurred when we made the turn onto the courthouse square in Pittsboro. Entering the roundabout, the car horn mysteriously sounded by itself. When Mom straightened the steering wheel, the horn stopped. Sounding like a sick freight train, the horn seemed to have a mind of its own. Quick turns brought forth short bursts while sweeping curves produced long steady blasts. It was absolutely hysterical. For about ten minutes. Laughter soon turned into chuckles, then boring smiles, to out and out annoyance. Despite the wailing car, Suzie fell asleep on my shoulder.

Twilight gave birth to a bright orange sun and life began to stir. Dusty contrails creeped behind distant tractors in massive fields. Bed sheets and towels flapped on backyard clotheslines. A perfect April morning. Ideal for climbing trees, pinning baseball cards to the spokes of a bike and cruising through the neighborhood. A magnificent day to do just about anything, yet here I was, crammed inside a noisy cattle car aboard the Azalea Festival Express.

The giddy prelude to the annual pilgrimage quickly evaporated. The sudden reality of enduring a four-hour car ride packed like sardines inside a singing Pontiac quickly took over. Mile after mile of longleaf pines, billboards and tobacco barns passed by my window. In silence we drove on as the haunted horn announced our arrival to the waking countryside. The busy two-lane highway hummed with passing cars and pickups. A green road sign caught my attention.

"Fayetteville 16 miles"

Fayetteville. Fort Bragg! Home of the 82nd Airborne! Although the sign stirred a burst of welcome excitement, I quickly dismissed any hope. In all my years of suffering through this boring quest, I never saw anything resembling the military. The only part of Fort Bragg I saw were a few directional signs and pine tree jungles.

All of that changed in a flurry of oncoming traffic. The glaring headlights of a massive olive-colored truck bounced toward us. Behind the lead vehicle rolled a noisy convoy of trucks and jeeps. Rolling down my window, I leaned out, squinting into the whirlwind rush of a diesel gale while vehicles shot past me in thunderous roar.

"J.D.! Sit down 'fore ya fall out the wenda!" Mom yelled.

Rolling up the glass, I watched the convoy charge by, disappearing behind us. I was ready to go home. No doubt the passing fleet of trucks would be the highlight of the trip. The weekend could only go downhill from here. Regrettably, it didn't take long to find out my instincts were correct.

The horror began along a desolate stretch of highway flanked by solid green walls of longleaf pines. The small bowling ball that I'd carried around in my stomach since the massive breakfast began to shift.

Gentle swaying from the car sent hurricane warnings flying while dizzying fifteen-foot swells churned away. Laying my head on the backseat, I wiped cold sweat off my forehead with my nasty hands. Suddenly the aromatic hint of rotting fish garbage lit the fuse. The launch button was pushed!

Bracing myself, I mumbled a feeble warning that no one heard. Like a west Texas oil rig, I blew, plastering the back of the driver's seat. What had been a delicious breakfast a few hours ago gently cascaded down into a golden egg-stained puddle on the floorboard. Suzie's spring dress, purchased especially for the trip, caught the rebound. Screaming at the top of her lungs, she dove for the safety of Aunt Grace's lap!

Hitting the brakes, Mom pulled the car onto the shoulder of the road, pounding every rut and hole at fifty miles an hour. A second wave hit with full force. Bouncing to a stop, the Pontiac's horn sensed my pain, breathing a sad and lonely cry.

"Get out of the car!" Mom screamed.

Limp and weak, I pushed open the door. The rush of passing cars, just inches away, knocked me forward as I staggered to the shoulder. Rolling herself out of the car, Mom waddled towards me as I defiantly vomited at an approaching pickup. Dropping on all fours, I focused my attention on a crushed beer can and proceeded to heave my guts out. Between contractions, I promised God if He got me through this that I would never eat again the rest of my life! Leaving me for dead, Mom eased open the car door, gagging at the carnage left in the backseat. Suzie stood crying beside the car while Aunt Shelby wiped yellow splotches from her soiled dress with a sweater.

When the storm finally subsided, Mom handed me a paper bag that I held in my lap for the remainder of the trip. Bleary-eyed and exhausted, I laid my head back on the seat and fell asleep.

Waking from a much-needed nap, I was happy to discover that my fuming stomach had agreed to a ceasefire, but the heaviness in my gut told me the spewing volcano was still active.

After what seemed like a never-ending voyage in the belly of a Roman cargo ship, we reached the outskirts of Wilmington. Lost excitement quickly returned. Dreamy-eyed, Mom gazed in wonder like Dorothy beholding the Emerald City. Creeping along in bumper-to-bumper traffic packed with fellow azalea addicts, we came to a stop on the drawbridge.

Looking out the window, I stared at the murky Cape Fear drifting lazily on its way to the Atlantic. Ancient wooden pillars where piers once stood rose from the cloudy water along the waterfront. Centuries old brick buildings and church steeples stood watch while an army of spectators moved along its narrow streets.

Then I saw her. Docked on the opposite side of the river, the blue and gray outline of the USS *North Carolina* towered over the trees.

"Look y'all! There's the battleship!" Three massive sixteen-inch guns from the rear turret pointed menacingly towards downtown. The lofty conning tower reached high above twin smoke stacks. Draped in battle flags and antiaircraft guns, she was the prettiest sight I'd ever seen!

I never took my eyes off her until we crossed the bridge.

Searching for the ever-elusive parking spot, we drove for blocks. Hurried spectators, dodging traffic, rushed towards the parade route. Mom found a tight space in a gravel parking lot near an abandoned warehouse. Opening my door a little too hard, I placed a sizable dent in the side of a red Dodge.

Joining the mob of excited parade-goers, we headed towards downtown. As expected, the parade route was lined with shoulder-to-shoulder spectators. Hunting for an opening, we weaved through the crowd.

Pushing past a packed drugstore entrance, we paused beside a yellow police barricade. In the distance, the sound of a marching band erupted. The crowd quickly shifted. A hardened festival veteran, Mom saw her chance. With her bulging stomach leading the way, she waded through the masses like a bulldozer. Protective of their territory, the crowd hardly budged, forcing us to stop three rows from the street.

Surrounded by towering adults, I suddenly felt hot. The exhausting hike coupled with swirling smells of sauerkraut, pizza, and cigar smoke sent my stomach churning once again. Honestly, I didn't think it could happen. There couldn't possibly be anything left in my stomach!

Without warning, I bent over and let 'er rip. A pathetic aftershock compared to my early morning detonation, but my pitiful groan and splattering mouthful were all it took. The frightened mob quickly scattered, leaving us an unobstructed view of the street. Climbing onto a fire hydrant, I rested my hands atop Mom's shoulders as she stood in front of me. Suzie took a front row seat on the curb. The few brave souls who remained stood at a safe distance, eyeing my every move. The distant music from the band edged closer. Pounding drums and blaring horns grew louder as the marching band filed by.

Decorated cars, trucks, and floats of every description inched down the street. A series of convertibles, carrying pretty girls adorned in antebellum dresses and matching bonnets, followed behind yet another high school band. As with past performances I'd witnessed over the years, it was the absolute epitome of boredom. You mean I threw my guts out for this mess?

When the parade mercifully ended, we quickly joined the growing stampede rushing to their waiting cars. Arlie Gardens was calling. With everyone in the eastern time zone making a beeline for the same destination, the city of Wilmington became a huge parking lot. It was early afternoon before we rode triumphantly through the hallowed front gates of the sprawling grounds. I expected the "Hallelujah Chorus" to burst from the heavens at any moment.

Securing a space in a grassy parking lot, Mom retrieved the two picnic baskets that had been fermenting all day in the back of the car. Spreading several blankets under a tree, we dined on a post-parade feast of warm fried chicken, warm potato salad, warm coleslaw, warm green beans, and melted pecan pie, washing it all down with tepid bottles of Pepsi that promptly erupted upon opening.

Weak and starving, I inhaled two greasy chicken legs and a side of hot potato salad. Reaching for another leg, I wolfed down another dill pickle. In a matter of seconds, the evil rumbling in my stomach returned to the stage for a slimy encore. Searching for a place to explode, I dashed past two old ladies admiring the scenery. Pushing aside a young boy, I defiled a collection of "Pink Ruffles" whose drab foliage blended nicely with my green skin.

Perhaps it was the glow of the blooms or the radiant sweat ponding on my face. Whatever the inspiration, Mom grabbed Suzie and me for a series of group pictures. Looking for just the right pose, Mom situated both of us in front of the dripping bushes I'd just violated. Adjusting her pigtails, Suzie smiled sweetly for the camera. Wiping my mouth and nose on my puke-stained corduroy jacket for the umpteenth time, I managed a sickly scowl.

After the pitiful photo shoot, we spent the remainder of the afternoon strolling the sprawling gardens, admiring hundreds of azaleas bursting with every color of the rainbow. Drinking their fill from the eternal fountain of azalea exuberance, the Andrews Sisters finally relented and headed for the car.

Unfortunately, the mystic "calling" clouded the Andrews Sisters' thinking as minor details of the trip went overlooked. Once again as in years past, Mom forgot to make a motel reservation. Unless we wanted to sleep in the car, Wilmington was out of the question.

Passing endless "No Vacancy" signs, we ended up at Carolina Beach where we discovered the splendid half star accommodations of The Sand Dollar Inn and Motor Court. A tacky neon sign with several burned-out bulbs blinked a hazy red "vacancy." Exhausted, Mom wheeled into the gravel parking lot. Refusing to open the door, Aunt Grace protested that the spooky row of identical doors reminded her of the Bates Motel from the movie *Psycho*. Locking the doors, she waited in the car.

A balding guy in white undershirt and black suspendered trousers strolled out to greet us. With a cigar wedged in the corner of his mouth, he introduced himself as Mr. Hargrove. It just so happened Mr. Hargrove had a vacancy. Judging by the empty parking lot, he had lots of them. It took some convincing, but Aunt Grace finally agreed to get out of the car. Impressed that he graciously offered us the Governor's Suite marked with a black number "1" on the door, Mom summoned me to unload the luggage.

Skeptical of Mr. Hargrove's intentions, Aunt Grace spent the next half an hour carefully searching every square inch of the room, opening drawers and closets, peeking under beds and behind pictures for anything suspicious. Saving the bathroom for last, she took a white washcloth and carefully wiped the interior of the bathtub looking for crimson residue.

Reeking of cigarettes, the sparse accommodations included two tilting double beds, both offering the comfort of two bulging camel hump mattresses. Lucky me, I would have the dishonor of sleeping on a pull-out sleeper couch that looked as if it were rescued from a busy highway.

Unpacking her suitcases, Mom placed her clothes in an ancient dresser that had a brick for one of its legs. The wooden door to our spacious penthouse was aptly fitted with two chain locks and an oversized padlock. Peeling wallpaper featuring a collection of stained seashells finished off the room's dreary Great Depression motif.

Expecting to find a body silhouette drawn in chalk on the ratty carpet, I inspected the pull-out couch for traces of yellow police tape. A group of roaches on a family outing raced across the couch, burying themselves inside. The small refrigerator in a grimy corner roared like a motorcycle. A filthy two-burner stove sat next to a cracked porcelain sink.

Once settled into our luxury lodgings, Mom left for the grocery store to buy the ingredients to make her famous spaghetti. Suzie and I laid on a bed, staring at the aluminum foil wrapped rabbit-ears of a TV that didn't work. Rather than risk another eruption, I dined on ginger ale and crackers, wondering if the roach family would join me later for a nightcap. Although we were staying in a rat hole, I was so worn-out I could have slept soundly on a bed of rocks.

The next morning, I woke up starving and could have eaten the battered dresser's remaining three legs. It was the best I felt all weekend. With the annual calling fulfilled, the passion and excitement of the journey disappeared. Realizing they'd spent the night in a dumpster, the Andrews Sisters quickly packed, throwing things into bags and suitcases.

Pulling out of the parking lot, I smiled for the first time in two days. The nightmare was finally over. We were going home. If we hurried, I might get back in time to play Ambush with the guys.

Thank goodness Mom never went anywhere without her morning coffee. My stomach roared its approval as she pulled into the gravel lot of a local pancake house. Still, the thought of greasy bacon and eggs brought back gastric memories of my weekend barf fest, and after careful deliberation, I chose a comforting bowl of oatmeal. Once on the road, my eyelids began to dance and I fell asleep.

"J.D.? J.D.? Wake up."

Opening a droopy eye, I peered over the hood of the car. A large red and blue sign came into focus: "ENTRANCE: USS *NORTH CAROLINA* BATTLESHIP MEMORIAL." I had to be dreaming! Excited, the car horn harmonized with my shrill scream.

"Are we really stoppin'?"

"Well, you had a rough day yesterday. I thought this might perk ya up!"

Having only seen her once from the drawbridge, I was shocked at the size of the gigantic ship. The mighty sixteen-inch guns were as massive as the giant oaks in Ashley Woods, dwarfing tiny visitors who wandered around the deck. Finding a parking spot, Mom joined others in the ticket line while I admired the wondrous ship. Running back, I gave her a hug.

"What do ya think?" she grinned.

"Thanks Ma! I can't believe I'm really here!" Leaving the others behind, I dashed up a wide gangplank. With my heart beating ninety miles an hour, I stepped onto the deck for the first time.

"Here. Let me take your picture," Mom said, pulling the camera from her bag. "Stand over there next to that big gun."

We hadn't been aboard five minutes when I realized that rambling around a glorious battleship with three women and a five-year-old was for the birds. Ducking into a side stairwell, I took off on my own.

Convinced that this was what a playground looked like in Heaven, I crawled through gun turrets, navigated narrow steel ladders while exploring the decks below from bow to stern.

Descending another set of stairs, I sprinted to the bow, admiring rows of .50 caliber machine guns. Gigantic anchor chains stretched out on the deck like enormous reptiles. Leaning between the rails, I glanced down at the muddy water below. Working up a mouthful, I spit over the side, marking my territory.

Looking back at the ship's bridge, I shielded my eyes from the blinding sun. My heart sank, knowing we'd be leaving soon. But then again, maybe not. The floating arsenal beneath my feet had a million and one hiding places. Heck! I could stay here for days before Mom ever found me!

Exploring the main deck, I hurried over to a pair of twin .40 anti-aircraft guns. On the other side of the turret sat an older man in one of the gunner's chairs that reminded me of a tractor seat. Smiling, he waved his hand.

"Come-on up here boy! Let's me and you git dem seagulls!" He said, pointing to an incoming flock of birds gliding over the parking lot.

"Yes sir!" I said, climbing into the other gunner's chair. Reaching for the crank handles, I peered through the round spider web gun sight.

"Here day come!"

Suddenly the loudspeaker crackled, echoing through the ship!

"Battle stations! Battle stations! Man your battle stations!" An air raid siren added to the confusion. Men scattered on deck from thick steel doors, taking their combat positions. Looking through my binoculars, I saw the menacing black specks banking on the horizon.

"Zeros! Ten o'clock!" I yelled.

"Zeros! Ten o'clock!" repeated my gunner's mate who fed a stack of ammo into the twin .40s. A distant plane broke formation. Diving down, the speeding aircraft came in hard, aiming for the ship's port side. Yellow flashes erupted from his wing cannons! Eerie metallic sounds erupted as bullets ricocheted off the steel armor.

Winding the crank, I held the sight steady. Fiery sparks spewed from my gun tips that recoiled with every shot. Tracers told me my shots were too high. Adjusting the sight, I held the approaching plane in the center of the web. The steady *pom, pom, pom,* of my guns pounded away! Suddenly, a stream of black smoke trailed underneath the wounded plane.

"You got him sir!"

"He's headin' straight for us! A Kamikaze!"

The Zero's wingtips wavered as the plane bore down! Keeping my sights steady, I pumped shells into the dying bird, shearing off its propeller. Ducking for cover, panicked sailors left me alone in the turret. It was up to me to save the USS *North Carolina!* The crippled plane's engine sputtered as he came in. Lowering my guns level with the choppy sea, I gave him all I had. At the last second, the plane exploded, crashing into the sea just in the nick of time!

"J.D.... J.D."

Blinking my eyes, I turned toward Mom's voice. Holding the camera steady, she took the shot. Thankfully she was smiling. She had every right to skewer me for leaving to explore the ship by myself. Giving her my patented innocent grin, I knew I had her. No way could she stay mad at her cute little sailor boy.

"Buddy, we need to hit the road pretty soon. I hope he behaved himself," she said to the older gentleman.

"Oh, he's been just fine ma'am. Me and him make a good team! We've been knockin' birds out of the sky left and right. Ain't we boy?"

"Yes sir!"

Waving good-bye, I slid down from the gunner's seat. Ambling slowly toward the exit I took in every glorious detail of the amazing warship one last time, wondering if I would ever set foot on her deck again.

"Thanks, Ma, for lettin' me go," I said, lightly touching her hand. Craning my neck, I watched the ship disappear behind us as we sped down the highway.

The following weekend, Dad contracted a splendid case of Spring Fever and decided to grill out on an unusually warm Saturday night. A pleasant reminder that lazy summer days were just around the corner. Suzie and I chased each other around the backyard while Mom readied the patio table.

"OK y'all come on!" Scrambling to the patio, I was about to sit down when I spotted a wrapped gift laying in my chair.

"I gotcha somethin'." Mom smiled.

It wasn't Christmas or my birthday. Something was terribly wrong! Probably one of those weird hormone things that made pregnant women eat pickles and ice cream. But hey! A present's a present! Grabbing the package before she came to her senses, I ripped open the wrapping paper.

"Oh Momma!" I gasped. Cradled in my arms was a plastic model of the USS *North Carolina!* Holding the priceless gift in one hand, I hugged Mom with the other. Forgetting about supper, I ran inside, clutching the box.

"Hey! Where you goin'? We're gonna eat here in a minute!"

Flying down the hall to my room, I jumped on the bed. Separating the model's gray plastic pieces, I found the twin .40-gun turret where the man and I had fought off seagulls. There in the quiet of my room, I gazed at the amazing model, waiting for me to put it together. At that moment, all I wanted to do was climb the wide gangplank and stand once again on the deck of that magnificent battleship. To feel the salty breeze hit my face. Relive the excitement of turning the cranks of the twin .40s. Stand on its bridge and clamber through the decks.

It hit me out of the blue. I managed a sheepish smile at my amusing discovery. Staring down at the scattered pieces of the plastic model, I finally understood why the Andrews Sisters were consumed by their annual trip to the Azalea Festival. All those years, they'd simply been chasing after something they loved. Counting the days and weeks until the trip came around again. To answer The Calling.

And I'd made fun of them, dreading the trip with every fiber of my being. Now I knew exactly how they felt. My desire, of course, was to feast my eyes again on 35,000 tons of floating steel docked in the Cape Fear River. On second thought, serving as the Andrews Sisters' private bellman wasn't so bad after all.

Never again did I complain about the annual pilgrimage. In fact, I looked forward to it, hooked by a burning desire of my own. Waiting and dreaming for the siren song of budding bushes and gun turrets to call us once again. Touring the battleship became part of our annual tradition. Another fondly bookmarked chapter of our lives, reread again and again at the first signs of spring.

"I 'MEMBER THAT!" DAD chuckled. "You had that ship model put together in no time! Supposed to be a birthday present, but 'cha momma just couldn't wait."

"When did we stop goin' to the festival?" Suzie wondered.

"Once Aunt Grace had the twins, the Andrews Sisters tossed in the trowel, so to speak." Dad laughed. Pretending to listen, Mom stared sadly at the lifeless backyard, trying to remember.

Crumbs from Heaven

Relishing one last look at the backyard, we stepped back inside. With stories and memories leading the way, we lovingly explored every dusty corner and dark closet, sharing collective "remember whens." Making my way through the cased opening to the narrow hallway, I discovered the hideous den carpet bled down the hall like a polluted stream. Running my fingers along the dingy wall, I felt the faint sensation of running through this narrow passageway countless times as a boy. Peering into the hall bathroom, I marveled, seeing that the room had hardly changed.

"Y'all come here! The pink bathroom is still here!"

"No, it ain't," Suzie gasped, ducking under my arm. "Goodness it's awful! Dang if that pink tub ain't here too!"

"Hold on right there young lady," Dad snapped, bullying his way through the door. "It ain't *pink*... it's rosé! Your momma just had to have rosé tile in the bathroom. That was the stuff back then!"

"Rosé ain't nothin' but fancy pink Daddy."

An old man stared back at me from twin replacement mirrors above an outdated vanity. I recalled a little boy brushing his teeth, laughing at himself in a sequence of funny faces.

Suddenly a devilish smile washed over Dad's face.

"Hey ya'll! You remember—"

"*Yes Dad!* We remember," Suzie smirked, cutting him off.

"...the picture I took of you potty trainin'?"

Remember? Boy did we ever! Nothing unusual about the picture really. An embarrassing universal pose taken countless times by joyful parents, preserving an important childhood milestone for the ages.

I chuckled, recalling the details of the black and white photo. Mom smiles as she kneels beside two-year-old Suzie who sits proudly on the throne, naked as can be. Seeing Dad was about to take her picture, she raises her hand to wave. The second Dad took the shot, Suzie's misshaped hand gesture, captured for all time, appeared as if she were giving Dad the finger. Savoring Suzie's embarrassment, Dad shared the endearing picture with everyone in the free world.

Making our way down the hall, the three of them disappeared into Suzie's old bedroom while I continued on. A carpet of light pulled me toward the open door. Pausing at the entrance, I gazed inside my old room. The place where I slept, played, and assembled countless plastic models looked more like an oversized closet than a bedroom. Cobwebbed corners of bland taupe walls welcomed me back. I tried to recall their color when I was a kid, but couldn't remember. Two curtainless windows met each other at a ninety-degree angle in the back corner. Vinyl replacements now.

"Oh my," I sighed.

There they were. The sacred ceiling tiles, blasphemously covered in grimy popcorn spray. Brown water stains bled through several wavy squares just above the windows. Comforting friends whom I shared my deepest darkest secrets as I contemplated life's complexities. Always there. Patiently listening, never passing judgment.

A cheap ceiling fan hung overhead. I remembered the orange frosted glass globe that once hung there, offering a colorful scene of a cowboy on horseback, tipping his ten-gallon hat. Following the dirty baseboard across the now carpeted floor, my eyes found the empty shadowed corner. A heavy lump forced a swallow. It had set right there. The chestnut-stained corner cabinet materialized in front of me, summoning the ghosts of my grandparents.

My favorite picture of them came into focus as I stared at the blank space. One that still retains a prominent spot on the large server in my parents' dining room. A stark black and white eight by ten bordered by a thin silver frame. No pictures had been taken of their wedding day and they'd sat for the portrait shortly after they got married. Grandpa Harrison sits upright in a simple straight back chair, dressed in a dark suit, white shirt, black tie. His open coat revealing a buttoned-up vest. A full head of thick black hair is neatly combed back over his prominent forehead in a waxy sheen.

There is no mistaking his massive hands, roughly the size of baseball gloves, stacked in a formal position on his left knee. I remember as a kid placing my small hand up to his, stretching my fingers as far as I could. Both of us laughing as my short wiggling fingers barely reached the middle of his palm. Whenever I got out of line, one powerful stroke from Grandpa's right hand covered my entire backside.

Behind him in the picture slightly to his right stands my grandmother. Wearing a light-colored dress with a half-moon lace neckline, her tiny left hand rests on Grandpa's broad shoulder. Her short hair is swept back, covering her ears. As if forced to pose at gunpoint, the two of them frown sternly at the camera. No lines, age spots, or wrinkles in their smooth skin. They were young. Their life together just beginning.

Although this photo of the two is by far my favorite, it is not at all how I remember them. Already in their sixties when I was born, my grandparents had lived an entire lifetime before I came along. It was always hard for me to ever imagine them as being young. I guess that's why I love that one picture of them so much.

Another lump. Another swallow. Suddenly I remembered a different time and place. An unforgettable spring night long ago, when I truly took the time to examine my grandfather's mighty hands, seeing for the first time the scars of time.

THAT NIGHT HIS GIANT hands appeared nothing like they did in the prized picture that I came to know and love. Worn from a lifetime of working, the grooved skin of Grandpa's fingers seemed slick and rubbery. Buttery folds wrapped around his crooked knuckles as if the skin had outgrown his fingers.

Cracked yellow nails stained by nicotine hung on the tips of his fingers like faded blooms. Age splotches scattered across his face. A few remaining strands of fine white thread were all that remained of his wavy dark hair. Neatly spaced furrows stretched across his forehead like thin boards of a fence. I remember thinking how much Dad looked like him.

At six-foot-five, Grandpa resembled the Jolly Green Giant compared to Grandma, who barely stood five feet tall. They lived in an old wooden two-story with wraparound porch just down the street from the church in an older section of town. The dark brown recliner in the den facing the TV was reserved for Grandpa, just like the wooden rocker between the double windows was Grandma's favorite chair. Nestled in the left side of Grandpa's chair laid an old worn Bible with its own share of lines and creases.

Although Grandpa couldn't read very well, if the Spirit hit him, he'd open his Bible and quote passages without any trouble. I always found that strange, so once after reading several verses to Suzie and me, I asked him.

"Grandpa, how come you can read the Bible but can't read much else?"

"Lord just speakin' to me, I reckon."

"What does the Lord say to ya?" Thinking hard about the question, he closed his Bible and leaned forward in his chair.

"Well, it ain't like I hear Him with muh ears. I hear Him with muh heart. Ain't 'cha ever felt somethin' right cheer?" he said, tapping his chest. "Like someone was a talkin' to ya? Tryin' to tell ya somethin'?"

"Well… I guess," I stammered. "One time I climbed out on a limb of a tree an' thought 'bout jumpin'. Then somethin' told me it was too high. That I might hurt myself. Is that what 'cha mean?"

"That's it!" he shouted, slapping the arm of his chair. "That was the good Lord tellin' ya right then and there you'd get hurt if ya jumped."

"Well… right after that, Bucky jumped off the same limb and sprained his ankle. Why didn't the Lord say somethin' to him?" Pausing for a second, Grandpa carefully chewed the inside of his jaw.

"Well… I reckon Bucky weren't listenin'. Gotta be quiet and listen with ya heart to hear what the Lord's gotta say."

The reserved of the two, at least to the casual observer, Grandma rarely got a word in edgewise since Grandpa talked a mile a minute.

Still, Grandma Harrison was not one to be crossed. A timeless lesson I painfully learned one evening during supper.

I remember her that night, scurrying around the kitchen, wearing her favorite flowery dress. A white apron with colorful images of red long stem apples tied around her waist. One of many that hung just inside the pantry door. Grandma treasured her apron collection like some women would a closet full of shoes. Although it was only the two of them, she made homemade biscuits every day as if cooking for a house full. Suzie helped her set the table while us men folk sat in the den watching TV. The smell of warm buttermilk biscuits, mashed potatoes, and fried chicken drifted through the house.

"Y'all come on," Grandma announced.

Taking his seat at the head of the table, Grandpa bowed his head. With clasped fists pressed against his forehead and elbows on the table, he prayed the same heartfelt blessing word for word that he prayed at every meal. His humble pleading prayer always struck me funny back then. Suzie and I peeped at each other and giggled.

Describing a new piece of furniture he was making, Grandpa held up his empty tea glass and shook it. Grandma quickly laid her fork down and got up from the table. Retrieving a porcelain pitcher, she stood beside Grandpa and poured him a fresh glass of tea. Returning the pitcher to the counter, Grandma again took her seat. No words were exchanged. How impressive. What a neat trick! Seeing the efficiency of the gesture, I wondered if Dad and I should start rattling our glasses at home. It just might speed things up at suppertime.

Twisting my fork in a mound of mashed potatoes, I pondered the ice trick. If I were to introduce this new dinnertime ritual at home, I best try it out with Grandma first. Sort of a practice run, making sure I was doing it right. Downing the rest of my iced tea, I lifted my empty glass. A quick shake sent the ice rattling. At that moment, my grand-mother's eyes went from light blue to fiery red.

"Boy! Git yourself up from this table right now! Git in that bed-room and don't come out till I tell ya!"

Sitting on the four-poster bed with my stomach growling its dis-pleasure, I decided that maybe the ice trick wasn't such a good idea after all. If Grandma reacted that way, then sure as the world, Mom would come at me with a meat cleaver.

My grandparents hadn't always lived in the big white house on Third Street. Most of their younger days were spent on a farm north of town. Like a lot of folks, they lost their home during the Depression and ended up moving around while Grandpa worked odd jobs to sup-port a family with six children. When the war started, Grandpa found steady work at Knight's Furniture. A few years later, my grandparents bought the house with the wraparound porch.

Quite the craftsman, Grandpa could build just about anything and was all the time making furniture for the church. The wooden commu-nion table in the sanctuary was made right there in his cluttered work-shop. For a wedding present, he built my parents a corner cupboard, stained a light oak finish, to match their dining room table.

Over the years, Grandpa gained quite a reputation as one of the best furniture makers at Knight's. All that came to an end the day his foot became caught in a conveyor belt. The accident nearly cut off his right foot and would have killed him if it hadn't been for Mr. Luther. Enduring months of skin grafts and operations, Grandpa was finally able to put weight on his foot. Unable to work like he used to, Grandpa lost his job. "Retired," he told everyone.

Working side by side at Knight's Furniture for twenty years, Lu-ther Snipes and Grandpa became the best of friends. Nearly as tall as Grandpa, Mr. Luther's dark blue coveralls he wore every day hung loosely over his narrow frame. Grandpa always joked that Mr. Luther was so thin he could hide behind a flagpole and no one would ever find him. I never saw him when he wasn't wearing a faded green cap with John Deere in peeling yellow letters on the front.

In those days, work was about the only place the two ever saw each other. The high-pitched shrill of factory whistles marked not only shift changes but ended the day's veiled harmony. At quitting time, Mr. Luther, along with other black folks, headed to the unpaved roads and shacks on the west side of town. After Grandpa got hurt, Mr. Luther came to see him almost every day when he got off work. The two of them always ended up in Grandpa's workshop.

What I enjoyed more than anything was listening to them "jaw back and forth" as Grandpa put it. Having the southern vernacular down to a crude science of mumbles and slurs, their conversations would certainly require an interpreter for those north of the Mason/Dixon Line. To some, theirs was the voice of ignorance and laziness. To me, their garbled dialect sang a soothing, comforting song. A warm relaxed cadence that made me feel safe for some reason. When Mr. Luther pronounced my name, it came out "Jady" in a rich baritone.

You'd never know it by looking at him, but Mr. Luther was nearly ten years older than Grandpa. Although the closest of friends, Mr. Luther always referred to my grandpa as "Mr. Billy." Never Billy or Bill. And my grandmother was a respectful "Miss Sally." When she came around, Mr. Luther always removed his hat, revealing tiny specks of thin coiling gray hair.

One afternoon, I tagged along, joining them in Grandpa's workshop. A blazing summer sun cooked its rusting tin roof, turning the dusty room into an oven. The open window above a long workbench offered little relief. Squinting through the hazy smoke of a cigarette clamped in his teeth, Grandpa ran a sheet of sandpaper along an imperfection on a wooden drawer. A smudged pair of glasses rested on the end of his nose. Mr. Luther inspected another drawer under a naked light bulb whose shadows swayed on the floor.

"Mr. Luther? Can I ask ya somethin'?"

"Mmm."

"Why do ya come over here after work? Ain't 'cha tired after workin' all day?"

"Iss ain't work," he mumbled, never looking up. "'Sides..." nodding toward Grandpa, "'at ol' gray mare right dare needs muh help."

"I don't need your help ol' man!" Grandpa snapped, the Winston bouncing up and down with his words.

"Jady... if I didn't come over and hep Mr. Billy, he'd wouldn't know which end of a hammuh duh hole!"

Back and forth they went. A perpetual skirmish that ignited every time they spent time together. Unaware they were saying something much deeper, I laughed at their sparring as they tried to outdo each other.

Before his accident, Grandpa never cared much for fishing. He'd rather spend his time hunting with Dad. Walking through the woods toting a shotgun behind a bird dog was far more challenging than the sedentary boredom of waiting for some indecisive fish to bite. With Mr. Luther's help, Grandpa became quite the angler. And of course, I quickly became his fishing buddy.

Grandpa taught me the sometimes painful process of baiting a hook along with the nasty art of cleaning fish. Over the years, Grandpa and Mr. Luther crafted quite a collection of cane fishing poles, sanding them just right, applying rich lacquer and sealer. Lazy Saturdays spent as a member of the Three Musketeers, as Grandpa called us, remains one of my fondest childhood memories. One fishing trip knocked at my heart as I leaned against the bedroom wall, succumbing to the memory.

As I DID MOST times before a Saturday fishing trip, I spent Friday night at Grandpa's, tossing and turning, dreaming of a giant bream teasing my cork. The next morning Grandma fixed us sandwiches for lunch, wrapping them in tin foil and placing them in a dented blue Pepsi cooler. Emptying every one of Grandma's silver ice trays, I packed the cooler with soft drinks. When I wasn't looking, Grandma slipped three slices of fresh pound cake into the cooler, a surprise for later.

Without saying a word, Grandpa tossed me the keys to his brown two-toned Rambler. Opening the trunk, I placed the cooler and a black tackle box inside while Grandpa wedged our cane poles into the car, their thin tips protruding out a backseat window.

Driving across town, we turned onto a rutty unpaved West Tenth Street. As usual, Mr. Luther stood waiting at the end of his dirt driveway holding his cane pole and a tattered tackle box tied shut with a rope. Behind him stood a worn, small shingle-covered frame house with a sagging front porch. A rusted metal chimney snaked from the roof. A sad old mutt of questionable heritage laid curled up in the shade of a large sycamore, next to a beat-up Chevy truck.

I didn't know the details back then. Kids weren't told such things. I learned later that Mr. Luther lost his wife to cancer years earlier. His children lived somewhere up north. All Mr. Luther had to his name was the rundown house, Knight's Furniture, that old truck, the mangy mutt, and my grandpa.

Jumping in the backseat, I held onto the fishing poles while Mr. Luther sat up front. Grandpa's straw hat lay beside him on the front seat. And of course, he never went fishing without wearing his lucky fishing shirt: an eternally-stained faded blue long sleeve with a hole in one armpit that seemed to get bigger every trip. Straps from his gray overalls looped over his shoulders and crossed in the back giving him the appearance of an aging train engineer.

The twenty-minute ride to Uncle Delbert's seemed to take forever. Passing one field after another, I stared out at the rolling landscape that I'd seen dozens of times. The loud rush from the open windows spawned an interior dust storm when Grandpa turned onto a twisting gravel road. Easing the car down a narrow path beside one of his younger brother's tobacco fields, Grandpa surveyed the sea of dark leaves.

"Delbert'll be irrigatin' if we don't get some rain soon."

"S'posed to come up a cloud saffnoon," Mr. Luther said, squinting into the sun.

Overhead limbs brushed the top of the car as we bounced over petrified ruts. Parking the car in our usual spot on the pond's west side, we gathered our gear along with a cardboard box of worms Grandpa bought on the way. The mid-morning sun wrapped us in a humid coat. Sweat plastered the shirt to my chest as I shooed gnats from my eyes. Mr. Luther never sweated and today was no different.

"Hot un duhday," Grandpa said, navigating dirt clods with his favorite cane, a carved likeness of a snake wrapped around a golden rod. After his accident, Grandpa became deluged with canes from family and friends. The one he carried this morning was one Mr. Luther made. You always knew where Grandpa was by finding his cane. If the cane was nestled in the armrest of his recliner, Grandpa was somewhere in the house. If the cane was missing, he was outside in his garden or workshop. Leaning on the pistol grip handle, he shuffled along, favoring his right foot.

Our favorite spot at the narrow end of the pond waited under the leafy arms of a leaning hickory. The sun's stark reflection gave the water a silvery sheen. Reaching the bank, I set the blue cooler down next to a small creek that fed the pond. I'd just picked up my pole when something rustled the water's flat surface.

"Look y'all! They're jumpin'!" I hollered, dropping my pole in excitement. Grabbing a worm from the cardboard box I quickly baited my hook. Throwing out my line, I watched the rings run away from the cork. After all that fuss, nothing. Not even a nibble.

"Where day go?"

"Sump'm musta skeered 'em," Mr. Luther sighed.

"Reckon it's Big John?" Grandpa asked, pulling a pack of Winston's from his shirt pocket.

"Who's Big John?" I asked as Grandpa lit his cigarette.

"Ya mean I ain't never told ya 'bout Big John?" he said as the smoke from his cigarette ran away in the hot breeze.

"Boy, ol' Big John's duh biggest fish I ever seen. Lives right cheer in Delbert's pond."

"How big is he?"

"Don't rightly know. What Luther? Nine...ten foot maybe?" Mr. Luther slowly nodded, scratching the top of his head through his hat.

"First time I ever seen 'im, I's standin' 'bout where you are. Delbert was tellin' me'n Luther 'bout 'im when out of duh blue, muh cork went unduh like a rock! Wahduh started churnin' roun' duh cork in a big circle like," he said, making a stirring motion with his finger. "Then quick as lightnin', dis big ol' black fish jump clean outta duh wahduh!"

"*Naw!*"

"Mad as a hornet too! Jump five foot in duh air! His mouth so wide open I seen what he ate for breakfast. And right dare, stuck in his jaw was muh hook. And him just a starin' back at me with them big red eyes uh his. Red as hot coals! Then he fell back in duh wahduh! *Whoosh!* Soaked us all. Broke muh pole slap in two!"

"My gosh," I said, staring out over the pond. "You reckon Big John is still out dare?"

"Lordy yeah! He's still out dare ahright. Ain't nobody been able to catch 'im. Sneaky rascal. For years, me and Delbert tried. Mornin's, evenin's. It was like ol' Big John knowed what we's thinkin'. Sometime when duh light's just right, I'd see him swimmin' tord duh bank like a long croc, weavin' back and forth in duh wahduh," he said, snaking his hand across his lap.

"One night me and Delbert 'cided we's gonna catch ol' Big John once and for all. Clean 'im up, feed eh'body at church for Homecomin'. We waited till midnight and come walkin' through dat field right dare. Delbert led duh way carryin' a lan'ern. All uh sudden, he jumped up in duh air, screamin' to high Heaven!"

"What was it?"

"He come iss close to steppin' on a fat coppuhhead, big as muh arm," he said, holding the tips of his finger and thumb an inch apart. "I ain't never seen ol' Delbert jump 'at high in all muh life! Well, we tippy-toed on past real quiet like, keepin' our eyes peeled. Put Delbert's boat in over yonduh unduh at bent hick'ry. Pushed off real slow. Couldn't hear nothin' but crickets and frogs. Heh. You shoulda seen ol' Delbert, skeered as could be, peekin' over duh side of duh boat. He's up front holdin' at lan'ern over duh wahduh whilst I paddled. His hands uh shakin' so bad at lan'ern was justa swingin'!" I giggled at Grandpa's description.

"I paddled us real slow right out dare'n duh middle. We's baitin' our hooks with some fatback when all of uh sudden sump'm rammed duh bottom of duh boat. *BAM!*" he said, pounding his fist into his palm.

"Then here it come again! *BAM!* Next thing ya know we done turn'd over! Lan'ern went one way we went anothern. Black as tar. Couldn't see nothin'! Well, we commenced to swimmin' for all we's worth!"

"How 'bout your foot?"

"Boy, I thought duh Lord done heal me! I's so skeered and swimmin' hard as I could, muh foot didn't bother me nary a bit. Like I said, I's a swimmin' up a storm when all uh sudden, I felt sump'm nibblin' at muh toes!" he said, wiggling his fingers. Cold chills ran down my arms on the hottest day of the year as I hung on his every word. "I just knew ol' Big John had me. Gonna bite muh toes off or maybe eat muh whole leg! Somehow, we got to duh bank alive. We laid dare, pantin' like a couple uh tarred coon dogs." Pausing, Grandpa took the last pull off his cigarette and thumped it in the pond.

"Never saw Delbert's boat no more after dat. Reckon it's at the bottom of duh pond or Big John done ate it." Leaning over the arm of his chair with his voice nearing a whisper, he looked me straight in the eye. "Boy, lis'n to me. What I told you's 'tween us. Don' 'cha go tellin' nobody, ya hear?"

"Oh, naw sir! I ain't tellin' nobody! Cross my heart and hope to die, I ain't! Where you reckon Big John is?"

"Ain't no tellin'. He could be a swimmin' close to duh bank, lookin' for sump'm to eat. Or maybe he's out dare in duh middle somewhere.

Ya know duh pond's four hun'derd foot deep out dare." Mr. Luther peeked out from under his John Deere cap at that one.

Squinting into the murky water, I wondered if Big John might be cruising near the bank. Barefooted, I backed up a few steps just in case. Edgy and excited, I tugged at my line, hoping to coax a bite. From then on, every ripple and splash was a red-eyed monster about to strike.

By noon, we hadn't caught much so we gave our poles a rest and ate lunch. One thing I learned on these excursions was that fishing and eating don't mix. No matter how hard I tried to keep my hands clean, the lunch Grandma packed always tasted like a worm sandwich.

After the break, we moved down towards the dam. Sick of cork watching, I was about to pull in the line when I felt a nibble.

"Look y'all!"

"Eee...zee boy, wait till it goes unduh," Grandpa said calmly. Suddenly the cork dived out of sight. The tip of my pole bowed under the strain.

"Jerk it!"

"It's him! It's Big John," I yelled, backing up the bank. Suddenly the monster splashed near the surface, then dove under, taking my heart with it. With shaking hands, I watched my line dance in the water, straight and taut.

"Dat's it! Bring 'im in." Grandpa said, leaning in his chair. There on the end of the line shook a nice-sized bream. "Woo hoo boy! It ain't Big John, but 'at's a nice un!"

"Good eatin' right dare." Luther nodded.

"He's a foot if he's an inch!" Grandpa laughed.

Excited, I dug the hook into my finger as I hurried to bait another worm. As soon as my cork hit the water, it disappeared again. The line frozen straight.

"Got one!"

"Jady!"

Pulling him in, I tossed the fish into the bucket.

"How dat happen?" I wondered. "They weren't bitin' at all and now I done got two!"

"I know why!" Grandpa said, wiping his face with a red bandana. "Duh good Lord been watchin' ya boy. He knowed ya wanna catch a fish real bad. So, He let 'cha catch not one, but two. Justa let ya know He's a lis'nin'."

"Really?"

"Duh good Lord loves blessin' His children, son. This here's justa small blessin'. Lord's table's mighty big. Hope to eat dare someday. Sometime when duh Lord's got some leftover blessin's, He takes His big hand and brushes a crumb or two off His table and lets 'em fall all 'round ya. Justa let ya know He's thinkin' 'bout 'cha."

"Really! You mean the Lord just threw me a crumb? From Heaven?"

"Hole on a minute. You got two fish. At's two crumbs!" He winked.

I never forgot Grandpa's animated story. Whenever some unexpected surprise occurred, I thought of what Grandpa said that hot summer afternoon.

Although he enjoyed fishing, Grandpa's first love had been hunting before his accident changed everything. Dad and I still took him crow hunting now and then. A few weeks after Grandpa's Big John story, the three of us piled into Dad's DeSoto along with his hunting buddies, Billy Mac and Mr. Clyde, for a crow hunt.

Driving out in the middle of nowhere, we parked the car on a deserted dirt road surrounded by thick pines. It'd rained the night before and a light fog held stubbornly to the ground. Besides keeping an eye on Grandpa, my job was to operate a battery-powered record player attached to a large loudspeaker with a fabric cord.

Lugging the record player, I inched along sideways, looking back at Grandpa as he made his way slowly through the woods. Leaving his cane in the car, he stumbled along, grabbing tree limbs with one hand and carrying his shotgun in the other. Pausing at a small clearing, he leaned against a tree, out of breath.

"You OK?"

"Oh yeah... I'm fine," he said, with a slight smile.

Setting the record player down beside a rotted fence post, I dropped to my knees. Selecting the only record on the day's playlist, I placed the slightly warped 45 recording of crows in a feeding frenzy on the small turntable and waited for the signal. A few minutes passed when Dad's voice echoed through the woods.

"OK J.D.!"

Turning on the power I cranked the volume up high, sending a sharp burst of feedback into the quiet morning. Placing the needle on the record, I stuck my fingers in my ears.

The crazed screams of a thousand cawing crows blasted from the dull gray speaker. In no time, black apparitions sped past overhead breaks in the trees. Suddenly the woods exploded. Frenzied noise from the record player and rapid gunfire filled the morning air with a sense of panic. Slow on the draw, Grandpa raised his shotgun. By the time he aimed and fired through the open tree canopy, the swift birds were long gone.

I felt so sorry for him. He'd say later, like he did after every hunt, that it didn't matter whether he hit anything as long as he got to fire his gun. I knew it still bothered him, knowing he couldn't hunt like he used to. Watching him fire and reload, I said a little prayer, hoping he'd hit something. Grabbing another handful of shells from his coat pocket, he peeped over at me with a half-hearted smile. Realizing the futility, Grandpa quit aiming altogether. Pointing his gun skyward, he fired as fast as he could.

Out of nowhere, the unluckiest crow in the state of North Carolina flew into Grandpa's line of fire. Folding into a black ball, the crumpled bird fell through the pines, landing in a thicket. From the look on Grandpa's face, you'd have thought he had just hit a grand slam in the bottom of the ninth to win the World Series. Raising his shotgun in the air, he let out a triumphant yell. Answering with a holler of my own, I lifted both arms in the air like a football referee signaling a touchdown. As we celebrated, Grandpa mumbled something I couldn't make out in the chaos of noise. When he smiled and pointed to the sky, I knew what he was saying... *Crumbs from Heaven!*

One of the things I loved about my grandfather was that he was never too busy to spend time with me. Most grownups never paid me no mind. It didn't matter what he was doing, he'd ask me to tag along. Maybe it was a combination of age and his bum leg, but Grandpa never got in a hurry about anything, taking life slow and easy. A trait I wished I'd inherited.

Of all the moments spent with him, one cold February morning stands out above the others. An occasion that didn't seem all that important at the time, but would gain meaning later, providing me with a priceless memory. I'd spent another Friday night at my grandparents' house, something I did every chance I got. When I awoke the next morning, I could hear Grandma stirring around in the kitchen.

"Mornin' sleepy head," she said, putting dishes in the sink. Seeing his cane was missing from the recliner, I ran to the window. Smoke twisted from the small metal chimney atop the workshop. "He's been out dare since sunup. Tol' me to tell ya to come help when ya got up." Inhaling my breakfast, I jumped up from the table. "Put on a coat or you'll catch pneumonia!" She warned. Doing an about-face, I grabbed my jacket. A cold overcast morning hinting of snow greeted me as I stepped out on the back porch.

The workshop door that desperately needed oiling announced my entrance. Grandpa's cane leaned against the wall, just inside the door. With his back to me, he stood at his workbench in a pair of dingy overalls and long-sleeved flannel shirt. Flanked by yellow light bulbs that hung from the ceiling, he looked like a surgeon standing over an operating table.

"Day's haff gone boy. Almost eight-thirty," he said, never turning around.

"Sorry."

Standing near a simmering woodstove, I worked up a mouthful. Spitting on the hot black globe, I watched it fizzle into a white stripe. Floor-to-ceiling clutter filled the ashen room littered with unruly piles of lumber. Lathes, table and band saws along with other contraptions connected by a maze of extension cords hugged the walls. Wood shavings carpeted the creaky floor. Wrenches, screwdrivers, and hammers of every description dangled haphazardly from rusty nails. And Mom said my room was messy! Ancient headboards and an old spinning wheel wrapped in dusty cobwebs hung from the rafters. Forgotten projects Grandpa would get to one day. A large triangular tabletop leaning against the workbench caught my eye. It was unlike anything I'd seen him make before.

"What's that?" I asked, rubbing one of the edges.

"Corner table for duh church. Here… hand me dat tape," he nodded towards a dusty shelf. Staring over his glasses, Grandpa leaned on the bench.

"Trick is…" he said, pulling the measuring tape. "Ya just… can't… git… in no hurry." Writing the dimensions on a wooden block, he rolled up the tape. "OK. Let's me and you git to work on duh legs. Hand me dem three pieces yonduh."

"Let's move over here…" he said, sitting down at a machine. "Now you watch and then I want 'cha to help me." Clamping one of the wooden pieces into an odd-looking device, he flipped a switch. The wooden stick spun around like the axle of a speeding truck. Picking up a small chisel, Grandpa winked and wiped his forehead on his sleeve.

"Now for a little magic," he shouted over the noise.

Slowly, Grandpa touched the whirling wood with the metal tool. The room exploded in a deluge of shavings, coating him in the dusty confetti. When the machine powered down, I was surprised to see the splintered lumber was now a smooth rounded table leg.

"Wow! Look at that!"

"Come here and I'll show ya how to do it."

Nervously standing in front of him, I eyed the strange contraption. Clamping another strip of wood in the machine, Grandpa again flipped a switch. Holding my hands in his, he guided the tool along the spinning wood as I squinted through a shaving-specked snowstorm. When he turned the power off, I looked up and busted out laughing at Grandpa's dust-filled eyebrows.

"What's so funny! How 'bout you?"

Giggling, I brushed my flattop, sending an avalanche of shavings to the floor. I'd helped Grandpa lots of times when he was working in his workshop, handing him one thing and then another. But this was the first time he'd ever allowed me to help build something. Like he said, it was magic!

It was Grandpa who gave me Yankee, a spirited cocker spaniel puppy for my birthday, surprising both me and my mother. Since he'd gotten the puppy from his cousin in Pennsylvania, I felt obligated to name him Yankee. Having been part of the conspiracy from the start, Dad was delighted with the new addition to our family. Left out of deliberations, Mom was more than a little miffed. Taking some old blankets, I fixed him a bed in the garage.

It didn't take long before Yankee had me wrapped around his little paw. Being a loving and caring puppy, he often left random presents on the garage floor for us to discover. Once, with her arms full of groceries, Mom not only stepped in one of Yankee's little gifts but managed to track brown footprints all over the kitchen floor. Of course, she blew a gasket.

"She'll get over it," Dad promised. After a few weeks, his prediction came true. Yankee's sad eyes eventually broke through Mom's icy wall, grabbing her by the heart.

My constant companion, Yankee followed me everywhere, sizing up folks who got a little too close. Developing a love for car chasing, he'd take off out of the yard at the sight of an approaching vehicle. Never giving up, Yankee would chase a car down the street, biting at the tires.

"Wonder what he'd do if he ever caught one?" Dad would always ask.

As Yankee grew older, he often disappeared for days at a time. Then out of the blue, he'd show up on the doorstep. His sudden absences worried me at first, but Dad assured me that he was probably out a courting some nice lady dog.

One morning as I left for school, Yankee was nowhere to be found. Figuring he was on one of his little vacations, I didn't think much about it. He'd turn up sooner or later. A few days turned into a week. Dad and I drove around town searching for him. Suzie and I crafted colorful "missing dog" posters out of crayons and construction paper, taping them to power poles.

As soon as school ended each day, I hurried home, hoping to find him waiting for me. Wherever he was, I just hoped he was all right.

Sitting in my tire swing on another worrisome afternoon, I knew something was terribly wrong. Fighting back the tears, I wondered if Yankee was gone for good. I hated to admit it, but there were times when I simply forgot about him. Too busy playing with friends, I ignored his frisky cries, jumping in circles, inviting me to play.

I loved him. So why didn't I pay him any attention? He'd always been there and I guess I took it for granted that he always would be. Suddenly, a horrible thought kicked me in the gut: *What if Yankee ran away looking for someone else who'd spend more time with him?* Tears came quicker. Kicking the shallow trench under the swing, I promised God that if He would bring Yankee home that I would play with him every day.

Then came that bright Sunday afternoon. Fully attired in army gear, I was on my way to meet the guys. I'd just stepped out of the garage when I froze. Stumbling up the driveway towards me was Yankee. Most times, he'd run to meet me, jumping and pawing. Placing one paw in front of the other, he limped along.

"*He's home y'all! Yankee's home,*" I yelled.

Sprinting to him, I fell to my knees. Crusty red cuts covered his face and legs. His body shivered with each rapid pant. Licking my face once, as if to say "I'm home," was all he could muster. Suzie came flying out of the house followed closely by my parents. Wiping tears away, Mom laughed and cried at the same time.

"Let's have a look here boy," Dad said kneeling. "Looks like he came up on the short end of a long fight." Yankee whimpered when Dad picked him up and carried him inside the garage. Placing a plate of food down beside him, I watched him tear into it as if he hadn't eaten since he left home. Turning, I looked up into the bright sky.

"Thank you, God. Thank you," I said out loud. This was more than a crumb. This miracle was a whole loaf of bread! I called Grandpa to tell him the news.

The next morning, Mom took Yankee to the vet. After his terrifying experience, he stuck around the house, never wandering too far. Thankfully it wasn't long before Yankee was back to his old self again. Sadly, the same thing could be said about me. Returning to my "too busy to play right now" habits, I promised myself that I'd spend time with him later. How quickly I'd forgotten the pain. The loneliness. Praying just to see his face and those black eyes again.

It happened on one of those weekends that always seem to come at least once every March. When temperatures shrug off spring, climbing into the eighties, teasing us of summer days to come. Kids in shorts and T-shirts played in the streets as if it were July.

Our squad had formed an impromptu wagon train, pulling younger kids along the curved streets. Starting out with Buster Parkland's red Radio Flyer, we picked up more wagons as we snaked through the neighborhood. Pretending to take tickets, we sat kids down, two in each wagon.

We were climbing the hill in front of Junior's house when a long squeal of tires echoed through the tall pines. Probably Eddie Stephenson showing off that souped-up Mercury of his. Our parade had just reached the hilltop when Connie Sue came tearing down the street.

"J.D.! J.D.!" she screamed out of breath, "Yankee got hit!"

Dropping the wagon's black pull bar, I blew past Connie Sue in a full run. She was crying.

"*No, no… Please Lord no!*"

Ducking under a clothesline, I fell, busting my knee. Hurrying through a side yard, I exited onto the street. Standing beside a car, Dad spoke with a man I'd never seen before. Jumping the ditch, I cringed at the large white towel laid over a motionless mound. Two crossed auburn paws stuck out from underneath.

"Yankee!" I screamed, falling onto the towel.

"Will, I'm so sorry. He just come runnin' alongside the car like he always does, barkin' and carryin' on. Next thing I knew he somehow got under the car."

"Aw, it ain't your fault Jess. Yankee's all the time chasin' cars… I reckon he finally caught one." He said, peering down at me. Locked in a tearful embrace, Mom and Suzie kept their distance.

That night we held a funeral, burying Yankee in the backyard next to the storage shed. My teary eyes locked onto the fresh mound of dirt while Mom said a prayer. A sharp ember burned in my stomach. *What if I'd been playing with him? He wouldn't have chased the car. He'd still be—*

The startling touch of Dad's hand on my shoulder ripped me away from one nightmare, plunging me straight into another.

"J.D., people are startin' to come in. Better get in line."

Yankee, fishing trips, Mr. Luther and Grandpa, came rushing by in the blinding light of a thousand lightning strikes. Staring again at the open casket, I gazed at the yellow stained fingernails of Grandpa's crooked hands one last time. Hands that taught me how to seed a garden and bait a hook. Busy hands constantly in motion, never tired, laid neatly crossed over the front of his navy blue suit, covering his belt buckle. His tranquil face reminded me of the times he'd fall asleep in his recliner. Tonight however, there was no snoring. No gaping mouth. Tight lips stretched across his face in a strange, almost frightening pose. Everything about him appeared so neat and tidy.

Standing there beside the dark casket, I thought about last Saturday. Punishing myself again just as I had countless times over the past few days. Bucky and I were walking across my front yard, admiring a toy bazooka he'd gotten for his birthday that shot plastic rockets. We were just about to head over to Ashley Woods to try it out when Grandpa pulled in the driveway.

"Hey boy!"

"Hey Grandpa!"

"Thought I'd surprise ya! Hop in and we'll go pick up Luther. Time for duh Three Musketeers to head out to Delbert's!" Excited to surprise his grandson with an afternoon of fishing, Grandpa's face shined like polished silver. His eyes glowed with pure joy.

"Oh… Uh," stammering, I looked at Bucky then back at Grandpa. "I'd like to, but me and Bucky are goin' to play with his new toy."

That was it. No "goodbye" or "Thanks Grandpa, maybe some other time." No nothing. I just walked away with Bucky, leaving him sitting in the driveway. Three days later, he was gone. That was the last time I ever saw him. Till tonight.

He died of a heart attack. Mr. Luther found him on the floor of his workshop. Our family gathered later at Grandma's where I sat cross-legged on the floor of the cigarette smoke-filled den. Slamming car doors were followed closely by hurried footsteps on the wooden porch.

Soft knocks came at the kitchen door. Strangers carrying foil-covered plates and casserole dishes came and went, hugging Grandma and telling her how sorry they were.

Thankfully, no one paid me any attention. Being seen and not heard was just fine by me. For some strange reason, the TV was on with the sound turned down. Some sort of police show drifted across the screen, one I didn't recognize. Something terrible had happened. People's mouths moved but I couldn't hear what they were saying. A man in a hurry ran out to his car and sped off, throwing a cloud of dust in the air.

Staring at the silent TV, I couldn't figure out for the life of me what was going on. A stunning portrait of what my life had become. Over the course of nine days, I'd lost both Yankee and my grandpa. The world was now a cold dark place surrounded by sad strangers. Like the muted TV, nothing made sense. Looking at Grandpa's recliner, I noticed his cane was gone.

"Come on son. We need to go," Dad said, softly nudging my shoulder. The sharp perfume of freshly cut flowers floated through the large open room as I joined my family at the end of the receiving line. We would be the last of the Harrisons to shake hands with sad mourners who glanced at their watches and headed for the door. People from church and the neighborhood shook my hand and told me how tall I was getting. Staring at the floor, I ignored the hushed conversation. I hated it. I hated everything.

Suddenly, a sheepish black face peeked around the corner of an open door. Smiling for the first time in days, I watched Mr. Luther stare nervously around the crowded room like a kid on his first day of school. Hatless and dressed in a worn blue suit, he seemed just as strange and out of place as Grandpa. His eyes met mine as he offered a modest wave. Keeping his hands neatly folded in front of him, he slowly moved along as the line filed past the open casket. Giving Grandpa a nervous glance, he quickly turned away.

Bowing politely, Mr. Luther offered Grandma a simple handshake. Without hesitation, she stood on her tiptoes, pulling him toward her in a tearful embrace. Unsure of what to do with his hands, he lightly touched her arms, wanting to pull away. In an awkward pose, he stood there, listening intently to her whispers. Slow to release him, Grandma reached for another tissue.

Moving down the receiving line, Mr. Luther nodded respectfully, offering a quick handshake, trying his best to get to us as fast as he could.

"Mr. Will, I's so sorry 'bout Mr. Billy."

"Dad loved ya like a brother, Luther. You meant the world to him. Hadn't been for you, we might have lost him a long time ago." Mr. Luther bowed his head. His boney Adam's apple floated in his neck as he swallowed. "Listen, Luther. I tried to call ya but didn't know your number."

"Ain't got no phone, Mr. Will."

"Oh… uh… it would mean a lot to us if you'd be a pallbearer tomorrow." Mr. Luther's bottom lip trembled.

"'At's what Miss Sally just axe me. Honor'd tuh, Mr. Will."

Nodding at my mother, Mr. Luther instinctively reached to tip his cap that wasn't there, quickly dropping his hand.

"Hey Jady. I's so sorry." Fighting tears, I gazed into his soft brown eyes, wondering if I'd ever see him again. Leaning forward and wrapping my arms around his thin waist, I buried my face in his shirt and sobbed. His broad hand gently rubbed the top of my head.

The next morning, a somber Pastor Larkin stood at the pulpit and said nice things about Grandpa to a half-filled sanctuary. When the service concluded, attendants wheeled the casket up the aisle. A hard rain fell through a foggy blanket of clouds. Headlights from the procession of cars illuminated the gray lifeless morning.

Wipers slapped the base of the Pontiac's windshield as if hammering a nail. Squinting over the steering wheel into the soupy mix, Mom followed the line of cars turning into Oak Ridge Cemetery. Suzie and I sat quietly with her on the front seat.

From the blanket of crying clouds to the army of black suits and dresses, the whole world seemed to have grown dark. Although it was close to noon, the dreary morning felt more like dusk than midday. Domes of umbrellas bloomed from opening car doors. The reverent crowd marched to the waiting cover of a green tent, lined with rows of metal folding chairs. Pallbearers, mostly older men from the church except for Mr. Luther, carried the wooden casket from the rear of the hearse.

Holding umbrellas high, somber attendants ushered family members to the shelter of the tent. Standing with my cousins behind the last row of chairs, I leaned inside but still got soaked. The casket topped with greenery and carefully arranged long stem red roses seemed suspended in the air, floating in a misty fog.

Opening a small Bible, Pastor Larkin slowly began to speak, but all I could hear were rain pellets pounding the overhead canvas. Like the muted TV in Grandpa's den, all I could see were his lips moving. I thought of my tenth birthday just a few weeks away. Tears trickled down my cheeks when I realized Grandpa wouldn't be there. Every year, Grandpa, Dad, Mr. Luther, and I gathered for a whole Saturday of fishing at Uncle Delbert's. A birthday tradition that would surely disappear from my life just like everything else.

Somewhere in the crowd, I spotted the back of Dad's head. His coat collar hugged tightly around his neck. I wondered what was going through his mind. How it felt to lose his father. The thought made me shiver in the rain. Although I knew he was sad, Dad never let on. When I thought about it, I couldn't remember Dad ever crying about anything. Death must be easier to handle for grownups.

Saturday May 4th dawned bright and sunny. A light breeze brushed over our patio while my army buddies dressed in full battle regalia gathered at three cloth-covered card tables. Pointy birthday hats with rubber band chin straps waited atop paper plates at each chair. Are you kidding? Mom must have thought I was turning five. No soldier worth his salt would replace his plastic helmet with something so ridiculously childish. Waiting for their chance to inhale cake and ice cream, the guys fidgeted in their seats while Mom lit the candles.

"OK! Make a wish!" someone yelled. My eyes met Dad's. What in the world could I possibly wish for? Wishes were nothing but cute little dreams, enticing curious giggles at birthday parties. Nothing that I wished for would ever bring back Grandpa or Yankee. Everyone waited as I sat there staring blankly at the burning candles. When nothing came to mind, I took a deep breath and blew them out.

In no mood for celebration, I went through the motions. After the party, I carried the mountain of meaningless gifts to my room. Staring at the colorful boxes laid out on my bed, I realized it was quiet for the first time all day. Over the past few weeks, I'd discovered that I didn't like quiet much anymore. A soft knock came at the door.

"Hey pal," Dad said softly, peering through the door. "Somebody here to see ya."

Stepping to the door, I looked up into Luther's smiling face.

"Happy burfday Jady." There in Luther's outstretched hand was Grandpa's favorite fishing pole.

"Grandpa's?"

"Mr. Billy'd want 'cha to have it. Ain't forgot how to use it, have ya?"

"Oh no sir," I said, reaching for the pole as if it might break when I touched it.

"We'll find out 'cause me, you and ya diddy goin' to Uncle Delbert's next Saerdy." Dad grinned and nodded as I looked wide-eyed at both of them. Holding the pole in one hand, I grabbed Luther around his skinny waist.

"Pal, there's something else... from Grandpa," Dad said. Looking past the two of them, I recognized the tall triangular corner cabinet, stained a light chestnut brown, standing at the end of the hall. Gold hardware shined on the large front drawer. Three small shelves rose from the tabletop, perfect for my collection of paint bottles, brushes, and other modeling supplies.

"That's... that's the one me and Grandpa built! I helped 'im make the legs! Told me he was makin' it for the church."

"Naw. Mr. Billy's makin' it for yo burfday da whole time. Almost had it done. Put duh last coat uh shellac on muhself."

"Then it's from you too? Ain't it, Mr. Luther?"

"Yeah, I reckon it is," he chuckled.

The two of them maneuvered the piece through the door while I made room in the back corner. To my surprise, Grandpa showed up for my birthday after all. Smiling I looked up at the ceiling tiles. Crumbs from Heaven. Like Grandpa said, the good Lord swept His mighty hand across His generous and compassionate table. And I'd bet anything that Grandpa was seated right beside Him, grinning from ear to ear.

As promised, the next Saturday morning, Mr. Luther, Dad, and I packed our gear into the trunk of the DeSoto along with Grandpa's rusty blue Pepsi cooler. Turning off the main road, Dad unknowingly followed the same path that Grandpa always did, maneuvering the car down the brushy side of a newly plowed field.

I tried to remember the last time I'd laid eyes on our favorite fishing hole. Probably sometime last fall with Grandpa and Mr. Luther. Water bugs shot across the pond's surface shimmering in morning sun. Sitting down on a log, Mr. Luther wasted no time baiting his hook.

"Cool day. Outta be bitin'."

"Might even catch ol' Big John," I said.

"Whose Big John?" Dad laughed.

"You mean I ain't never told ya 'bout Big John?" I grinned.

Mr. Luther shook his head and smiled that smile of his.

"I BET I KNOW what you're thinkin'." Dad's sudden voice startled me. An unintended shout in the empty room. I grinned at his response. "Didn't the cabinet set right there?"

"Sure did," I sighed. "Pop? Whatever happened to Mr. Luther? I honestly don't remember him after Grandpa died." Dad smiled sadly at my question.

"A year or so after Dad passed away, he came by my office. Said he was movin' up north to live with one of his children. Baltimore, I think. That was the last time I heard from 'im."

"Well one thing's for sure. If there're fishin' holes in Heaven, he and Grandpa are casting their lines out about now." We chuckled softly at the thought.

"Where's the cabinet now?"

"In my study. Filled with rows of dusty books. Walk by it every day and to be honest, I forget it's there."

"Well, I reckon we all take a lot of things for granted," he said, leaning against the wall. "Look at me. Never smoked a day in my life and here I get lung cancer… then there's ya momma." He said, reaching again for his bandana. "I was hopin' this little trip would help some. Been nice to hear her laugh again," he said, his eyes filling. "I think that's what I miss most about her… us… is the laughter."

"Pop…" I started, staring at the floor, then back at him. "Suzie and I been talkin'—"

"Yeah, I know," he interrupted. All my life, I'd looked into Dad's eyes, searching for answers that he always seemed to have. For the first time, his tired lost eyes stared back into mine.

"There's somethin'…" he began, pushing the door closed. "Somethin' I need to tell ya. I guess now's as good a time as any." He swallowed. "I ain't told ya momma yet so this is 'tween me and you," he said, keeping his voice low. "I've decided I'm done with chemo." My chest squeezed tight as I fumbled for words.

"Don't 'cha think we need to discuss this?"

"What's there to discuss? Hell! Chemo ain't helpin' at my age.

Throwin' up for days is worse than the damn disease. I've felt the best today than I have in six months. You know me." he smiled. "I'm gonna live til I die! I'll be fine."

Suzie pushed open the door.

"Hey, y'all 'bout ready to go? Mom's getting tired." Retracing our steps through the house, we paused in the living room where our adventure first began.

"OK, y'all." Suzie announced, thumbing her cell phone. "Let's stand in front of the fireplace." Squeezing together, the four of us smiled as Suzie raised her phone for the obligatory selfie.

Joining in the group smile, I wondered when we last had our picture taken together. Filled with fleeting sunsets and steak dinners, I was sure my cell phone didn't contain a single photo of my aging parents. Hesitating at the front door, we stood in silence.

"That was fun." Mom smiled, walking out as if she were exiting a dress shop. Like a sad child taken from a carousel, Dad, hungry for one more ride, gazed back, surveying the details of the dusty room one last time.

Babies, Bullies and Baseball

Another coughing jag grabbed Dad as he slid into the backseat. Suzie reached inside the cooler, retrieving another bottle of water. "Feels better to sit down," Dad puffed, taking hurried swallows.

"Want to head home?" Suzie asked, backing the car out of the driveway.

"Let's ride by the church while we're out."

Crossing over Fifth Street, we cruised through an older section of town. Lazy rocking chairs and wooden swings relaxed on shady front porches of well-kept century old bungalows. English ivy scaled picketed fences covering defenseless front yards in blankets of thick green.

A handful of cars sat scattered across the blacktopped parking lot of Maybin Baptist Church on the eve of another Sunday service. Blooming annuals and burgeoning azaleas rose from a carpet of brown mulch surrounding the church in a colorful moat. Mom smiled at the beautiful ornate windows lining the sanctuary's wooden exterior.

"Still the prettiest stained glass I ever seen," she sighed. "Sure do miss it."

Turning left at the corner we rode slowly down Third Street, stopping in front of my grandparents' old house. Black patches of mildew splattered the north side of the white vinyl two-story. Several white pickets were missing from the wraparound porch. Gone were the massive oaks that once carpeted the front yard with millions of acorns every fall. A silver and black Harley leaned on its kickstand in the gravel driveway next to an older blue truck.

"Is that Grandpa's Harley?" I winked.

"Not quite his style," Dad chuckled.

"Could be Grandma's. She was always the feisty one," Suzie chimed in.

"I don't know. I imagine her as more of a convertible muscle car type!" I laughed.

A pain shot through my chest seeing a soulless metal outbuilding intruding on the hallowed ground where Grandpa's workshop used to be.

"Who lives there now?" I wondered.

"Don't know. Been sold several times over the years," Dad said, taking another swig from his water bottle. Leaning against the window, Dad offered a few quick selections from his standard menu of embellished childhood tales, including the often-celebrated account of raising a pet squirrel. Having languished through these repetitive narratives my entire life prompted another double dose of guilt. Sooner rather than later, these tired stories that I knew by heart would forever be silenced.

Circling the block like a group of curious tourists, we drifted past the open expanse of a city park where Maybin High School once stood before being demolished in the early 70s. Mom perked up at the dazzling azaleas that formed a multicolor perimeter.

"There's your azaleas Mom!" I pointed.

A tennis foursome scurried across an asphalt court in a spirited rally. Crossed-legged moms conversed on green benches while children chased each other through the plastic tunnels of a huge playground.

"Hey, Suzie Q! Ride by the ball field," Dad directed, with a sudden burst of energy. Our meandering slow turn onto Second Street grabbed the attention of an older woman tending a promising flowerbed. Wiping her forehead, she returned my wave. Leaning forward with her face against the backseat window, Mom offered her hand as well.

Rolling to a stop at a padlocked gate, we peered in amazement through a silver chain link fence framing the open expanse of grass that stretched for two city blocks. Surprisingly, Tiger Field looked nothing like we remembered. Rows of modern stadium lights peered down from mighty steel towers. The ancient wooden grandstand was long gone, replaced with graceless sections of metal bleachers. Barren and unmoving, the pride of old Maybin High School, where countless touchdowns and home runs were scored, sat alone and sad. Seemingly uncomfortable with its modern look.

"Look at that," I said, shocked at the sight before me. "It looks like a brand-new park!"

"Mercifully they tore down the old field house," Dad remarked. "That run-down shack was fallin' apart back when I was in school."

The noon sun ran behind a bank of cotton ball clouds, casting a pale shadow across the deserted baseball diamond. Lazy childhood summers of sweat-soaked T-shirts and tattered baseball gloves returned as I gazed at the infield's coppery sand.

"Oh, if that field could talk," Dad mumbled softly as he stared out over the open ground.

"Amen," I chuckled. "Spent many a summer day playin' youth baseball on that field," I began.

I REMEMBER IT WELL. The summer of '63. The year Mom gave birth to Eddie. The countdown to my little brother's arrival took a heavy toll on our mother. Always the first on Circle Drive to sport the latest women's fashion, Mom poured through pages of *Vogue* and *Vanity Fair*, searching for the perfect look. Unfortunately, Dottie Harrison fell kicking and screaming from the ranks of local trendsetter as her tummy transformation became her most prominent feature.

Fittingly, Edwin Allen Harrison entered the world on the anniversary of D-Day, June 6th, changing our lives forever. The day Dad brought them home from the hospital, Suzie and I watched through the large picture window in the living room. When the green Pontiac appeared we scampered out the back door.

"Hey! I missed you two," Mom smiled from the front seat. Holding a bundled blue blanket, she hugged us with her available arm. Dad reached into the backseat, retrieving her suitcase.

"Ready to meet your little brother? Say 'hey' to little Eddie," she said, pulling open the blanket.

Leaning inside the car, I froze. Snuggled in Mom's arms was the ugliest thing I'd ever seen! With eyes firmly shut, Eddie resembled a giant salmon-colored mole.

"Let's go in the house and I'll let 'cha hold 'im."

Hold him! Are you kidding? I've picked up dead squirrels that looked better! Once inside, Mom took a seat on the couch holding the squirmy rodent.

"Here J.D.," she said, lifting Eddie, blanket and all. "Be gentle, now." My hands shook as I took him in my arms. "Easy now... hold his head up."

Ensuring the blanket maintained a cootie-proof barrier, I gently laid the thing in my lap, balancing the back of his head on my closed knees. Opening one eye, Eddie glared at me like a possessed cat. Ticked that I woke him, his scrunched face turned pinkish red and he began to cry.

"Lift him up, honey," Mom gestured. Laying his tiny chin on my shoulder I held Eddie close to my chest. That did it. As if I'd turned off a light switch, he stopped crying.

"Well now. Aren't you a natural. I think I've found a babysitter!" Suddenly a warm trickling sensation melted through my shirt.

"Git 'im off me! Git 'im off me!"

Calmly, Mom took the diaper off her shoulder and proceeded to push warm spit-up into my favorite Roy Rogers T-shirt, which I promptly threw in the trash can when Mom wasn't looking. Of course, the messy introduction to my baby brother was just a warm-up, so to speak. A few days later, I was scarred for life.

Running into the den from playing outside, I stopped dead in my tracks. With two blue diaper pins wedged between her teeth, Mom mumbled baby talk to her fidgety infant who had just taken the mother of all craps. And there she was. Changing him right there on the den couch! Then I saw it. A nasty mustard-filled diaper that convinced me to swear off the yellow condiment forever.

Up to her elbows in the raw sewage, Mom worked feverishly while Eddie laid on his back, flailing his arms and legs. Then the unthinkable happened. Like an out-of-control water hose, Eddie whizzed right in Mom's face! Surprised, she just laughed about it. Traumatized, I never allowed my mother to kiss me again under any circumstances.

And just like that, my world took a horrible turn. Everything at the Harrison house revolved around little Eddie. No more running, yelling, or slamming doors. The TV was kept constantly on low volume or turned off altogether. Accustomed to a riotous world of constant noise, I spent most of my time playing outside, rarely coming home until dusk. By the time I adjusted to my new routine, my parents finally came to their senses. Leaving me to my own devices for the summer was just too risky. There'd be less neighborhood damage if I were under someone's watchful eye.

Like every other boy in town, I spent most of the summer playing youth baseball at Tiger Field. Convinced that sports would instill important life lessons, my parents firmly believed that baseball would teach me the value of teamwork, fair play, and sportsmanship. What summer baseball really taught me was how to cuss, fight, and if time permitted, play a few games.

Tiger Field, home to Maybin High's football and baseball teams, came alive during the summer, hosting baseball and softball games from early morning to almost midnight. The whole town came out on steamy summer evenings to watch strapping young men and old geezers with beer bellies play fast-pitch softball. Hot humid days found the park crawling with young boys locked in fierce competition on and off the field.

Relieved that I was in the capable and loving hands of Mr. Carson Turner, Mom spent the rest of her summer attending to Eddie's turbulent bowels. Balding with a middle-aged inner tube around his waist, Mr. Turner was in charge of youth baseball, overseeing everything from scheduling games and practice times to umpiring. Happy to get rid of their boisterous kids for a few hours a day, parents rarely showed up at the park. Except for Dicky Mitchell, who ran the concession stand, it was just Mr. Turner and hundreds of screaming boys.

What parents didn't know was that summer baseball at Tiger Field was akin to a daylong prison riot. Like drunken cowboys on a rowdy Saturday night, kids ran wild, looking for trouble. Fights were commonplace and only the strong survived. Unable to police the mayhem, Mr. Turner steered clear of most fights and squabbles unless someone got seriously injured or killed.

Every kid got into a fight at some time or another. Winning or losing wasn't as important as how one handled one's self in the throes of fisticuffs. A worthy performance might win over the masses, avoiding future encounters. There were few rules when it came to these impromptu slugfests. Participants could bleed, cuss, and yell all they wanted, but if anyone broke down and cried, they were finished.

Holding little Eddie in her arms, Mom waved goodbye to me from the front porch as I rode off on my bike with the guys on the first day of baseball practice. First day jitters had us jabbering away, wondering how good our team would be this year. If past performance was any indication, our beloved Southeast Braves would once again finish near the bottom of the standings.

The closer we got to the ballpark, the louder our nervous chatter became. There was, however, another ominous, unspoken motive for our restless babble. Each of us knew full well there was a distinct possibility of getting into a season-ending brawl on the first day of practice.

Last summer our shortstop, Sparky Patterson, broke his hand in an opening day fight and missed the entire season.

Making the turn onto Second Street, we fell in line with other rag-tag ballplayers on their way to the park. Rows of bikes leaned haphazardly near the front gate of a ramshackle wooden fence that surrounded the field. The sounds of excited yells and cracking bats kindled the unstoppable rush as we shuffled inside.

A proper entrance, especially on the first day, was crucial to one's long-term survival. Like busting open the swinging doors of a raucous saloon, a tough first impression might save one from a black eye or busted lip. Swaggering through the gate like a hired gunfighter, I sneered at anyone who dared look my way, dispelling any signs of weakness.

Unfortunately, not everyone strolled into the ballpark that morning with guns drawn. Distinguishing new kids from salty veterans was easy. Huddled nervously in the shadows of the wooden grandstand, a terrified group of kids stared at their unfamiliar surroundings. One boy who looked to be about eight years old made the fatal mistake of wearing a bright orange T-shirt tucked into a brand-new pair of dark blue Wranglers. No doubt his mommy had neatly dressed him that morning before he came to the ball field. Poor kid. He might as well slap a sign on his back that read, "Beat the snot out of me!" Ballpark bullies would smell this kid a mile away.

Although it was still early morning, a line had formed in front of the cinderblock concession stand. The warm smell of buttered popcorn and hotdog chili tempted us as we paraded by. Snow cones were in high demand from early patrons lined up with money in hand.

Leaning on the counter inside the shelter, Tricky Dicky Mitchell, sporting a Saint Louis Cardinals baseball cap and dirty white T-shirt, mumbled something to a kid as he took his order. Three hundred years old and wiry as a steel brush, Dicky's sunken narrow face covered in sweaty gray stubble gave him the painful look of a starving donkey.

Suddenly a commotion near the grandstand shook us from our collective John Wayne impersonations. A circle of boys quickly formed around panicked screams. Oh boy! The first fight of the season! Scampering over, we joined the growing ring of spectators. Squaring off inside the makeshift loop Leon Bright and Kenny Daniels were locked in a vulgar argument as to who would play shortstop for their team this summer.

The curious language of profanity inviting outlandish impossibilities and challenges drew me closer. The hushed crowd hung on every expletive. Listening to their vulgar barbs, I tried to pick up a few pointers. Two foul mouth authorities, Leon and Kenny didn't disappoint. Poetic filth flowed from their tongues in a tirade of obscenities. Rumor had it that Leon had memorized the scandalous lyrics to the song "Louis, Louis."

Catching Kenny off guard, Leon unleashed a tapestry of offensives. Envious of Leon's oration possessing both perfect inflection and style, I listened in awe at the master. Completing his address with just the right quantity of grit and anger, Leon spewed a spitty mist in Kenny's face. Nice touch.

All eyes turned to Kenny, hoping for an equally belligerent retort. Obviously shaken, Kenny felt the heat of fifty waiting eyes. Unable to respond, he spit at Leon and stormed off. It was a watershed moment. In the first contest of the season, Leon had set the bar for profanity at an all-time high. Basking in his victory, Leon blocked playful arm punches from impressed spectators.

After witnessing Leon's amazing performance, I suddenly felt profanely inadequate. Telling people where to go and what to kiss was pretty much the extent of my offensive repertoire. It was high time I visited the field house before I embarrassed myself.

Tucked in a back corner behind overgrown bushes and poison ivy stood the gray wooden field house. Its clapboard exterior hadn't been painted in decades and its door had long since rotted away. Stepping inside, I almost puked at the sour blend of sweat and pee. Two naked light bulbs hung from the ceiling. Wooden benches crisscrossed the cracked cement floor. A boy carelessly aimed from three feet away at one of the urinals. Peering from a haunting corner sat a clogged-up toilet filled to the brim with a vile mixture of brown horror. Staring at the porcelain god's gaping mouth, I knew it was just a matter of time before some unfortunate kid's head would be forced into that hellhole in a shocking baptism that occurred at least once a week.

Along with several other curious patrons seeking to brush up on their vocabulary, I squinted at the crude markings on the dingy walls. Every inch of the field house's rustic interior was plastered with every expletive known to man. As if looking at fine art, I studied the sacred sayings, carved verses, and stick pictures. Every school year before the start of football season, an embarrassed Principal Shambley ordered the walls painted a bright white, temporarily erasing the vulgarity. Presented with a fresh canvas gifted bards and artists applied their trade and in no time, the walls were once again covered in filth.

Running my fingers over the splintery surface, I searched closely, looking for Leon's impressive outburst. Discovering several of his quotes near a nasty sink whose water had been permanently cut off, I spent several minutes in deep concentration. After a few rehearsals, I felt confident that I could humiliate Lucifer himself!

Shielding my eyes, I exited the field house into the blinding sun. The first day spectacle of organized chaos was well underway. Coaches ushered confused players to their assigned teams and practice fields. Standing next to a rusty burn barrel, our pathetic coach, Dennis "The Menace" Strong, yelled at our team. A pimply-faced tenth grader who constantly scratched his butt, Dennis' vast knowledge of baseball could easily fit inside a small thimble with plenty of room for a finger or two. I hurried over just as Coach Dennis concluded his inspirational scream.

"All right! Listen up you bunch of weenies! Get your sorry asses to the south diamond and make it snappy!" After a few hours of shagging fly balls and fielding grounders, most kids headed for the exit, thankful to have survived the first day. Along with other thrill seekers, Billy Ray, Skeeter, and I stuck around the park eating hotdogs and watching other teams practice, hoping a fight would break out.

Grabbing two hotdogs all the way and a Pepsi from Tricky Dicky, I took a seat with the guys under the covered grandstand. Beyond the chicken wire screen in front of us, Stevie Guthrie's twelve-year-old team, the Northwest Rangers, practiced on the big diamond, where the big games were played.

Tall and lanky with a blond crew cut, Stevie was the best shortstop ever to grace Tiger Field and could hit a ball a country mile. Admired by all, Stevie had been declared the unspoken guardian and protector of younger kids, keeping goons like Buster Carmichael in check.

A broad-shouldered chunky twelve-year-old, Buster, the bully of bullies, had terrorized summer baseball for as long as I could remember. A foot taller than most kids, Buster's monstrous size was quite imposing. With his black hair slicked back in a greasy ducktail, he resembled a deranged Elvis Presley.

Like a badland's gunslinger, Buster strutted around the park searching for weak victims to devour. The ongoing feud between Buster and Stevie was the highlight of summer baseball. The ultimate clash between good and evil, waiting to erupt, hung over the park like an approaching thunderstorm. Day after day both of them simmered in the hot sun until neither could stand it any longer, facing off in a winner-take-all bout.

Sitting with others on the bleachers, I was about to take another bite from my hotdog when loud shouts came from behind the grandstand. Boys backed away, making a path. Emerging from the shadows of the stands, Buster strutted along, carrying a kid over his shoulder like a sack of feed. I couldn't miss the bright orange T-shirt and new pair of Wranglers.

"Put me down," screamed his victim, beating Buster on the back with his fists. We found out later the boy's name was Jimmy Bullard. The snickering crowd trailing behind knew exactly where Buster was headed. Scrambling down the bleachers, we fell in with the raucous mob.

As expected, Buster disappeared with his screaming victim through the open field house door. By the time we got there, the baptism was over. Pushing his way through the crowd, Jimmy burst from the field house. His orange T-shirt now stained a nasty coffee brown. Coughing and crying, the young boy ran through the park and out the front gate.

At first, the nasty ceremonies were funny, but over the years they'd lost their luster. No one said anything as the crowd dispersed, wondering who might be next.

I figured we'd seen the last of the little boy in the bright orange shirt following his hideous induction into the Toilet Bowl Hall of Fame. Most rookies who experienced the baptism were too embarrassed or scared to come back. To my surprise, Jimmy showed up the next morning with baseball glove in hand. Sporting an untucked low key T-shirt,

Jimmy strutted into the park like he owned the place. I had to hand it to him. The boy had guts.

After a couple of weeks of boring practices and scrimmage games, I thought our team looked pretty good. Fresh off two victories, we were excited to be playing our next practice game on the big diamond. Leaning on the dugout fence, we were joking with each other when the team we were about to play came strolling up.

"Hey Billy Ray! Ready for a butt kickin'?"

I didn't have to turn around to discover the identity of the lame-brain running his mouth. Everyone knew the annoying screechy voice of Darrell Kirkland who sounded like an angry blue jay.

"Only butt that's gonna get whooped is yours!" Billy Ray retorted.

"Oh yeah?"

"Yeah!"

"Says who?"

"Says me!"

While Billy Ray and Darrell continued their stimulating discussion, I turned around to find Wally Keck staring up at me. A pathetic weasel, Wally stood four feet tall on his tiptoes and weighed about four hundred and fifty pounds. He was so chubby he had to hit the ball to the fence just to leg out a single. A Buster Carmichael wannabe, Wally's modus operandi was sneaking up behind unsuspecting victims, pushing them to the ground, and sitting on them until they gave him money for candy. Once, after a morning of rotund extortion, Wally stole enough money from other kids to buy every pack of SweeTarts from the concession stand.

"What 'chu lookin' at butthead?" He sneered.

"I'm... not sure."

I didn't want to get into it with Wally, but when he pushed me against the dugout fence, I had no choice. From observing the plump southpaw in previous scuffles, I knew Wally always went for an early belly punch. It happened in a flash. Wally yelled something about my mother, rared back, and went for my gut. Sidestepping his sluggish swing, I hauled off and punched him as hard as I could in the left ear. Grabbing the side of his head, Wally called me a name I'd never heard before and stormed off. Like most ballpark fights, it was over in a few seconds. From the smirking faces of my teammates, I knew I'd won significant style points.

A few days later our team was just finishing up practice when some kid came running up.

"Hey y'all!" He panted, out of breath. "Stevie and Buster... they gonna fight... in The Ring!" Dropping our gloves, the team bolted from the practice field. Even Coach Dennis joined the fray. We couldn't believe it. It was only mid-June. The earliest Stevie and Buster had ever fought. Usually, they didn't tangle until late July!

By the time we reached the concession stand, a huge crowd had already formed in a makeshift circle. The Ring, as everyone called it, was an out of the way spot hidden behind the grandstand. Littered with cigarette butts and candy wrappers, the barren dusty swath was reserved for serious bouts only. A playful air of excitement rippled through the raucous crowd that stood three deep. Billy Ray, Skeeter, and I managed to score a spot next to an overflowing trash can teeming with yellow jackets.

A wild cheer arose when Stevie stepped inside the antsy ring of spectators. Loosening up, Stevie rolled his arms in rapid windmills to "attaboy" shouts from adoring fans. Crawling out from the shadows of the grandstand like a snake, Buster slithered into The Ring to a smattering of boos. Meshing his fingers, Buster cracked his knuckles, sneering at his opponent. Motionless, both combatants began the all-important prefight ritual of staring each other down. A tense hush fell over the crowd.

Like gunfighters in a western, Stevie and Buster slowly marched toward each other. Wild shouts echoed through the park, growing louder with every step. As if on cue, the two stopped ten feet apart. Stevie suddenly hesitated. Cocking his head, he backed away. Confused spectators squirmed in disbelief. Oh, my gosh! Was Stevie Guthrie, protector of the free world, backing down?

Smiling to the crowd behind him, Stevie raised his hand and beckoned. A gasp rose as a small figure stepped into The Ring wearing a bright orange T-shirt and new Wranglers. Like David and Goliath, Jimmy swaggered straight for Buster. Pausing only a few feet away, Buster towered over Jimmy like a giant grizzly.

"What 'chu gonna do, ya little shrimp?" Buster snickered. A satisfying grin washed over Jimmy's face.

"*Git 'em!*" Jimmy yelled. Suddenly the crowd bolted, collapsing on Buster like a breaking wave. Pushing him to the ground, kids rushed in from all sides seeking a piece of the action. Joining the crazed mob, I grabbed Buster's jerking right leg.

"*Lemme go!*" Screaming and cussing, Buster bucked like a wild calf. Turning the tyrant over on his belly, we lifted him off the ground. No one thought to bring along flaming torches or pitchforks. Stevie grabbed Buster in a headlock.

"Hey Buster. You're sweatin'. Let's go wash your face!"

"*No! No! Lemme go!*"

Of all those wondrous summers spent at Tiger Field, I'd never seen anything like it. An exhilarating and liberating moment. Tired of living in fear, the riotous mob had taken all they could from Buster Carmichael. Advancing to cheers and applause, we paraded the doomed prisoner past the concession stand where Tricky Dicky gave an eager thumbs up. Suddenly Mr. Turner appeared out of nowhere. Our spirited procession came to an unexpected halt.

"Mr. Turner! Mr. Turner! Make them lemme go!" Buster yelled, trying his best to break free. Realizing what was about to happen, Mr. Turner glared at the parade for a moment. Slowly a wide grin stretched across his face. Turning around as if he didn't see us, he quickly walked away.

"*No! No!* Mr. Turner! Help me!"

Having lost his final appeal, Buster committed the unthinkable and began to cry. It was over. We could have dropped the whiny rat right then and there. The bully of bullies had openly wept in front of his accusers. Of course, that made the trek to the death chamber that much more entertaining.

An enthusiastic line formed on both sides of the dirt path leading to the entrance of the field house. Navigating Buster's squirming body through the open door, we carried him inside the muggy room packed with onlookers. Jimmy, the happy executioner, waited next to the porcelain basin. The crowd relented as Stevie forced Buster to his knees in an unyielding headlock. Realizing there was no way out, Buster begged for his life.

"No, you can't do this! Stop it!"

"Pretend it's chocolate milk!" chuckled Stevie.

Stepping forward to do the honors, Jimmy grabbed the back of Buster's trembling neck in one hand and a handful of greasy hair in the other. With all the strength he could muster, Jimmy stuffed Buster's horrified face into the brown murky slime that surged over the rim in a disgusting fecal tidal wave. Holding him under for a second or two, Jimmy eased up.

Exploding from the muck, Buster's oily head resembled a slick Tootsie Pop!

"How 'bout another!" Jimmy laughed, ramming Buster's head again into the vile mixture. Coming up a second time, Buster threw his matted hair back, slinging wet excrement on the fervent crowd. Coughing and spitting with his eyes tightly shut, Buster tried to speak. Before he could say anything, Jimmy pressed again.

"One more time!"

After the third plunge, Buster came up choking. Stevie released the soaked prisoner who slumped to the floor. Unsure if Buster would come up swinging, the cautious crowd backed away. Coated in brown sludge, Buster scrambled to his feet, only to slip and fall to the wild approval of the bloodthirsty mob. Regaining his balance he staggered out the door. That was the last time we ever saw the likes of Buster Carmichael.

After the "Great Baptism," as it became known, things were much different around Tiger Field. There were the occasional fights and scuffles, but no one dared to step forward to fill Buster's sewage-soaked shoes. With Buster out of the way, everyone's attention turned to the last few practice games and the official start of the season.

Whether the venue is the hallowed confines of Yankee Stadium or some dusty country pasture with feed sack bases, every ballpark has its legends. Over the years, Tiger Field produced its share of fabled players whose athletic prowess, embellished with time, were on the lips of every kid who stepped on the diamond.

By far, the greatest player in the history of summer baseball was Delbert Swinney. Six-foot-tall and thin as a rail, it was believed that

Delbert was around fourteen years old, but rumor had it he was going on sixteen. He'd failed so many grades over the years, no one truly knew Delbert's real age. Somebody said he was already shaving.

A lanky redhead with a million freckles, Delbert didn't cast much of an imposing figure, except for those terrifying moments when he stood on the pitcher's mound gripping a baseball in his left hand. The gangly southpaw didn't possess a diverse pitching repertoire, but he didn't need one. The only pitch Delbert had mastered was a Mach four fastball that blew by hitters in a high-pitched hiss.

Eric Wells, a wiry kid who held summer baseball's record for stolen bases, was the only batter that ever got a hit off the flaming left-hander. Able to retrieve the treasured ball from Mr. Turner, Eric kept it under lock and key in a display case in his bedroom.

Delbert pitched for the feared Southwest Cowboys, a team of rag-tag ruffians who grew up in the tough streets around the ballpark. Faceless brutes who'd just as soon smack the crap out of you as look at you. If every one of them didn't end up in prison, they just might make it one day in the big leagues.

When Delbert took the mound, crowds packed the bleachers. Curious spectators weren't there in hopes of witnessing another base hit miracle against Delbert's flaming fastball. What the masses came to see was the outside chance that Delbert might uncork a wild pitch and accidentally hit and kill a batter.

No one had any idea what would happen if a kid were struck by one of Delbert's lethal pitches. It had never happened. Not yet anyway. Thank God Delbert's team played in the twelve-year-old age group. Still, strange and unexplained events occur during summer baseball that defy human understanding.

The morning was hot and steamy. Westward clouds warned of a brewing thunderstorm. Everyone was excited. The last of the scrimmage games would be played that morning before the season officially began tomorrow. Sweat filled my eyes as our team warmed up. Thrilled to be playing our last practice game on the big diamond, we joked and teased each other, knowing rival teams would be watching from the grandstand. Coach Dennis called us together in the dugout for a pregame pep talk and broke the news.

"Boys!" Dennis always called us "boys." Not "men," not "team," just "boys." Like we were sniveling brats crawling on the floor surrounded by mounds of Play-Doh.

"Today I have a challenge for you. Challenges… uh… make us great players." Clearing his throat, Dennis groped for words. "Boys. This is our last scrimmage before the season starts… so… to see how good we are… we're goin' to play the Southwest Cowboys. This should get us primed and ready for the season."

Expecting him to say we were going to play some cupcake team, it took a few seconds for Dennis' words to register in our feeble brains. *The Southwest Cowboys! That's Delbert Swinney's team!* I suddenly realized that *we* were the designated cupcake team!

For the first time in his life, Coach Dennis had been right about something. We *were* a bunch of little boys. *About to become dead little boys!* Panic spread down the bench. Our third baseman Roger Scott threw up in his glove. Skippy White and Gene Sneed jumped off the bench, sprinted from the dugout and out the front gate of the ballpark. Disgusted, Coach Dennis cowered over us as we trembled in fear.

"Listen here ya bunch of babies! I know they're older and they have Delbert, but don't tell me y'all are *skeered!*" The puddles under the bench weren't the results of a morning shower! Why would anyone in their right mind concoct such a murderous idea? I'll admit, there remained a very remote possibility the slaughter might prove just how good our team was, but there was a much greater chance that the massacre would maim us as young children. Whatever the motive, Dennis "the Menace" Strong had finally gone over the edge. Scratched his butt and sniffed the evidence one too many times.

A master of inspiration, Coach Dennis yelled insults that nobody heard. Stunned and glassy-eyed, we all wished were someplace else as our entire lives passed before us. I thought about the Christmas that I got a go-kart and the fun times fishing with Grandpa and Mr. Luther. Thanksgiving mornings hunting with Dad. It had been a good life; short, but good.

Looking up and down the bench, I studied the faces of the condemned as Coach Dennis strolled to home plate, giving Mr. Turner our lineup and the names of our next of kin. At the far end of the dugout, Petey Moon blew a fat bubble from a mouth full of bubble gum. His black P.F. Flyers swung back and forth under the bench as if he were running in place.

Petey was the one kid on the team who couldn't hit a baseball if it were the size of a watermelon. Whenever our team got a big lead, Coach Dennis would stick Petey in right field and pray nobody hit the ball to him.

The idea came to me in a flash. *Hey! Why don't we sacrifice Petey!* Make him bat first. Maybe Delbert will unleash a screaming fastball upside his head. With a headless ten-year-old lying dead at the plate, surely Mr. Turner would stop the game. We'd all live!

Petey's eyes met mine. The bubble popped, cloaking his smirking lips in a shroud of pink. Petey knew good and well that he didn't have a snowball's chance in hell of getting into the ball game. He'd watch the carnage from the safety of the dugout. After the mindless slaughter he'd go home on his bike instead of stuffed in a body bag.

All activity at the ballpark ceased. Tricky Dicky closed the concession stand and climbed into the bleachers with a toothless grin. Like bloodthirsty Romans entering the Colosseum, teams and coaches gleefully filled the bleachers to witness the massacre.

"Play ball," shouted Mr. Turner, taking his umpire position behind home plate. Delbert strolled to the mound while the rest of the Southwest Cowboys charged the field. The usual false chatter of "attaboy" and "here we go" that preceded most games, morphed into tearful whispers of the Lord's Prayer.

Glaring from the mound, Delbert repeatedly threw the russet-colored baseball into his glove, waiting for his first victim. Leadoff hitter Marshall Wyatt would be the first to die. Trembling from head to toe, he shuffled towards home plate like the Cowardly Lion. Tears streamed down his cheeks.

Delbert went through his standard ritual, pinning his glove under his left armpit while rubbing the ball down in his hands. Violently kicking the dirt around the pitching rubber, he looked like an angry bull ready to charge. Pausing for effect, Delbert grinned at Marshall, revealing a mouthful of green teeth. With the bat on his shoulders, Marshall stood at the plate shaking like a jackhammer.

Starting his windup Delbert pulled his skinny right leg tight to his chest. With his left hand cocked back behind his head, Delbert's whole body exploded toward the plate. The smoking rocket sizzled through the air, breaking all laws of physics, bursting like a shotgun blast in the catcher's mitt.

Swinging at everything Delbert threw, Marshall thankfully struck out on three pitches. Slinking back to the dugout, he pointed to the heavens, giving thanks. Delbert retired the side on nine blistering fast-balls and our team gleefully took the field.

For the time being, we were safe from Delbert's powerful arm and if I had anything to do with it, we'd stay in the field till next Tuesday. Regrettably, as Delbert's counterpart for the Southeast Braves, I reluctantly lumbered my way to the mound. Any other time I'd step on the pitching rubber, dreaming for a moment, of standing before a sellout crowd in Yankee Stadium, reveling in thunderous applause and wild cheers as my name was announced as starting pitcher. Dizzy Dean and Pee Wee Reese were up in the broadcast booth, calling the play by play to fifty million television viewers. Today, however, I had no such aspirations.

There was absolutely nothing fast about my fastball. My sorry excuse for a pitch moved at such a snail's pace, batters could count the seams as the ball glided towards the plate. After watching Delbert hurl blistering rockets at frightened hitters, I wondered how impressed the spectators would be with my pathetic toss. It didn't take long to find out. The Cowboys hit me like a rented mule. After batting around twice without an out, Mr. Turner motioned to our team to come in and bat.

Jackie Booker led off the top of the second. Although he couldn't catch a cold in the outfield, Jackie could smack the fire out of a baseball. Much to his misfortune, he was also a natural born smartass. Strutting towards the batter's box like a barnyard rooster, Jackie yelled junk at Delbert. I had to admire him. Witnessing the last painful moments of his short life, I thought how much I had enjoyed playing ball with him. Holding his hand up to call time, Jackie stepped out of the batter's box, calmly taking a few practice swings. A real pro. I was determined to remember him that way.

Swinging at Delbert's first pitch, Jackie fouled the ball to the back-stop. Our bench erupted. The crowd in the grandstand gasped in surprise. Jackie Booker had drawn wood on a Delbert Swinney fastball!

"Attaboy Jackie! Come on! You can do it!" I yelled.

Amazingly, Jackie hung in, working Delbert to a full count. Our team leaned nervously on the dugout fence, wondering if, by some miracle, we were witnessing history. Then it happened. The crack of the bat sent our whole team jumping. A slow dribbler crawled to the second baseman who flipped the ball to first base for the easy out. Our dugout emptied. Running onto the field, we surrounded Jackie in celebration as if he'd hit a grand slam.

When it came my turn to face the Grim Reaper, I stumbled to the plate as if I were walking the plank of a pirate ship. As I approached the batter's box, catcher Lee Nash lifted his catcher's mask and spit on the ground.

"You throw like a sissy, Harrison."

I was both honored and extremely frightened that Lee Nash actually knew my last name. Anybody who could crouch behind home plate and catch Delbert Swinney's fastballs had to be tough as nails.

"Thanks Mr. Nash," I muttered with a silly smile.

Delbert shot me his patented stare before going into his windup. Raring back, he unleashed a pitch that I never saw but distinctly heard. The high-pitched shriek of the projectile whistled by my head, exploding into Lee's mitt. Swinging purely in self-defense, I took a cut.

"Strike one!" yelled Mr. Turner.

OK. Only two more! Wasting no time, Delbert loaded and fired another missile. This time I was ready. Swinging the bat before Delbert let go of the ball and twice more for good measure, I missed everything. Twisting out of the batter's box, I lost my balance and fell down.

"Strike two!"

Taking a deep breath I braced for another pitch. So far, Delbert had been accurate, but I wasn't about to take any chances. Halfway out of the batter's box, I swung wildly as the third pitch sizzled by.

"Strike three!"

The grandstand howled at my pathetic performance. I didn't care. Feeling the warm sunshine on my face, I skipped back to the dugout, happy to be alive. Passing me on his way to the plate, Skeeter sleep-walked by me like I wasn't there. With prayerful fingers crossed, our team watched as Skeeter stepped inside the batter's box. Even Coach Dennis seemed mildly concerned. At fifty pounds soaking wet, Skeeter was so skinny Delbert Swinney's fastball might cut him slap in two! Standing in the box with his eyes shut, Skeeter's stringy legs shook like spaghetti noodles in a tornado.

Delbert's first pitch sailed off course, hitting the ground five feet in front of the plate. The sizzling ball bounced off the dirt, nicking Skeeter's pants on its way to the backstop.

"*AAAAAAGGGGH!*" Skeeter yelled, spinning around and diving to the dirt. It was, by far, the grandest display of blatant cowardice I'd ever witnessed. Rolling on the ground from side to side, Skeeter grabbed his right leg in agony, screaming his head off. Calling time, Mr. Turner stepped out from behind the plate.

"Y'all come git 'im," he mumbled, shaking his head at Skeeter's spineless behavior. Milking it for all it was worth, Skeeter put his arm around my shoulder and limped off the field as if his leg was severed. Laughing under his breath to a nice round of applause, he hobbled on one leg until he reached the bench.

After another embarrassing inning, Mr. Turner mercifully ended the game. I'm not sure how many runs the Cowboys scored that day;

certainly more than any of us could count. Surprisingly, nobody was killed or maimed, including Skeeter, who made a remarkable recovery after the game.

Huddling in the dugout, we laughed at ourselves. Like soldiers who'd survived a suicide charge, we'd lived to fight again. It was a moment that would live with us forever. The day the Southeast Braves faced down the legend himself, Delbert Swinney, and lived to tell about it.

THE SUN REAPPEARED, BATHING the field once again in bright light. I pictured a tall lanky redhead walking off the mound as a team of excited little boys danced in the opposing dugout.

Dad recalled the usual stories of his high school days on the gridiron, including one where a brawl broke out during a game. In the confusion, Dad accidentally slugged Principal Shambley, who had taken the field to stop the fight.

"I don't know about y'all, but I'm gettin' a little hungry," Suzie mumbled.

"I could eat a little somethin' myself," Dad answered. "How 'bout you, Momma?"

"That's fine."

"I know just the place." I smiled.

The Eyes of Sissy Ledbetter

Waiting for the light to change at the busy intersection of Fifth and Main, I studied the weathered brick exterior of what used to be Knight's Furniture Company, wondering if I were truly seeing the giant building for the first time. Like most things growing up, I never paid that much attention. The bustling three-story complex had towered over downtown forever and I figured it always would. An immortal and unchanging fortress whose benevolent spirit wrapped Maybin in a comforting blanket of assurance and promise. The prominent smokestack that bellowed charcoal-colored clouds over the town had long since disappeared, along with the green blanket of English ivy that consumed its west wall.

Converted to upscale apartments after the plant closed in the 90s, its gigantic windows that once spotlighted an army of sweaty workers, including my grandfather, stood shamefully embellished with flowerpots and various knickknacks. Another slice of Maybin's soul swallowed by time.

Turning right, we followed a miniature traffic jam down Main Street to the edge of town. The familiar neon sign displaying a smiling pink pig atop a one level brick building appeared in the distance. After all these years, The Grill's enduring parking lot remained a rutty expanse of dusty gravel. Somehow the local eatery had survived the onslaught of plant closures and restaurant chains. Blue smoke drifted from the weathered brick chimney filling the air with the sweet aroma of barbecue.

"That's what Heaven smells like," Dad said, taking Mom's hand as he closed the car door.

"Amen to that!" I chimed in.

Garbled conversation and clanging glassware met us at the door. A row of hunched backs and propped elbows sat bunched together at the lengthy lunch counter. The cavernous dining room hadn't changed much since I was a kid, still possessing its greasy blue-collar charm. Yellowed portraits of cowboys and cattle drives hung askew on amber knotty pine walls. Booths decorated with plastic checkerboard tablecloths sat crammed against scruffy chair rail brandishing wounds from decades of abuse. The unsteady blades of two out of sync ceiling fans twirled lazily overhead. A stained cardboard sign taped to the side of the bar read: "Seat yourself."

Mom glanced around the cluttered room, trying to convince herself that she knew the place. A white-haired man in suspendered trousers, leaning on a cane, recognized Dad. While the two of them compared ailments, I thought of my first summer job in high school. Wearing a white apron and folded paper hat that displayed a red Coca-Cola logo, I'd once flipped burgers behind this same counter.

A muddled cork message board peppered with a thousand pushpin business cards hung beside last year's wall calendar. Seemingly out of place on the scrambled panel, a colorful flyer caught my attention. An array of hand-drawn flowers and ribbons framed the brilliant red lettering. A masterpiece only a schoolteacher could have perfected.

SOUTH MAYBIN ELEMENTARY ANNUAL SPRING FLING
FRIDAY NIGHT, MAY 6TH
THE FUN BEGINS AT 6:00!

Why the flyer brought the treasured memory to life, I don't know. Maybe it was the exaggerated calligraphy reminding me of scribbled notes we passed in class when the teacher wasn't looking. I shook with laughter.

"What's the story this time? Human sacrifice?" Suzie whispered.

"Tell ya when we sit down."

Sliding into an empty booth on the back wall, we didn't bother opening the same oily menus that hadn't changed in seventy years. The familiar rush of The Grill's syrupy sweet tea pouring into our red plastic glasses stirred its own set of fond memories. I always felt the local diner's supercharged version of this southern staple should be served with a warning label. Strong and sweet, a single glass of the maple-colored liquid contained enough caffeine to inspire an impromptu triathlon in the sleepiest of customers.

"I sure have missed this," Dad said, chugging half a glass before coming up for air. Settling in with barbecue sandwiches, hushpuppies, and endless refills of the aforementioned incendiary beverage, we picked up where we left off. Stories opened forgotten doors, revealing cherished nuggets of time. The "spring fling" flyer got me started.

THE WANING DAYS OF that remarkable summer found me at the pinnacle of my game, if ten-year-olds can achieve such a thing. All was right with the world on hot sultry days sprinting through the underbrush of Ashley Woods, chasing my friends in glorious games of Ambush. A rising and sophisticated fifth grader, I stood primed and ready to join the coveted ranks of South Maybin Elementary's fashionable Big Kid Fraternity. Standing atop the mountain, surveying my untouchable kingdom, I had no idea that in a few short weeks, events and situations would enter my life, forever altering its course.

On the eve of another school year, I huddled in the den with my parents, enduring yet another stupid School Summit. Laughing inside, I suffered through Mom's standard warnings and threats with surprising composure. I was a fifth grader for goodness' sake. I didn't need her silly advice.

Discovering Miss Hawks would be my teacher, I knew my final year at South Maybin would be a cakewalk. A moderate when it came to punishment, Miss Hawks was one of those "cool" teachers who wanted to be everybody's best friend. A trait I planned to exploit every chance I could.

The next morning, I strutted through the front doors of South Maybin proudly brandishing an arrogant preteen swagger. Thankfully this would be my last year at this pathetic kiddie school before Junior High came calling. Cologne and deodorant were just around the corner.

Passing other children in the hall, I sensed something was very different. The moment I set foot in my classroom I knew things had changed. Although my dopey Ambush squad looked dumb as ever, I had to admit that the girls in class seemed the prettiest they'd ever been. Having spent the past four years of school suffering through their bizarre and unusual customs, I couldn't understand why in the world they looked so... well... cute! I cringed at my revelation.

There were a million reasons for my concern regarding this unusual observation. First of all, girls were just plain weird. And of course, there was the ever present "Cootie Question." No one really knew what cooties were, but with a name that disgusting, the frightening and peculiar condition everyone feared had to be awful. Cautiously, with mild curiosity, both sexes observed the other from a safe distance.

And that's the way it had always been. A neat and tidy arrangement with discernible limits and parameters that no one in their right mind would dare infringe. Just as we were getting settled into the new school year, my rather naïve perception of the world quickly turned upside down.

Out of nowhere, a sudden and unnatural metamorphosis consumed the entire fifth-grade. I watched in horror as smitten boys lost their collective minds in the presence of giggling girls. Sacrificing every ounce of dignity, guys who'd loathed the opposite sex their entire lives became babbling idiots in the presence of cute dresses and prissy hair bows. Boys who'd once pulled stringy pigtails and laughed about it suddenly turned into goofy morons. With their "showoff buttons" firmly pushed, enamored daredevils risked bodily injury in exchange for a simple smile.

Before I knew it, South Maybin Elementary went to hell in a handbasket. Palpable excitement gripped the playground as kids huddled together, feverishly whispering about the latest smitten couple. Of course, this despicable decline in moral standards only strengthened the squad's resolve. We were soldiers with tough-guy images to protect. Girls would not be tolerated!

I knew the rules and had every intention of following them to the letter. But with temptation lurking around every corner, I found myself gazing at girls more and more. A rather disgusting trait that I just couldn't shake for the life of me. After weeks of secretly peeping I'd become quite the master, perfectly disguising my stolen glances. Of course, this strange addiction would have to remain a deep dark secret. There was no way in the world I could ever admit my horrible sin to the guys. I'd never hear the end of it. I might even get kicked out of the squad. Banished from playing Ambush forever.

For a few weeks, I successfully kept my feelings bundled up inside until one fateful day at recess. Everyone had gathered for a few minutes of freedom under the big oak that stood behind the school. A rallying point for kids who played under its dappled branches, the big oak became the perfect base for games of tag or a goal line for quick games of football.

Standing by the tree minding my own business, I had just taken a bite of my Nutty Buddy when several girls marched up the hill. As she passed me, Brenda Wells looked straight into my eyes and started laughing. In some ways it wasn't that surprising. Why kids stared at me and laughed was something I never fully understood. A simple indignity I'd gotten used to over the years.

But there was something different about her playful snicker. Dang if her cute giggle didn't run me up a wall for some reason. Unsure of how to respond, I broke out into an uncontrolled chuckle of my own. Pausing, Brenda cocked her head, smiled, and waved at me. Suddenly my knees began shaking. Her laugh haunted me the rest of the day.

At recess the next afternoon, Brenda and her girlfriends turned and walked straight towards me. Just like yesterday. Taking a deep breath, I smiled and waved as she passed by. Ignoring me as if I were a discarded candy wrapper, Brenda strutted right past me. No smile, no wave, no interest. I was right. Girls are weird!

Then out of nowhere, the Chester Beasley Incident, as it became known, changed everything. A truly intolerable fifth grader, Chester proudly served as South Maybin's chief tormentor of anything female. Short, stocky, and rough as a cob, Chester was the youngest of eight children who lived on a dairy farm. His dirty blonde hair stayed plastered down with so much Brylcreem that a Category Five hurricane couldn't muster a single waxy strand out of place. A master of improvisation, some of his best work occurred at lunch and recess when no girl was safe from pulled hair or dead bugs in her chair.

One morning, as the class tolerated Miss Hawks' southern nasal twang, I glanced over at Chester. From the sneaky smirk on his face, I knew something was up. Reaching into his ratty jean pocket, he produced a piece of bubble gum: a Class A felony! It was better to be caught with an open can of beer than a stick of spearmint! While the girls sat hypnotized by Miss Hawks' every word, the guys elbowed each other as the master went to work.

Unfortunately for her, Diane Smith sat directly in front of the monster. Sitting attentively with pencil in hand, she stared straight ahead, captivated by the mind-numbing lesson. Her long brown hair draped over her shoulders, falling across the back of her chair. Chewing the gum to the proper consistency, Chester pulled the slick wad out of his mouth. With surgeon-like precision, he bonded Diane's hair to the back of her seat. She never felt a thing. In gleeful anticipation, we waited.

"Miss Hawks? Can I sharpen my pencil please?"

"Yes, Diane."

Twirling her legs around into the aisle, Diane attempted to stand. A painful scream quickly followed as she fell back into her seat. We lost it. It was the funniest thing I'd ever seen! Of course, Chester was taken to the office and beaten senseless.

It wasn't a week after Chester's exciting demonstration of the countless applications of bubble gum that our class was enjoying a sunny afternoon at recess. We'd gathered for a quick game of football using a crushed paper cup. Chester was missing. Hunting for our prized tight end, Skeeter and I spotted him under the big oak. Standing next to the demon was Diane, sporting a shorter hair cut after the bubble-gum episode.

"Look Skeeter! Poor Diane's gonna git it again!" I laughed. From a distance, Skeeter and I took it all in. Smiling sweetly at his victim, Chester slumped forward with his thumbs stuck inside his belt loops. Nervously kicking the ground with his filthy brogans, he dropped his head. *What an actor! Let's see. Will he knock the popsicle out of her hand or kick dirt on those shiny black shoes?*

Suddenly Chester raised his arm towards Diane. This is it! Here he goes! Without warning, Chester grabbed Diane's hand.

"Oh my gosh! He's gonna throw her down the hill!" Skeeter gasped.

After a few awkward seconds, nothing happened. Twisting in place, Diane flashed a blushing grin. Unable to comprehend the moment, Skeeter and I stood there like a couple of garden statues. No way! Chester Beasley and Diane Smith were holding hands. On purpose!

Distraught, both of us lumbered back to the classroom, our heads hung in defeat. Word of Chester's conversion spread like a raging wildfire. Morale at South Maybin hit an all-time low. The passing of our fearless leader left us nothing to believe in. All hope was gone.

Chester's tragic fall from grace somehow triggered other despicable acts. There were confirmed reports of other boys and girls holding hands and several eyewitness accounts of couples kissing. On the mouth!

The big oak quickly transformed into a cheesy Lover's Lane where couples met, stole kisses, and carved their initials in the tree's massive trunk. Incredibly, cooties' strange and mystical powers magically disappeared. Shot down for all time by Cupid's flaming arrows. Every day, someone I knew lost his soul to an alluring female. And I had been worried about the prospect of nuclear annihilation.

With innocent children dropping like flies, the nauseating epidemic eventually reached the unreachable. Junior Kenyon, an Ambush legend possessing nerves of steel, a boy I'd fought beside since I was seven, became the next casualty. The day he and Linda Sue Hunsucker were caught holding hands outside the cafeteria shook our squad to the core. A secret meeting was held to discuss the proper punishment. Debating his immediate court-martial, we decided instead to make Junior's life a living hell. Another stern example to would-be defectors who might contemplate the same twisted evil. Embarrassing him at every turn, we tried our best to break him. The walk home after school became prime time for abuse.

"Everybody meetin' up later for Ambush?" I asked as we made the turn onto South Third Street.

"Gotta mow the yard then I'll be over," Skeeter sighed.

"Hey Junior? You playin' or writin' love letters?" taunted Billy Ray. "Better call Linda Sue. Make sure ya can play. Wouldn't want to make ya sweetie mad!" As he did during every blistering attack, Junior bit his lip and took it. Without the slightest rebuttal, he trudged along staring down at the street.

The next day, below the constant hum of the lunchroom, we pounced on him full force. Still in the early stages of courtship, Junior and Linda Sue hadn't mustered the courage to sit together during lunch. True love took time. Sitting at an adjacent table with Sissy Ledbetter and Wanda Gail Taylor, Linda Sue stole glances at Junior. Billy Ray started the silly song.

"Junior and Linda sittin' in a tree." The rest of us joined in, keeping our voices low.

"K-I-S-S-I-N-G."

"First comes love, then comes marriage."

"Here comes Linda with a baby carriage!"

Bowing her head in embarrassment, Linda Sue gazed down at her lap while Junior ignored the teasing and kept eating.

We'd just finished the song when Miss Hawks stood up from the teachers' table, signaling it was time to return to class. The sound of grinding chairs erupted as everyone bolted for the trash cans. Locked in our daily competition to avoid being the last one to dump their tray, we pushed and shoved our way toward three large plastic trash cans under the tray return window.

Fighting my way to the middle of the bustling mob, I felt a hard push against my left arm. Figuring it was Billy Ray attempting to cut in front of me again, I turned to let him have it.

"Watch out smart…" The words hung in my throat.

To my shock I discovered it wasn't Billy Ray who bumped me. Instead, I found myself staring into the sweet face of Sissy Ledbetter. Sparkling powder blue eyes gazed back into mine. Cute bangs lightly kissed her forehead while perfectly painted freckles dotted the crest of her soft round cheeks. Honey blonde hair, flipped up at her shoulders, framed the stunning picture.

Gently, the corners of her soft lips raised into a dazzling smile. Then I saw it! A tiny gap appeared between her top front teeth. Just like mine! Struggling to breathe, my heart shifted into overdrive. My knees became wavering palms in a storm. With a wet sponge for a tongue, all I could muster was an awkward grin.

Lost in the moment, I plowed into one of the garbage cans, spilling the contents of my tray on the floor. Surrounded by snickering faces and pointing fingers, I bent down to clean up the mess.

"I'm... I'm sorry!" Peering up through a sea of knees, I didn't see Sissy anywhere.

Somehow I made it back to the classroom under my own power. Lightheaded, I slumped into my desk like a lifeless sack of potatoes. Those eyes! That face! That smile! Until five minutes ago I hardly knew she existed.

Lost in an enamored fog, I never heard the jumbled sounds of shuffling books. Locked onto the goddess three rows over, I watched as she opened her reading book, carefully turning the pages with her tiny hands. Not a wrinkle in her pretty pink dress. The white line of a thin belt wrapped perfectly around her waist. Slowly, she fingered a lock of her beautiful blonde hair. *What in the world was happening to me? I've never felt this way before!*

"J.D."

She'd been in my class every year since the first grade. Why hadn't I noticed Sissy before today?

"J.D.!"

Had we ever talked to each other before?

"J.D. Harrison!"

"Huh?" I managed to a chorus of giggles.

"What's the answer?" Miss Hawks glared.

"Ma'am?" More snickers.

"I asked you a question young man, but since you were busy staring at Sissy, you didn't hear me." A collective gasp ripped through the room. Inventing shades of red, my mouth flew open.

"*No! No!* I wasn't lookin' at... I was... I was... starin' out the window, Miss Hawks! Honest I was!" I'd done some pretty stupid things in my short life, but this ranked right up there with the time I stood in front of the entire Bible School Assembly, proudly holding up the American flag with my fly open. Embarrassed, Sissy never looked up from her book.

When the bell rang to go home for the day, the Princess never acknowledging my existence, strolled out of the classroom with the others. Hoping to get in one last look, I pushed my way through the hall of crazed kids. Rushing out the front door, I squinted into the blinding sunlight.

PUNCH! Pain shot through my left shoulder.

"Can't you hear?"

"Huh?"

"HUH!" Billy Ray screamed a foot away from my ear, drawing laughter from the guys. *"I said are you playin' Ambush!* Wake up stupid!"

Suddenly Billy Ray's beady eyes met mine. My stomach squeezed together in a tight fist as his thin lips slowly curled into a sinister grin that I'd seen a thousand times before. I knew exactly what was burning in his twisted mind.

I'd been caught staring at a girl. A cardinal sin! And Billy Ray was going to let me have it! Just as he opened his mouth, Skeeter raised his leg and ripped one, sending everyone into hysterics. After years of attending Skeeter's impromptu concerts, I was convinced the boy was born with a trumpet up his butt. If presented with the right combination of chili beans and Pepsi, I was sure he could blow "Reveille." The gauntlet had been cast down. With everyone busy trying to outdo the other, Billy Ray's attention quickly turned to straining. I was safe, for now.

Unamused by the environmental disaster exploding around him, Junior shuffled down the street like a sad puppy. His weary eyes glued to the sidewalk. From the faraway expression on his face, I knew there was someplace else he'd rather be. With his girl Linda Sue. For the first time in my life, I knew exactly how he felt.

That night at supper, all I could think about were those beautiful eyes staring back at me. Sitting at the table with my chin in my palm, I twisted my fork through a plateful of Mom's famous spaghetti.

"You OK pal?"

"Oh yes sir!" I said, perking up. Oh Lord, if Dad ever suspected a girl was part of my life, I'd never hear the end of it. I'd rather suffer through an evening of dentistry with dull garden tools than endure his teasing!

Later that night I crawled into bed with my mind racing ninety miles an hour. Those gorgeous blue eyes gazed back at me from the dark shadows of my room. Locking my hands behind my head, I again sought the wise counsel of the ceiling tiles. Strange and thrilling emotions I'd never felt before bounced back and forth, pulling me one way then another, shattering the world as I knew it. Unable to comprehend it all, something inside burned away. A desire that I'd never known before, pushing me to do the unthinkable.

Somehow, some way, I had to summon the courage to ask Sissy to be my girlfriend. Considering the only major decision I'd made in my ten years was picking out what I wanted for Christmas, this was by far the biggest choice of my young life. One that carried with it tremendous risk and consequences. Was I willing to commit like Junior and give up my wonderful life as a soldier…all for a girl? Could I handle the squad's brutal wrath and endless teasing? Pondering my fate, I thought of Sissy's smile, those blue eyes and seductive gap in her front teeth. At that moment there was no question what my choice would be. The quest was on!

Next morning, I sprinted up the front steps of the school. Rushing through the classroom door, my eyes fell on Sissy. Sitting at her desk, she giggled about something with Wanda Gail, who sat in front of her. Wearing a light blue dress, her pretty blonde hair was gently pulled up in a cute ponytail. *Dang if she didn't look better than she did yesterday!*

Our eyes met for a split second. Her lips never stopped moving as she continued her conversation. Unable to summon the courage to speak to her, I fumbled listlessly through the day like a lost lamb. What was I supposed to do? How do I get Sissy's attention without being obvious? The guys would never let me hear the end of it! Needless to say, it was time I did some serious homework. If I were going to capture Sissy's heart, I'd better learn how.

The following day, I began an extensive training regimen, observing various methods and techniques of other infatuated couples. After considering several lovebirds as my case study, I zeroed in on Frankie Clark, a refined fifth grader who'd been going with Vickie Townsend for a whole month. Surely, he knew all there was to know about love.

At lunch I observed Romeo in action. Sitting in their usual seats near a cafeteria window, Frankie brandished a wide grin as he set his tray down beside Vickie's.

OK. Remember to smile a lot. Check. I thought, making mental notes.

In amazement, Vickie reached for her plate and laid her yeast roll on Frankie's tray. He didn't even ask for it. She just gave it to him! Where in the world do you find the perfect girl like that? In return, Frankie handed Vickie his apple.

All right… very important. Trading food… Check. Perhaps Sissy likes spinach!

That afternoon at recess I followed the two heartthrobs to the playground. Vickie waited patiently under the big oak for Frankie who arrived carrying two cherry popsicles. After carefully unwrapping the frozen treat, he presented it to her as if he were offering an engagement ring. And napkins! He thought to bring napkins. This would require a slight adjustment on my part since I was accustomed to wiping any excess residue on my shirtsleeve.

In a daze, I didn't say much on the walk home from school. Thankfully the guys never noticed my preoccupation. Skeeter quickly grabbed everyone's attention, describing the cool details of the Mattel Thunder Burp machine gun he'd gotten for his birthday. Out of habit, I casually glanced towards town at the Fourth Street intersection. A few blocks away, several men leaned on shovels beside a churning cement truck. Doing a quick double take, I almost blurted it out but quickly caught myself. Searching my friends' faces, I knew no one had seen the truck but me. If anyone suspected there was wet cement to defile, we'd have raced each other down the street to be the first. Making the turn onto Circle Drive, I searched for an excuse.

"OK. See y'all in a bit!" Skeeter said, running home.

"Me too!" Billy Ray yelled.

"Uh… Can't play today," I mumbled. "Gotta help Dad… uh… wash the car!"

Slamming the screen door, I offered Mom a cursory "hey." Tossing my books on the couch, I bolted for the garage.

"Be back 'fore six ya hear? We're havin' liver and onions!" Thanks for the warning! I considered for a moment running away, but enduring life on the road without Sissy wasn't an option. Pedaling down Circle Drive, I blew through the busy Fifth Street intersection, eliciting an angry car horn. Making the turn onto Fourth Street, I rode unnoticed by the humming cement truck spewing its gray soup into long rows of wooden forms. Continuing down the block, I searched for a good spot.

Studying the fresh canvas, I dropped to my knees. Maybe someday Sissy and I would make it official, displaying our love for all to see on the big oak. For now, this would have to do. My own little secret. Dragging a crooked stick through the tacky mud, I drew a giant plus sign between our initials, surrounding the declaration with a crude heart. Swallowing hard, I smiled at the masterpiece.

The next morning I couldn't get ready for school fast enough. Professing my love for Sissy for all eternity in wet cement bolstered my confidence. An eager little boy with a determined face stared back at me from the full-length mirror on my closet door. All I had to do was break the ice, employ my intoxicating charm and get her talking.

Following Sissy around school like a little puppy, I waited for just the right moment. When our class returned from the library, I fell in behind the goddess. Sissy's soft hair bounced gracefully on her shoulders as she skipped down the hall. My heart melted like an ice cube on hot pavement. Rounding a corner, a book slipped from Sissy's arms, falling to the floor in an echoing thud.

This was it! My big chance! All I have to do is reach down, pick up the book, and hand it back to her. That should get us talking! As I stood there methodically plotting my move, Roger Coffee scooted past me. His high-water pant legs hit him six inches above his ankles, revealing a pair of white socks. A dark-haired bookworm, Roger was one of those quiet kids in class who rarely spoke above a whisper. Bending down, he scooped up the book and handed it to Sissy. Her blue eyes glowed.

"Thank you, Roger. You're so sweet!" *You stupid idiot! What the hell were you waiting for?*

The unexpected intrusion immediately pushed my preadolescent paranoia pedal to the floor. What if Roger entered the picture? Not another boy. *The last thing I needed was competition!* Time to get this loser out of the way.

Lining up to go to lunch, I slipped in behind Roger.

"Hey Rog. Look up there." I said, nodding toward the front of the line. "There's Sissy and Wanda Gail."

"Uh huh." Obviously, Roger was quite the conservationist. If I wasn't careful, he just might sweep Sissy off her feet with a witty assortment of vowels.

"Rog," I said, shooting a wink. "What do ya think of Wanda Gail, huh? Cute as a button, ain't she?"

Cocking his head, Roger stared through his droopy eyes, frowning at my question. How in the world did this clown make straight A's?

"She's purdy, I reckon. But she ain't as purdy as Sissy."

"Yeah… but… but… Rog… look at Wanda Gail and those pigtails!"

"What's her real name? I forget."

"Huh."

"Sissy."

"What 'cha mean?"

"Sissy ain't her real name. Sissy's just a nickname. Dang, what is it? Anna… something…"

What? I thought her name was Sissy! You mean I'm in love with a girl and don't even know her name? Flustered, I grabbed my daily portion of gruel and plunked down with the guys.

Twisting my fork around my plate, I tried my best to recall Sissy's real name. Heaven knows I couldn't ask anybody. With romance at a fever pitch, kids were on high alert, looking for the first hint of a budding relationship. If the guys ever suspected I had a thing for Sissy, I was a goner!

With all the confusion surrounding Sissy Ledbetter, including her name, one thing was certain. There wasn't the slightest hint of cooties behind those beautiful eyes. Still the dreaded disease was alive and well at South Maybin and Becky Simmons was without a doubt, Cootie Queen.

A curly haired redheaded demon with black eyes, Becky resembled a crazed Shirley Temple. Every day at recess when the Queen went on the prowl, every boy remained vigilant. And with good reason. Sensing the slightest distraction, Becky would sneak up behind some unsuspecting boy. Locking her prey in those burly arms of hers, she repeatedly kissed her victims, soaking them in a wet sheen of cooties.

Unfortunately, Skeeter became Becky's latest victim. Arguing with Billy Ray one day under the big oak, he let his guard down for a split second. Tiptoeing up from behind, Becky struck like a rattlesnake. Clutching Skeeter in a viselike grip, Becky went to work, kissing the back of his neck, soaking his shirt collar in a ring of slimy spit. Being kissed by Becky Simmons was a slow and cruel way to die. In stunned silence, the class gathered to witness the execution.

Locked in the Queen's steadfast grip, Skeeter's entire head disappeared, smothered from view by Becky's bouncing red curls. Summoning unknown inner strength, Skeeter pulled himself free. Screaming at the top of his lungs, he galloped around the playground, scrubbing the wounded area with his shirtsleeve. As the death rattle began, he fell to his knees in a pitiful moan, scouring his face with dirt. Needless to say, everyone avoided Skeeter the rest of the week.

Continuing my observations of Frankie and Vickie's devoted routine, I slowly began to understand the mysterious ritual of courtship. Then came that fateful night when the pieces finally fell into place. I was sitting on the den floor watching a western with Dad when a cigarette commercial appeared on the screen. Unlike most boring advertisements, a beautiful woman with blond hair just like Sissy's caught my attention.

Fashioning a sweater a few sizes too small, she couldn't take her eyes off a man smoking a Marlboro. While the mustached man puffed away, the woman flashed her eyes, giving him these funny looking grins. Her whole face lit up! I couldn't remember Mom ever looking at Dad that way, but again, he didn't smoke. Wait a minute! Do cigarettes really make girls smile like that? Grinning back at the smitten lady, the man held the cigarette between two fingers as the swirls of smoke circled in front of his face. Suddenly it hit me.

Flying down the hall to my bedroom, I tore through a dresser drawer, finding the pack of candy cigarettes: "Jolly Viceroys." Standing in front of the mirror, I held the candy stick beside my face with two fingers, just like the Marlboro Man. Cocking my head, I winked for good measure. This was it. My secret weapon! That night I slid under the covers with new-found self-confidence. Tomorrow would be the day I make my move on Sissy Ledbetter!

Getting dressed the next morning, I practiced my alluring gestures in the mirror one last time. Placing two "Jolly Viceroys" in my jean pocket, I couldn't wait to get to school. After careful deliberation, I decided to pull the trigger at recess. Following Sissy, Linda Sue, and Wanda Gail at a distance, I watched the three of them gather underneath the big oak. Taking a deep breath, I charged up the hill.

A sweet smile broke out on Sissy's face as I approached. Lord help me! With a bass drum pounding in my chest, I slid my hand in my jean pocket to retrieve a candy cigarette. To my horror, all I felt were tiny pieces of broken candy! Rattled, I pulled out the first piece I touched. Placing the short nub between my fingers, I leaned my other hand on the tree. My knees felt like rubber. OK. *Here goes nothing!*

"Hey y'all," I said seductively.

"Hey J.D." Sissy's round face retreated to her shoulders like an embarrassed turtle. Biting her bottom lip, she grinned, sending freckles dancing under her eyes. Thoroughly hypnotized, I never heard the scream.

"I GOTCHA!" Two powerful arms from behind locked around my chest. Jerking from side to side, I tried my best to break free!

"Mmm, mmm, mmm, mmm, mmm," Becky hummed. Kissing the side of my neck, she worked her way hideously around my head! Warm drool clogged my ears, dulling my piercing screams! Drowning in the Queen's deadly venom, I twisted and pulled, biting her arms. Falling to the ground, I pulled the beast down with me!

Pivoting like a lioness, Becky went for the kill. With her bony knees digging into my stomach, she kissed me right on the mouth! After several slippery licks to the face the monster relented, leaving me in a wet slimy heap. With my eyes tightly closed, I felt my skin dissolving in acidic cootie-infused dribble. My classmates stared down at me as if I were roadkill. Officially crowned Cootie King, the guys boiled me alive for the rest of the day.

Next morning I lumbered down the hall to my classroom, wondering what hell awaited me, when I spotted Denny Taylor peeking around the classroom door. Serving as lookout, Denny watched for Miss Hawks to return from the office. As I entered the room, I quickly discovered the need for a sentry.

Huddled together like a football team, the entire class pressed together in the back of the room. Suddenly everyone broke into crazy laughter. The reddening faces of Marsha and Willy slinked away from the crowd, ignoring playful congratulations. Joining the group, I peered over Skeeter's shoulder. Sitting in the middle of the throng, Betty Sue Thomas smiled wryly at her latest revelation.

"OK, who's next?" she laughed, holding a folded piece of notebook paper in both hands like a bouquet of flowers.

Upon closer inspection, I noticed different words and numbers, crudely written in crayon, decorated the sides of four folded paper spikes.

"Me! Me!" shouted Cathy, moving closer.

"OK, pick one." Betty Sue smiled.

Pressing a nervous finger to her lips, Cathy pondered her choices to the hum of the curious crowd.

"I pick... *like!*" she squealed. Kids cowered in gleeful expectation as Betty Sue lifted the fold from her lap. In unison, kids spelled "L-I-K-E" as Betty Sue opened and closed the magic paper. Fascinated, the class watched as Cathy made her selections. After several agonizing moments, Betty Sue slowly opened the flap.

"Freddie! You like Freddie!" She yelled, with a wide grin.

Screaming, Cathy buried her sheepish face in both hands. Wishing the declaration were true, sleepy-eyed Freddie gawked longingly at Cathy, revealing his missing front teeth. Throwing caution to the wind, I jumped in.

"Hey! I wanna try!" I said, pushing my way to the front. Time to send the ball spinning on the roulette wheel one more time. Like a lost gambler down to his last chip, I was positive a bountiful jackpot was just one more spin away. What was there to lose? Maybe, just maybe, Sissy's name would come up.

"Which one?" Betty Sue grinned. Taking a deep breath, I blurted it out.

"*Love.*"

Cringing at my scandalous choice, my classmates pulled in tighter. My stomach churned away while beads of sweat broke out on my face. This was it. My entire future with Sissy Ledbetter lay hidden somewhere inside the mystic folds of a single piece of paper!

Choosing the numbers, I held my breath while Betty Sue worked her magic. Playing the crowd like a sleazy midway con artist, she milked it for all it was worth. Abruptly stopping her hands, Betty Sue cautiously opened the flap.

"*Come on!*" someone shouted. Betty Sue's eyes lit up.

"*Oh my!* It's... It's Becky Simmons! J. D. loves Becky Simmons!"

"Attaboy Cootie King!" Billy Ray yelled.

Becky's smile reminded me of a rabid possum. I wanted to crawl in a hole and die. Why was this happening to me? I was cursed. That's all there was to it. When it came to Sissy Ledbetter, everything I did turned to crap. Such is the strange and unpredictable life of a fifth grader. One minute you're at the bottom of the heap, thinking life can't get any worse, when out of the blue your fortunes take an unexpected turn.

Before the bell rang to end another miserable day in the life of J.D. Harrison, Miss Hawks stepped to the front of the classroom holding a stack of envelopes.

"Class, I have a surprise for you. Well, it's really Sissy's surprise," she said, exchanging smiles with the deity. "Sissy is having a birthday party and she's inviting the whole class."

You would have thought Miss Hawks had yelled "free ice cream!" The place went nuts. Suddenly my heart leaped in my chest as Miss Hawks handed out the invitations. Of course! A birthday party is the perfect place. Having all that time together without the shackles of school, surely I could win Sissy's heart! It was too good to be true. Another grace-filled chance had fallen into my lap. *Crumbs from Heaven,* my grandfather used to say. I tore into the envelope.

You are cordially invited to Angela Ledbetter's Tenth Birthday Party
Saturday afternoon, October 26th
4:00-7:00 p.m.
106 Corbett Ridge Drive
There will be lots of games and fun for everyone!
We're having a bonfire and a weenie roast!

ANGELA! SISSY'S REAL NAME is *Angela*! "Angel" with an "A." What a beautiful name. Angela Harrison sounded even better!

Dad surprised us that night with barbecue, slaw, and a pack of buns from The Grill, putting Mom in a good mood. With Eddie snuggled in the crease of her elbow, she opened a jar of pureed peas. Unable to contain my excitement, I handed Mom the invitation. Puzzled, she began reading the card out loud, stopping before she finished the first sentence.

"Oh, that's Harriet Ledbetter's daughter," she said, as Eddie's wrinkled face recoiled at the disgusting spoonful of snot.

"You know 'em?"

"Sure. Harriet's been a member of our garden club for years."

"Her father's a lawyer in Hillsboro," Dad said, taking a sip of tea. Par for the course. Everyone in my entire family knew the Ledbetters but me!

"What are you gettin' Angela for her birthday?" Mom quizzed. In all the hoopla, the thought of buying Sissy a present had never crossed my mind. Great! Another detail to worry about. Why was love so complicated?

"I don't know," I shrugged.

"Well, ya got time to think about it. You can buy it with your allowance. I'll help you pick out somethin'," she winked. Mom was forgetting one minor detail. Most of my allowance was being garnished to reimburse the town for a broken streetlight. Paying restitution to a municipality at age ten didn't leave much discretionary income.

Sitting at my desk before class started the next day, I glanced across the room at Sissy, who remained locked in another whisper session with Wanda Gail. In an unexpected moment of confidence, my shoulders flew back. A strange power pushed my feet into the aisle, drawing me to her. Putting one foot in front of the other, I ambled over to her desk.

"Hey Sissy."

"Hey J.D.!" One look from those stunning eyes and I lost it. So much for coolness.

"I just wanted to let ya know that I'm comin' to your birthday party," I said, as if I were attending a funeral.

"I'm glad!" she beamed. With that I slithered back to my desk.

For the next week I spent every waking moment racking my brain about a birthday gift. Whatever I selected would have to be perfect. Something that would knock her socks off. After school one afternoon, I rushed to my bedroom and hurriedly counted the loose change I kept in a mason jar. Oh wonderful! What amazing gift could I purchase with a whopping buck ninety-two? Wait! The couch! Of course! Once, during a rather intense wrestling match, Suzie and I pushed all the couch cushions onto the floor. To my surprise I found fifty-eight cents. I brushed by Mom as I ran down the hall.

"Hey! How was school? Land sakes, J.D.! You got a hole in your knee again?"

"Football."

"Honey, that's the second pair of jeans since school started and I'm out of iron-on patches!" Ignoring her irritation, I pulled the cushions off the couch and threw them on the floor. "What in the world are you doin'?"

"Lookin' for money… for Sissy's gift."

"Oh yeah! That's right. The big party's this weekend!" Along with four paperclips, a pencil, and several hairpins, I salvaged thirty-three cents.

"Can you help me find a gift for her, Momma?"

"Sure, I will!" My sudden excitement triggered one of Mom's patented dry smiles. I wasn't fooling Dottie Harrison. Hoping to avoid her nosy interrogation, I slinked into the kitchen. Trailing behind, Mom crossed her arms as she leaned against the counter.

"Why do ya call her Sissy? Isn't her name Angela?"

"Everybody calls her Sissy," I said, pouring a glass of grape juice.

"She cute?"

"Momma!"

"Tell ya what. I got choir practice tonight. But tomorrow when you get home from school, me and you'll go down to Rose's and see what we can find for Sissy. OK?"

"Thanks, Ma," I said, setting my empty glass in the sink. "Oh, Ma? You ain't gonna say nothin' to Dad, are ya?"

"No, honey. This is between you and me," she winked.

Closing my bedroom door, I threw on my army gear for the day's battle. Suddenly out of the corner of my eye, I spotted the ball sitting on the bookshelf. Why didn't I think of it before! I'd asked the Magic 8 Ball some pretty stupid things over the years, but it was time to get serious! Shaking the mysterious orb with both hands, I placed the black ball under my chin and closed my eyes.

"Does Sissy like me?" I whispered. Excitedly I turned the ball over, waiting for the ghostly white response to appear.

"Don't count on it," it read.

"AH!" Shaking the ball long and fast, I placed it again under my chin. Time to ask the Big Question!

"Will Sissy ever be my girlfriend?" Gently rolling the ball over in my hands, I peeked with one eye.

"Yes, definitely!" It was official! The mystical gods had spoken. Sissy Ledbetter was destined to be mine!

As promised, Mom accompanied me to Rose's 5 and 10 the next afternoon. The swinging double doors slapped behind us as we entered the store. The pleasant aroma of popcorn and roasted nuts drifting from the candy counter made my stomach growl. Creaking wooden floors trumpeted our every step.

"Hello Miss Dottie." came Mr. Fletcher's deep voice. I always liked Mr. Fletcher, the store manager whose thinning hair and piercing eyes reminded me of my grandfather.

"Hey there, Pete. Looks like you got your hands full today."

"Always busy," he said, arranging items on a shelf. "My goodness! Is that J.D.? Boy'll be taller'n Will 'fore you know it!"

Offering a hasty wave, I scurried past. Weaving my way through the store, I peered jealously down the long corridor of the boys' toy section that I knew like the back of my hand. Before entering the forbidden girls' department, I searched every aisle, making sure no other guys were in the store. Where was Mom? I couldn't go traipsing down the girls' toy aisle unattended! Running through the store, I found her in housewares engaged in lengthy conversation with Mrs. Porter. Please! Not Mrs. Porter! The woman could talk the ears off an elephant!

Ignoring my waves, Mom listened intently as her chatty friend described in boring detail her latest problem with gout. If I didn't do something, they'd talk all day. Easing over to a display of pots and pans, I looked up and down the aisle. Nudging a frying pan to the edge of the shelf, I looked around again. No one.

CRASH!

The pan slammed against the wooden floor sending its top spinning like a giant coin. The sound of angry high heels quickly followed.

"J.D.! What's gotten into you!"

"I'm sorry. It was an accident," I said, picking up the pan.

Rushing through the store, I ran back to the girls' toy aisle that looked as if it had been painted with fifty coats of Pepto Bismol. There were pink baby carriages, pink stoves, pink refrigerators, and pink tables stacked with plastic pots and pans. Row after row of baby dolls stared back at me. Shelves crammed full of board games, coloring books, and tea sets. Identical pink bicycles with tasseled handlebars stood like a row of soldiers at attention. Hidden somewhere in this girlish passageway lay the key to Sissy's heart. I just had to find it.

"Think she'd like a book?" Mom asked, meandering behind me.

Oh, how romantic! Nothing says "I love you" quite like a stupid book. That should reel her in! The more I considered the myriad of choices, the more confused I became. What do ten-year-old girls like anyway?

Suddenly, my face lit up! There at the end of the pink corridor stood a long wooden table piled high with stuffed animals. An endless assortment of cuddly creatures of all shapes and sizes, from furry teddy bears to plush elephants. On the edge of the table laid a golden Pooh Bear dressed in his customary red sweater. Reaching over I picked him up.

"Oooh… J.D.! Sissy'll love that!"

"Think so?"

"Oh yes! How much is it?" Turning him over, I examined the tag on Pooh's sweater.

"$2.80! I ain't got that much," I pouted, placing Pooh back on the table. Dang if love ain't expensive! Just like Sissy, the cute little bear rested just beyond my reach. Undaunted, I picked Pooh up again, unknowingly hugging the bear. "Momma! This is it! I just got to get Pooh for Sissy!"

"You still got time to round up some money."

The day before the party I was still fifty cents short. On the walk home, I scoured ditches and sidewalks for lost change. Suddenly a shiny coin flickered in the middle of the street. Risking life and limb, I darted out in front of an oncoming car, scooping up the nickel at the last second. Hearing the screen door slam, Mom came in from the kitchen.

"How was your day?"

"OK I reckon. Momma, Sissy's party's tomorrow and I still ain't got enough money for Pooh."

"Aw, really? That's too bad… Have ya checked the couch?"

"I did the other day."

"Well, look again. Ya never know."

Moping over to the couch, I pulled a cushion to the side. To my amazement, two quarters shined back at me.

"*Momma! Look!*"

"Well, I'll be!" Her sneaky grin didn't fool me in the least.

"Thanks Ma," I said, smiling back.

"What 'cha thankin' me for? You found it!" She beamed. "Now let's me and you go down to Rose's and get Pooh!"

Strutting out the double doors of Rose's Department Store that afternoon with Pooh tucked firmly under my arm, I felt a wonderful sense of relief. I thought about the long frustrating climb that had consumed me since the tray-dumping incident, when I first gazed into those beautiful blue eyes. Sitting Pooh down on the seat beside me, I looked out the window and smiled. After weeks of uncertainty and embarrassment, my fortunes with Sissy Ledbetter were about to change!

It's My Party and I'll Cry If I Want To!

The swelling moan of a train passing through downtown a few blocks away grew louder, penetrating my semi-conscious fog of sleep. Lying under the covers listening to the westbound's roar, I contemplated the twisted path my life had taken for the past month. Trying to make sense of the feuding emotions that had tossed me around like a helpless pinball. But that was all behind me now.

Throwing back the covers, I rushed to the corner windows of my bedroom. Peeking through the wooden blinds, my eyes rebelled at the sun's reflection glistening off the thick morning dew. Misty maples glowed in hues of yellow and burgundy. Typical Saturday morning noises of rustling dishes and a blaring TV drifted down the hall.

Changing into my army fatigues, I braced for another round of interrogation. Grunting a terse "morning," I sat down at the table.

"Mornin'! You gotta big day today," Mom said as she washed dishes. "What 'cha wearing tonight? Supposed to get cool."

"I don't know."

Concentrating on the orange box of Wheaties, I crammed down a bowlful and sprinted for the door. "Remember. We gotta wrap Sissy's present! Don't stay out all day!"

"Yes ma'am."

Flying out of the garage, I pedaled for Ashley Woods. A lump rose in my throat as I laid my bike down in the ditch alongside the others. Shadows from the tall pines closed in around me as I hurried down the familiar worn path. Hearing the squad's playful voices echoing through the trees, I wondered if this would be the last time I'd ever play Ambush. In just a few hours the truth would be revealed at Sissy's birthday party. The whole world would know.

Joining the battle, I sensed something very different in the guys. Sidetracked by the upcoming party, typical concentration and determination from our zealous band of wanton killers drifted away in the morning breeze. No one seemed to take the game seriously, cracking jokes instead about Sissy's party. The plastic machine gun that had always fit perfectly in my hands now felt childish for some reason. What was happening to us?

Pausing briefly for lunch, we played well into the afternoon. When hostilities ended, I jumped on my bike and was about to head home when Skeeter's voice came from behind.

"Hey J.D.! Wait up," he shouted, running towards me. "Gotta show ya somethin'!"

Glancing nervously over his shoulder into the dark woods, he retrieved a note from his jean pocket. His hands shook as he unfolded the paper. "Ya gotta help me!"

"What's wrong?"

"Cross your heart and hope to die ya ain't gonna tell nobody!"

"OK... Cross my heart. What is it?"

"Got this here note yes'day when the bell rang." Staring again into the woods, he handed me the note. "It's from Sherry."

"Sherry? Sherry Whitesell?"

"Yeah!"

Dear Skeeter,
I like you. Do you like me?
Check one
___ yes ___ no
Your friend, Sherry Whitesell

First Junior. Then me. Now Skeeter? Checking the sky I expected to find pigs circling overhead.

"Why didn't you ask Billy Ray?" I smirked, knowing his wimpy answer.

"He'd ride me to hell and back and ya know it. Can't tell nobody 'cept you. Figured you'd keep a secret."

"What 'cha tell her?"

"Ain't told her nothin'! She dropped the note on my desk when the bell rang and took off."

"She'll be at Sissy's party."

"I *know*! What am I supposed to do?"

"Well, do ya like her?" Shifting from side to side as if he were about to wet his pants, Skeeter shot me a panicked gaze I knew all too well.

"I... don't know. I... I... think so... I ain't rightly sure!"

"Tell ya what. Stick with me at the party. We'll figure it out. I promise." Leaving Skeeter sulking in the street, I hurried home. I had enough problems of my own to worry about.

Eddie's soft cries floated through the screen door as I parked my bike in the garage. Stepping inside, I found Mom pacing around the den with my little brother in her arms.

"Eddie's not feeling good. Think he's comin' down with somethin'. Listen, go look in the bottom of my closet. There's a box of wrappin' paper in there. I'll wrap Sissy's present soon as I get him down for a nap."

Scampering to my parents' bedroom, I pushed the sliding closet door to one side. Shoved behind a massive collection of high heels was a large box filled with wrapping paper and spools of ribbon. I was almost to the bedroom door when I stopped dead in my tracks. There on top of Dad's dresser set several bottles of cologne. A tantalizing bonanza of manly fragrance guaranteed to drive women wild. *That's it! The icing on the cake!* Pooh *and* cologne and Sissy might just propose to me right there!

Placing the box on the bed, I stood motionless in front of the dresser, pondering the array of choices. What scent would have Sissy drooling? Standing on my tiptoes, I grabbed a cream-colored bottle of Old Spice. Pulling the plastic stopper, I recoiled, recognizing the pungent scent Dad splashed on his face every Sunday before church. Nah... going to Sissy's party smelling like my father wouldn't cut it. Reaching for a short stubby bottle of English Leather, I examined the claret-colored horse saddle on the label. Horses? Oh sure, reeking like a two-ton Clydesdale would surely win Sissy's heart! Next to a bronze change holder stood an ice-blue bottle of Aqua Velva. Then I remembered. *There's something about an Aqua Velva man!*

Grabbing the bottle, I twisted off the black plastic cap and took a sniff. My eyes quickly teared up at the powerful rush of potent aftershave. If the malodorous explosion didn't suffocate her first, the strong scent would certainly get Sissy's attention. But wait a second. Splashing a handful of the lethal concoction on my face would be like setting off fireworks, confirming what Mom already suspected. And if Dad got a whiff, so to speak, God help me. I'd never hear the end of it!

Suddenly the wooden floors groaned down the hallway. Quickly placing the bottle back on the dresser, I backed away.

"What's takin' so long?"

"Uh... I was... lookin' at the wrappin' paper... tryin' to pick out the right one."

"Bring the box in the den. And be quiet. Eddie's asleep." Clutching the box, I stared one last time at the inviting blue bottle.

"OK. Let's find some really pretty paper," Mom said softly, placing the box on the dining room table.

"Uh... I gotta... find a pair of jeans to wear."

"The only clean pair ya have is in your bottom drawer," she whispered.

How in the world was I gonna pull this off? I wondered, sprinting down the hall. I couldn't just lug around a bottle of Aqua Velva at the party! Rummaging through my toy closet, I ran across a small forgotten water pistol. The plastic gun fit perfectly in the palm of my hand. Glancing down the hall I dashed into my parents' bedroom. Taking the bottle from its perch, I stood over the bathroom sink, carefully filling the gun with the blue liquid. Checking the stopper and trigger, I hid my secret weapon in my dresser drawer.

After a hot bath, I carefully selected a green and white striped short-sleeved shirt and blue jeans as my dazzling ensemble. I was tucking in my shirttail when a knock came at the door.

"You need any..." Mom's question died when she stepped into the room. "Why J.D. Harrison! You look absolutely handsome!"

"Ma!" Taking a knee, she looked me over.

"OK, the gift is on the table," she said, adjusting my collar. Dodging her efforts like a boxer, I flinched when she rubbed my flattop. "Remember to say, 'Yes ma'am' and 'No ma'am', 'please' and 'thank you.' And don't forget your jacket. It's gonna get cool." Making sure I was without blemish, she turned to leave. Pausing at the door, Mom again admired her little man.

"We'll leave in a few minutes," she said, with a wistful smile. Retrieving the water pistol, I crammed the gun in my back pocket.

Standing beside the dining room table, Mom gleefully presented me a beautifully wrapped purple package topped with a stunning pink bow. A semi-professional gift wrapper, Mom spent countless hours during the holidays delicately dressing each present with neatly wrapped paper and color coordinated ribbon, only to have her handiwork ripped to shreds in five seconds on Christmas morning. I could tell she'd taken her time on Sissy's gift.

"What 'cha think?"

"Wow! That looks great Ma!"

"Don't forget to sign the card." Beside Mom's festively decorated masterpiece laid a colorful balloon-covered card exclaiming "HAPPY BIRTHDAY" in bold black cursive. Peering inside, I read the message: "HAVE A WONDERFUL BIRTHDAY!" *That's it? What hopeless romantic came up with that zinger?*

Flicking the pen, I hesitated. How should I sign the card? "Your boyfriend?" "Your prince?" Settling on just "Your Friend," I wrote my entire name, "J.D. Harrison," ensuring Sissy wouldn't confuse me with the hundreds of other J.D.s who might show up at the party. Careful not to disturb the wrapping paper, I slid the card under the gift's pink ribbon.

Stepping gingerly out to the car as if I were carrying a gallon of nitroglycerin, I gently placed Sissy's gift on the back seat. Jumping in the car with the style and grace of a water buffalo, Suzie slid dangerously close to the wrapped gift.

"Don't you mess up my present," I said, pointing back at her.

"I ain't!" she said, sticking out her tongue. Caressing Eddie in a blue baby blanket, Mom stepped slowly out to the car.

"Here J.D., Eddie's sick. You'll have to hold him on the way over."

"Ma, he's nasty! I took a bath and everything!"

"Take your brother!" She glared.

Shrinking back, I reluctantly took the tiny bundle of germs in my arms. Rivers of snot hung beneath his nose like olive drab socks on a clothesline. Always a bizarre smorgasbord of odors, Eddie could give a skunk a run for his money. The constant cloud of noxious fumes never seemed to bother Mom. Noses must quit working when you become a parent.

"Here," Mom said, handing me a tissue. "Wipe his little nose."

Quite the snot enthusiast, I dealt with my own green goo on a daily basis. But this was deadly germ-infested baby snot I was toying with. As if poking a hornet's nest, I dabbed Eddie's nose, creating a slick sheen on his chubby cheeks.

Afternoon shadows brushed by my window as we turned onto Fifth Street. Shade from the overhead canopy of monstrous oaks made it feel later in the day. Tidy neighborhoods became open fields and piney forests. Sagging barbed wire tethered weary fence posts as we drove through the country. Jerking in my arms in fits of sleep, Eddie's protesting moans faded from the blue bundle.

A drum solo began inside my chest when the car's turn signal began. Plumes of dust followed us down the twisting graveled curves of

Corbett Ridge Drive. Pressing my nose against the window, I marveled at the rambling brick ranches and two-story houses with manicured lawns and neatly trimmed shrubs. Mom slowed the car at a black mailbox marked "106."

"Look Ma! They got a paved driveway! With reflectors!" Flanking both sides of the driveway entrance, the red plastic dots atop twisting aluminum stakes looked almost as snazzy as painted tractor tires! A sure sign of southern nobility. High on a hill, past a thick forest of pine trees, stood a sprawling white brick ranch. My sudden exuberance was quickly tempered by a familiar stench. Glancing down, I stared in horror at Eddie's straining face.

"Stop the car! Stop the car!" I yelled.

"What's wrong?"

"*Take 'im!* He done crapped in his britches!" I screamed, holding my brother away from me as if he were on fire.

"Land sakes J.D., hold on!" Mom huffed. Handing her my fetid brother, I sniffed my left arm, catching a putrid whiff.

"BABY STINKY! I GOT BABY STINKY ON MY ARM!"

"Mercy sakes J.D.! Calm down," she puffed, "I need to change his diaper."

"Ma! I'll be late for the party!"

"Boy, there ain't gonna be no party if you don't hush up!"

The story of my life. Close, but no cigar! Thanks to Eddie's free flowing bowels, I would be the last one to show up for the party. With my luck, Roger had already made his move on Sissy!

While Mom performed the unholy cleansing, I reached over the seat, pulling Pooh to safety. Suzie held on to the car door for dear life. A vile odor not of this earth filled the car. With the unspeakable horror completed, Mom drove into the driveway that circled in front of the stately house. Clutching the present, I dived out the door.

"I'll pick ya up at seven. Have fun!"

Watching the Pontiac disappear down the driveway, I retrieved the water pistol. Smelling like an open sewer, I pumped the trigger, soaking my defiled shirtsleeve. The strong blast of fragrance not only obliterated any traces of odor but took with it the last vestiges of oxygen. Sneezing and coughing, my lungs screamed for air. Fearing I might explode when they lit the birthday cake, I squeezed the excess cologne from my shirt.

A huge one-story ranch stretched in front of me like a gigantic battleship. Picture windows garlanded with black shutters towered over neatly cut boxwoods. Berms of barren rose bushes bordering a stone walkway led to the front steps of an expansive porch guarded by two angry lion statues. Pink balloons tethered to wrought iron handrails danced in the breeze.

"Come in! Come in!" Standing by the double front door, a smiling lady in a rose-pink dress waved her arm. I detected Sissy's eyes.

"I'm J.D. Harrison."

"Yes! Your mother told me you were coming." Suddenly Mrs. Ledbetter recoiled as I brushed past.

"Mercy me! That's… some kind of aftershave!" she grinned.

"Thank you." Wow! If Mrs. Ledbetter loved the scent, surely Sissy would be blown away!

"Come with me. Everyone's down in the basement."

Walking down a long hallway, I admired an entire wall covered with family pictures. *If Pooh comes through for me, maybe someday our wedding portrait will hang there!* Mrs. Ledbetter opened a basement door, triggering a garbled explosion of noise. A record player blared from somewhere. Following her down the wooden stairwell, I watched in amazement as screaming kids, locked in excitement overload, darted through the cavernous basement in a semi-riot.

Miles of pink ribbon dangled from the tall open-joisted ceiling. Balloon-strewn tables covered with snacks and goodies stretched in front of an army of arm-crossed moms leaning on a back wall. The juicy red contents of a glass punchbowl in the center of the cheerful display called my name. Below the bowl, a streaming banner stretched the length of three tables, declaring "HAPPY TENTH BIRTHDAY ANGIE!"

Gazing over the sea of children, I studied the clusters of ponytails and colored hair bows for signs of the goddess.

"Here J.D., let me have your jacket."

"Thank you, Mrs. Ledbetter."

Unsure of what to do next, I stood at the base of the stairs, holding Sissy's present. Through the noisy clamor, I heard her voice.

"Hey J.D."

Turning around I suddenly lost control of my lips. My ten-pound chin dropped open as I shamelessly gawked. At the top of the stairs stood the prettiest sight I'd ever seen. Sissy's bright red short-sleeved dress with sweeping white collar lit up the room. A stunning halo of strawberry blonde hair encircled her smiling face. The tantalizing gap in her front teeth beckoned me. Doing my best Rhett Butler imperson-ation, I leaned on the banister for support.

Slowly she descended the wooden staircase. Her right hand gliding gently atop the railing. A pair of shiny black shoes with silver buckles leading the way. Fittingly, the song "Just One Look" blasted from the record player. Her baby blues gazed into mine as she reached the bot-tom of the stairs.

"Hey." Surprised that I could form a syllable, I stood there like a statue. A disturbing frown quickly washed away her dazzling smile.

"What's that smell? Is that you?"

At the tender age of ten, I lacked the critical aptitude to sense disapproval in a woman's voice. A rather peculiar skill that I would never fully master. Naturally I took her question as a compliment.

"Yeah." I blushed, kicking the bottom rung with a nervous shucks y'all grin. "I gotcha a present."

"Oh J.D.! You're so sweet. Follow me!"

Holy smokes! There really *is* something about an Aqua Velva man! Where was she taking me? New York? Los Angeles? Raleigh? Slaloming through the crowd we paused beside a table in the back corner of the basement. At long last we were alone. This was it. The moment I'd waited for. Sheepishly peeking from her bowed chin, Sissy fumbled with a crease in her dress. An unexpected flicker of brain activity sent words forming on my bloated tongue!

Struggling to speak through the violent sandstorm that swept down my throat, the primal utterance dribbled through my trembling lips! "Uhh...can I... ask ya a question?" I stammered. Her blue eyes doubled in size as she nodded. "Will ya... can ya... uh... tell me... why everyone calls ya Sissy?" I choked! I just couldn't do it!

"Oh. When my brother was little, he couldn't say 'Angela,' so he called me Sissy. Now everybody does." Completing my shining moment as a spineless failure, I nodded like a bobblehead. What's next for me? Diapers? A pacifier? Maybe a nice rattle?

"OK... well... put it with the rest of 'em." With that, Sissy disappeared into the crowd. Lost in an infatuated fog, I hadn't noticed the mountain of birthday gifts piled on the table beside me. In need of a stiff drink, I laid the present on the table and lumbered towards the refreshments. Reaching for a cup of punch, I felt a tug at my shoulder.

"J.D." Like a spy passing secrets, Skeeter leaned over. "Sherry smiled at me while ago. What do I do?"

"Did ya smile back?"

"Uh… no," he said, dropping his head. Skeeter was one of my best friends, but I swear his IQ was just a few notches above his shoe size.

"Did ya say anything to her?" Before Skeeter could answer, Billy Ray came charging up.

"Come on y'all! We got… a… great game of tag goin'!" he puffed out of breath. "There's a big… water fountain… out back… we're using for base. Dang, I need some punch!" Wiping his sweaty forehead on his shirtsleeve, Billy Ray stepped toward the refreshment table. "Hey y'all! Look at Junior," he snorted.

In the center of the basement sat a canary-colored couch filled with would-be lovebirds. Watching for the slightest signs of affection from timid couples sitting just inches apart, curious classmates examined their every move. At one end squirmed the squad's two favorite sweethearts, Junior and Linda Sue. With both hands locked in a death grip on the arm of the couch, Junior looked as if he were holding on to the handrails of the Titanic. With her eyes glued to the ceiling, Linda Sue's hands twisted nervously in her lap. Literal wallflowers desperately wanting to dance, but too scared to make the first move.

"Reckon he'll try and hold her hand?" Billy Ray laughed, playfully punching Skeeter's shoulder. At that moment, Billy Ray's eyes slowly narrowed as he gazed at the anxious couples. His facial expression went from hysterics to confusion as he pondered his own question. A small crack suddenly appeared in the impenetrable armor of a boy who demanded attention every second of the day. Always the one at the front of the line, Billy Ray ran the show, pure and simple. The kid who "got you first" in Ambush. The one who had to be the quarterback or the banker in Monopoly. An authority on everything, Billy Ray was always right or he'd take his little ball and go home. A boy who wouldn't take a backseat to anyone or anything.

The peculiar scene of lovesick couples grabbed Billy Ray by the throat. As if a curtain slowly opened, exposing a brightly lit stage and thunderous applause, he stared in amazement. An exciting performance was about to begin and for the first time in his life, Billy Ray realized he was sitting in the audience instead of parading in the spotlight.

Someone lifted the noisy tonearm of the record player. Clamor and laughter faded. Standing in front of the giant punchbowl, Mrs. Ledbetter waved her hand in the air.

"Hello everyone! Welcome to Angie's birthday party! We're so happy all of you could come. I see you've found the punch and cookies. Mr. Ledbetter is out back gettin' things ready for our weenie roast. Before we cut the birthday cake, we have a few things to set up so y'all go out in the backyard and play. Have fun!"

The basement quickly emptied as kids bolted for the sliding glass door. Somewhere in the wild stampede, I detected the blur of strawberry blonde hair and bright red dress. Standing on the patio nursing two smoky charcoal grills, Mr. Ledbetter waved at the exodus. Running outside with the others, Skeeter and I came to a stop, stunned by the baffling sight before us.

Never in all my five years of school had I seen such a display of mass insanity. Nothing, not even the blatant absurdity at recess, came close in comparison. Maybe it was the pale silhouette of the full moon peeking over the horizon in the late afternoon sun, casting some celestial spell, coaxing timid boys into brazen foolishness. Perhaps, deep in the infinite blackness of space, the stars found themselves in some crazed alignment, unleashing pent-up emotions, sending wild-eyed boys into fits of mindless lunacy.

Free from the stern frowns of surly teachers, cocoons of self-doubt and insecurity peeled away as smitten boys darted across the yard. Cute pigtails and dresses incited impromptu cartwheels and somersaults accompanied by primal screams of madness, offering a pitiful glimpse of future manhood in its purest form.

What happened next forever altered the course of history, changing the sacred Ambush fraternity forever. Later that night I thought I heard the towering trees of Ashley Woods weeping in a lonely breeze.

Hanging upside down by his knees on the crossed Ts of an empty clothesline was the Clown Prince himself, Billy Ray Satterfield. Gawking at the brainless trapeze artist was Ruby Faye Sharpe, a cute brunette with gaping dimples.

"Is that... Billy Ray?" Skeeter stammered.

"Dang if it ain't!"

A stalwart rock, immune from the crashing waves of feminine temptation, Billy Ray remained the last holdout. Witnesses said later they felt the earth tremble beneath them, while others swore they heard trumpets. A monumental day forever burned in the annals of South Maybin Elementary, surpassing the infamous Chester Beasley Incident. As if beholding the birth of a new solar system, curious kids rushed over. Standing shoulder to shoulder, the entire class watched in astonishment.

Rocking upside down with his arms crossed over his chest, Billy Ray's sandy hair hung from his head like dirty icicles.

"Watch this!" he yelled.

Twirling off the bar, he landed in front of Ruby Faye. Momentarily stunned by the shameless exhibition, she quickly regained her senses and scampered away.

"*Hey!* Where you goin'?" Enamored, Billy Ray raced through the yard in hot pursuit. Of all the marvelous and wonderful events I'd experienced in my ten years on the planet, watching Billy Ray grovel like a helpless three-year-old stands alone at the top of the list. Ebenezer Scrooge finally awoke from his fitful sleep. The Grinch had seen the light.

"There she is," Skeeter whispered, elbowing me on the arm. Standing with a group of girls near a pink playhouse, Sherry glanced at us from across the yard. Scared out of his mind, Skeeter's face melted into a weary frown. Wait a second. Maybe all the boy needed was a little shot of courage!

"Hey Skeet! Think this would help?" Reaching inside my back pocket, I exposed the plastic handle of the water pistol. "It's full of Aqua Velva!"

"Aqua Velva! The smelly good stuff?"

"One shot and Sherry'll be all over ya!" Skeeter's eyes lit up like a Roman Candle.

"Shoot me, J.D. Shoot me right now!"

"Not here. Follow me!"

Scampering around the corner of the house, we took cover behind a tree. Pulling the pistol, I aimed at my trembling victim. With his arms opened wide, Skeeter raised his chin and closed his eyes. Wincing at the four quick shots to the chest, he peeked at me with one eye.

"OK! Turn around!" Pumping the trigger, I blasted an ice-blue stream down Skeeter's narrow back, forever washing away a distinctive yellow streak. Like Popeye opening a can of spinach, Skeeter's worried look vanished in Aqua Velva's potent mist.

"Thanks J.D., here goes!" Never looking back, Skeeter bolted across the yard towards Sherry. Watching him stride headlong into the unknown, I felt both happy and sad, like an anxious parent sending a child off to school for the first time.

"OK everyone!" Mrs. Ledbetter shouted from the patio. "Y'all come inside! Time to sing Happy Birthday!"

Kids sprinted to the basement that had been transformed into a sprawling banquet hall. Place settings of celebratory paper plates and plastic cutlery set perfectly spaced on white cloth-covered tables stretching the length of the room. Balloons, hats, and noisemakers laid at every chair. Quite impressive! For my tenth birthday I was lucky to get cake and ice cream served on Mom's dinky card table.

In the center of the royal dais stood Sissy's throne marked by a folded paper sign: "Birthday Girl." To my surprise my tan jacket hung on a chair next to the guest of honor.

Grinning, I understood why Mom kept reminding me to take my coat. A key element of the conspiracy arranged earlier by Mom and Mrs. Ledbetter. Something we'd laugh about later. Sunk down in a chair at the far end of the table, Roger stared back in surprise. Giving him a quick smirk, I offered a haughty wave.

Applause greeted Sissy as she took her seat beside me. The army of moms quickly dispersed to their battle stations. A lively chorus of blowout horns sang a sickening refrain as kids discovered the annoying party favor. Protruding and retracting horns stretched across the table like a group of happy frogs snatching flies.

Tapping Sissy on the shoulder, I blew my party horn, unfurling the crumpled paper in her face. Closing her eyes, she raised her hands in playful defense as the feathered end tickled her nose. The simple gesture changed everything.

Somehow, the unapproachable aura that had surrounded her melted away in a sea of silly laughter. The shy girl who playfully twisted the ends of her hair. Whose head sunk between her shoulders at the slightest embarrassment. The one who bit her lower lip and grinned as if she knew some deep dark secret wasn't so elusive after all.

Since that fateful day in the cafeteria when I first looked into those blue eyes, Sissy Ledbetter had been the unattainable prize sitting high atop an unreachable shelf, put there by insecurity and emotions I'd never felt before. *What had I been so afraid of?*

"OK everyone, let's sing!" a voice shouted.

"Happy birthday to you!" Taking her cue, Mrs. Ledbetter crept toward the table balancing a huge birthday cake the size of a lady's hatbox. Ten flaming candles wavered with every step. Maneuvering around the room with his fancy Polaroid, Mr. Ledbetter fired off pictures.

"OK. Angie, make a wish!" Mrs. Ledbetter coaxed. Standing at her chair, Sissy leaned forward. A quick flash captured the moment she blew out the candles followed by a thunderous ovation. With silver cake cutter in hand, Mrs. Ledbetter supervised an assembly line of cake and punch. The appearance of food sent any remnants of manners flying out the window as eager kids attacked the plates before them like hungry vultures. Mustaches of white icing appeared on giggling faces.

One of those silly frosting-filled expressions belonged to Skeeter Crabtree. Sitting to his left, grinning from ear to ear, was Sherry Whitesell. He'd done it! With a little help from the magic water pistol, Skeeter mustered the courage to give Sherry the answer to her love letter she'd hoped for.

A few seats down, with her hands over her ears, slumped an annoyed Ruby Faye. Billy Ray's newfound love interest was so angry, I thought she might explode. Across the table, Billy Ray barked like a rabid dog, trying to get her attention.

"Hey…! Hey…! Hey!" he shouted. I'll admit. The boy had charm. Disgusted, Ruby Faye ignored Billy Ray's not so subtle advances. Empty plates and balled up napkins soon covered the tables, while Rin Tin Tin continued his screaming mating call.

"OK! Time to open presents," Mrs. Ledbetter announced. Metal chairs screeched against the concrete floor as kids dashed to the gift table. Leaving me high and dry for a bunch of cheap gifts, Sissy led the way.

"J.D.! Wait up!" Frantic and sweaty, Billy Ray pushed his way around the table. "Where's the smelly stuff?"

"Huh?"

"The water pistol! Skeeter said you shot 'im with smelly stuff." *Gee, thanks a lot Skeeter!*

"Gimme some!" he growled.

Staring back into his demanding eyes, I felt the familiar twinge of self-doubt. My paper-thin wall of resistance began to crack like it had a thousand times before. As long as I could remember, I'd always given in to the bully, allowing him to run roughshod over me at every turn, yielding to his every whim.

A trace of panic in his trembling voice sent a small flutter of a budding backbone twitching under my shirt. Holding the carrot in front of the jackass' sweaty face felt good for a change. Reaching in my back pocket, I exposed the pistol.

"Maybe later," I said, flashing a sarcastic grin. Leaving him in an angry pout, I ran to join the others.

Surrounded by eager onlookers, Sissy examined the festive table piled with colorful gifts. This was it! The last hurdle. The final lap of the Indy 500. Everything rested on Pooh's golden shoulders. The present of all presents! Holding my breath, I watched as Sissy reached for a small gift with red bow.

"This one's from… Sammy!"

A few "oohs" went up as the tearing paper revealed a green and gold box of Crayola crayons. Thankfully, it was only the standard box of thirty-two. Nothing to get excited about. I'd been a little worried had it been a box of sixty-four with a built-in crayon sharpener! Taking her own sweet time, Sissy read each card aloud, graciously thanking each person with her signature syrupy smile. The suspense was unnerving. If this had been a boy's birthday party, the table full of gifts would have been ripped opened in two minutes!

Halfway through the mountain of gifts, I was happy to see that nothing came close to touching Pooh. Just the standard birthday fare: a few books, a couple of games, nothing sophisticated. Every time Sissy reached for another present, she seemed to ignore the purple gift with pink bow. I chuckled out loud when some poor slob gave her a baby doll. You're kidding me! Sissy wasn't a little girl anymore. She was ten years old for heaven's sake. And who took the time to wrap a stupid Hula Hoop!

Gradually the tabletop reappeared as the gifts dwindled down. With just two presents left, Sissy pressed a puzzled finger against her lips. Dang if she didn't pass over mine again! Opening the next to last gift, she read the card.

"This one is from… Roger!" At age ten and destined for greatness, Sissy had fully mastered the important female aptitude of playing two would-be suitors against each other like a fiddle! Holding my breath,

I watched her tear open the paper, exposing a raggedy used shoebox. Crammed inside was a silly stuffed cat. Upon closer inspection, I could tell the skinny feline was nothing but a cheap furry ball of crap. Couldn't have cost more than a buck, tops!

"Oh, thank you, Roger!" Sissy blushed, rubbing the cat against her cheek. Smiling at the last gift, Sissy's curious eyes found me in the crowd. *She'd waited.* Saving mine for last! Ripping off the paper, her face lit up.

"I can't believe it! *Pooh!* My favorite!" Twisting from side to side, Sissy held the bear tightly in her arms. 'Her favorite' she'd said. Pooh had done it!

"Wow!" beamed Mrs. Ledbetter. "What wonderful gifts! You're all so thoughtful!"

Hugging Pooh, Sissy made no attempt to join the others who milled around, gawking at the presents. With my confidence turning barrel rolls in the stratosphere, I tapped her on the shoulder.

"Want some punch?"

"Sure!"

With my heart pounding a thousand times a second, I floated to the punch table. The long frustrating climb was finally over. Standing proudly on the summit, I stared back at how far I'd come. Bidding farewell to the uncertainty and insecurity on the jagged cliffs below, I handed Sissy a cup of punch. There was only one more thing left to do. Plant the flag atop the mountain, declaring my everlasting love!

"Thanks for Pooh," she said, biting her lower lip. "That's really sweet." For the first time, I stared into the eyes of Sissy Ledbetter and didn't flinch.

"Sissy... Can I ask ya somethin'?"

"Uh huh," she whispered, her head sinking into a shy shell.

Suddenly I felt something move in my back pocket! Reaching back, I grabbed tightly to someone's wrist! Spinning around, I glared at Billy Ray who had managed to pull the water gun free from my pocket!

"Let go!"

"Give it here!"

"Let go!"

"You let go!"

"Boys! Boys! Stop that right now!"

Mrs. Ledbetter's warnings went unheeded. There was much more at stake than a silly water pistol. Locked in a fight to the death, nothing else mattered. Our eyes met in a resolute stare as the decisive battle that had been brewing for years came to a head. Kids scrambled to witness the violent tug of war.

Determined, both of us pulled with all the strength we could muster. Suddenly a wet sensation bled into my clamped fist! Somehow, in the melee, the pistol's trigger was pulled! Losing my grip, I fell backwards, slamming hard into the refreshment display. The impact sent the ladened table shifting onto two shaky legs.

Grasping for something to break my fall, I grabbed the dangling tablecloth, dragging down Sissy's birthday banner along with an avalanche of cookies and chips as my butt bounced on the floor! The leaning table fell back into place sending the sloshing punchbowl's turbulent contents raining down, drenching me in a cold red slush! Tipping one last time, as if trying to regain its balance, the rocking glass bowl tumbled from the table, shattering into a billion pieces!

Piercing screams echoed in one long cry followed by sickening silence. Paralyzed by the heat of a thousand eyes, I couldn't move. Somewhere in the blurred confusion, I detected a pair of shiny black shoes with silver buckles. Looking up, I watched Sissy's trembling hands touch her cheeks. Tears filled her beautiful blue eyes.

"I'm… I'm… sorry," I cried over and over through sobs of my own.

The rest of the evening became a muddled nightmare. Sitting in the front seat of the car, I watched Mom and Mrs. Ledbetter talk on the front porch. Sissy was nowhere to be found. *Why did I grab the gun? Why didn't I just let Billy Ray have the dang thing!* None of this would have happened! Not only had I ruined Sissy's birthday party, but any chance of a budding romance lay shattered along with the punchbowl on the basement floor.

I fully expected a firing squad to be waiting for me when I got home. Without saying a word, my parents followed me down the hall as I bolted to my room. There was absolutely nothing they could possibly do to me that I hadn't already done to myself. After a halfhearted lecture, Dad, Mr. Belt, and I gathered for a required session. To my surprise, Mom cried along with me.

Next morning, Mom never called me to go to church. Pretending to sleep, I heard the soft click of the latch as she slowly closed my bedroom door. Muffled noises and short commands of our standard Sunday morning ritual carried on without me. The sharp report of the closing back door left me alone in an eerie stillness. Throwing back the covers, I peered through the blinds into a dreary fall morning. A foggy drizzle draped trees in its silent grip. Dew-covered spiderwebs dotted the yard in hundreds of white clusters.

Throwing on some clothes, I scampered through the garage, leaving the back door unlocked. It seemed as if everyone in the neighborhood had vanished. There wasn't a single car on the road. Sunday morning papers waited in lonesome driveways. Everything remained quiet and still. Sounding like a window fan, the wheels of my bike churned hard on the wet pavement. The damp air penetrated my shirt as I blew through the haze.

Picking up speed, I turned onto Fourth Street. Laying my bike in the ditch, I searched the squares of the soggy sidewalk, finding the crude water-filled heart. Dropping to one knee, I ran my hand over our initials. In the quiet, I heard the rain racing toward me through the trees. Then the bottom fell out.

Getting ready for school the next morning, I knew good and well the worst of this never-ending nightmare waited for my arrival. J.D. Harrison would forever be the laughingstock of South Maybin. Riding to school in silence, Mom pulled into the traffic circle.

"It'll be OK," she whispered.

Dismissing her soft assurance, I opened the car door. Ignoring stares and giggles, I stared glumly at the sidewalk. Pointing fingers and whispers followed me down the hall. Taking a deep breath, I stepped into the classroom.

Raucous morning babble ceased. Shocked to discover I was still alive, the room full of open mouths resembled a choir holding an endless silent note. My eyes found Sissy. Waving at me without raising her hand off her desk, she offered a sad smile. Shuffling quickly to my seat, I stopped in the aisle. Laying in my chair was the yellow water pistol. Billy Ray's calling card. Snickers rippled through the room.

Thank goodness Skeeter sat in front of me. The only trusted friend that I had left on the entire planet. Watching him come out of his fearful shell at Sissy's party was some consolation. If it hadn't been for me, he would have never gotten into the game with Sherry. I'd been there for him. Putting his arm on the back of his chair, Skeeter turned around.

"Boy J.D.! That was the dumbest thing I ever seen!" he whispered. "Ya broke the punchbowl and everything... ruined Sissy's—"

"Shut up Skeeter!"

My eyes never left Miss Hawks the entire morning. When writing period started, everyone reached into their desks, pulling out pencils and paper, prompting the daily ritual of note passing. Feigning attentiveness, determined hands reached over shoulders and behind desks, exchanging folded messages. One's sacred duty during this clandestine operation was to make sure notes were passed along to their intended addressee.

The familiar stab of creased paper pressed between my shoulder blades. Without looking, I took the note from Junior. Letters rarely came addressed to me. I was simply another lonely pole in a long telegraph line. I was about to send the note on its way when I noticed my initials printed on one side. Pretending to write, I unfolded the letter.

Hey J.D. How about a cup of punch?
Sissy

IN A FULL-BLOWN PANIC, I looked three rows over. With swirling tongue, Sissy pressed her pencil hard against the paper on her desk as she wrote. Then I saw him! Billy Ray collapsed on his desk laughing under his breath. With a defiant stare, I gave him the finger. Letters came and went. Another one fell on my desk in front of me. Grabbing the note, I passed it back to Junior. A tap hit me in the back.

"It's for you," Junior whispered. Snatching the letter out of his hand, I glared again at Billy Ray. Dadgummit, I wasn't falling for his crap again! I'm goin' to kill that boy someday!

Ripping open the paper, I read the note.

Dear J.D.
I like you. Do you like me?
___ Yes ___ No
Your friend,
Sissy

FOR A SECOND, THE words bounced around in my brain like hot kernels in a popcorn machine. Another stupid note from Billy Ray. I almost lunged across the aisle! Looking again at the message, it finally sank in. *Cursive! The note was written in cursive!* Billy Ray could barely print his stupid name much less string two letters together! My head snapped to attention!

From across the room, Sissy's eyes met mine. Slowly her mouth turned into a gorgeous grin. The beautiful gap in her front teeth had never looked so good. A thunderous Fourth of July fireworks finale erupted in my chest! *SISSY LEDBETTER LIKES ME!* For the rest of the morning, Sissy and I exchanged giggling glances from across the room. By lunchtime the entire class knew about our secret.

Picking up my tray, I exited the cafeteria serving line. For all I knew our tantalizing entrée for the day could have been greasy roadkill and gravy. I never bothered to look. Gazing across the packed tables, I smiled at the amazing sight before me. Junior and Linda Sue huddled next to each other, engaged in silly laughter. Skeeter and Sherry ogled between bites. The transformation from shy little kids to daring preteens was well underway. Next year at this time, we'd all be at Maybin Junior High.

To my surprise, Sissy saved me a seat. Setting my tray down beside hers, I smirked at Billy Ray and the other pathetic failures pouting at the losers' table. I was reaching for my fork when Sissy placed her yeast roll on my plate. I knew then and there that I had found the girl of my dreams!

Brandishing a newfound confidence, the slings and arrows of envious classmates bounced off me like bullets off Superman's chest. Sissy was mine and that was all that mattered.

Holding hands on a cold December day, Sissy and I searched for an unscathed section of bark. Taking my pocketknife, I carved our initials for all eternity on the big oak. Admiring our handiwork, we turned to each other. Playful smiles washed over our faces. It happened in a split second. With our eyes wide open in surprise, we pressed our lips together in a rather awkward kiss, followed by sneaky giggles!

"YOU BROKE... THE PUNCHBOWL!" Suzie howled.

"A crowning achievement, don't ya think? Right up there with bustin' out the streetlight!"

"Lordy mercy! I 'member that," Dad roared. "Your momma was so embarrassed."

"What happened to you and Sissy?" Suzie grinned, twisting the straw in her glass.

"Of course, the details are kinda sketchy, but as I recall, we were a hot number till Christmas vacation. Then we faded into the sunset."

"You're kiddin'! All that aggravation for a couple of weeks!"

"Hey! Never underestimate the burnin' lust and unbridled passion of a ten-year-old. Besides, two months was considered a long-term relationship by fifth-grade standards." I chuckled, fingering another hushpuppy. "I remember the afternoon when we left to go home for Christmas. Sissy and I stood at the flagpole in front of the school, vowin' to the stars above to pick up right where we left off. When we returned from Christmas vacation, she forgot me quicker than last night's dream. She probably ended up with Roger!"

Suzie followed with a silly high school tale of her own, recalling the time she threw up in her date's car on their first and last night out. After another "y'all need anything" from our server, I noticed we were the only ones left in the quiet dining room. Sliding his elbows onto the table, Dad rested his chin on his clutched hands.

"What y'all think?" he asked. "Was my experiment a success?"

"Wished we done this years ago." Suzie nodded.

"I've had the time of my life." I smiled. "How 'bout you, Mom? Had a good time?"

"Oh yes! I've had just the best time!"

"That's what I wanted to hear!" Dad grinned, putting his arm around her shoulder.

"OK... Pop. How 'bout you?" I asked.

"Today was absolutely wonderful. Somethin' I really needed. We needed," he said, still with his arm around Mom, pulling her closer. "Glad we did this."

"I gotta hand it to ya though," I said, picking up the grease-stained ticket. "Of all your spur of the moment surprises over the years, from Christmas Eve rides to piano birthday presents, today was by far your best!"

"Guess I saved the best for last, huh?" he smiled. His chilling response took Suzie and me by surprise. Thankfully, Mom didn't hear him.

Plans

Basking in the afterglow of the day's events, the ride home remained pleasurably silent. Clusters of white clouds muted the sun's glare, sending shadows drifting over the highway. Despite endless refills of The Grill's potent sweet tea, Mom and Dad succumbed to the soft lullaby of the car's racing tires and drifted off to sleep.

Slowly the twinges of sadness that had simmered beneath the joy of the morning made its inevitable appearance. Although Dad's adventure granted us the lighthearted joy of childhood memories, the trip unintentionally accentuated the unavoidable path ahead. We'd skirted things far too long, banging our heads against a daunting brick wall that Dad defiantly constructed with impenetrable bricks of stubbornness and fear. Now the once impregnable fortress appeared to be crumbling.

Like an exhausted climber, Dad trekked slowly up the back porch steps. Making his way to the den, he collapsed into the welcoming arms of his recliner. Wearing her wide-brimmed sun hat, Mom inched down the sidewalk, nurturing her tender annuals while Suzie and I observed from a pair of rockers on the front porch. Watching her bent over, struggling to caress each plant, I knew it wouldn't be long before the simple joy of deadheading flowers would join the ever expanding list of fading pleasures. Wiping her forehead on her sleeve, she eventually gave in to the heat of the afternoon.

"Too hot!" she moaned. Disappearing inside, she returned with a tray of glasses filled with her famous lemonade. Following close behind, Dad joined us on the porch. Gathering his thoughts, he gazed at the yard from the relaxed cadence of his rocker. A quick wind gust sizzled through the young leaves of nearby maples. I tried to recall the last time we sat together on the porch. A long overdue moment, taken for granted a thousand times in the past, once again felt comforting.

"Well, I guess it's time we had a little talk," Dad began with a half-hearted grin. Avoiding eye contact, he gazed straight ahead as he spoke. "Strange. I don't know how many loans I made down at the bank over the years. Thousands, I reckon. Spent my whole life helpin' other folks plan their futures and never took the time to think about mine." he chuckled. "Somethin' I'd get 'round to one day. Embarrassin' when you think about it." Offering supportive smiles, no one spoke as Dad offered his confession.

"Corny to say, but I guess life got in the way. Or maybe I let it take over. I honestly thought there would always be time. I didn't think we had the time back when we were raisin' kids, payin' bills and mortgages. Walkin' through our old house this mornin', I could almost see y'all runnin' around the den barefoot, laughin' and playin' with each other. Next thing ya know ya'll are in college, married, kids of your own, grandkids. Where does the time go?" Taking another sip, he placed his glass on a small table. "After a while, ya get to kickin' the can down the road. Unintentionally, intentionally puttin' it off, if ya know what I mean." Craning his neck, he nodded at a black shepherd's hook hiding in the dappled shade.

"Kinda like that hummin'bird feeder over yonder," he said, motioning to a red glass feeder. "Put 'em up the other day. Ya momma's got seven of 'em scattered around the yard. Every spring, we stare out the windows at those feeders waitin' for the hummin'birds to come back. Days maybe weeks go by. Nothin'. Then one day ya look out and see that first hummin'bird! We'd get all excited. Then here they'd come! Ten sometimes more at a time, just a chasin' each other 'round the feeders. Then summer'd set in. We'd get busy runnin' here and there. Keepin' the feeders full becomes a chore. Ya kinda forget about the beauty and magic of those little birds after a while. Next thing ya know, ya look outside one September day and they're gone. We knew that day would come. But still ya get to missin'em. Wishin' they hadn't left so soon. Nothin' left but lonely feeders hangin' on the poles." Taking another sip of lemonade, he looked at me. "What was the phrase Grandpa used when somethin' good and unexpected happened?"

"Crumbs from Heaven," I smiled.

"That's it. Ya grandpa knew it then, just like I do now. 'Live every day to the fullest' they say. Ya hear it all the time. But we never do. Why can't we? It's almost like somethin' blinds us somehow from understandin' this simple phrase, 'specially when we're young. Somethin' about gettin' older brings things into perspective. Never forget that everything—*and I do mean everything*— in life is so fleeting." His eyes almost pleading as he spoke. "When you think about it, all those stories and memories we shared this mornin' and a million more just like them were all crumbs from Heaven. We just didn't know it back then. Every moment we have on this earth is precious. Be thankful for every last one of them. I don't have many left. But ya'll do." He said, nodding at Suzie and me. "Make the most of 'em."

My chest burned as I listened to him. Waiting. Fully expecting him to reveal his decision about chemo with Suzie and Mom. With no intention of spoiling the day, he never mentioned it. One step at a time.

In the shade of the front porch on that warm April afternoon, the four of us crept down that elusive path once more. Weary of fighting, Dad grudgingly relented, agreeing in principle to our suggestions. Suzie agreed to make the calls, including one to her husband David, saying she was staying a few more days.

Driving half-heartedly down the long gravel driveway, I gazed in the rearview mirror at the sprawling brick ranch as the three of them lingered on the front porch. Part of me wanted to stay. Something I hadn't felt in a long time. To sit on the porch without glancing at my watch. Feeling the breeze brush against my face. Exchanging the blare of car horns for the soft inflection of a dove's coo somewhere in the woods. Listening to nature's quiet while Dad shares his treasured stories once more.

Detouring through town, I turned onto South Drive. Small saplings back in the day now stood tall and full, blanketing the school's fenced playground in dappled shade. Except for a few aesthetic improvements, the one-story brick building looked very much like I remembered. Making a slow turn in the traffic circle, I noticed the big oak had disappeared, making room for a maze of mobile classrooms. Chuckling at my sudden sadness, I slowly pulled away.

Stories and smiles played again and again while towering pines and gaudy billboards drifted past the shoulders of I-40. I thought of the cancer devouring Dad's body, wondering how many visits, how many moments he had left. Although Mom enjoyed our little outing, more than likely she wouldn't remember the trip by tomorrow. But she'd laughed. We all laughed.

Specks of rain dotted the windshield as I questioned what forty years of chasing the next real estate deal had stolen from me. Or like Dad said, maybe I'd willingly given it away. Shrugging off the momentary flicker of homesickness, I thought of my 8:30 tee time tomorrow with Ronnie. Time for revenge after the thrashing he handed me last time. Lynne was standing at the open refrigerator when I got home.

"Hey! Everything OK?" she asked, opening a Diet Pepsi.

"Got a lot to talk about. How was the bridal shower?" I asked, giving her a kiss. Rolling her eyes, she offered her patented cynical glare.

"Why does one consider hosting a wedding shower for two middle-aged whiners? Give 'em a year, tops. Guy's a total loser. Worse than the first one. The clown showed up at the end wearing a tank top, cut off blue jeans, and sandals. He's fifty years old and dresses like he's fifteen."

"How does Kim feel about it all?"

"If it would get her forty-five-year-old daughter out of the house, I think she'd be thrilled with pending nuptials to Charles Manson! Ready to eat? I'm starvin'!"

Traversing the elevated bridges to downtown, we corralled our favorite corner booth at Emilio's on the waterfront. The black Cape Fear crawled past the window like a sinister beast in the setting sun. Sipping a glass of my favorite cabby, I managed an abridged, yet somewhat animated version of the day's incredible adventure.

"Your dad agreed!"

"In principle. Details have to be worked out, but at least he's open to talkin' about it."

"That's surprisin' coming from someone who won't trust anyone with his checkbook," she noted, dipping another piece of bread in a saucer of olive oil. "What makes you think he's gonna go along with the prospect of movin'? He's fought y'all every step of the way."

"I'm sure he's thought about it for a while; he just won't admit it."

"How about your mom? What did she think?"

"That's one of the details. Not sure where that'll go."

"Wonder what changed his mind?"

"I think our little trip today was the icin' on the cake. Walking through our old house, relivin' the past, gave him a frightenin' glimpse of the future, if that makes sense. He knows they can't stay out there in that big house in the middle of nowhere by themselves much longer. Suzie's checkin' on all the legal stuff, makin' sure everything's in place." Twisting the stem of my wineglass, I swallowed hard. "He confided in me that he's quittin' chemo."

"What?"

"I know."

"How did Suzie and your mom take that?"

"He hasn't told them. At least not while I was there." Meditating for a moment, we sat in silence as I poured myself another glass.

"Jay..." Lynne asked, looking down at the table then back at me, "do you think... with the cancer returnin' and all... that your dad's given up?" The question ripped me from my wine-induced haze. I'd never considered the possibility. It wasn't like him. The ever-invincible optimist, Will Harrison never quit anything in his life. I didn't have an answer. Her question haunted me the rest of the night.

It was close to nine when we pulled into the driveway. Opening the door, I was startled by the telephone's ring. It had to be Dad. But he never calls this late. A panicked ache grabbed me as I executed a hurried cabernet hopscotch to my office. Sure enough, Dad's number appeared on the plastic display.

"Hey Pop! Everything all right?"

"Hey pal! You get back OK?"

"Yes sir. Just got in from dinner."

"Hey, listen! I got another idea!"

Sitting down in my desk chair, I listened as his lively voice described in detail his next great quest. Of course, my attendance was required and I cheerfully accepted the invitation. Placing the phone back in its cradle, my tired eyes settled on the dusty corner cabinet. Forgotten books, office clutter, and crumpled stacks of paper lined its auburn shelves. Once again, that cold winter day long ago returned. When Grandpa and I reveled in a whirlwind of wood shavings in his cluttered workshop.

Rising from my chair, I studied every inch of the cabinet's details, admiring my grandfather's craftsmanship. Remembering the placement of every model airplane and ship, I ran my fingers across the dusty shelves, wondering how long it had been since I'd touched this treasured piece.

"Everything OK?" Lynne asked, standing in the doorway.

"Yeah. Everything's just fine. It was Dad."

"I figured," she smiled.

Reaching for my cell phone, I called Ronnie. Enduring his playful accusations that I might be sprouting chicken feathers, I canceled our golf outing. Clearing the shelves' clutter, I stepped down the hall. Finding a dust rag and furniture polish under the bathroom sink, I gently cleaned the cabinet's coppery finish.

CPSIA information can be obtained
at www.ICGtesting.com
Printed in the USA
BVHW051514020323
659559BV00013B/934